NUCLEAR FAMILY

KATE DAVIES is a novelist, screenwriter and writer of children's books. Her first novel, *In at the Deep End*, won the Polari Book Prize and was shortlisted for the Bollinger Everyman Wodehouse Prize. She lives in East London with her wife and son.

Also by Kate Davies

In at the Deep End

NUCLEAR FAMILY

KATE DAVIES

THE BOROUGH PRESS

The Borough Press
An imprint of HarperCollins*Publishers* Ltd
1 London Bridge Street
London SE1 9GF

www.harpercollins.co.uk

HarperCollins*Publishers*
Macken House,
39/40 Mayor Street Upper,
Dublin 1
D01 C9W8

First published by HarperCollins*Publishers* 2024
1

A catalogue record for this book is available from the British Library

Hardback ISBN: 978-0-00-853661-9
Trade Paperback ISBN: 978-0-00-853662-6

'This Be The Verse' and lines from 'Lines on a Young Lady's Photograph Album',
'Aubade' and 'An Arundel Tomb' by Philip Larkin reprinted with permission from the
Larkin estate
Extract from 'The Mother' reprinted by consent of Brooks Permissions

Typeset in Sabon LT Std by Palimpsest Book Production Ltd, Falkirk, Stirlingshire

Printed and bound in the UK using 100%
Renewable Electricity by CPI Group (UK) Ltd

For my mum and dad

They fuck you up, your mum and dad.
They may not mean to, but they do.
They fill you with the faults they had
And add some extra, just for you.

But they were fucked up in their turn
By fools in old-style hats and coats,
Who half the time were soppy-stern
And half at one another's throats.

Man hands on misery to man.
It deepens like a coastal shelf.
Get out as early as you can,
And don't have any kids yourself.

'This Be The Verse'
Philip Larkin

Family plot

That winter, before the argument that changed everything, Lena was happiest eating sandwiches in Kensal Green Cemetery. She ate them once a month or so, on a bench in the shade of an oak tree, with her twin sister Alison, her father Tom, and her mother, Sheila. Though her mother didn't actually eat the sandwiches, because she was dead.

Sheila Delancey
1952–2017

The words on the temporary wooden cross didn't really do her mother justice. Which wasn't the wooden cross's fault. How were you supposed to distil someone's life into an epitaph? Especially someone as alive as her mother had been? She'd had a New York accent and she'd talked quickly, as if she knew her time was running out. She'd dyed her hair pillar-box red and she'd worn a lot of waterproof mascara (just as well, because she'd cried easily – Lena had once reduced her to tears by describing the

1

plot of the musical episode of *Buffy*). She'd called everyone 'baby', and she had been a biochemist before she had children, and every year she'd stayed up all night to make Lena and Alison a birthday cake each. 'Why should you have to share? We should teach girls to have desires! To take up space!' she would say, before swearing at her Italian meringue. She had entered the *Great British Bake Off* once, but she didn't make it past the second round of the selection process (probably because of the swearing). If only she'd been chosen. Imagine all the footage they'd have of her, just doing ordinary things: wearing oven gloves and setting a kitchen timer and flirting with Paul Hollywood.

'We have to sort out a proper headstone,' Lena said, on the second Sunday in December, as the remaining Delanceys sat side by side, gazing at the grave. 'Maybe something slightly less enormous than that one.' She nodded to the marble column that marked the grave next to her mother's. A couple – Barry and Nigel – were buried there. An optimistic vase sat at the foot of the ledger stone, forever empty.

'It'll have to be quite big, or it'll look out of proportion,' Alison said. They had finished their sandwiches and had moved on to plum tart (Alison's contribution to the picnic – she made a lot of frangipane when she was approaching an illustration deadline).

'Have you seen how much headstones cost?' Tom said, brushing crumbs from his beard.

'It's not really an optional expense, Dad,' Lena pointed out. 'I can pay for it, if money's an issue.'

'It's not the money, Lenny. It's the principle.' Tom reached for a second piece of tart and Lena moved the Tupperware away from him. He had a sweet tooth and an angina diagnosis; an unfortunate combination. 'Bloody vultures, these memorial masons, preying on the recently bereaved.'

'I'm not sure we count as "recently bereaved" any more,' Alison said.

Alison had a point. Two years, three months and twelve days had passed since the night in the hospital when their mother's internal organs had shut down one by one, as though someone was flicking off the lights. Sometimes Lena felt like she was still standing there, blinking in the darkness. There aren't many silver linings to losing your mother unexpectedly on an ordinary Tuesday, but the happiness Lena felt when she was with her father and her sister was definitely one of them. It was the fierce sort of happiness you only experience when you're aware of the abyss that's waiting on the other side, just out of sight. Before, she had taken her parents for granted. Before, she and Alison had mostly communicated via Mariah Carey GIFs and the yellow heart emoji. Now, some of her favourite Sunday afternoons were spent sitting between Tom and Alison on a wooden bench, grumbling about memorial masonry.

'I like simple gravestones. Like Blanche Bridge's,' Tom said, showing them an image on his phone: a white headstone covered in dense black text. 'The writer. Have you read her work? She's buried in Kensal Green somewhere. You know we're related to her?'

'Yes, Dad,' Lena said.

Tom's face fell a little. He had always been a mansplainer, but Lena had only noticed in recent years, since there had been a word to describe it.

'Be nice if your mum's headstone echoed hers in some way, is what I was thinking,' he said, defensive. 'Seeing as

Kensal Green is sort of the family plot.' Tom was proud of his ancestors. Apparently, the Delanceys were descended from a long line of writers, stretching back to Edmund Delancey, a dreadful Elizabethan poet who had written obsequious odes to Elizabeth I: *My heart doth rage / Yet my mistress stays; / Would my courage / Could her soul amaze.* Then there was Richard Delancey (real name Eleanor) who wrote fat Victorian novels about parsonages that weren't as good as George Eliot's. Blanche Bridge was a wonderful writer, though – she'd written light comic novels at the turn of the century, and was rumoured to have had an affair with Vita Sackville-West before Virginia Woolf came along. Tom was a writer, too – he'd had a few short stories published in his twenties – and Lena had always thought she might write a novel one day, seeing as it was in her blood.

'I can ask Jim if he'll give us mates' rates,' Alison said quietly. (She said everything quietly. She did not take after their mother.)

'Who?'

'Jim. He was at art school with me, but he's retrained as a stonemason. He specializes in gargoyles.'

'Ideal,' Tom said. 'It'll be my grave too, soon enough.'

'Dad.' Lena wished he wouldn't joke about that sort of thing.

'What? We've all got to die eventually. By the way, when I go, I'd like a bench dedicated to me. But not here. On Hampstead Heath.'

'Stop it,' Alison said.

'Or a charitable foundation in my name.'

'You only get one of those if you die young,' Lena said.

Alison laughed at that. Their father didn't. 'Right, that's it,' he said. 'I'm cutting you out of my will.'

'You have to actually write a will before you can cut us out of it,' Lena pointed out.

'Yeah, yeah.' Tom crushed the silver foil from his sandwich into a ball. 'Anyway, you horrible lot. What do you want for Christmas?'

'For you to write a will,' Alison said. 'It's totally irresponsible, not having one.'

'You're ganging up on me.' Tom wasn't smiling now.

'What do *you* want?' Lena asked him.

'A new set of arteries would be great.'

'I'll see what I can do.'

They sat on the bench in silence for a while, as the oak leaves shimmered in the wind, thinking about mortality. At least, that's what Lena was thinking about. That, and how small their family seemed: small enough to fit on a bench, now, if you didn't count Adam, her husband, and Suria, Alison's wife. Even if you did count them, they could probably perch on the arms, or something. Family gatherings were too quiet and polite, these days. It wasn't a coincidence that she and Alison had both started trying for a baby.

'I was a bit mean to Dad today,' Lena told Adam that night. She was lying with her legs up the wall, even though she knew the wall thing was a myth.

'I'm sure you weren't,' Adam said. 'You're never mean.' He was lying with his legs up the wall, too, in solidarity.

'I was a bit. I had a go at him again, for not writing a will. And I told him off for eating pastry.'

'Only because you love him.' Adam took her hand in his. 'I reckon we've made a baby this time. That sex felt really procreation-y.'

'I don't know,' Lena said. 'I'm thirty-five. My eggs have probably all shrivelled up—'

'Thirty-five isn't old!'

'I found a white pubic hair the other day.'

'So? I've got loads of them. I prefer to think of them as silver plated.'

'Platinum pubes,' she said.

'Exactly. And look at how smooth your hands are! You're extremely biologically young. Basically a teenager.'

She laughed and turned to look at Adam as he sat up, pushing his messy golden hair out of his eyes; he looked particularly handsome in the warm light from the bedside lamp, his fine nose and square jaw in sharp relief against the shadows. Lena liked herself more when she was around Adam. That's why she had fallen for him all those years ago, at a Bristol University Conservation Group meeting. She hadn't actually intended to go to the meeting – she'd stumbled into the wrong room on the way to a hip-hop dance class, and there he was, giving an impassioned speech about the plight of the greater mouse-eared bat. He had smiled at her and she'd felt a flash of warmth, a thrill of energy, and that had been that. He had asked for her number and she had laughed all the way back to her halls, thinking, is it supposed to be as easy as this? Their relationship had been easy ever since. They had said 'I love you' after three dates and moved in together straight after graduation, and they'd eaten such delicious sushi on their honeymoon in Tokyo that Lena sometimes still thought about it, late at night. Over the years, they had started to argue about the recycling bin, and they had started calling each other 'Donkey' and 'Pony' during a trip to Vauxhall City Farm and couldn't seem to stop, and whenever they went through

Clapham Junction on the train, Lena knew Adam would look out of the window and say, 'My parents lived here in their twenties. On Lavender Sweep, just up there.' And until they had started trying, sex had become a special-occasion thing, like going to the theatre. They'd always enjoyed it, and resolved to do it more often, but it was easier just to stay on the sofa, watching BBC crime dramas and scrolling through Instagram, envying people with kitchen extensions. Still, he always laughed at her jokes, no matter how many times he'd heard them, and at dinner parties she often caught him looking around the table, marvelling at the way she entertained people. She was lucky to have him, even though he sometimes called her 'Pony' in public. 'You're the best person I've ever met,' he sometimes told her. She never said it back, because she had Alison. He was definitely in her top three, though.

'Want to go again?' Adam said now.

'All right. And then I better do some Christmas shopping.'

Lena sat on the sofa while Adam took a shower. *Paddington 2* had just started on BBC One. The bear was desperate to buy the perfect present for his Aunt Lucy; Lena sympathized. She was browsing the Moleskine website, wondering whether her father might like a monogrammed notebook, when a GoogleAd popped up, advertising Genealogy DNA test kits. Not a terrible idea for a Christmas present, actually; her father had always wondered whether his ancestor, Edmund Delancey, was descended from French merchants, or whether he'd just changed his name to make himself sound more aristocratic. *Give the gift of family history this Christmas!* the advert said. *23 pairs of chromosomes. One unique you!* Karla, a fellow associate in the litigation team, had got her DNA results a few weeks previously and discovered that although she had an Australian passport, her genes were mostly Scottish. Now she was threatening to host a Burns supper. 'I might have a go at making haggis,' she'd said. 'I've always loved offal. Now I know why!' Lena had told her that Suria, who was actually Scottish, hated haggis and bagpipes and, indeed, kilts, but Karla wasn't bothered. 'She should take a DNA test, too. She sounds pretty bland. She's probably English.'

If there hadn't been a special offer, Lena might not have bought the DNA tests. If her father hadn't mentioned Blanche Bridge earlier that day, she might have panic-bought him an engraved pen or a pair of noise-cancelling headphones. But there was, and he had, so she tapped her card details into the Genealogy DNA website. All over the world, strangers were doing the same, innocently buying incendiary devices that they would wrap beautifully and leave under Christmas trees, ready to detonate on the twenty-fifth of December.

Special occasion

'Alison, see if I conceive a baby while you're looking at Instagram? I'm going to murder you—'

'I'm not. I'm emailing Jim about Mum's headstone—'

'Can you put your phone away, please?'

Alison did as she was told. She stared at the floor of the cramped consulting room, averting her gaze while the embryologist fiddled around with a catheter.

Suria was lying on a bed that reminded Alison of a sex swing she'd once tried out with an ex-girlfriend: ergonomic, but hard to get in and out of. The swing had been black, though, and this bed was cream. Everything in the fertility clinic was pastel and twee, the opposite of sexy. Which was appropriate, really, as there was going to be zero sex involved in the making of this baby.

For the third time in twelve months, Aoife, the nurse, crouched between Suria's knees and said, 'Could you slide your bum towards me a bit? Grand, that's it.'

Suria nodded, sullen, and shifted forward. She had taken against Aoife at their very first appointment; Aoife had said, 'Been anywhere nice on holiday? You've a lovely tan,' and refused to believe it when Suria told her she wasn't tanned, she was just half-Malaysian. Alison took Suria's hand and thanked the universe that her wife was willing to go through all this – catheters and speculums and strangers staring into her vagina and casual racism – so they could be a family. Alison couldn't wait to carry her children on her shoulders, to embarrass them at the school gates, to accuse them of treating the house like a hotel, and her longing for a baby increased with every round of IUI and every negative pregnancy test, but she was very glad she wasn't the one with her feet in the stirrups.

Emily, the embryologist, handed a vial of sperm to Alison. 'Just check it's got the right code on it for me.' She smiled a tight smile.

Alison checked the code against the receipt from the sperm bank, reading it forwards and backwards and forwards again, the way she checked her bank details every time she invoiced a client. 'It's the right sperm,' she said. Although she wondered, briefly, if it would really matter if there were a mix-up.

'Has that ever happened?' Suria asked. 'Has anyone ever been impregnated with the wrong sperm?'

'Jesus, not at this clinic! That we know of!' Aoife said. Emily, who was drawing the sperm into the catheter, said nothing. 'Here we go!' Aoife said. 'Little pinch, OK?'

'This is actually quite painful.' Suria's shoulders were hunched.

'Not as painful as giving birth,' Emily said. 'Or so I hear. Haven't done it, myself.'

'Nor me. Don't fancy it,' said Aoife, cheerfully, from between Suria's legs.

Me neither, Alison had wanted to say. She couldn't bear the idea of maternity clothes and breastfeeding and midwives calling her 'Mum', as though she had given birth to an entire team of NHS professionals. She didn't mind that she wouldn't be related to her child, because she loved plenty of people she wasn't related to – and this way she'd get to be a parent without having to push an actual human being out of her vagina.

'All done!' Aoife said, snapping off her gloves. 'I'm thinking good thoughts for you. A positive pregnancy test in time for Christmas. Or – whatever festival you celebrate.'

'It's not exactly a romantic way of making a baby, is it?' Suria said, taking Alison's hand, as they walked down Harley Street. 'A racist nurse stabbing my cervix with a catheter.'

The sun was setting, though it was only four. Workers in high-vis jackets and Santa hats were emptying dustbins into the back of a roaring lorry.

'Would it be more romantic if we went to Fischer's for hot chocolate?' Alison asked.

Suria checked her watch. 'Aye, OK. *EastEnders* doesn't start till seven thirty.'

Fischer's was a decadent-feeling Austrian restaurant with tiled walls, leather booths and portraits of eccentric Europeans. They sat at a table beneath a huge, old-fashioned railway clock. Suria's mood had swung upwards, and she smiled so broadly at the waiter, as he placed their cups carefully on white saucers, that he asked, 'Special occasion?'

'Yes!'

'Well,' Alison said, as the waiter walked away, 'we'll know in two weeks whether it's a special occasion or not.'

Suria stood up. 'Meet me in the women's toilets in, like, two minutes.'

'Why?'

'Just do it. Wait a bit, though, so it doesn't look weird.'

As Alison sat, looking at the paintings of women dressed in bustles and men smoking pipes, the waiter approached again. 'Is it her birthday? Your friend?'

Why not, Alison thought. 'Yes.'

The waiter nodded and smiled.

Alison pointed to the Ladies. 'Just going—' She had never been able to say the word 'toilet' without blushing.

Suria pulled her into a cubicle. 'Take your jeans off.'

'No!'

'OK. You can do me.' Suria was already unbuckling her belt.

'There are other people here!'

'So? We used to do this—'

'When we were, like, twenty-five—'

'Pretend to be twenty-five.'

Suria braced herself against the cubicle wall. She looked hot, and Alison missed being young and spontaneous, so she knelt down and said, 'Fingers?'

'Tongue!'

Alison hesitated. 'It's weird, though. There's sperm up there!'

'Yeah, but above the cervix. It's not like you'll be able to taste it.'

A revolting thought. Fortunately, grief had taught Alison to compartmentalize. She used her tongue.

Suria grabbed a handful of her hair – painful but a turn-on, the way things sometimes are. 'I'm going to come—'

'Shh!'

They heard a flush from the next-door cubicle.

'Don't stop!'

Alison started to fuck her, two fingers, then three, and then Suria was shuddering, hands still in Alison's hair.

'Better?' Alison asked afterwards, as she washed her hands and face.

'Better,' Suria said, zipping up her jeans.

Their hot chocolates weren't hot any more.

'Worth it,' Suria said, sipping hers.

'You've got a chocolate moustache.' Alison reached across to wipe it away. As she sat back in her seat, she noticed the waiter walking slowly towards them, proudly carrying a piece of chocolate cake with a sparkler in it, as though he was taking part in a small but important parade.

'Happy birthday to you,' the waiter sang.

'Happy birthday to you!' sang the other customers.

'Happy birthday dear—'

'Suria,' Alison clarified.

'Happy birthday to you!'

Suria blew out the sparkler. 'Sorry. Bit hormonal,' she said, as the waiter took a step back, alarmed. 'These are happy tears.'

Later, they curled into each other on the sofa and watched *EastEnders*. The Slater family were shouting at each other about Hayley, who had, apparently, done a runner. But Alison wasn't really paying attention.

'Stop double screening,' Suria said, frowning at Alison's phone.

'Sorry. Just a minute.' Jim had replied. *What an honour to be asked! Kensal Green's a lovely spot to be buried.*

She texted her sister and father. *Jim's up for making Mum's headstone.*

Her father replied right away. *And I'm attempting to write a will!*

'Please put your phone down—'

'Hang on.' Another text from her dad. *Shall I just leave the house to both of you jointly? I feel like King Lear, dividing my kingdom in two.*

Lena replied, *You could always hold a competition to see which of us loves you more? That always ends well.*

Suria was reading over her shoulder. 'What are they on about?'

'Shakespeare in-jokes.' Alison tossed her phone on to the sofa.

'Pretentious wankers. Can't we have Christmas just the two of us this year?'

Alison shook her head. 'I love the pretentious wankers.'

Will (or won't)

Tom sat at his untidy desk, searching his inbox for the email Lena had sent, over a year ago now, with the details of a solicitor who could help him draw up his will. He was supposed to be working on a short story, but the words wouldn't come – and besides, his daughters were right, it was high time he sorted out his estate. Not that there was much of an estate to sort out: all he had to leave them was the house on Dyne Road, which had been remortgaged so many times that he couldn't afford to retire. He and Sheila had always spent more than they'd earned. One unforgettably horrible morning when the girls were about eight, bailiffs had arrived at the door. He'd made Lena and Alison crouch behind the sofa until the coast was clear. He knew it was unforgettably horrible because they still talked about it, sometimes. Lena had been terrified of debt ever since. His fault, in other words, that she'd become a corporate litigator.

Still, the house was now worth a disgusting amount of money, thanks to gentrification and Kilburn's excellent transport links. Lena occasionally tried to persuade him to sell up and buy a two-bedroom flat so that he could retire, but that was unthinkable. He was rooted to it, like the buddleia growing in the brickwork. He only really knew who he was in the context of NW6. There was the Kiln Theatre, which used to be the Tricycle, where he and Sheila used to go for a glass of wine and a movie on Sunday nights. There was his daughters' old nursery, shut down shortly after they left because inspectors had found rat droppings in the baby room. And there was Dyne Road itself, a terrace of Victorian houses, neat as teeth. Most of the other houses in the street were shinier and whiter than his. Number 14 looked as though it could do with a trip to the hygienist. He ought to pay someone to give it a lick of paint – another thing he hadn't got around to.

A removal van parked up outside the window. The woman who'd bought the ground-floor flat next door was moving in. Recently divorced, according to Mr Walcott at number 18. Tom stood up to get a better look at her. She was about his age, with grey hair, a leather jacket and a fondness for pot plants, judging by the contents of her removal van. She turned and saw him staring and gave him a quick wave. How humiliating. He waved back, then tugged the curtains closed and sat down again. He hoped she hadn't noticed his unironed shirt, or his unkempt hair, or the mess in his office: electricity bills and newspapers and half-drunk cups of tea. No wonder he hadn't got round to writing his will, when so many other things were demanding his attention. He pushed the papers together and added them to the pile on the floor behind him. An old copy of *The Times* fell open on the puzzles page; he picked it up and spent a good ten minutes solving a cryptic crossword clue (*Alarming disclosure of beauty (9))*. Then he tossed it aside and turned back to his inbox.

There was the email – the solicitor had actually replied, attaching forms for him to fill in. But now he remembered, why he hadn't got around to completing them: they asked for the value of his pension (fucked if he knew), his funeral plans (morbid), the names of his executors. Anyone would do as an executor, as long as they weren't a beneficiary, but he didn't have many friends these days; he'd lost touch with most of them since Sheila's death, and he hadn't bothered to make new ones. Compared to his wife, everyone seemed as boring and unappealing as newsreaders. It wasn't much fun, taking stock like this. What did he have to show for his life, apart from the house, two daughters, shelves of books and piles of bills and a surprisingly large collection of Christmas decorations? What words would his daughters choose for *his* headstone, when his time was finally up? He liked to think of himself as a good person – he'd marched against the Vietnam War, and he always voted with less fortunate people in mind, and he'd never cheated on Sheila, apart from that one time at the Christmas party when he'd kissed Natasha from Inter-Library Loans, but Natasha had come on to *him*, and he'd told Sheila about it straight away, and she'd forgiven him, so it didn't count. But then there was the secret. He had decided, long ago, that his children were better off not knowing the secret, but it was always there, fluttering at the edges of his consciousness, persistent and irritating as a moth. Perhaps he ought to add it to his will – would a solicitor charge extra for a confession clause? No. Writing it down would be like giving it a physical form, the equivalent of saying 'Beetlejuice' three times. (His daughters had made him sit through that film every bloody

Halloween. He missed fighting with them about the remote control.) He was the only person who knew the truth, now that Sheila was dead. Better to let it die with him.

He minimized his inbox and turned back to his short story. He wasn't ready to face any of it – his death, the possibility of his children finding out the truth (worse than death, that would be) – and it was naive, anyway, to pretend you could tie up the loose ends of a life in neat little bows. Better to die messy and intestate, to create a ripple: proof that you used to exist.

Bang

The argument took place, as family arguments often do, on Christmas Day, after the turkey but before the Christmas pudding. It wasn't the first disagreement of the day: that morning, Lena had told her father off for eating a Lindt chocolate reindeer. She had found the wrapper in the bin while she was throwing away the turkey giblets.

'It's Christmas!' her father had said. 'Give me a break, Lenny!'

'Dad, I've been asking you for, like, twenty years to stop calling me that—'

'Lenny's a great name. Lenny Henry, Lenny Bruce—'

'Both men.'

'Leni Riefenstahl!'

'Famously a Nazi.'

Her father was brandishing a box of All-Bran. 'This is what I'm supposed to eat for breakfast. With skimmed milk. Have you ever tried skimmed milk? It tastes like diluted bird shit. For breakfast, I had fucking twigs, doused in diluted bird shit. I had to get the taste out of my mouth somehow.'

The glossy white kitchen her parents had installed in the Nineties looked dated. The pale wood and hard edges and the MiniDisc player mounted on the wall reminded Lena of a room in a museum, a snapshot of a glorious time in the family's past that everyone was pretending wasn't over.

She looked around the kitchen for back-up. Alison seemed very absorbed in peeling parsnips, and Suria was standing at the stove, frowning at a saucepan of cranberries, her apron spattered with red as though she was ready to go onstage for the final act of *Sweeney Todd*. Adam made a cross in the bottom of a Brussels sprout. He said, 'I'm sure one hollow chocolate reindeer won't do Tom any harm.'

'Thank you.' Tom smiled at Adam, who shifted in his chair, delighted. Adam had been trying to win her father over for fifteen years, without much luck. Once, after half a bottle of wine, Tom had told Lena he found Adam 'exhaustingly good', because he was a primary school teacher, and he was always trying to recycle things, and he insisted on playing the folk fiddle in public. 'Hasn't he heard of electric guitars?' Tom had asked. 'Or does he only approve of carbon-neutral instruments?' He had laughed so hard at his own joke that wine had dribbled out of his nose.

Lena joined her father at the kitchen table and tried not to think about how grey his skin was beneath his stubble, which was also grey. He seemed to have faded since his angina diagnosis, like one of the family photographs on the fridge. 'Just FYI,' she told him. 'You have to live until me and Alison are at least seventy-five. We cannot lose another parent.'

'A Christmas guilt trip,' he said, looking away. 'Very festive.'

'I'm serious, Dad. You're not allowed to eat the roast potatoes.'

'You're not in charge of me! I'm not in a nursing home yet.'

'If you don't behave, I'll put you in one.'

'You dare.'

'There's one in Highgate with a creative writing club. Obviously we'll have to sell the house to pay for it—'

'Such cruelty! And from my own flesh and blood.'

'I'll boil you some new potatoes instead.'

'A life devoid of roast potatoes isn't worth living.'

'And no pigs-in-blankets. I've got you some Linda McCartney sausages—'

'Bloody Linda bloody McCartney's sausages.' He shook his head. 'What are we having tomorrow night, Yoko Ono's fish pie? Jerry Hall's hot cross buns? Actually, I wouldn't mind a feel of Jerry Hall's buns—'

'Dad, you're disgusting,' Alison said, throwing the parsnip peelings into the vegetable bin.

'Thank you.' He crossed his arms, pleased with himself.

'This turkey,' Tom said, when they sat down to lunch, 'is a fucking triumph.'

Lena looked around at her family, at the kitchen flickering in the candlelight like an old film, and told herself to remember the moment so she'd be able to look back on it later. She hadn't done that enough, before.

'So moist!' said Adam, about the turkey. 'And I've never actually enjoyed Brussels sprouts before, but with the bacon and the chestnuts—'

Lena caught Suria rolling her eyes at that, but Adam didn't notice.

'And the carrots! I could write a sonnet about these carrots!'

'Please don't,' Suria said.

'No. Right. I should leave that to Tom.'

Tom cleared his throat, as if considering the sonnet idea. 'I've never been a big fan of the sonnet form.'

'Oh god,' Alison said, filling up her wine glass.

Tom helped himself to new potatoes. 'This puts me in mind of my favourite literary Christmas.'

'Here we go,' said Alison.

'Which one's that?' Adam asked.

'You have to guess.'

'*A Christmas Carol*!'

'It won't be that. Too obvious,' Lena said.

'Exactly,' said Tom.

'*Christmas at Cold Comfort Farm*,' Alison said.

Tom shook his head.

'I can't think of any other novels set at Christmas,' said Lena.

'There are loads,' Suria said. '*A Christmas Wish. Christmas at the Cupcake Café. Bridget Jones's Diary* is Christmassy at the end.'

'Novels Dad will have heard of,' said Alison.

'Ah. I didn't say it was a novel. My favourite Christmas in *literature*.'

'I give up,' said Alison.

Tom smiled. '*Sir Gawain and the Green Knight*! "Þis kyng lay at Camylot vpon Krystmasse, with mony luflych lorde, ledez of þe best—"'

Lena pushed her chair back.

'I haven't got to the good bit yet!'

'You recite Middle English, you lose friends.'

'Keep going! I'm enjoying it!' Adam said.

But Tom was tinging his glass with his knife. 'We should have a toast!' he said. 'To absent friends.'

'To absent friends.'

'To Mum,' said Lena, because that's what everyone was thinking anyway.

'To Sheila.'

'To Tom!' Adam said.

'Oh come off it,' Tom protested. 'I'm not dead yet.'

'To family,' said Suria.

'To family!'

And it must have been getting a bit too maudlin for Alison, who preferred people to express their emotions alone, behind closed doors, where they wouldn't hurt anybody, because she said, 'Shall we have a break before Christmas pudding, and open the presents?'

The Delancey family tradition was that the youngest person got to hand out the Christmas presents. Alison had been the youngest (by twelve minutes) for the last thirty-three years, but somehow she'd maintained her enthusiasm for the ritual. She handed a package to Suria, then sat down to watch her open it.

'Slippers!' Suria said, standing up to kiss Alison's cheek. 'Just what I wanted.'

'Bloody hell,' Tom said, spreading his arms across the sofa. 'How old am I that I have children who give their partners slippers for Christmas?'

'To keep my feet dry when I'm taking out the bins,' Suria said, sliding her feet into the slippers.

'God, that's a depressing present,' Tom said.

Suria's phone started to ring. 'It's my cousin, sorry, back

in a minute.' She shuffled out of the room (the slippers were a bit big).

Lena unwrapped a book. 'Thanks! *Milkman*. I've been meaning to read this.'

'Hope it's good,' Alison said.

'It will be, it won the Booker Prize,' Lena said, reading the back.

Tom held out his hand. 'Let me see what's considered literature these days.'

As he was reading the back cover, shaking his head, Alison handed him a present. 'From Lena.'

'Lucky me!' He put the book on the floor and opened the gift: a glossy white cardboard box, decorated with green leaves. 'What is it?'

'A DNA test kit,' Lena told him, leaning forward the way you do when you know you've given someone a present they'll love. 'You spit in a tube and send it off in the post, and they tell you where your ancestors are from, and how Neanderthal you are.'

Tom nodded. 'Interesting. Thank you.' He didn't seem that enthusiastic. He put the box on the floor and rubbed his hands together. 'Right. Next present.' Lena was a little disappointed.

'A DNA test kit,' Alison said, unwrapping Lena's gift. 'What a surprise!'

'I don't know if these things are such a good idea,' Tom grumbled, reading the small print on his DNA test. 'They collect your data. You're putting your genetic material in the hands of organizations you know nothing about.'

'Don't take the test, then,' Lena said, sulky.

'I don't think any of you should take it.' The urgency in his voice silenced the room. He looked up at them all. His

24

face looked as though it was collapsing. 'Please don't take the test.'

Lena felt something shift inside her. Her father famously never said please and thank you.

'Why shouldn't we take it?' Alison asked.

'Because I said so,' he said, the way he had when they were little. 'Just – don't. OK?'

'But why?'

Lena was beginning to panic. 'What's going on, Dad?'

He couldn't look at them.

Something was very wrong. 'You're dying,' she said, just to get the words out, to get it over with.

But he shook his head. 'Your mother said this would happen.'

'We're adopted,' Alison said, as though that made sense of everything, as though they should have known it all along.

Tom said, 'You're not adopted . . .'

But everyone could hear the ellipsis.

'Can we stop guessing, please?' Alison said. 'Can you just tell us what's going on?'

And Lena couldn't have told you how she knew, what it was that made it obvious, but everything shifted into place, like a key in a lock, like a contact lens, and she could see.

Her father looked broken. It was breaking Lena's heart to see him so broken. She smiled at him, even though she didn't feel like smiling, but if she stopped, she wasn't sure when she'd start again. 'Are we going to find out you're not our father, or what?' she said, so he could deny it.

He cleared his throat. 'I am your father,' he said. 'I'm just not—'

'Not *what*?' She hadn't meant to shout. The words hung there as her father looked down, hands open on his lap, like he'd given up.

'I'm just not biologically related to you.'

A silence.

Lena's heart was furious in her ears. 'Oh my god,' she said. 'Oh my god.' She held her hands in front of her mouth to stop herself saying it again.

'Maybe I should give you some space—' Adam was saying. But no one was listening to Adam.

'Did Mum have an affair?' Alison asked.

'No!' Tom said, looking offended, as though it wasn't a completely logical question.

Lena couldn't bear it, and she didn't understand, and she just wanted him to make it all go away, so she kneeled by his chair and said, 'Tell me it's not true. It's not true, is it, Dad?' She shook his leg. 'You're my daddy.'

'Of course I'm your daddy.' He was crying, wiping away his tears with the back of his hand, like he was angry with them.

'You're not making any sense,' Alison said.

He was still looking down at his hands. 'We tried to have children for years, but nothing was happening, so we went for tests and it turned out my sperm count was zero. So. The hospital matched us with a sperm donor.'

Lena's mind was full of static. Her body felt full of static, too. Fizzing with it. 'But then why,' she said, touching his arm. 'Why do you love us?'

'I love you because you're my daughters,' he said. He couldn't look her in the eye, though.

'Why didn't you tell us?' Alison asked. Her voice was unsteady.

'The doctors said it would be better if you never found out.'

'Who was the donor?' Lena asked.

'They didn't keep records,' Tom said. 'But they were mostly medical students. They tried to match them by appearance—'

'So we can never find out who our actual father is?' Lena was walking, directionless, ping-ponging from the sofa to the Christmas tree to the window to the piano that nobody played. Adam put out a hand to stop her. She shook him off.

'*I'm* your father!'

Lena knew she was crying, because she couldn't see properly, but she couldn't really feel anything any more, because she was outside of herself, and she didn't know what her self was any more, either, because her father was a stranger. She thought of the video they had watched in their Reception year at primary school. 'A stranger is someone you don't know. Don't accept sweets from a stranger. Don't get in a stranger's car.'

'Look,' Tom said, standing up. 'I'm still your dad—'

Lena looked at Alison, and a thought struck her. 'Wait – is Alison my full sister?'

'You're twins. Of course she's your full sister.'

A rush of relief. She looked for herself in Alison's face. But Alison had their mother's eyes, and Lena had green eyes like their father – except they weren't her father's eyes, they were a stranger's eyes, and she felt more lost than ever. Something exploded inside her, a ripping sort of rage that tore the future from the past and left her in the present, falling, nowhere, lost.

Alison covered her face with her hands. 'This is so fucked up. This is all so fucked up.'

The living-room door opened. Suria was back, holding her phone, looking around at them all – at Alison, sitting shellshocked in the armchair, and Lena, still pacing – sofa to window to piano – and Tom, who looked worn out, shrunken, ashamed, and Adam, who was standing next to the bookcase, picking up books and putting them back again, as though he hoped one might be a portal into another dimension – and she said, '. . . Everything OK?'

Lena pushed past her and ran upstairs to her childhood bedroom and locked the door. The walls her father had painted over and over again as her tastes had changed, white to pink to black to white again, felt flimsy, like a filmset. The books, still on the bookshelves, that he'd read to her each night seemed sinister. He had been acting a part every time he'd kissed her goodnight, and she had been acting too, only she hadn't known it. Anger and grief propelled her forwards and she threw the books to the ground, but the sound they made when they hit the carpet was too muffled, too polite for her fury, so she ripped one book from its cover, roaring as she tore out the pages. She regretted it immediately. She'd chosen the copy of *Bleak House* her father had given her for her sixteenth birthday. She sat there on the floor, the yellowing pages scattered around her like dirty snow, crying and crying, because there was no greater crime in the Delancey family than destroying a book, but she wasn't even part of the family any more, and she hated her father, because she loved him so much.

She lay on her old single bed and closed her eyes. She reached down and found the initials she'd carved into the frame, running her fingers over the indentations, reassuring herself she still existed, because she couldn't be sure of anything any more. She wished and wished and wished she could unknow what she now knew, which was that she didn't know anything at all.

Unnatural disaster

There was a bang, as Lena's bedroom door slammed shut. Then the sort of quiet you get after a natural disaster. It was quiet in Alison's head, too, and it was never quiet in Alison's head, unless she was at the end of a kickboxing class or in the middle of a particularly good orgasm. Her father's eyes were closed. She felt a surge of fury and a slamming sense that she wasn't safe. She had never felt unsafe with her family before.

Adam turned stiffly to face the room. 'Do you think— maybe we ought to give you all some time to talk? Suria, I can give you a lift. I've only had one glass of wine—'

Someone's hand was on Alison's shoulder. Suria's. 'Do you want me to stay?' Alison felt herself shake her head, as though someone else was doing it for her. She caught sight of herself in the mirror above the fireplace and she stood quite still for a moment, brain cauterized, staring at her reflection, into the void of her identity. All useful worry prompts action; all other worry is useless, she told herself. There was nothing she could do. There was nothing anyone could ever have done, apart from tell the truth. So her brain shut the anger away, the way it had after her mother's death, putting the feelings into storage so that she could carry on living.

She stood there, and her father sat, still, silent, on the sofa, as Adam and Suria tiptoed around them, pushing unopened presents into bags, saying goodbye in hushed voices, like mourners leaving a funeral. She walked her wife to the door and watched from the doorstep as Adam's car pulled away. She made herself think, 'My dad's not my dad,' trying to feel it. But she didn't want to. Because he *was* still her dad. As much as she'd ever be her child's mother. Was it really just a week since she had checked the code on the vial of sperm in a Harley Street consulting room? She had wondered, then, if it really mattered whether it was the right sperm or not. Sperm was just an ingredient they needed to create their child – it would melt into insignificance once their child existed, the way butter disappears into a sponge cake. She hadn't thought that much about the man who'd produced it.

Alison found Lena on her single bed, her back to the door, curled beneath the duvet. She climbed on to the bed and hugged her sister from behind, the way she had after Lena's failed drama school audition and her first break-up and every time they watched *Beaches*.

'Has everyone gone?' Lena asked.

'No one really fancied hanging around for the Queen's speech.' Alison closed her eyes, her breath rising and falling along with Lena's.

'What's Dad saying?' Lena asked, eventually.

'Nothing. He's tidying the kitchen, humming under his breath.'

Lena turned to look at Alison. Her face was puffy with

31

crying. 'Shall we get some fresh air? I need to get away from him.'

'Don't say that—'

'Please?'

The stairs creaked as they walked down to the front door, but their father didn't call out or try to stop them leaving.

They walked in silence, side by side, through the eerily empty streets of their childhood. The windows of other people's houses glowed like television screens. Teenagers on a sofa, legs on the armrests. Families pulling crackers, red-faced with central heating. A couple shouting at each other, two children crying, like a dystopian John Lewis advert. 'At least they're having a shit time, too,' Alison said, to lighten the mood. Lena didn't react. Alison realized her sister was crying. She wondered if she ought to be crying too, and she blinked a few times, a sort of experiment. Nothing.

'I hate him,' Lena said.

'You don't.'

'I'm allowed to hate him tonight, if I want to.'

'OK, but you'll forgive him eventually,' Alison said, because she needed everything to be OK. Her fury hadn't lasted – it rarely did. What could she say to make her sister feel better? Ahead, the spire of St Gabriel's reached into the air, like it knew all the answers. A man was sitting on a doorstep, a paper crown on his head, a cigarette in one hand. 'All right, girls?' He looked from Lena to Alison, then back again. 'Wait, are you sisters?' They ignored him. 'It's Christmas! Give us a smile!' Alison grinned, because she didn't like to disappoint people.

*

And then they were back at the house, and Lena was unlocking the front door, and Alison's heart was hammering, because she knew that Lena was going to insist on the three of them sitting down and talking honestly about their feelings.

Tom was pottering around the kitchen as though nothing had happened. 'The prodigals return! We never had the Christmas pudding! I've just put it in the microwave.' He turned and smiled, but she could see in his eyes that he was a little afraid of them, now.

Alison would have happily gone along with his act and offered to put the kettle on, but Lena sat at the kitchen table, palms flat on its surface, as though she was chairing a meeting. 'Dad. You just told us we're not related to you. We need to talk about it.'

Alison sat down next to her and looked down at the stains on the table, black rings from long-ago cups of tea. Their mother hadn't believed in putting things on coasters.

Tom pulled out a kitchen chair and sighed as he lowered himself into it. 'What is there to talk about?'

'I mean – you and Mum lied to us our whole lives—' Lena said.

He frowned, affronted. 'We did not—'

'You literally did—'

'Technically, we never lied,' he said, raising a finger. 'We just – didn't tell you the whole truth.'

'That's a lie of omission!'

Alison was starting to close down, the way she did whenever things became too heated. Party-popper streamers littered the floor, like ticker tape for an election nobody had won. She got up from the table and picked them up, for something to do. She often used housework as a way

33

to get out of difficult conversations. Her bathroom was spotless.

'The doctors advised us not to tell you,' Tom was saying. 'I am sorry about that—'

'Thank you!' Lena leaned back in her chair. 'An apology!'

Tom folded his hands on the table, case closed. 'I have to say, I do feel better, now it's out in the open.'

'Oh, *you* feel better. That's OK then.' Lena was trying to catch Alison's eye, but Alison was staring at the streamers in her hands. She didn't want to take sides. She didn't know whose side she was on.

'We were put in an impossible situation, Lena! I hope you never face a dilemma like that—'

'It wasn't a dilemma, Dad! It's never OK to lie to your children!'

'That's easy for you to say.'

Lena swung towards Alison. 'Have you not got anything to say about this?'

Alison wished Lena didn't have to be so melodramatic, so fond of arguments and sentences that ended in exclamation marks. Yes, their father was in the wrong, but why couldn't Lena put herself in his shoes? They were both waiting for her to say something. She sat back on her heels. She wasn't very good at putting things into words. 'I guess—' she started. 'I mean, ideally you wouldn't have had to tell us like this, Dad. Because ideally it wouldn't have been a secret in the first place.'

Her father looked defeated. 'Your mother never told you either!'

'Yeah, but she's dead, though, isn't she?' Lena said, and Tom looked dangerously watery-eyed, and Alison just wanted to get out of there, but she knew Lena would follow her if she left, so she walked to the cupboard under the sink and rummaged around for the dustpan and brush.

'I'd honestly forgotten about it,' Tom was saying. 'I'd completely put it out of my mind.'

'You obviously didn't, or you wouldn't have freaked out about the DNA tests—'

'*Most* of the time I forgot about it. The doctors told us to have sex after your mother had the treatment so that there would always be some doubt about who the biological father was. Even though – zero sperm count, so.'

'Shitty advice,' Lena said.

Alison swept the remaining streamers into a pile and tipped them into the bin. Lena was watching her. She was going to have to rejoin the conversation.

'I'm not a bloody time traveller, Lena!' their father was saying. 'I didn't know everyone was going to end up giving each other DNA test kits for Christmas like something out of fucking *Star Trek*!'

'Oh, right, so this is my fault—'

'That's not what I said! I just don't know why you're so worked up about this. It doesn't matter that much, surely, whose DNA you have?'

'Of course it matters!' Lena was staring at him. 'How can you not see that this matters?'

Alison sat down at the table again. Her father was bent forward. His white hair was thinning at the crown. His hands were so lined they could have been drawn by an art student who'd just discovered crosshatching. This whole thing was worse for Lena, no doubt about it. Lena had always been proud to take after their father – gregarious, green-eyed, fond of crosswords, puns and Eighties alternative comedy – whereas Alison was used to being an outsider.

It had always been a family joke, how shy Alison was, compared with the rest of them. 'No idea where you get that from! Not me, anyway!' Tom had said, after yet another parents' evening ended with a teacher saying, 'She just won't join in with the rest of the class.' But Tom was the one who didn't fit in, Alison realized now. Not biologically, anyway. And as she looked at him, bowed over the table, braced against their anger, she felt a pang of protectiveness.

'It doesn't matter to me,' she said.

'What doesn't?' Lena asked.

'Whose DNA we have.' Their father had parented them. It was as simple as that. Lena had a tendency to overcomplicate things.

Lena shifted away from her and stared out into the garden, furious.

'Come on, Lena,' Alison said. 'Dad was there when we were growing up.'

'I was,' Tom said. 'I read you bedtime stories. I changed your nappies—'

'Don't try and make me feel sorry for you!' Lena said, turning around, savage. 'I want to know where I came from!'

Tom laughed, without smiling. 'What, north-west London?'

'You know what I mean! Who's our biological father? Who is he?'

'The donor's not our father,' Alison said.

'He is.'

Anger was Alison's least favourite emotion of all, but here it was, rising inside her, leaving her spluttering and sweaty and inarticulate the way it always did. 'You can't say that—'

'I'm sorry, but that's the reality of the situation—'

'Our genes don't make us who we are.'

'They do. That is literally all they do.'

'So if I have kids with Suria, I won't be their parent?' Her voice sounded like someone else's, loud and penetrating. Like Lena's, actually.

A beat. Lena sat up straighter. 'I didn't say that—'

'You basically did—'

'Girls!' Tom said, banging his hands on the table, his eyes red-rimmed. It was awful, seeing him like that.

Alison took a breath to calm herself. She picked up the pepper grinder from the table. The pepper grinder existed. She existed, and Lena existed, and there was no point wondering what the pepper grinder would be like if it was made of wood instead of glass, because then it would be a completely different pepper grinder.

'Pudding's probably ready,' Tom said, crushing a festive napkin in his fist. 'Who wants brandy butter?'

'You can't have brandy butter, Dad,' Lena said. 'Think of the cholesterol.' She put her head in her hands and started to cry.

The sky was black by the time Alison got back to Leytonstone, except it wasn't really black, more of a deep sludgy brown, because it never gets that dark in London. She stepped over the piles of letters in the hall addressed to people who no longer lived there, and the upstairs neighbours' cat, which was mewing and rubbing itself on the skirting board. Everything was the same as it had been before. She wasn't, though. Suria was sitting on the sofa, reading a book by lamplight, like a Victorian. Suria was very into the Victorians. She had a nineteenth-century-style nightie, which Alison hated – it was like going to bed with an elderly ghost – and she'd recently bought an uncomfortable fainting couch from eBay, which unlucky people had to sit on at parties. Alison hated the fainting couch even more than the nightie. Interior design was usually her domain and she favoured clean lines, pale wood, cupboards without handles, no fuss. But relationships were about compromise so she tolerated the fainting couch, just as she tolerated the cheese plant with its roots that trailed messily on the floor.

'Come here,' Suria said, shifting up the sofa. 'How are you feeling?'

Alison sat down. She felt tired, more than anything. The truth was trickling into her slowly, like sand through an hourglass. 'Fine,' she said. She was fine, really. At least, she would be, if she decided to be.

Suria put her book face-down on the arm of the sofa. 'How's Lena?'

'All over the place.' Alison picked up the book and pointedly saved Suria's place with a bookmark.

'No change there, then.' Suria smiled, sympathetic. 'I guess you probably have a better perspective on the whole thing than Lena does. You get what it's like to need a sperm donor.'

And the anger was back. 'Yeah, but there's a reason you're supposed to tell kids they're donor conceived as soon as they're born, so they don't end up having an identity crisis.'

'You think she's having an identity crisis?'

'Seems that way.'

'Are you?'

Alison leaned against the sofa cushions and closed her

eyes. Her brain was on fire. 'Can we just go to sleep? I don't want to talk about it.'

'Of course we can. It's all going to be OK, OK?'

Alison nodded and wished she could believe it. Because a bomb had gone off in her family and they were hurtling away from each other, twisted and vicious as shrapnel.

Later, while Suria was in the shower, Alison unlocked the back door and walked out into the garden in her bare feet. The icy patio stung her toes and the pain wiped her mind clean. Her phone rang. She almost didn't pick up, because it was Lena, and she didn't want to think or talk about any of it any more. But she had never ignored a phone call from her sister.

'I feel like an orphan,' Lena said.

'Well, you're not.'

'But don't you feel like we've lost Dad?'

'I don't know. No.'

'I guess it's more like we never had him.'

Alison sat on the rotting wooden bench the previous owners had left in the garden. She could feel the cold and damp through her pyjama trousers. She was caught in the middle, somewhere between her sister's insistence that everything was different and her wife's assumption that everything was fine. 'There's nothing we can do to change what happened,' she said.

'Why aren't you angrier?'

'Because – what's the point in being angry? Anger's not a useful emotion. It won't change anything.'

'Emotions aren't supposed to be useful, Alison—'

'I just – I don't think thinking about it is going to make me happy.'

'You can't just choose not to think about it.'

'I can, actually. I have a meditation app that tells me my mind is like the sky and my thoughts are passing clouds.' Inside the house, the bathroom light flicked off. Alison was suddenly very tired. She wanted oblivion. 'I better go—'

'Are you around, before New Year? Do you want to do something?'

'We're leaving for Glasgow tomorrow—'

'Oh, yeah.'

'We're back for New Year's Eve, though.'

'I'm not sure I'm in a New Year's Eve kind of mood this year,' Lena said.

'OK, then. We'll do something after that.'

'Night. Call me if you can't sleep.'

Suria fell asleep quickly, the way she always did, snoring and pulling the duvet to her side of the bed. Alison was horribly awake, staring up at the ceiling, but was the ceiling there any more? Hard to tell, in the darkness. She might as well do some work, she decided, so she padded to her office: the box room at the back of the house. Once she and Suria were parents, her desk would be replaced by a cot. She might as well make the most of it now. She was halfway through illustrating a non-fiction book about inspiring women. She had just finished the rough artwork for Madonna. Next up, Malala. But her hand was clumsy, and the pencil was blunt, and she couldn't get Malala's expression right.

What if her children felt the way Lena did? What if they resented her for bringing them up without their biological father? She hadn't really thought about that. She had been so focused on becoming a parent, the happy ending. But that wasn't an ending, really, was it? It was another kind of beginning. She and Suria hadn't spent that long choosing their donor. In the end, they had chosen sperm from an American company, because UK sperm banks don't provide photographs of the donors. 'Life is easier for attractive people,' Suria had said, as they'd browsed the catalogues. They'd picked Royston (not his real name), a neurologist who looked a little bit like Alison and a little bit like Eighties Tom Hanks, because everybody loves Tom Hanks. Alison had felt a twinge when they'd listened to an audio clip of him talking about his motivations for donating – 'Money is a factor, sure, I'm not gonna lie, I still haven't paid off med school' – but he was clever and attractive, and her kids would look like they belonged to her, and that was what mattered. And during the implications counselling the fertility clinic provided (one session, via Skype), the therapist had said their child would be fine with being donor conceived, because they'd never know any different. The child would be brought up as part of a community of donor-conceived kids with queer parents, and having two mums and no dad would seem completely normal.

She picked up her phone. She had an email from Jim, about the designs for their mother's headstone, a message from a time when other things had mattered. *It might be a while before I can get to it – my studio was flooded in the storms last week. But let's kick things off with a call when I've got that sorted. Hope you've had an amazing Christmas!* Laughing darkly, she closed the email. She Googled *donor conception* and found a support group on Facebook. She scrolled through the posts, horrified by the anger and the grief of the donor-conceived adults. The more she read about American sperm banks, the more uneasy she felt. There was no legal limit on the number of families one man's sperm could create in the States, and some men donated sperm over and over again at multiple clinics, for years – an easy way of making thousands of dollars. There were donor-conceived people who had found hundreds of half-siblings. Some had discovered they had been to school with their half-brothers or at university with their half-sisters without realizing it. Some of them said they felt like science experiments, like designer babies, like they'd been genetically engineered. A few wished they had never been born.

She scrolled to Lena's number. But she knew what Lena would say, and it was too late. Suria might be pregnant already. They would find out, one way or another, in a week's time. She closed Facebook – she was fine with being donor conceived, so her children probably would be, too. The fertility counsellor had told them they couldn't expect to feel more than '60 per cent comfy' with their choice of donor, anyway. Which is pretty much how Alison felt in life, as a gender non-conforming woman: never more than 60 per cent comfy in any given situation. Always ready to drop her wife's hand on a dark street. Always awkwardly dressed at weddings.

The reservation system on the Glasgow train wasn't working the next morning. Alison and Suria found seats in the quiet coach, facing the wrong way. An angry-eyed man with tiny glasses was sitting opposite Alison, sipping coffee, frowning at the *Daily Telegraph*. Suria picked up an old copy of the *Metro* from the empty seat and started to read. 'I feel like we should be joining in the Extinction Rebellion protests,' she said. 'I want to be able to say we did something, when our children ask.'

Alison nodded. They'd know, soon, if the treatment had worked. Only a 16 per cent chance. Better to assume it wouldn't. But hope was burning in the pit of her stomach. Oh, it was awful, the way it drugged you and filled your thoughts, leaving you giddy and sick. The certainty of disappointment was easier to bear.

'See if my mum has a go at us for not having weans yet? What'll we tell her?'

'Let's not talk about this on the train,' Alison said, still looking out of the window. Electricity pylons loomed over the fields, casting menacing shadows. They were out of London, but they weren't properly in the countryside yet.

Suria opened her rucksack and pulled something out. She prodded Alison's thigh to get her attention. She held up a pregnancy test.

'Suria!'

'I bought it in Boots when you were getting the sandwiches.'

'We can't take a pregnancy test at your parents' house!'

'Why not?'

They argued about it until the angry-eyed man said, 'Excuse me,' and pointed at the Quiet Coach sign.

'Really sorry,' Alison said, as Suria sulkily zipped the pregnancy test back into her rucksack.

'You shouldn't have apologized,' Suria said, a few minutes later, as the man stumbled down the carriage towards the toilet, steadying himself on the seats. 'He's just an old homophobe.'

But Alison felt sorry for him. He was like her dad – vulnerable, pretending he wasn't. 'Maybe he just doesn't need to hear the ins and outs of our private lives when he's trying to read the paper.'

'Shall I spit in his coffee?'

'No. Bad karma.'

Suria nodded, one hand on her belly.

Suria's mother, Fiona, was waiting on the concourse at Glasgow Central. She moved more slowly than she had the last time Alison had seen her. She seemed shorter, too, and softer, as though she had melted. She hugged Suria first. 'Darling. How fantastic to see you.' Alison stood by, hands in her pockets, waiting her turn. Fiona hugged her briefly, then turned back to Suria, taking her daughter's face in her hands. 'Let me look at you. Why do you have to cut your hair short like that?'

'A bob isn't short.'

Alison felt very aware of her short back and sides.

'You had such pretty long hair when you were a wean. You should have seen her, Alison.'

'Mum, leave it.'

Fiona limped a little as they walked towards the car. 'Your dad'll be pleased to see you,' she said to Suria.

'Will he.'

'We missed you at Christmas.'

Alison got into the back seat. She crossed her legs, so she'd take up less space.

'I'll warn you: he looks a wee bit peely-wally.' Fiona got into the car in slow motion.

'What's wrong with him?'

'Oh, he's having problems with his circulation, because of his diabetes. He's got ulcers all over his toes. They're not getting enough blood. Don't tell him I told you that.'

She smiled at Alison through the rear-view mirror. 'How's your poor dad doing?'

'He's OK, thanks,' Alison said in her daughter-in-law voice, which was posher than her usual voice. 'No toe-ulcers, anyway, I don't think, so—'

'Is he still smoking, too, aye?'

'When he thinks no one's looking.'

'Honestly, these men, they're asking for trouble, smoking their entire lives.' Fiona turned the key in the ignition. 'Now then. Let's get youse home, where you belong.'

Suria's parents lived in a pebble-dashed bungalow in a street full of bungalows, all with neat front gardens and net curtains. They'd moved there when they retired, thinking ahead to when they wouldn't be able to climb stairs. The ceilings were too low and the rooms were too small. Or maybe it just felt that way to Alison. Suria's parents had always been very polite and done their best to make her feel at home, but they had a tendency to smile at her sadly, as though they were disappointed Suria hadn't yet left her for someone with a Y chromosome. Tonight, Ahmad was in his usual chair, watching *It's a Wonderful Life*. Alison bent down to give him a hug and felt his shoulder blade, too close to the skin.

'Hello! Welcome, welcome!' He smiled (sadly) at Alison and pushed himself out of his chair. 'Let me make you a cup of tea.'

'Oh, no bother, Dad, let me do that,' Suria said.

'Away with you,' Ahmad said. 'Sit down. You've come all this way to see us, least we can do is put the kettle on.'

So they sat down, and watched as Ahmad shuffled to the kitchen sink, the kettle dangling from one hand.

45

Fiona sat down opposite them, pulling a face – 'Just my arthritis' – and pushed a plate of sausage rolls towards Alison.

Alison bit into one. The pastry was clammy from the fridge.

Fiona closed her eyes as she ate. 'Oh, it's such a treat to eat a sausage roll and not be at a funeral.'

'So it is,' Ahmad said, putting teabags into cups.

'Mrs McIntyre, from number 78, died last week. And do you remember Mhairi, from nursery? The one with the pigtails?'

Suria nodded.

'Aye, well, her mother died at the weekend, too. Cancer.'

'Tell her about David,' Ahmad said, grim-faced, as he filled the cups with boiling water.

'Dead. Only sixty-two. Cancer again. I only ever see my friends at funerals.'

Ahmad handed Alison a cup of tea. She wished it were whisky.

They settled on the sofa after dinner and watched the end of the film. Ahmad pointed at Jimmy Stewart. 'He's dead, and all.'

'I think all the actors are dead at this point,' Suria said.

'Just as well, the way the world's going.'

Fiona cranked round in her chair to look at Suria. 'You're going to be thirty-five, next birthday.'

'Don't.'

Alison started to clear the plates away. She didn't want to be in the living room when the argument really got going.

'I didnae say a word.' Fiona handed her plate to Alison without looking at her.

'I know what you're about to say.' Suria crossed her legs.

'You've got to admit, you're not getting any younger. If you have children after the age of thirty, you're more likely to die of breast cancer. And if you'd seen what Mrs Robinson went through—'

'Well, then. I'm already doomed.'

Alison had made it to the kitchen. She stacked the plates in the dishwasher as noisily as she could, but that wasn't enough to drown out the raised voices.

'I know what you're thinking,' Fiona was saying. 'But I have no problem with youse two having children together.'

'You've never been a good liar, Mum—'

'I don't mind! I just think youse need to hurry up and get to a clinic, or what have you, before your ovaries shrivel up and disappear. That can happen, you know! It happened to Lindsay, Mrs Brady's daughter!'

'We're already having treatment,' Suria said.

Alison paused, a fork in her hand.

'You?' Fiona said to Suria. 'Or—'

'I'm going to be the one carrying the baby.'

'Well. That's good news. We have great genes in this family.'

Alison decided not to be offended. Her genes were a mystery now, after all.

'I mean – we don't though, do we?' Suria said. 'Dad's got diabetes.'

'Aye, well, if you eat enough Greggs chicken bakes, your genes don't stand a chance.'

Suria locked herself in the bathroom after her parents had gone to bed. Alison sat in the hall and waited. They didn't piss in front of each other, unless it was an emergency. (Suria's rule, to keep things sexy. And yet, the nightie.) 'I don't know if I can pee on demand,' Suria said, from behind the toilet door.

'Think about waterfalls,' Alison said. She could hear a rustling. She closed her eyes. She couldn't bear the waiting.

'Not working. It's always hard to piss under pressure.'

'Are you in your usual wee position?'

'I'm crouching.'

'Sit on the toilet like you usually do, but dangle the test in the bowl. To trick your body.'

'Disgusting.'

'Just try it.'

Alison could hear a pattering, then a hissing.

'I've pissed all over my hand.'

'It'll wash off.' Silence. Alison's pulse picked up. 'Are you looking at the stick?'

'Just one line so far.'

'Well, yeah, but it hasn't been three minutes yet.'

'If we're not pregnant, we can get pure wasted at New Year.'

'If *you're* not pregnant.'

'If I'm not pregnant, we'll go to Sainsbury's tomorrow and buy a fuckload of goat's cheese.'

Alison couldn't bear to sit still any longer. She pushed herself up from the floor. 'Anything yet?'

Suria didn't reply.

'Suria?'

'Not pregnant.'

Alison leaned against the wall. She had let herself hope. She shouldn't have done that. The secret to happiness was low expectations. She pushed the door. It didn't move. 'Let me in.'

'No.'

Silence.

'Come on—'

The door juddered as Suria unlocked it. She was still on the toilet, the toes of one foot curled around the toes of the other. 'I really thought it would work this time.'

Alison took the test from her and checked, just to be sure. One line. 'It might be a false negative?'

'It's not.'

Suria blew her nose.

Alison sat on the edge of the bath, trying not to look as disappointed as she felt. 'It'll be OK. We'll try again.'

'I don't want to try again.'

'I know. But like you said, we can get wasted with Ed and Abeo at New Year—'

'I don't want to get wasted! I want a baby!'

'I'm just trying to find an upside—'

'There is no upside!' Suria stood up and pushed her way out of the bathroom.

Alison stayed there, balanced on the bath.

From down the hall, Fiona called, 'Are you girls all right?'

'Fine, Mum!' Suria shouted.

Alison heard a door creak shut. Then she crept back to the spare room. Suria was lying on the bed, on top of the duvet. Alison lay down next to her.

'I just want it to be over,' Suria said.

'I know.' Alison held her hand and wished she were better at knowing what to say. 'I'm sorry,' she said eventually.

Suria rolled to face her. 'No. *I'm* sorry. I know I'm being a bitch.'

'I thought we were phasing out gender-specific insults.'

'Aye. So we are.' Suria thought for a moment. 'I'm an arsehole.'

'A twat.'

'Twat means vagina.'

'Shit, so it does.' Alison thought for a moment. 'You're being a wanker.'

'Is "wanker" gender neutral?' Suria asked.

'Of course it is!'

'*That's* why there's always a buzzing noise coming from the bathroom when you're in there.'

Alison laughed, a little too loudly.

'Do you think we should do one more round of IUI?' Suria asked. 'Or go straight to IVF?'

Alison felt too hot. She stood and opened the window, and as she breathed in the clean Scottish air, she wondered what to say to her wife. IUI was one thing – the pills Suria took to stimulate her ovaries meant she cried at cat food adverts, but the procedure itself was straightforward (the nurse just injected sperm into Suria's uterus) and a cycle was a bargain at £800. Whereas IVF involved injections and operations under general anaesthetic and cost about ten grand a go, and what if it was all for nothing?

'Want to have sex instead of a conversation?' Suria asked.

'Your parents will hear us.'

'I'm not expecting the sex to be that good, hen,' Suria said. Which felt like a challenge.

'You never know,' Alison said. 'You're very sexy when you're in Scotland.'

'Am I, now?'

Alison pulled Suria towards her. 'Shall we do some *Monarch of the Glen* role-play?'

'Aye, no bother.'

'Now you just sound like Billy Connolly.'

'Nothing wrong with Billy Connolly. My mum's got a thing for Billy Connolly.'

'Exactly.'

Suria knelt up and pulled her T-shirt over her head.

'I haven't had a shower yet,' Alison pointed out.

'I like it when you're fusty.' Suria straddled Alison and started to kiss her stomach.

'New moves,' Alison said. 'Should I be worried?'

'Can you please stop commenting on what I'm doing and just go with it?'

'Sorry.' Alison closed her eyes, and it was working, she was getting into it, she wasn't going to think about the negative pregnancy test any more—

'Fingers? Or just tongue?'

'Oh, you're doing me first, are you?'

'Just answer the question.'

Alison opened her eyes. Suria was looking down at her, and she was stupidly beautiful, this woman who had, for some reason, agreed to become her wife, and one day they would both be dead, and before that there would probably be hip replacements and lower back problems and (if things worked out) a baby or two, so really, their days of having exciting sex were numbered. Seize the day, Alison told herself. Out loud, she said, 'Fingers, no tongue. From behind.'

Suria raised her eyebrows. 'That's a bit of a departure.'

Alison pulled her jeans down. 'Well, you know. Seeing as we're shaking things up, and it's nearly New Year's Eve.'

*

The next morning, they went out for a spontaneous brunch in Finnieston, because it's hard for people with babies to go for spontaneous brunches. On the way, Alison texted Lena to let her know Suria wasn't pregnant. Lena sent a row of kisses back.

Alison and Suria sat in a window seat. The winter sun was warm on their backs. As they ate their bagels, a man walked past their table clutching a screaming toddler who was upset that his chocolate ice cream wasn't brown enough. Suria put her head in her hands and Alison looked at the ceiling, blinking back tears. It was silly, really, to grieve someone who had never even been conceived, but it felt like grief all the same.

They fuck you up,
your mum and dad

The house on Dyne Road was silent and dark that New Year's Eve, apart from the lamp in Tom's office and the tapping of his fingers on the keyboard. He didn't see the point in turning the heating on just for himself, so he was wearing fingerless gloves and a woolly hat. In a way it was a good thing Christmas had ended early. More time on his own, to write. He'd read an article about a woman who'd got her first book deal in her seventies. It wasn't too late. Except what was the point in writing, when no one wanted to read his words? He'd had a couple of short stories published in the Eighties – he'd started writing at university when he'd realized his best friend, a performance poet, was getting a lot more sex than he was – but these days, literary magazines were edited by 21-year-old girls, and they all thought he was a dinosaur, irrelevant, just because he didn't write stories in patois. And if he were to try, they'd accuse him of telling a story that wasn't his, of course. He wrote two words and deleted them again, and he wondered what he could say to his daughters to make them feel better. He decided there was nothing he could say, so it was better to say nothing at all.

He heard shouts and whoops from his next-door neighbour's flat. Someone had smashed a glass. He pushed his chair back and walked to the window. The woman who'd just moved in was having a party. She'd slipped a note through his door telling him to call if the noise got too much. Gone were the days when neighbours actually invited each other to their parties. The smokers were standing in the garden, loud with wine. Most of them had grey hair. They ought to know better. Tom knocked on the window.

A man in a woolly hat, holding a beer, looked up and smiled at him. 'Happy New Year!'

Tom waved back. He felt like he was drowning.

If Sheila were still alive, they would have been hosting a party, too. They had thrown a New Year's bash every year, and everyone had come – Sheila's friends, mostly, because he'd never had many of his own – and the kids had stayed up past midnight, sipping the adults' cocktails. He found the photograph album on the bottom bookshelf and opened it to the pictures of the legendary party of '89: Heroes and Villains. There he was, dressed as Margaret Thatcher, his fist tight around a champagne flute, shiny-faced, miserable. He never smiled in photographs. He didn't want a reputation as a person who enjoyed himself at parties. The trouble was, when he didn't smile, his skull was too visible beneath his skin and he looked like a memento mori, there to ruin everyone's fun the way death always does. Sheila looked wonderful, even dressed as Nixon, spiky with opinions and jokes. It was utterly, utterly wrong that he'd outlived her. A ludicrous plot twist a good editor would have insisted on changing. And not even a hint of dramatic tension: she was there one minute, gone the next, before either of them had any idea what was going on. The girls hadn't even said goodbye. Sheila had said it wasn't worth dragging them to the hospital, and by the time they got there, she was unconscious: it turned out she had sepsis, and that was that. Stupid fucking meaningless way to go. But still. No point thinking about it. He just had to keep buggering on.

Sheila would have been so angry with him for the way he'd handled everything. She had always wanted to tell the twins the truth. When she was pregnant, she'd borrowed a book aimed at adoptive parents from the library. For the whole of her third trimester, she'd banged on about the importance of telling the babies their conception story before they could speak. This was supposed to be for the parents' benefit, to get them used to talking about it, so that it would never become a secret, so they would never have to say, 'Sit down, children. There's something we have to tell you.' But Tom couldn't stand the thought of his girls growing up lionising the 'very kind man' who'd helped create them (people always referred to sperm donors as 'very kind men', as though the ability to wank into a beaker automatically made you a good person) – and anyway, once the twins arrived, Sheila was too busy being vomited on and weeping from sleep deprivation to write the girls a lovingly person-alized picture book about the difference between a sperm donor and a father. She had brought it up again when the twins were three, but Tom had persuaded her they were too young to understand. And they had argued about it again when the girls were fourteen, but fourteen is such a difficult age, and he could see where that would lead, to slammed doors and underage sex and both of them shouting,

'You're not my real dad!' when he asked them to unload the dishwasher. He had persuaded Sheila that they should wait – he'd promised they would tell Lena and Alison eventually, before they had children of their own – but they'd both left it so bloody late. So yes – Sheila would have been furious with him. But she was dead. No point getting sentimental about it. Not that there was anything wrong with a man being sentimental. He just preferred it when that man wasn't him.

None of this was his fault, anyway. He hadn't chosen to have useless sperm. He hadn't chosen to sit in clinics, humiliated, while doctors spoke euphemistically about 'treatment options', as though a stranger's sperm was just another drug, like the fertility medication they had given his wife before they realized it was all his fault. He'd cried every night about it for months, grieving the children he would never have, the ones who were half-him, half-Sheila, but quietly, so his wife wouldn't hear him. That had been before he met the babies, though. He couldn't have loved them more. The doctors had told him to lie, so his name would be on the birth certificate, so it wouldn't say *Father Unknown*, so he wouldn't have to adopt his own daughters. Yes, he should have listened to Sheila, and yes, he would regret not telling the kids the truth for the rest of his life, but hindsight is a wonderful thing. And anyway, Sheila wasn't the one who people would look at differently, if they knew. She wasn't the one their children would look at differently.

Sheila had gone to a women's support group when they had started looking into the possibility of using a sperm donor, but back then there hadn't been an infertility support group for men. And what good would it have done, anyway, sitting sheepishly in a dark corner of a pub with a handful of other infertile idiots, comparing horror stories about windowless rooms, filing cabinets full of porn, wipe-clean sofas and medical orgasms? Talking about it wouldn't have changed the outcome, the shame of it, the pain of feeling your masculinity blistering like a bad paint job as a nurse said, 'I'm afraid it's your sperm that's the problem, Mr Delancey. Or rather, your lack of them.'

Things were different now, of course. The young men he worked alongside at UCL library discussed their emotions on social media, kissed each other on the cheek, wore pink T-shirts with impunity. But Tom was pinned to the past by his upbringing the way his grandmother had been, sitting bolt upright in her whalebone corsets while her daughter was out marching for women's liberation.

Tom had tried to make himself forget, but as the years had passed the secret had felt heavier, weighing on him like a stodgy meal, though higher in his body, in his heart. Every six months or so he woke up sweating from a nightmare: that his daughters had found out the truth, and they didn't want to know him any more. There's a relief that comes along with the horror, when a nightmare comes true. He had felt it when his wife died, because he didn't need to worry about her dying any more.

No point dwelling on it, he told himself, as he stared at his laptop. Alison had seemed quite understanding, and Lena would come around. She was like her mother. Her mother had always come around. He silenced the voice that said this time it might be different.

The party next door was getting louder, and the second-hand laughter made him feel lonelier. Which was silly; he had chosen to stay home alone. He had turned down an invitation to the pub with his university friends – he couldn't bear the idea of them asking how his Christmas had been. He'd never told any of them about how his children had been conceived. It wasn't the sort of thing that came up at dinner parties in the Eighties. He hadn't even told his parents – they hadn't been that sort of family – and now they were dead, too. He and Sheila had sworn that the family they created would be different, better, closer, and he'd gone and fucked it all up.

He pulled open the curtains. The moon was full, perfect, clean. It never aged. At least it never seemed to. The moon had looked just like this the night Lena and Alison were born. He'd seen them lying, bloody, new, on Sheila's chest and he'd felt a burst of love, like an artery exploding, a dangerous, immediate fierceness.

DNA didn't matter to him.

Philip Larkin had written something about the moon. Tom scanned his bookshelf for Larkin's collected works. From the corner of his eye, he could see Lena's grade three piano certificate, framed; Alison's MA from the Cambridge School of Art; their graduation photographs.

DNA didn't matter to him.

He found the book. The cover was brown, but the spine had faded to a mossy green. He turned to the index and looked up the poem he was thinking of: 'Sad Steps'. He read it, comforting himself with someone else's melancholy. He flicked through the rest of the book. It fell open at 'This Be The Verse'. No wonder; he had read it to his daughters over and over again when they were younger, and they had loved it, the outrageousness of it. He took a photograph of it now and sent it to Lena. She knew him well enough to know that was an apology.

He wasn't in the mood to write any more. He closed Word and searched YouTube for the exercise bloke his GP had recommended. After an advert for stir-fry sauce, a young man with an Essex accent appeared on the screen, shouting about beasting it and going hard and smashing the workout. The man started squatting. Tom felt exhausted just watching him. He shut his laptop.

Down in the sitting room, he turned on the overhead lights. Too bright, Sheila had always said, and insisted on lighting about fifty standard lamps instead. She'd been right about that, too. He walked around the room, bending down to turn on the lamps, wondering when bending down had become so difficult, marvelling at how big the room seemed to have become. Before the girls left home there had never been enough space on the sofa for everyone, and they had argued constantly about what to watch on TV, what to listen to on the record player, why he still insisted on using a record player. No complaints now. He walked up to it and swiped the dust off the lid with his shirt sleeve. He flipped through his records and pulled out *Sticky Fingers* by the Stones. There was a zip on the front of the sleeve, rusty and stiff with age. He slipped the record out, put it on the turntable and lowered the needle.

He danced to 'Brown Sugar', nodding to himself, lips pursed, feet shuffling, and thought back to the first time he'd heard this song, in the squat he'd lived in after university – damp walls and an outside toilet, vats of home brew on the kitchen shelves, the air always heavy with weed. That's where he'd met Sheila, at a party (every night had been a party in 1979), shimmying in her fake-fur coat (the squat didn't have central heating). He remembered the way she'd let him hold her, the way they'd slow danced to 'Sway', how exciting it had been when he'd made her laugh.

The song ended, and 'Wild Horses' started, and Tom felt maudlin. It's hard not to feel maudlin when you hear the opening chords of 'Wild Horses,' even if you're not a seventy-one-year-old with angina, a dead wife and two angry daughters. Maybe he should have had that thought the other way around, daughters first – maybe that was part of the problem. Standing alone in his living room, Tom Delancey closed his eyes and swayed and remembered the weight and warmth of Sheila's head on his shoulder, and he hugged himself, because no one else would do it for him.

He had forgotten to draw the curtains. Jessie Collins, his new next-door neighbour, glanced in as she stumbled outside to say goodbye to her friends. She pulled her leather jacket tighter and stood there for a moment, watching him dancing on his own, his arms wrapped across his chest. Poor old sod. She'd made a New Year's resolution to befriend someone through Help the Aged or to do whatever people do at food banks. She'd knock on the door in the morning, she decided, and see if he needed any help with his shopping.

Panic at the over-forties disco

Lena woke up on New Year's Eve and for ten blissful seconds the world was as it should be, and she was still related to the people she'd thought she was related to. And then she remembered. She felt as though she was floating outside herself – it seemed like the sort of thing that happened to other people, like the premise of an Audible Original podcast. She'd felt like this once before, the morning after her mother's death. Except that tragedy had done what tragedies are supposed to do: it had brought the rest of the family closer together. Which wouldn't happen this time, because her sister didn't agree that it was a tragedy, and it was all her dad's fault.

Adam brought her a cup of tea in bed before he left for his weekly folk fiddle class. He was worried about the fireworks. 'The bangs can stress birds out so much they fall out of the sky, dead,' he said. And then, 'Sorry. Dead pigeon chat isn't going to cheer you up, is it?' He hesitated at the door and smiled, a little shy. 'This might be our last New Year's Eve as non-parents.'

'Yeah, it might be!' Her period had come that morning. She had never been so happy to ruin a pair of underpants. How could she have a child when she had no idea who she was?

Adam frowned. 'Sorry. Was that an insensitive thing to say?'

'No, not at all.'

He hadn't noticed her relief. He'd assumed she shared his disappointment, because they shared almost everything else. Even a toothbrush, sometimes; she could never remember if hers was purple or turquoise.

She couldn't be alone with her own thoughts yet, so she flicked through familiar films as she ate breakfast, and showered, and put on her make-up: *The Holiday*, then *One Hundred and One Dalmatians*, though she turned that off at the point when Pongo and Perdita discover their puppies are missing. She couldn't cope with stories about parents and children, no matter what species, any more. Was Pongo really the father? The puppies would never know for sure.

Even on years when she hadn't discovered her whole life had been a lie, Lena felt miserable on New Year's Eve. She'd spent too many of them in rubbish pubs that charged you £20 just to get in, counting down to midnight half-heartedly, Ed Sheeran wailing in her ears, so every year she created a New Year's Eve WhatsApp group and sent her friends a photo of an Airbnb in Cornwall. Someone, usually Suria, would say Cornwall was too far away, and could they go to Devon instead? Ed and Abeo would write *Please can we get a dog-friendly place so Oscar can come!!* and Izzy would say *I'm allergic to dogs,* and she'd add a crying emoji and a dog emoji to try and lighten the message but it would still come across as passive-aggressive, and Alison would say *I'm up for whatever!* to try and keep the peace, but by that point everyone would have gone off the idea of a joint holiday, and Ed and Abeo would book to go away on their own – much less stressful – and Lena would spend the night with Adam, eating shepherd's pie on the sofa, watching the celebrations on television, quietly longing for the days of £20 pub entrance fees and disappointing snogs. This year, Alison and Suria were meeting up with Ed and Abeo, but Lena was going to stay with Izzy – she needed to get out of London. Adam had sounded relieved when she told him she was going to Waterbeach, and she didn't blame him. Now he could go to a party with his folk-fiddle friends instead of staying home with her and stroking her back as she stared into the mirror, wailing, 'Who am I? I don't recognize my chin!'

Lena left the flat about four and walked down Holloway Road to the Tube, looking at every man she passed, wondering. She focused on the white men in their late fifties and early sixties, men with light green eyes like hers. London was full of them. She felt, for the first and (she hoped) last time in her life, like Sophie from *Mamma Mia*, wide-eyed and confused and surrounded by countless potential fathers. None of them looked anything like Colin Firth, though, which had to be a good thing. She didn't want to accidentally fancy her own father. The donor had been a medical student, so he might be a consultant by now. Perhaps he was a celebrity doctor – one of the experts that regularly appear on morning talk shows, telling middle-aged women not to get too reliant on sleeping pills. Or maybe he'd given up medicine and turned his talents to something else. Perhaps he'd written a medical memoir; lots of healthcare professionals did that sort of thing now, didn't they, telling funny, moving stories of life on the NHS frontline to make enough money so they'd never have to be on the frontline again. Some of the men smiled at her as she walked past. One looked her up and down. She stopped making eye contact with strangers after that.

There were no father candidates on the train to Waterbeach. She sat across the aisle from four middle-aged women in party hats, drinking miniature bottles of wine.

'Do you want one?' the blondest woman asked her.

'Don't worry—'

'Go on! It's New Year! We have too many!'

'OK then. Thank you!'

They passed her a small bottle of chardonnay and a plastic cup, and when she burst into tears, they were very nice about it.

Izzy opened the door, swiping her fringe out of her eyes. Joe, her ten-month-old son, was strapped to her front. Izzy had been Lena's wildest friend once – she'd come out as bisexual at the age of fifteen, which Lena had thought was incredibly cool, until she'd found out Izzy was secretly shagging Alison. They had drifted apart for a while after Izzy dumped Alison for a boy named Rob, but they made friends again at Bristol, after running into each other at a house party. Izzy had offered Lena some MDMA and they had ended up on a park bench, staring at the Clifton Suspension Bridge, crying about how beautiful engineering could be – a very bonding experience.

Izzy wasn't wild any more, though. She was a mother

now. She commuted to London twice a week. She had recently confessed to buying cardigans from the Boden catalogue. 'My friend,' she said. 'How are you?'

'Not great.'

'Come here.' Izzy opened her arms for a hug, but Joe was flailing about, so Lena rested her head on her old friend's shoulder. Izzy smelled sweet and milky, like a baby. 'I don't know what to say,' she said.

Which reminded Lena of the conversations she'd had after her mother's death: the desperation people had felt, grasping for words of comfort when they should have known no words would do. The loneliness of talking to a friend who usually tells you about their sex life, or the state of their marriage, or how many Jaffa Cakes they've eaten, but now can't think of anything to say except, 'I'm sorry for your loss.'

Lena felt a sticky little hand in hers. She looked down. Peggy, Izzy's three-year-old, was staring up at her. Her mouth was smeared with brown. 'Chocolate,' she said. 'Look like runny poo.'

Lena would have been happy with a quiet night in, but that evening, as she stood in the shower, looking down at her body, trying to remember what shape her mother's kneecaps had been, Izzy let herself into the bathroom and said, 'Let's go clubbing. Mark says he'll stay in with the kids.'

'Get out! I'm naked!' Lena covered herself with the shower curtain, then immediately regretted it. She peeled the cold, clammy plastic off her thighs.

'Nothing I haven't seen before.' Izzy sat on the toilet seat. Lena could tell from the angle of her gaze that she was looking at her breasts.

'Stop it.'

'Stop what?'

'Judging the size of my tits.'

'You've seen mine plenty of times.'

Which was true. That was how Lena knew that friends judged the size of each other's tits.

Izzy didn't move. 'I miss having small, normal nipples.'

'Get out! Get out!'

'When you agree to come clubbing with me.'

Lena turned off the shower. 'I'm not in the mood.'

Izzy handed her a towel. 'It might take your mind off things.'

'I don't think so.' Lena wrapped the towel around herself and walked, dripping, to the spare room. Izzy followed. Lena turned on the hairdryer. Izzy was still talking. Lena flicked the hairdryer off. 'Yes?'

'There's a Nineties night in Cambridge that only costs five pounds. I always feel young when I go, because everyone else is in their forties.'

Lena shook her head.

'You can stay in with the kids if you want. I'll go with Mark. If Peggy wakes up and realizes we're not there, she might vomit all over her pyjamas. But I'll leave some clean ones out, so you can change her—'

And so it was that an hour later, Lena found herself standing in a church hall on the outskirts of Cambridge, clutching a can of Grolsch, dancing to music she'd been too young to dance to the first time around. Moving her body reminded her who she'd been, before she realized she didn't know who she was. Everyone else looked like they were remembering who they used to be, too, before they became parents. As the opening chords of 'Smells Like Teen Spirit' roared out from the speaker, Izzy ran to the middle of the dance floor and started to leap around, throwing her hair forwards, playing air guitar. Lena had never seen Izzy play air guitar before. She'd been under the impression that the only people that played air guitar were 60-year-old men with mullets. Maybe you lose the ability to dance after you procreate, along with your sense of shame. Maybe air guitar was another lesser-known side effect of childbirth, like your hair falling out, and bleeding non-stop out of your vagina for six weeks.

One by one, the air-guitar-playing women left the dance floor and dashed off in the direction of the toilets. Izzy made it to the second chorus before she handed Lena her drink and ran after them. Lena knew what was going on. She'd once pissed herself during a trampolining class, and she didn't even have childbirth as an excuse.

'Have I missed the countdown?' Izzy asked, as she jogged back from the toilet.

'No.' Lena handed Izzy her gin and tonic.

Izzy took a sip. 'Great sense of solidarity in the toilet queue. Everyone's talking about their pelvic floors.'

'Did you make it in time?'

'No. My knickers are soaking.' Izzy reached down to adjust her tights.

Lena looked out at the writhing bodies, dimly aware that another night she'd have felt a cold clutch of panic at this dystopian vision of her future: middle-aged men moving their arms up and down, hands in fists, like they were milking cows; white women attempting to twerk, squatting as though they'd been caught short on a woodland walk. She tried to dance, but that just made her feel heavier. She started to cry. 'Sorry.'

'Don't apologize. You've got a lot going on.'

Lena nodded, and linked her arm through Izzy's.

'Are you going to try and find the sperm donor?'

'I don't know. Alison doesn't want to.'

'Alison's never been very good at dealing with her emotions though.' Izzy sipped her gin. The end of her relationship with Alison clearly still stung, even though Izzy had been the dumper, even though she had once told Lena that neither she nor Alison had known what women did in bed, so they'd spent most of their sexual relationship just rubbing up against each other like Barbie dolls.

Alison wasn't the only reason, though. 'I don't want to upset my dad,' Lena said. 'Even if he is a lying bastard.'

'You shouldn't have to worry about your dad's feelings.'

'I do, though—'

'But your parents are the ones who decided to use a donor.'

A couple on the dance floor were snogging like teenagers. The man slid his hand up the woman's T-shirt. The woman pushed it down. A man in double denim was watching them, looking slightly disgusted. He caught Lena's eye and smiled.

'I know the whole situation's shit – but isn't there a part of you that's a little bit excited?' Izzy asked.

'Why would I be excited?'

'I don't know – you might have loads of half-siblings, right? They could be anyone.'

Lena didn't know why Izzy was smiling, because she'd never heard anything so horrifying. She looked back at the man in double denim, and she couldn't be sure, because of the low lighting, but his eyes seemed to be the same colour as hers – and now the room seemed very loud and much too warm, because you're more likely to be attracted to your relatives than your non-relatives if they're total

68

strangers, aren't you? She thought about how many dozens of half-siblings she probably had, and some of them might live in Cambridge, because they had been conceived in London and London was an expensive place to live so they'd probably moved out in their twenties, and what if she'd already had sex with one of her brothers without knowing it, and she couldn't really breathe, and her legs weren't working the way legs ought to work and she was sitting on the dance floor and Izzy was standing above her, one hand on her shoulder, shouting, 'Can someone bring me some water? I think my friend's having a panic attack.' And the man in double denim was crouching in front of Lena, telling her to breathe slowly, to count her breaths. She noticed that his eyes weren't the same colour as hers after all, and she felt a little better – but when she managed to get her breath under control, she was so embarrassed at causing such a scene that she burst into tears again. The people who weren't having panic attacks were counting down – 'Ten! Nine! Eight! Seven! Six!' – and the man was saying, 'You're going to be OK.' Izzy was sitting on the floor next to her – 'Five! Four! Three! Two! One!' – saying, 'Happy New Year, darling,' and the man said, 'Let's hope it's better than the last one.' 'It can't be any worse,' Lena said.

She was wrong, though.

Izzy ran Lena a bath when they got back to the house. Lena lay in the water and phoned Adam to say Happy New Year.

'How was your night?' he asked. She could hear a clattering in the background. 'Just making myself a sausage sandwich. Bit pissed.'

She told him about her panic attack, tried to make it into a funny story, but he said, 'Lena. That's awful,' and she started to cry again. She told him she didn't want to talk about it, so he told her about his night – about Martin Carthy turning up unexpectedly at the folk club, and the songs he'd sung, and the way everyone had hugged each other at midnight. 'Martin didn't actually hug me, but I hugged Nell – you know, the woman who runs the night? And she hugged Martin. So that's one degree of separation.' He laughed at himself. 'Get me. "Martin." Like we're on first-name terms.'

The skin on Lena's fingertips was wrinkling. 'I love you,' she said.

'Because I'm a strong and manly man?'

'If you were, I wouldn't love you.'

'That's reassuring.' She could feel him smiling. 'Can't wait till you get home.'

But she was glad she wasn't at home. Sleeping in Izzy's uncomfortable spare bed, using the borrowed hairdryer, smelling of someone else's shampoo, she felt less like she didn't belong in her own life.

She stayed in the tepid bathwater after she'd said goodbye to Adam, and Googled *I've just found out I'm donor conceived*. There were first-person accounts from people like her, interviews given to the *New York Times*, the *Mirror*, the *Telegraph*:

My shock at discovering I was a sperm donor child
I've just found out I'm a sperm donor baby
I'd got to the bottom of a secret

Strange and comforting to read her own feelings in someone else's words.

I felt that the rug had been pulled out from under me

It's like living in The Truman Show

She read everything she could about sperm banks and sperm donors and found herself on a message board for donor-conceived people, most of whom were angrier than her, furious with their parents and even more furious with the donors.

He should have thought through the consequences of his actions before he sold his spunk for beer money.

My mother was planning to tell me on her deathbed. She told me not to tell my dad that I know, because it'll upset him.

The donor doesn't want to meet me. How dare he? He won't even send me my fucking medical history.

I heard from my bio dad today. He called me 'Miss Fazlali'. His email was so cold. My heart is breaking.

Lena wasn't angry with the donor. He wasn't responsible for her conception, for the lies that had been told. She would rather be half her mother and half a stranger than no one at all. She felt polluted by the fury of people like her. She didn't want to be like them. She had no choice.

She needed to talk to someone who understood, so she typed:

Hello everyone, my dad told me I was donor conceived on Christmas Day (Happy Christmas to me). I want to find my biological family but I have no idea where to start – any advice gratefully received.

Dots appeared beneath her message at once.

The best way to find relatives is to take a DNA test. Welcome to the ride – it's a rollercoaster, but everyone here knows what you're going through.

That exact thing happened to me three years ago. Welcome to the club. Found my first half-sister two months ago.

She was about to get out of the bath when her phone buzzed with a message from her father. A photograph of a page from a poetry book:

> *Man hands on misery to man.*
> *It deepens like a coastal shelf.*
> *Get out as early as you can,*
> *And don't have any kids yourself.*

He was blaming his terrible parenting skills on his mum and dad, and he couldn't even do *that* in his own words. She put her phone on the floor and let her head sink below the water. She waited until her lungs burned before she burst up to the surface. Her phone was glowing: another message from her dad. *Come for lunch on Saturday, if you like.*

Izzy must have noticed the bathroom light. 'Lena? You still in there?' Lena dried herself and opened the door. Izzy was in her pyjamas, holding a pile of Joe's babygros. She leaned on the doorframe. 'You OK?'

Lena nodded. 'Sorry for crying on you.'

'Oh god, don't. I cried at a documentary about reindeer migration last night. Some of them were pregnant—' She shook her head. 'I was going to apologize to you, actually.'

'Why?'

'I'm worried I make motherhood seem a bit bleak. It's not. It's the best thing I've ever done.'

'Bet it's a bit bleak at four in the morning.'

'It actually isn't.' Izzy smiled, thinking about her children. The sort of smile you see on documentaries about cults.

'I don't think I can deal with the pregnancy hormones at the moment,' Lena told her.

'Alison and Suria are still going ahead with it, though, aren't they? They're still planning on using the sperm they bought?'

Lena sat down on the toilet seat. 'Yeah. I think so.' She hated the idea of it, the thought of this genetic bewilderment being passed down to a new generation. Maybe there was some kind of alternative to using a sperm donor. Maybe she could persuade her sister to think again.

An avalanche of strangers

It was two minutes past midnight on New Year's Day, and Alison was shouting along to 'Auld Lang Syne' in a crowded pub in Bermondsey, one arm around Suria's waist, another around a stranger's bony shoulders. She was sweltering in a fair isle jumper – an early start on her New Year's resolution to dress more like Billy Crystal in *When Harry Met Sally* – but she was grateful for the crowds and the pub's aggressive central heating, because everyone seemed to have mistaken the tears on her cheeks for sweat. Everyone, that is, apart from Abeo, who was frowning at her from the other side of the Auld Lang Syne circle, equally sweaty in a tweed jacket and bow tie. He had taken tweed up at university the way other people take up veganism and class-A drugs.

She tried to smile, but she couldn't quite manage it, because the year had ended, and she still wasn't a parent. She had never failed at anything so spectacularly, apart from the Introduction to Improv course that Lena had once signed her up for, to 'help her overcome her fear of public speaking'.

'I'm fine!' she yelled at Abeo above the music, because he had broken away from the drunken, swaying bodies. 'I'll be fine in a minute!' But he already had one hand on her forearm and he was shouting in her ear: 'Want to get some air?'

The pub backed on to the Thames, and the terrace was crowded with couples and groups of friends, ostentatiously enjoying the fireworks. Alison and Abeo leaned over the railings and stared down into the blackness of the river. Flashes of white and green and red lit up the water as she told him about the failed IUI treatment.

'I'm so sorry, darling,' Abeo said, hugging her. He was a big hugger – friends, colleagues, Pret baristas, the parking warden who let him off a fine once, no one was safe – whereas Alison preferred not to be touched at all, except during sex. 'Are you going to try again?'

'Don't know. The fertility clinic said that if IUI is going to work, it should only take three rounds.'

'Don't take this the wrong way,' Abeo said, 'but are you *sure* you want to have kids? I sort of feel like – one of the best things about being queer is that we get to opt out of all that—'

Alison told herself not to get angry. 'We're sure.'

'And you wouldn't consider just adopting?'

'It's literally Suria's job to deal with adoptions that don't work out. "Just adopting" isn't a thing.'

Abeo nodded. 'Of course it isn't. Sorry.'

She looked down at the reflections of the fireworks, blurred by the water.

'You wouldn't want to get pregnant yourself? If Suria's struggling?'

Alison couldn't read his expression properly in the darkness. 'Can you really imagine me pregnant?'

'I don't see why not.'

'Seriously?' He had come with her to buy a binder to wear to their university ball, so her shirt would sit flat under her tux. He knew she'd demanded to join the football team at primary school, even though it was boys only, and that she'd shaved her head as soon as she'd turned sixteen, with Lena's pink plastic razor. And that was just the gender stuff. Never mind her hatred of being touched, her phobia of hospitals—

'I know it wouldn't be easy—'

'Would *you* do it? If you could? Would you get pregnant?'

Abeo crossed his arms, thoughtfully. 'I would, actually,' he said. 'If I wanted a baby badly enough.'

How to make him understand? Her body just *knew* she wasn't supposed to carry a baby, the way it knew when she was hungry, the way it forced her eyes to droop when she stayed up working till 3 a.m. 'Suria's eggs might not be the problem,' she said. 'Maybe it's the sperm's fault.'

Abeo said something then, but Alison couldn't hear him over the music from a party boat motoring past them down the river. She asked him to repeat himself and he said, 'I was just saying – you could always use some of Ed's sperm, if you like. It's not like he's doing anything with it. Don't you think he'd make a good-looking baby? Plus he's a doctor. And he can play the trombone!'

Alison wasn't sure what to say. They had never seriously considered asking a friend. There's a reason people use sperm banks. It's a nice, clean, anonymous, controlled process. And she had heard something awful on Radio 4 about a man donating sperm to his friends, then suing them for custody of the kid—

'Or you can have my sperm, if you want it,' Abeo said. 'I just thought you'd want a white donor—'

'Only because *I'm* white—'

'It's fine, darling, I get it.'

An awkward silence.

'Talk to Suria about it, anyway,' he said.

'Talk to me about what?' Suria was stumbling out on to the terrace, a wine glass in each hand.

'She'll tell you later.' Abeo took the glass from Suria's left hand and kissed her cheek.

'I've been looking for you everywhere,' Suria said. She gave Alison a messy kiss. 'I've drunk all your drinks. Come and sing karaoke. We're doing a duet.'

'I don't sing in public—'

'Please?'

'Abeo will do a duet with you. Won't you, Abeo?'

'Aye, OK, Abeo, let's go.' Suria was slurring. 'We're doing "I know him so well". I'm Elaine Paige, you're Barbara whatshername. The Scottish one.'

Abeo put an arm around her and led her back inside. 'I'd be honoured. One of my clients played the Barbara Dickson part in *Chess* at the Coliseum last summer. Quite a short run. You know it's literally about a chess match?'

The door into the pub swung shut behind them. Alison walked back to the railings and stared down into the river again, except the fireworks had petered out and there was nothing to see but blackness.

London looked hungover on New Year's Day, full of regret. The Christmas lights were feeble against the grey morning sky. Shop windows screamed desperately about sales and the poinsettias were half-price at M&S, along with the Brussels sprouts and the musical tins of shortbread. Alison was hungover, too, but she hoped that would soon be a thing of the past: she was on her way to meet Lena in a Swedish café that sold stodgy cinnamon buns and very strong, very expensive coffee. She was early, so she wandered up and down the backstreets of Soho for a while, trying to remember the night before. She remembered arriving at the pub in Bermondsey. She remembered Abeo's bow tie, and Ed's faded Coca-Cola T-shirt, and Abeo kissing her and saying, 'This is Ed's idea of making an effort.' She remembered all the wine, and singing 'Auld Lang Syne', but the rest of the night was blurry. She did remember her conversation with Abeo on the terrace, though. It's not every day someone offers up their husband as a sperm donor.

The Swedish café was a soothing place, full of trendy people in oversized jumpers comparing New Year's Eve stories and laughing, quietly, so as not to reactivate their headaches. Lena was sitting in the window, staring vaguely into the street. She waved when she saw Alison. She was wearing a familiar checked shirt.

'Isn't that mine?' Alison asked, taking off her coat.

'I'll give it back, once I've washed it.' Lena pulled out a stool for her. 'Got you a coffee.' Lena seemed thinner than she had at Christmas. The skin beneath her eyes looked bruised.

'I'll get the buns, then. Cardamom or cinnamon?'

'Sit down for a minute first.'

So Alison did. 'How was last night?'

'Not amazing. Me and Izzy went out, but I saw this bloke with green eyes on the dance floor, and I thought he might be our half-brother and I totally freaked out.'

Alison nodded. Best to change the subject. 'I meant to say, Jim's sent me some examples of his work.'

'Who?'

'That bloke I went to art school with. I told you, he's up for making Mum's gravestone—'

'I don't want to talk about Mum's grave.'

'Would a bun make you feel better?'

Lena ignored the question. 'I just can't stop thinking about not being related to Dad.'

Alison was far too hungover for this conversation.

'Don't you have anything to say about any of this? At all?' Lena said.

'I think I want to pretend it never happened.'

'But it's blowing my mind! How is it not blowing your mind?'

Alison closed her eyes. 'Please let me get a bun, for my hangover.'

'Are you still going to use an anonymous sperm donor?'

Alison could feel her face reddening. 'Sperm donors aren't anonymous any more. The kids can find out who they are when they're eighteen.'

Lena was staring at her. 'Alison!'

'We don't have another option.'

'Can't you see how fucked up that is? Suddenly discovering who your father is when you're eighteen?'

'Our kid won't have a father!' Alison said. 'And *Dad*'s our father, not some sperm donor we've never met.'

'But he's not, though, actually, is he?'

'Yes! He is!'

People were definitely staring now.

'You're in denial.'

'I'm not!' Lena could be so fucking patronizing some-times.

'And your kids won't have a dad at all, and it's not like they won't notice—'

Alison couldn't believe the words that were coming out of her sister's mouth. 'Can you hear how homophobic you sound?'

'But that's just – reality! This is the world we live in. Every family in every cartoon has a mum and a dad. When your kids go to nursery, all their friends will have a mummy and a daddy, and they'll come home and say, "Why do we have two mums? Why don't we have a dad?" That's just what's going to happen, I'm sorry—'

'They might decide they don't want to know about the donor at all—'

'Of course they'll want to know!' Lena slapped the table for emphasis. The coffee in Alison's mug rippled in response.

Alison forced herself to take a breath. 'The fertility counsellor told us most people aren't that interested in their genetic family, if they're told the truth from the very beginning—'

'A counsellor employed by a fertility clinic with a finan-cial incentive to get you to buy the treatment they're selling?'

'Lena—' Alison was flushed, stuttering, furious.

'You know the donors aren't obliged to have any kind of relationship with their genetic offspring at all? And you know that if you buy sperm from a commercial sperm bank, your kids might have *literally hundreds* of half-siblings around the world? You know there's no worldwide limit on the number of families one man's sperm can create?'

'If *you* want kids, you can just fuck Adam—'

Lena shook her head. 'I just think it's wrong to bring up a child without them knowing where fifty per cent of their DNA came from—'

'Plenty of people grow up not knowing who their biological father is.'

'Not intentionally, pre-planned, before birth—'

'Are you saying a child needs a mother and a father? What are you, a fucking Catholic priest?'

'That's not what I'm saying—'

'It literally is!'

Alison's hangover was worse than ever. 'Please can we talk about something else?'

'Just one more thing. Just one thing.' Lena's eyes were shining. 'Please don't buy sperm from one of the big American sperm banks, or the big Danish ones. The donors are more likely to be lying about their medical history, because they're getting paid—'

Alison looked out of the window. She didn't have any fight left in her. A couple walked past, a man and a woman, two babies in a double buggy.

'Please. If you're going to do it, get sperm from the UK—'

'We've already bought the sperm.'

'But Suria's not pregnant! It's not too late!'

Alison felt limp, the way she always did at the end of an argument.

'You can get a refund if they haven't shipped the sperm, I've checked. Please, UK sperm banks are better regulated. And the donors don't get paid. At least use a UK sperm bank. *Please*, Alison.'

'I'll talk to Suria.'

But Lena had never known when to stop. 'Or use a known donor. It's much better to use a known donor, so the kids will never have to wonder who their biological father is.'

Alison looked down at her hands. Her heart hurt. 'If the kids have a father, what would be the point of me?'

Lena was shaking her head. 'You'll be their mother—'

'Suria will be their mother. I'll be a random person they're not related to who's always telling them to tidy their rooms.'

'Come on,' Lena said. 'Don't be so black and white about it. I'm not saying Dad's just a random bloke.'

'You're the one who's being black and white.' Alison wanted to shake her sister, until her old personality settled back into her, like flakes in a snow globe. Instead, she said, 'So. Are you going to look for *our* donor, then?'

Lena picked up Alison's empty coffee cup. She put it down again. 'I just kind of – I feel like I have to.'

Alison felt her brain open, just for a second – and it really hit her, the truth that there was an alternate reality existing alongside this one, and that, technically at least, she had another father. For a moment, she let herself imagine what it would be like to meet this man, and any other children he had, a whole new family, and who knows what they'd be like – homophobic, maybe, or interested in stamp collecting, or ukuleles, or conspiracy theories. The donor probably wouldn't want to meet them anyway, because he had been promised anonymity, and she wouldn't be able to take the rejection – but it would be even worse if he *didn't* reject them – and she felt like she was about to be buried in an avalanche of strangers. She said, 'Don't tell me if you find him.'

Lena looked at her. 'Why not?'

'I just— I just don't want to know.'

But Lena was shaking her head. 'I don't want to have any secrets from you!'

'Then leave it,' Alison said. 'Just leave it. You don't need to hunt this guy down. You don't need to do that to yourself. Or to him, or to Dad.'

Lena's eyes were closed, her eyelids fluttering the way they had the morning of their mother's funeral as they had waited for the burial to begin. Alison hadn't been able to watch as the undertakers lowered the coffin into the grave, but Lena had thought it was important to face it, just as she had thought it was important for them to see their mother's body, so they could accept that she was gone. And wherever Lena went, Alison went, so she had stood there, looking down at her mother, so still, almost as pale as the hospital sheets, only it wasn't her mother any more. The white, waxy, empty face still came to her in dreams. She could have done without seeing it, in other words. 'Please can we stop talking about this now?'

Lena nodded. 'Can I use your DNA test? If you don't want it?'

Alison wanted to say no – wanted to beg her not to take the test – but what was the point, if Lena had made up her mind? 'OK,' she said. 'But seriously, if you dare tell me anything you find out—'

'I won't.'

A beat.

'But I don't know why you've got such a problem with knowing the truth.'

Alison didn't either, really, except that it felt essential, like self-preservation. 'I don't want to fuck up my sense of self.'

Lena looked blank. 'But surely if we find out who we are it'll *give* us a sense of self—'

'No! I've already got one! I don't want a new one! And I don't want to be bombarded with internet weirdos who think we have something in common just because we're technically related—'

'But we might be, like— part Thai or something!'

'I really don't think we are.'

'German then! We might be really German.' Lena's eyes were wide with the possibilities. Why couldn't she see how terrifying all of this was?

'I just – I don't want to know.'

'Fine.'

An awkward pause.

Eventually, Lena asked, 'What kind of bun do you want?'

They walked up to the counter together and stood several feet apart.

A woman in an apron smiled at them. 'Can I get you girls a coffee?'

Alison looked down at the empty sheets of baking parchment, sticky circles where the pastries had been. 'Are there any more buns?' she asked.

The woman shook her head, apologetic. 'Some guy just came and bought them all.'

'Fucker,' Alison said.

The woman in the apron laughed. Then she looked at Lena, and stopped laughing. 'I'm really sorry. If you come back tomorrow, I'll put some aside specially—'

'I'm fine.' Lena wiped her face with the back of her hand. 'I just really – I was really in the mood for a Scandinavian pastry.'

*

'I'm still in the middle of your onion, aren't I?' Alison asked, as they left the café.

Lena had read about the Relationship Onion in some self-help book or other. She'd introduced the concept to Alison soon after Izzy dumped her. 'The people you're closest to are in the middle of your onion, and less important people are on the outer layers,' she'd said, sitting on the edge of the bed as Alison sobbed into her pillow. 'Izzy was in the middle of your onion, but you can mentally move her further out, where she can't hurt you any more.'

'I want to peel her off the onion altogether—'

'Sure. She's the old rotten onion skin,' Lena had said then. 'Put her in the bin.'

Now she said, 'Of course you're still in the middle of my onion. You basically *are* my onion.' But they didn't hug as they said goodbye.

The argument played in a loop in Alison's head as she rattled back to Leytonstone on the Central Line, trying and failing to concentrate on an article about the Brexit negotiations in the *Evening Standard*. Lena must still be in shock. She didn't *really* believe Alison and Suria shouldn't have children. She couldn't. The sister Alison knew would never be so hung up on biology, so conservative, so narrow in her definition of what a family was. Lena was in the wrong. Wasn't she?

Just a week ago, starting a family had seemed like a straightforwardly good thing to do, like eating less red meat or signing up for an allotment. But finding out she was donor conceived had complicated things, even though she was trying her best not to think about it. She wished she'd never seen the Facebook forums, never read the posts from people who felt it was their human right to grow up knowing their biological parents and siblings, who thought paying men for their sperm ought to be illegal. She hated that she was doing something that so many people believed was unethical. But what choice did she have, really? Her desire to become a parent felt almost physical, a lump in her chest, a spot in her vision, always there.

Of course she wished there was an alternative to using a sperm donor. She had a green pension, and she only bought organic free-range eggs, and every time she needed a new T-shirt it cost her upwards of thirty quid because she had given up buying fast fashion. Perhaps she ought to try a bit harder to find an ethical sperm bank. Did such a thing exist? If only it were the Seventies – she and Suria would have lived in a squat in West London, like her parents had, and raised their children in a queer commune, taking it in turns to do childcare and host CND meetings. She wouldn't have had as many control issues in the Seventies. She'd definitely have been more politically active. She'd have been beaten up by the police more often, though, probably.

Maybe she ought to take Ed and Abeo's offer seriously.

'What do you think about using a known donor?' Alison asked Suria that night, as they ate spaghetti carbonara by candlelight, listening to Carole King.

'I honestly don't think we should indulge Lena. She needs to try harder to see this situation from our point of view.'

'I'm trying to think about it from the kid's point of view. And lots of donor-conceived people think known donors are way better—'

'Do you know anyone who'd be up for giving us sperm?' Suria had dropped a bit of bacon on her Victorian nightie.

'Shit.' She pushed back her chair and walked to the sink, dabbing the white cotton with a piece of damp kitchen roll.

'Well,' Alison said, putting down her fork, 'we could ask Ed.'

Suria looked up. 'What?'

'Abeo said he might be up for it.'

'When? Last night?'

'Yes.'

'But Ed didn't offer himself?'

'I mean – no. But Abeo wouldn't have brought it up if they hadn't talked about it.'

Suria sat down again, her hands clasped. 'This could be amazing. This way, we'd know the donor wasn't a total weirdo.'

'Just a partial weirdo. You know Ed fancies Dominic Raab?'

'No!'

'I know.'

Carole King started to sing 'You've Got a Friend'.

Suria was smiling now. 'Aye. Let's do it.'

'As in—'

'As in, let's ask Ed, when we see him next.'

Alison's heart sped up. 'You really think it's a good idea?'

Suria laughed. 'You suggested it!'

Alison untangled her spaghetti and wished she could do the same with her thoughts. Because she did think it was a good idea for children to grow up knowing their biological family, but she didn't want to feel left out, to be irrelevant in her child's life. And it would be wonderful to form a big, queer family, but what if they fell out and she lost her best friends?

'It'll be fine,' Suria was saying. She'd said the same thing about the Brexit vote, though, and after Trump was elected, and before Alison failed her fourth driving test. 'If Ed and Abeo say no, we'll have done our best, and we can go ahead and use a donor with our conscience clear. OK?' She put spaghetti in her mouth, like a full stop.

Lonely old pensioner

Tom was woken on the second of January by the doorbell. He turned over and checked his alarm clock. Almost ten in the morning. He had once been the sort of man to leap out of bed at six to make himself a smug cup of coffee and get a head start on the day. No longer. All he had to look forward to now was slowing down, stiffening up, and a funeral that his daughters might not even attend. He'd read about municipal services organized by the council for people who die without money or friends. That'll be me, he thought, and pulled the duvet up around his chin. The doorbell rang again. He swore, heaved himself upright and wrestled himself into yesterday's clothes.

There are certain perils associated with being at home during daylight hours, prime among which is the risk of being asked to sign for your neighbours' parcel deliveries. He looked through the peephole: he wasn't going to be caught out again. A woman was standing on the doorstep. She was wearing a Barbour jacket, and her grey hair was

Kate Davies

piled on her head and held in place, somehow, by a pencil.
He was sure he had seen her somewhere before.

'Hello,' he said, as he opened the door.

The woman smiled. Nice teeth. 'I've just moved in to
12b, so I thought I'd introduce myself properly.' She reached
out a hand. 'I'm Jessie.'

'Tom,' he said, shaking it. His voice sounded dusty with
disuse. He cleared his throat.

'Happy New Year!' she said.

'Yes,' he said.

She pointed at his boots. 'Snap.' She was wearing DMs,
too. 'It's just you here, is it?'

'It is.'

She nodded. She looked into the hallway, probably to
reassure herself it wasn't stacked with corpses. 'I just wanted
to say that if you ever need anything, just let me know.'

'Need anything?'

'If you need me to add anything to my Sainsbury's delivery
for you—'

She thought he was a lonely old pensioner. Which he
would be, he realized, if he'd ever bothered to sort out his
pension. But she wasn't much younger than he was. In
fact— 'Jessie . . . Collins?'

She looked taken aback. 'Yes . . .'

He laughed. 'It's me. Tom Delancey. From Haldane Road.'

She covered her mouth with her hand. 'No!'

'Afraid so.'

'Fuck me!' she said.

'It's a bit early for that,' he said, and then wished he
hadn't, but she didn't seem to mind. She looked as impressive as she had in the early Eighties, though her hair had
been dark brown then. She hugged him the way she had

90

all those years ago, when she'd moved in to the squat round the corner and he'd helped her steal electricity from the National Grid.

'Tom Delancey! I'm mortified— I can't believe I just offered to help you with your groceries—'

'It's fine. The picture in my attic is getting more handsome by the second.'

'I'm so sorry—'

'Whereas you haven't changed a bit.'

'Bollocks. I went on the anti-Brexit march the other day, and two people asked if they could take a photo of me, and thanked me for marching, because I'm so bloody old.'

'I'm impressed that you're still out marching.'

'Keeps me young.'

'I should try it, clearly.'

She laughed again. 'Well. Isn't this nice, being neighbours again? We should have a cup of tea one day.'

He thought about the way he'd had to clear his throat to say hello. He said, 'We should. I would really like that.'

Lena arrived for lunch with armfuls of paper bags. Somehow, without Tom noticing, she had become an adult, with a sensible haircut and a proper handbag and enough money to buy organic groceries. This morning, she looked more like her mother than ever. Same wavy hair, same disappointed expression when she looked at him. She usually had her mother's smile, too, but she wasn't smiling today. Tom tried to hug her, but the paper bags got in the way. Instead, they nodded to each other. Politely, as though they were rival croquet players, or feuding horticulturalists.

'Lena.'

'Dad.'

He watched with alarm as she unloaded the shopping bags on to the kitchen table. A distressing array of lentils and green vegetables; something in a white packet that looked horribly like tofu. 'You didn't need to bring food. I'm having flashbacks to my hippy days,' he told her.

'You didn't have heart problems when you were a hippy,' she pointed out. 'I'm making you a lentil and kale salad for lunch. With goat's cheese in it.'

'Is this my punishment?' he asked, half-hoping she'd say, 'What for?'

She ignored him and put the tofu in the fridge on the shelf next to the cured meats. She turned to look at him, one hand on the open fridge door. 'Salami?'

'I am not giving up salami.'

'You have to.'

'I'd rather die. There aren't many pleasures left in my life—'

She held up a block of Cheddar.

'It's just cheese!'

'It's a lump of fat! It's not even nice Cheddar! It's not worth it!'

'Go away.' He crossed his arms.

'You're lucky I'm talking to you at all.' She took a sieve from the cupboard and poured the lentils into it.

'Oho! Ohoho!' He rocked back in his chair. He was aware that a novelist might describe his laugh as 'blustery'. He stopped pretending to laugh and tapped his fingers on the table. 'I'm very glad you're talking to me.'

She ran the lentils under the tap.

'You haven't forgiven me then, I take it.'

She turned off the tap. She didn't reply.

'You'll never guess who's moved in next door,' he said.

She looked up.

'Jessie Collins. We were squatters together! What are the odds?' It wasn't working. Lena wasn't smiling. 'Come on, Lenny. I can't change what happened—'

'I know you can't.' Her voice was hard. The way Sheila's had been, when he'd told her about Natasha.

She tipped the lentils into a saucepan and threw the sieve into the sink.

'You should have put the water in the pan first,' he told her.

'I know how to cook lentils.' She put the pan on the hob and said, 'Did they tell you anything about the donor, at all?' Straight to the point. Just like her mother, again.

'Why don't we eat first?'

Lena put her hands on her hips. 'I'm not really in the mood for small talk, to be honest.'

There was no avoiding the conversation. So he told her what he knew. 'The way it worked was they picked a donor – one of the medical students – who looked a bit like the father—'

'I always thought I had your eyes. And your way with words.'

He laughed, without smiling. 'If you'd read the rejection letters I get for my short stories, you'd be thanking your lucky stars you didn't inherit my way with words.'

Her face softened slightly. He didn't want her pity. Still, it was better than nothing. She opened a packet of kale and shook it into a colander.

'We're never going to eat all that.'

'It'll wilt.' She looked up at him. 'Where did you have the fertility treatment?'

'Sussex Hospital.'

'In London?'

'Near Euston, yes. It doesn't exist any more. The doctor's name was Sandringham. A woman doctor.'

'Woah. A *woman doctor*.' She was mocking him.

'It was quite unusual to be seen by a woman doctor in the Eighties, actually, Lena.'

'Then say "female doctor", Dad. Would you say "man doctor"? No. You wouldn't.'

She took her phone from her pocket and started typing something into it. What was she doing? Panic was rising in him now. He asked, 'Why? Why do you want to know about the doctor, anyway?'

She put her palms on the kitchen counter. 'I'm going to try and find the sperm donor.'

He tried to keep his face neutral, but it was chaos inside his head. 'I'm not sure that's a very good idea.'

'Well. It's not your decision.'

All this time, his greatest fear had been his children finding out they weren't related to him. But something worse had been lying in wait. What if his daughters found their biological father and realized Tom was a poor imitation of the real thing? What if this man was just like them: artistic and funny and fond of leafy vegetables? What if he was healthy and young? 'They didn't keep records,' he said, unable to hide the desperation in his voice. 'They actually destroyed them, on purpose—'

'That's so fucked up—'

'Yes, well. The government evidently agrees with you. They changed the law in 2005—'

'I know—'

'—so kids born now have the right to find out who the donor is when they're eighteen.'

94

'I know, stop *telling* me things as if I don't *know* them—'

'I don't know how much research you've done—'

'And even though they changed the law, you didn't tell us—'

'The law isn't retrospective! What good would it do, telling you? And how was I supposed to bring it up? "Oh, pass the salt, Lena. By the way, I'm not your biological father—"'

'No, you're right, much better to risk me finding out from a fucking DNA test—'

'You're not being very fair, Lenny.'

'STOP CALLING ME LENNY.'

The room sang with silence. A car drove past, bringing him back to himself. He cleared his throat.

'Sorry,' she said. The water in the pan of lentils was spitting and churning.

His heart was beating wildly, clamouring at him to do something, to find some way to make her see sense. He said, '*I'm* sorry, for what you're going through. But don't you think it would be better to leave it? Alison doesn't care about any of this—'

Lena laughed. Covered her eyes with her hands.

He was saying the wrong things, he *knew* he was saying the wrong things, but he couldn't stop, because he had to keep his family together somehow. 'Your parents are the people who brought you up. Strangers you've found on the internet are not your family. We're all related to people genetically! We're all fucking descended from the same woman in Africa, aren't we? Doesn't mean she's family—'

'You don't get to tell me who my family are.'

'Come on. I'm still your father—'

'You're not, though, genetically. That's the whole point. You're *not*.'

He couldn't breathe for a moment, couldn't believe his worst nightmare had actually come true. He loved her so much, he had always loved them both with all of his being, and that wasn't enough to stop his beloved daughter rejecting him. As easy as that. Like she'd just picked up her life and shaken him out of it, tossing away everything he'd done for her, the night feeds and the bedtime stories and the school drop-offs and the lectures about cigarettes and the bowls of porridge and listening to *Hancock's Half Hour* and the goodnight kisses and the trips to the doctor and the love and the love and the love.

She looked smaller after that, a little afraid of herself.

'I've always believed in nurture over nature,' he said, but the words sounded strangled, and he stood up and left the room before his body could betray him. He locked the bathroom door. He sat on the toilet seat and stared down at the white hair on the backs of his hands and thought back to the nights when she had pushed her mother away, saying, 'No, Mummy. I want Daddy.'

A knock at the bathroom door. 'I'm sorry,' she said. 'I'm just upset.'

He flushed the toilet, as though he'd used it. 'It's fine.'

'Come and eat this lovely salad with me.'

'Don't try and kid me. I've seen the ingredients,' he said, emerging into the corridor.

She hugged him. He wanted to kiss her on the forehead, but he hadn't done that since she was a teenager, so he patted her back instead. 'The thing is,' he said, into her shoulder, 'you have to remember how much we wanted you.'

She pulled out of the hug. 'Oh, Dad—'

One syllable, but it was everything. And to think that, once upon a time, he had tried to persuade the kids to call him by his first name. 'You're an idiot,' Sheila had told him, at the time.

'Thank you,' he said, now. 'Thank you, for calling me Dad.'

Lena took his hand as they walked to the kitchen. He hadn't held hands with anyone for decades – Sheila had never been a hand-holding sort of person – but there had been a few short, sun-drenched years when he'd held hands every day, crossing the road, or walking to the shops, or skipping through the park (he was a nimble skipper, even now). One little hand in each of his.

The salad tasted marginally better than it looked.

'Very chewy,' he said, gnawing on a leaf.

'It's supposed to have more dressing on it than this,' Lena said.

'What are the pink raisin things?'

'Dried cranberries.'

'They're helping.' He stole an extra one from Lena's plate. 'I'll try and make it up to you,' he told her. 'I'm going to be a better father.'

She nodded, the way Sheila had, every time he promised to give up smoking.

'I will,' he said. 'You don't really want to find this donor chap, do you?' He hated how needy he sounded.

She put down her fork. 'Yes, Dad. I do.'

'Won't it be nigh-on impossible, though? I don't want you to be disappointed—'

'I've got to at least try. And plenty of people find their donors, by taking DNA tests—'

'So, what, you just wait and hope that he takes the same test as you?'

'No. Even if I just match with second or third cousins, I can build a family tree, and work backwards to find out who my great-grandparents were, and then work forwards again from there.'

'That sounds quite labour intensive.'

'It is.'

Which was heartening. Lena was a corporate litigator. She didn't have the time to fanny around on ancestry websites.

'Alison's given me her DNA test, though. So I'll take that and see if there's anything interesting in the results. That's the first step.'

He nodded. He had to stop her. He had to find a way to stop her.

A *twenty-first-century Pandora's box*

Lena was suspended, halfway between who she'd thought she was and who she might turn out to be – and yet she couldn't bring herself to take the DNA test. Not yet. What if she didn't find the answers she was looking for? What if she didn't *like* the answers? The box sat on the kitchen counter, the glossy cardboard now dulled by splatters of curry and porridge and Heinz baked beans. Time was passing in fits and starts, seconds lasting weeks and days disappearing into weekends, and Lena's friends had already stopped asking how she was, the way people do after your mother has been dead for a couple of months and they think that you're probably over the worst of it, that it would only upset you to bring it up in conversation.

Lena worried how Alison was coping, but since the argument in the Swedish coffee shop, their conversations had become less frequent and more stilted. Alison insisted she was fine – and Lena felt fine too, most of the time. Sure, occasionally she woke up after a nightmare and started hyperventilating because she didn't recognize her own hand

and wanted to cut it off, but everyone had something going on, didn't they?

The only thing was, her libido had disappeared along with her sense of identity. Sex was for light-hearted people, people who could look at other human beings without wondering if they were related to them. And on the rare occasions she and Adam did have sex, she struggled to behave like a sexy person.

'Your arse feels amazing,' he said one night in bed. He started to kiss her but Lena couldn't take the intensity of it. She yelped and curled her hands into paws and pulled away.

Adam rolled on to his back. 'Why do you have to do that?' His eyes were closed. 'It isn't sexy when you pretend to be a cat.'

'Sorry,' she said, but she said it the way a kitten might.

'Stop it!'

'OK. I stop.'

'*Stop* talking in a baby voice!'

She turned on to her side, cringing.

'You were yourself a minute ago. You were an adult.'

'OK,' Lena said, taking a breath. 'I can be an adult.'

He started stroking her face again. His breathing was getting heavier. 'You're so fucking sexy.' He looked so serious. She tried to keep a straight face. She failed.

Adam stared up at the ceiling.

'Sorry, Donkey. I can't do it.'

'You can. And please don't call me Donkey during sex. You can't have kids if you act like a baby all the time—'

'I don't want kids right now anyway, Adam.'

'Oh.' He looked at her. 'Really?'

'I think I'm too traumatized for a baby at the moment.' She could see him trying to hide his disappointment, adjusting to a new vision of the future. '*Now* you talk like an adult,' he said, eventually. He kissed her on the forehead and started to get his clothes ready for the next morning, as if to prove what a grown-up he was.

She felt raw and exposed on the Tube as she made her way to the office for the first time in January. But the other commuters were caught up in their own lives, trying to remember how to do their jobs after two weeks eating Quality Street on the sofa, adjusting the new trousers they'd got for Christmas, probably wishing they'd asked for a larger size. As Lena walked from Bank Station to the office, she was swept along by all the other people who looked like her. She had never been so pleased to feel ordinary.

Copperfield and Bailey's London headquarters was the sort of building designed to make people like Adam angry, with out-of-season cut flowers on the reception desk and an unnecessary fish tank. Lena practised smiling as she swiped her pass on the entrance gate.

'Happy New Year!' Angela, the receptionist, said. Angela had bought Lena a tub of cellulite cream for her birthday, once.

'Happy New Year!'

Angela nodded and went back to her computer. Lena had passed as the person she used to be.

There was a pile of leftover Christmas chocolates by the kettle in the kitchen. A Post-it said, *Help yourself!* Lena took a mini-Twix back to her office. She still couldn't quite believe she was grown-up enough to have her own office. She had her own rubber plant, too, which she emptied her water glass into every Friday evening, and a view of the boring bit of the City of London. She ate her Twix as she stood at her window, forehead against the glass, wishing she was on the other side of it, somewhere in the streets below. She imagined the glass disappearing, imagined herself falling, peaceful, arms outstretched, the speed knocking the air out of her lungs before she hit the ground. And then she sat down at her computer and replied to an email about Anna's leaving collection.

'Good Christmas?' James, the senior partner, asked, as the litigation team took their seats in the boardroom for the midday progress meeting.

'Not really,' Lena said, and she told everyone, about being donor conceived. A mistake, she realized, as the room fell silent. James turned to Karla, as though she'd know what to say.

She didn't. 'Your dad's still your dad, though.' Karla fiddled with her necklace.

'I know.'

'And we all inherit traits from people we've never met,' James said. 'Everyone says I have my great uncle's nose. And I've never met the man.'

Lena nodded. Easier not to argue. Would they say the same to someone who had just discovered they were adopted? She knew it wasn't the same, but some donor-conceived people considered themselves to be half-adopted. It was intense, the isolation she felt, now that she knew she was donor conceived, because most people seemed to think it shouldn't bother her.

Silence for a moment. Then James said, 'OK – let's get started. Lena, can you give us an update on the Jerwood case?'

'Of course!' She pressed her tongue to the roof of her

mouth to stop herself crying, the way her mother had taught her to.

She spent the afternoon wading through disclosed documents; thousands of bank statements and emails and letters, most of them completely irrelevant, one of which might prove that the director of a Russian bank was involved in money laundering. She listened to podcasts about DNA and the ethics of donor conception as she worked. She had quickly become an expert on the fertility industry – because it was an industry, a lucrative one, with children as the products. She started throwing slang around on internet forums. She was DC (donor conceived). Her half-siblings were sibs, or diblings, though some considered that a derogatory term. Her donor was her bio dad. Tom Delancey was her social dad. Every day, several times a day, someone new would join the donor-conceived Facebook forum.

I've just found out I'm donor conceived. I'm 54.

I took a Genealogy DNA test, and it turns out my parents used a donor egg.

My mom flew to Florida to tell me, because she knew I was about to take a test.

The old hands welcomed the newbies to the group. They referred to the period between Thanksgiving and New Year as 'sibling season': DNA companies offered discounts, people gave and received tests for Christmas, thousands of new matches appeared on the sites in December, January, February. She felt like she belonged to a strange new club that she had never wanted to be part of. She was already part of the Dead Mum Club, and being donor conceived was a bit like that, except weirder. Because everyone lost someone, eventually, but not many people knew what it was like to have siblings that you'd never meet, to lose a parent who was still alive.

On the Tube home, Lena sat opposite a man with a neat beard and a checked blazer, holding a Jiffy bag. He looked around at the other passengers, then reached into the envelope and pulled out three stacks of brand-new British passports, bound together with elastic bands. He slipped two passports into his breast pocket. Three went into his right trouser pocket. He put the rest back into the Jiffy bag and folded it shut, holding it to his chest, as though he was worried someone might take it away. Lena looked at her own reflection in the grimy window. She couldn't see her eyes clearly because of the dark and the dirt, and she wondered whether her biological father was still alive, and what he'd died of if he wasn't, and whether she'd die from it too. She wondered whether there was a history of cancer in his family, or whether he got acid reflux like she did, and whether her half-siblings had IBS, too, and whether they sneezed when they looked at the sun, and whether they were any good at maths. She wondered where they were, and whether she would ever find any of them, and whether they would fill a Tube carriage, or a whole train, and her fingers tingled with the enormity of it all and as the train moved the vibrations travelled up through her legs, through her stomach, up to her throat and she felt it rattle inside her, the question, her body echoing with the absence of an answer.

Who am I?

*

Adam was in the kitchen when she got home, humming along to a Cajun fiddle tune, sweatshirt sleeves rolled up, taking jars and tins out of the cupboard and lining them up on the floor.

'Pony!' He jogged towards her and tripped on an ancient jar of chutney.

'Hello, Donkey,' she said, putting her arms out for a hug.

'Thought I'd do some spring-cleaning, before term starts again.' He held up a tin of harissa from 2010. 'The year we got together.'

'Maybe we should hang on to it till our tenth anniversary, celebrate with a bout of food poisoning,' Lena suggested.

He threw the harissa in the bin, then picked up the Genealogy DNA test from the kitchen counter. 'Do you want to keep this?'

Lena's heart beat faster: it was a twenty-first century Pandora's box. She read the words on the outside of the kit: *Welcome to you.*

'Can I make an observation?' Adam said. 'Every time you think about being donor conceived, you start to cry. And every time something distracts you, you cheer up.'

Lena sank into the sofa. Adam sat down next to her and reached into his tracksuit trousers to scratch himself. 'Adam. Gross.'

'Sorry.' He stopped scratching. 'Did you know that a bush cricket's testicles make up fourteen per cent of its bodyweight?'

'I didn't know that. Did I need to know that?'

He was looking at the DNA test, frowning.

'What?' she asked.

'Do you really think it'll make you happy, finding this man? And never being able to tell Alison he exists?'

Probably not, she wanted to say. But she had always been a curious person. She knew he was out there somewhere. She couldn't just carry on with her life, pretending he wasn't. What if she put off looking for him until it was too late?

'I just think,' he said, 'that sometimes it's possible to have too much information.'

'Well, yeah, about bush cricket testicles.'

He laughed.

'You think I should embrace denial.'

'Nothing wrong with a bit of denial. Whenever I think about Sunil getting promoted to Special Educational Needs Coordinator over me, I want to stab him with my compass.'

'Don't do that.'

'I won't. Mostly because I don't know where my compass is. But also whenever I think about Sunil, poncing around school with the headteacher—'

'Don't let Alison and Suria hear you say "poncing".'

'I won't. But you take my point.'

'I do.' She opened the box. She felt like she was stepping across a precipice.

'But you're still taking the test.'

She nodded. 'I'm not allowed to eat or drink anything for half an hour before I spit into the tube.'

'I'll set a timer for you,' Adam said, picking up his phone with his testicle fingers.

She placed the plastic tube, warm with her spit, in the box, then sealed it. She walked along Holloway Road, past women in sportswear heading to the netball court and boys riding BMX bikes on the pavement, to the postbox outside the church. She looked up at the great glimmering windows as she pushed the package through the slot. A choir was

106

practising, which added a pleasant sense of occasion to the whole thing. The DNA test made a satisfying papery slap as it landed on the pile of other letters, much more boring ones, invoices and birthday cards and direct debit instructions. Done. The singers faltered. A voice called out, 'Try that again. *Tutti*, figure seven.' She felt calmer, now that it was too late to change her mind.

The sun had set by the time she got home, and the living room looked cosy and messy, the standard lamps casting pools of warm light on the piles of books and newspapers, the rug her mother had bought them as a housewarming present, the sofa where Adam was sitting, left leg crossed over his right knee, as though it was an ordinary day. On the television, Monty Don was taking cuttings from some viburnum. Adam watched a lot of *Gardeners' World*. The flat didn't have a garden, but he wanted to be ready for when they bought their own place.

He stood and hugged her. 'I think you're very brave.'

She dropped to the sofa. 'Please don't divorce me if it turns out my biological father is a murderer, or Nigel Farage.'

'I won't.'

'Or – what if it turns out he's really into fracking?'

'I promise never to divorce you, even if your biological father turns out to be a massive fracking bastard.'

She kissed him. 'I promise not to divorce you, either. Unless you turn out to be my half-brother.' She felt a little thrill of horror at the possibility. Very unlikely, she told herself. Adam and his father both had large, distinctive foreheads and unusually tiny ears.

Adam looked alarmed, too. 'What do you reckon the odds are?'

'We'll find out in six to eight weeks, according to Genealogy DNA.'

'I took the DNA test,' Lena told Alison that Saturday, as they were getting changed after their weekly kickboxing class.

'I've asked you not to tell me anything about that,' Alison said.

'I haven't got the results yet, so there's nothing to tell.'

'OK. Can you pass me my towel?'

They were both trying very hard to pretend nothing had changed since their argument, but these days their WhatsApp exchanges were polite and GIF-free, and the subject of donor conception hung in the air during every conversation.

'You should get Suria to take one, too,' Lena said, peeling off her sports bra.

'Take what?'

'A DNA test. Before you guys have a baby. In case she and the donor are both carriers for the same genetic disorder—'

'Do straight people take DNA tests before they have kids?' Alison asked. 'No. So we shouldn't have to, either.' She sounded pretty angry, but at least they were actually talking about it. 'And anyway,' she said, 'we might not be using a donor.'

Lena looked up, her leggings halfway down her thighs. 'What?'

Alison leaned back against the lockers. 'We're going to ask Ed if he'd be up for giving us some sperm.'

Relief and gratitude. A strange sort of euphoria. Lena hugged her sister, then wished she hadn't: Alison had evidently put more effort into her jump kicks than Lena had.

'He hasn't said yes yet,' Alison pointed out, as Lena wiped her sister's sweat from her cheek.

A *silent fish pie*

Alison and Suria were planning to ask Ed to be their donor that night, over dinner. Alison had been feeling increasingly anxious all day. She had been for a run that morning to get the adrenaline out, and listened to a meditation podcast as she got dressed afterwards, breathing in for a count of four as she pulled on her jeans, breathing out for a count of six as she looked for a matching pair of socks, but her heart hammered on, relentless, as though it was trying to get her attention. Maybe it was warning her the whole thing was a bad idea.

'It seems ungrateful to ask for sperm when they're cooking us dinner,' she said to Suria as they stood outside the tower block where Ed and Abeo lived, arms crossed against the cold. 'Maybe we should wait, and cook for *them*—'

'So that they owe us something?' The door buzzed. Suria pushed it open.

'No—'

Suria walked through to the stairwell, but Alison hesitated, the way she had when she'd bungee-jumped from a crane in Peru, aged nineteen. There was a video somewhere, showing her stepping to the edge of the cage, then panicking and grabbing on to the sides, as the instructor shouted, 'Let go! It's too late to change your mind!' in Spanish.

'What if they say no, and it ruins our friendship?'

'They won't say no. Abeo literally offered.'

They were in the lift now, and the doors were sliding closed, and if they didn't ask Ed and Abeo they'd have to use the donor sperm—

'You look like you're about to boak,' Suria said, which wasn't very comforting.

'I feel like – you know when you ask someone out, or tell them you fancy them, and it turns out they're not interested, so you feel really dirty, like you're a predator?'

Suria looked blank. The lift pinged open.

'Oh god,' Alison said, as Suria knocked on Ed and Abeo's door.

'It's fine.' Suria tucked her hair behind her ears. 'I'll bring it up straight away. Get it over with.'

'How about we wait to see if it comes up organically in conversation?'

'I'll make sure it's totally organic.'

And before Alison could reply, Abeo was ushering them inside. He was wearing an immaculate cream shirt and perfectly creased mustard trousers. He must spend a lot of time ironing, Alison thought, as Oscar the border terrier barked at her territorially, as though he knew she had ulterior motives.

'Sorry about him,' Abeo said. 'I think he's going through puberty. Poor boy.'

Alison laughed, but she could feel that her face wasn't smiling the way she wanted it to.

'Where's Ed?' Suria said, taking off her coat.

'In the living room!' called Ed.

Suria went to find him. Alison could hear him apologizing for how hot the flat was, something about a broken thermostat, as she followed Abeo into the kitchen. She usually felt at home in Ed and Abeo's flat; she had spent so much time here over the years, sleeping in the spare room after bad dates and disappointing days in the studio; she knew where to find the bin bags and how Abeo liked to stack the dishwasher (Ed never did it properly). She had even helped pick the tiles for the bathroom floor. They shouldn't have listened to her. The hexagonal pattern she'd suggested was like a Magic Eye picture if you stared at it for too long, and she got a headache every time she used their toilet. But today, her breath was high in her chest and she leaned awkwardly against the granite worktop in the kitchen as Abeo crouched down and opened the oven. She felt as though she had tricked her way over the threshold. 'Fish pie's nearly ready,' Abeo said, shutting the oven door again, fanning the steam away.

'Shall I put this in the fridge?' She held out a bottle of cava, grateful to have a prop.

'Let's open it now,' Abeo said. 'I'm desperate for a drink. Ed's family came over earlier. I beat them at Monopoly, and it all got a bit tense.'

Alison followed Abeo to the living room, which was homely but a little too cluttered for Alison's taste; velvet sofas with woollen throws draped casually over the arms, framed posters advertising plays Abeo's clients had starred in, records and cards and odd bits of art stacked on the bookshelves. Ed's collection of Star Wars figures and Arsenal memorabilia had been banished to the spare room. Alison wondered if the baby would inherit Ed's terrible taste in clothes and interior design, or if that was a nurture over nature thing. She shouldn't be so shallow, she knew, but she couldn't help it: aesthetics were important to her. She nibbled the nuts Abeo had set out in little china bowls as she watched Ed fuss over Oscar. He would be a brilliant dad, she decided, though they weren't actually going to ask him to be a dad—

'Are you OK, darling?' Abeo asked.

'Yeah! Fine!' Alison ate a crisp, casually.

'You don't have to be fine.' This was one of the few annoying things about Abeo: like Lena, he thought that talking about things made them better. 'I spoke to Lena about it the other day. She sounds kind of traumatized—'

'Yes. Well. Lena and I are very different people.'

'As long as you know we're always here,' Abeo said. He raised his eyebrows at Ed, encouraging him to say something.

Ed just said, 'Yeah,' then lowered his eyes respectfully, as though he was trying to imagine how he'd feel if he discovered he wasn't related to his father.

Which is when Suria smiled at Abeo and said, 'While we're on the subject of sperm donation—'

Abeo sat up very straight. He looked as though he'd forgotten to turn the iron off.

'Suria,' Alison said, trying to catch her eye, because she could see what was coming.

But Suria carried on. 'Have you guys thought any more about it?'

Ed was looking from Suria to Abeo and back again, brow furrowed. 'Thought about what?'

'Doesn't matter,' Alison said.

'No, tell me.'

Abeo was playing with the bottle of cava, turning it in his hands so it caught the light. 'I just said – I told the girls you might be up for being their sperm donor.' He said it quickly and quietly, as though he was hoping no one would hear.

'Abeo!'

'It was your idea! Don't you remember?' Abeo said, as though Alison and Suria weren't there.

'I've literally got no recollection of this conversation.'

'We talked about it when we went to see that play about surrogacy at the Donmar. At the interval. We did, I remember it really clearly—'

'That was in 2013!'

'God, was it?' Abeo put a hand to his mouth.

'OK, forget it,' Suria said.

Alison desperately tried to think of something else to talk about, but her mind was blank, and Abeo was looking at Ed and saying, 'We could just discuss it quickly now? Seeing as we're talking about it already? You'd still be up for donating your sperm in theory, right?'

'Yeah, but we're not talking "in theory" any more,' Ed pointed out. He looked at Suria. 'How are you thinking it would work?'

'Let's leave it.' Alison had to get out of the room. 'I'm going to the loo,' she announced.

But the walls of the flat were very thin, and as she sat on the toilet, head in her hands, cursing the tiles on the bathroom floor, she could hear Suria saying, 'From what I've read, it's best to donate sperm through a clinic so it's all really clear, legally, where everyone stands—'

'Yeah, but were you thinking we'd co-parent?' Ed was saying. 'Or that I'd just be a sperm donor?'

'Co-parenting's probably too complicated. Like, it's not ideal, bringing up a child between two homes.'

'But we'd be part of the baby's life, wouldn't we?' Abeo said.

'Aye, sure, that's the idea—'

The situation was slipping out of her control. Panicking, she pulled the flush, but by the time she was back in the living room, Abeo was saying, 'I mean – if Ed's not keen, you can just have *my* sperm—'

'Abeo! I don't want Alison and Suria bringing up your child without us being involved!'

'It wouldn't be my child, though, that's the point.'

'I'd want to do it properly,' Ed said. 'So the kid would have two mums and two dads.'

'I didn't think you wanted kids,' Suria said.

'I didn't think I did.' Ed crossed his arms.

Suria looked at Alison, alarmed. 'I'm just not sure that would work.'

'Me and Suria would be the ones on the birth certificate,' Alison said, sitting down.

'But I'd still be the father, is what I'm saying,' Ed said.

'*Biological* father,' Suria said. 'Sperm donor—'

'And my mum would definitely want to know her grand-child.'

'We'd have no problem with that,' Alison said, just as Suria was saying, 'We'd need to draw up some kind of arrangement—'

Abeo stood up to take the empty wine bottle to the kitchen. Alison could see him through the door, standing, hands on hips, reluctant to come back in.

'And what if you both died?' Ed asked. 'In a car crash?'

'No current plans,' Alison said.

'Or carbon monoxide poisoning?'

'Please stop imagining us dying,' Suria said.

Abeo was back, with another bottle of wine.

'Look, you wouldn't have any legal parental responsibility,' Suria said. 'You'd be like godfathers, or uncles. No one would come after you for money—'

Ed's shoulders were around his ears.

'Let's just leave it,' Alison said. 'It's fine. It doesn't matter. It was just an idea.'

When Abeo went to fill Suria's glass, she said, 'I've had enough. Thanks.'

There was an unpleasant silence.

'You have other options, don't you?' Abeo said.

'Yes! Yes. We can use a sperm bank, like everyone else.' Another silence.

'Let's just forget about it,' Suria said. 'It would only work if everyone was totally cool with it, and you're clearly not totally cool with it.'

'We can talk about it more, over the next week or so,' Abeo said.

'No. Don't.' Suria stood up.

'Don't be like that—' Ed called after her.

'I'm fine!'

The toilet door slammed.

And then – *bing!* – the oven timer went.

'Fish pie's ready!' said Abeo, running from the room.

Ed followed him, muttering about water glasses.

Alison sat there alone. She poured herself another glass of wine and made herself smile, to convince her body she wasn't devastated.

*

Alison and Suria left early, after the silent fish pie. Abeo walked them to the door. 'Bye! See you soon, darlings!' he said, smiling and waving too vigorously.

'They moved the goalposts,' Suria said, as she and Alison walked down Finchley Road, hand in hand.

Alison didn't know what to say. She was pulsing with humiliation and rejection. She was angry with Suria for bringing up the subject of sperm donation at a dinner party, and furious with Abeo for putting them in such an awkward position, and she was angry with Ed, too, because *of course* he wouldn't be a parent if he didn't do any actual parenting, and she was raging, just raging, against nature, because two women ought to be able to have a child together without going through all this awful bullshit.

A red-faced man clutching a blue plastic bag stumbled out of an off licence and shouted 'Dykes!'

Alison walked faster. 'I can't believe Abeo didn't check with Ed before he suggested it.' She was going over and over the conversation in her head, trying to work out what she could have said to make it less of a disaster.

'Aye, well, I should have checked that *he'd* checked before we brought it up at dinner.'

'Well, I mean, yeah.'

Suria dropped Alison's hand. 'It's not my fault. OK?'

The drunk man was catching up with them. 'Let's see you snog then!'

Suria turned to face him. 'Fuck you.'

'Just ignore him.'

'We shouldn't have to ignore him!'

'You're going to get us beaten up.' Alison felt for her keys in her pocket, ready to use them as a weapon.

'He can't even walk in a straight line.'

116

Alison looked over her shoulder. The man was having an in-depth conversation with a plane tree. She relaxed a little. They were outside the Odeon where they'd been on an early date, to see *Carol*. Afterwards, in the queue for McDonald's, Suria had told her she hoped to have kids one day.

'You're sad,' Suria said. Suria had a habit of stating Alison's emotions, so that Alison could confirm or deny them, to save her having to verbalize them herself. Alison nodded. 'I feel like we've lost the baby. I know that's stupid.'

'It's not.'

The drunk man was weaving across the pavement.

'We'll just use the sperm we already have,' Suria said, as they waited at the traffic lights. 'You can't get messed around by sperm from a sperm bank.'

Alison nodded and imagined what Lena would say when she found out they were going to use donor sperm after all, and she felt almost dizzy with dread and disappointment, though she had drunk a lot of white wine very quickly while they were eating the fish pie in an attempt to dilute the awfulness of the evening, so that was probably a factor too.

The red-faced man was on the other side of the crossing, clutching the traffic light. 'Shirtlifters!' he shouted.

Suria laughed. 'That's gay men, not lesbians! Get it right!'

Later that night, while Suria was in the bath, Alison decided to get the conversation with Lena over with. She put on her coat and went out into the garden.

Lena picked up straight away. 'How did it go?'

'Not amazingly.'

'They said no?'

'Basically—'

'Fuck!'

'It was so embarrassing—' She closed her eyes, cringing as she remembered the look in Ed's eyes, half-disgusted, half-afraid.

'I'll talk to them for you!'

'Please don't. It's not going to happen.'

'So what are you going to do?'

Alison pulled the coat tighter around herself. Rain was starting to fall. 'You don't think the baby will automatically be fucked up, if we do use the donor?'

'Please don't do this, Alison! You'll be passing on generational pain—'

'I don't have any generational pain. What even is generational pain?'

'You do have pain, it just hasn't sunk in yet—'

'I really don't. I just— I want to have a baby.'

'Ed can't be the only option!' Lena's voice was rising up the octave, the way it always did when she was angry. 'Isn't there someone else you can ask?'

'No. We've been through all our Facebook friends and everything. Suria suggested this fifty-three-year-old bloke she works with, but apparently he has a crush on her, so.'

'There'll be other people. Let me have a think—'

'I'm not asking anyone else to give me their genetic material, Lena. Do you know how humiliating it is? It's a horrible thing to do. It's such a huge thing to ask of someone—'

'But if you put it out there that you're looking, people might offer! You could post something on Instagram—'

Alison laughed, though it wasn't funny. It wasn't funny in the slightest. 'Have you met me, Lena?'

'I could post something for you. One of my friends might be up for it—'

'Oh my god. No. We're going to use the sperm donor. OK?'

Lena didn't say anything.

'There are loads of donor-conceived people who aren't fucked up,' Alison said, into the silence. '*I'm* not fucked up—'

'You don't know if you're fucked up yet. And how will your child feel?'

'I don't know! And you don't either!' She was furious with her sister for refusing to see things from her point of view.

'You could find a known donor if you tried. You *could*. There are forums where you can match with people, kind of like dating apps—'

'The men on those forums are creeps who want to have as many kids as possible—'

'Not all of them!'

'We've made our decision.'

She heard Lena breathe out.

'I don't want to fall out with you over this. Please. Come on. We'll just have to agree to disagree.'

'But we never disagree,' Lena said, in a small voice. Which wasn't true. It was just that Alison didn't usually tell Lena when she didn't agree with her.

'You can say "I told you so", if our kid ends up being fucked up.'

A beat.

'I guess all parents fuck up their kids somehow.'

'They fuck you up, your mum and other mum,' Alison said, mimicking their father's voice.

119

Lena laughed.

They were silent, for a moment. Alison watched the steam from her neighbour's boiler disappearing into the air.

'What's the donor like, then? The one you're using?' Lena asked, eventually.

'His name's Royston. Except that's a fake name.'

'OK.'

'I know it's not ideal—'

'Do you know what he looks like?'

'He has brown eyes. He sounded quite nice in his letter. He describes himself as a podcaster, though.'

'Jesus.'

'Yeah, well. No one's perfect.'

Alison and Suria looked at Royston's profile again that night, as they lay in bed.

'Nice handwriting,' Alison said. Grasping at straws.

Suria studied his baby photo. 'He definitely doesn't look like a serial killer.'

'Ted Bundy probably didn't look like a serial killer when he was eighteen months old, either.' Alison adjusted the pillow. 'Why hasn't anyone invented synthetic sperm yet?'

'I'm sure someone's on the case.'

'I bet there's no funding for that kind of science. Bet the funding bodies are full of men who are too freaked out by the idea of becoming obsolete. There'll be artificial wombs and eggs before we get sperm. Bet you a tenner.'

'It's going to be fine,' Suria said, taking her hand. 'Using a donor is fine.'

'The kids might not think it's fine when they're in their thirties—'

'You can't make every decision as a parent worrying what your kids are going to tell their therapists.'

Alison nodded. She felt heavy. Defeated.

'We're not going to make the mistakes your parents made,' Suria said.

'No,' Alison said. 'We'll make different ones.'

Still got it

Tom had always felt at home in libraries. For a man who had once spent a night in prison for head-butting a policeman at a Rock Against Racism gig, he was very fond of peace and quiet and decorative plaster mouldings. He had worked at the Main Library of University College London for thirty-three years, going grey as the students remained young, new ones replacing old ones like newly minted coins. The job was lonelier than it used to be, though. In the old days, a student would approach the desk and say, 'I'm looking for the T. S. Eliot concordance,' and he'd chat to them about *The Waste Land* as he led them to the right shelf, and then he'd rush back to the desk because someone else would need his help – a lecturer who couldn't work out how to use the photocopier, or a graduate student wanting to pay a fine, or a first-year history undergraduate panic-borrowing every book in the library about the Balfour Declaration. These days, though, everything was online. The library was just a glorified workspace with free Wi-Fi. Tom didn't even need to issue books – there were machines for that. He could go for days without speaking to a student, except to tell them off for eating pizza in the rare books section, or riding a scooter through the stacks.

The library wasn't quiet this afternoon, though. There were a couple of Extinction Rebellion protestors in the quad, dancing and playing tambourines. He tapped his foot in time to the beat as he updated the rota on the white board. Kwaku's PhD thesis was due in a week, so Tom gave him the mid-morning shift on the issue desk, when the library was emptiest – everyone worked on their own stuff, when the desk wasn't busy. Priya, who was a part-time stunt double, applied for TV jobs, and Brian – actually, no one knew what Brian did. But they did know what he would wear to work each day: a trilby and three-piece suit in the winter months, a straw boater and linen shorts in the summer, no matter the weather. Tom had written about him, in one of the stories no one wanted to publish: he usually wrote short fiction when the library was quiet. Now, though, he had a much more pressing project.

He started with a Google search:

legal ways to prevent children finding biological father

The results were disappointing. Endless articles about adoption, and stepfathers' rights, and dreadful stuff about how easy it was for children to find their genetic parents now that home DNA tests were so readily available. Reading it all made his scalp itch. Time for a different tack. He pushed his chair back and walked out into the quad, taking deep gulps of February air. The sky was heavy and white.

The neoclassical architecture was grey. The only colour in the quad came from the protestors. One of them was wearing what looked like a hand-knitted bra. She'll catch her death, Tom thought, before he could stop himself. He put a finger in his ear to block out the tambourines as he made the phone call.

'Dad? What's wrong?' Alison sounded worried. Which was understandable. He didn't often ring his daughters for a casual chat at 3 p.m. on a Monday.

'Nothing! I just wanted to say hello.'

'Oh. OK.' She sounded relieved. Two policemen had joined the protestors. One police officer per protestor struck Tom as overkill, no matter how awful their taste in knitwear. He moved away from them to sit on the steps leading up to the library, and tried to work out how to broach the subject.

'Dad? You still there?'

'Yes! Yes!' He should have thought this through before calling her. He should have written himself a script. 'Are you at the studio, then?' he said, to fill the silence.

'Yep. I've got a deadline next week.'

'Good for you. Good for you. I've been meaning to ask – has your friend Jim started designing your mother's headstone yet?'

'Apparently he's had the flu, but he said he'd get to it as soon as he's better.'

'Good. Good. I thought we could send him a photo of J. G. Ballard's grave, one of my favourites – sandstone, so not too morbid.'

'OK.' She was impatient to get him off the phone. Of course she was; they were so busy, his daughters. Their lives were so full. He shouldn't waste her time. Before he could

124

work out what to say next, she said, 'Dad? Why did you actually call me?'

Tom took a breath. Get to the point, you old bastard, he told himself. 'Your sister's got it into her head that she wants to find this sperm donor character. And I think it's a bad idea.'

'Yeah.' She sounded tired. Bored of the conversation? Frustrated by Lena? It was always so hard to tell, with Alison.

'Do you think it's a bad idea?' he asked her.

'I mean – I don't want to find him, myself—'

'Excellent!' He sat up straighter. 'Excellent! Because I was hoping you might be able to talk her out of it.'

Alison didn't reply. The protestors were smiling and dancing and singing about how the planet would soon be too hot for human habitation.

'Alison? Are you there?'

'I am.'

'And . . .?'

'It's Lena's decision, Dad.'

Bugger. 'I was hoping you'd be on my side.'

'I'm not taking *sides*, Dad.'

'No, of course you're not.' You weren't supposed to pit your children against each other, were you? That was pretty much the first rule of parenting, wasn't it? He imagined Sheila watching him, rolling her eyes. 'Stop talking!' he imagined her saying. But he didn't seem to be able to. 'I'm just worried Lena's going to get hurt,' he said. 'This man isn't going to welcome her with open arms, whoever he is. He was promised anonymity for life—'

'I know. But you know what Lena's like.'

He looked down at his hands. 'I just thought she might listen to you.'

'You're the one she listens to,' Alison said.

He didn't say anything. He knew his voice would wobble if he did. Bloody statins, messing with his body chemistry.

He was taking the bins out that afternoon when Jessie appeared on her doorstep in slippers, holding a bag of recycling. 'I was hoping I might catch you!' she said, shaking the cardboard boxes and empty milk cartons into the green bin. 'How have you been?'

He didn't have the energy to pretend any more. He closed his eyes, one hand on the railing that separated his house from hers, and he cried. There was a lot to get out, it seemed. Somewhere in the middle of it all Jessie came over and started stroking his back, making soothing noises, and it reminded him of the way Sheila had calmed their daughters when they were small and inconsolable. He really gave into the tears after that, because life was such a fucking tragedy, one long Greek tragedy, and it's all the more tragic when you have a happy childhood and you love your wife and your kids, because then you have so much to lose, and that's one of the certainties of life, isn't it, that you lose it all? He just hadn't expected to lose it all so soon.

Jessie was ushering him back inside, following him into the house. He winced as he watched her notice the worn carpet on the stairs and the discoloured paint on the hallway walls, yellowish grey around the light switch from years of fingerprints. He ought to redecorate, but he so rarely had visitors – and now here she was, taking charge, leading him into the living room, clearing a pile of old newspapers from the sofa so she could sit down next to him, handing him a Kleenex. He blew his nose. 'Sorry.'

'No need to apologize.'

'I've just been – things aren't really going my way at the moment.' He cleared his throat. 'Anyway. Don't worry about me. I'll be fine.'

'Of course you will.' An awkward silence. 'Lovely sofa.'

'Thank you. Sheila chose it.'

'Such a great shade of green.'

He nodded, crushing the tissue and pushing it into his pocket. He wasn't sure what ought to happen next. Guests had always been Sheila's domain. 'Tea!' he said, remembering.

'So many books!' Jessie said, once they were in the kitchen, looking around at the cluttered work surfaces and the overflowing bookshelves. There were books piled up on the dresser, too, along with odd bits of artwork the twins had made at secondary school – wonky clay pots, unflattering lino-print self-portraits, dusty Christmas decorations made out of toilet-roll cardboard. He reached around the detritus and took down a couple of mugs. 'I forgot,' Jessie said, picking up a Saul Bellow hardback from the kitchen table. 'You're a man of letters, aren't you?'

'Well, I work in a library. And I write the odd short story, for my sins.'

He opened one of the white kitchen cabinets – the shiny plastic doors really showed up the dirt, he noticed now – and took out the tin of loose-leaf tea. He'd make a proper pot for a change, seeing as he had someone to share it with.

127

'I've just started a book club,' Jessie said, putting down the Saul Bellow novel. 'A feminist one. Just me and a couple of friends at the moment. We're only going to read books by women.'

'I'm a bit behind in my reading of women writers.'

She pulled out a chair and sat down at the table. Damn it, he ought to have asked her to sit down, oughtn't he? He was so out of practice.

'You and Sheila?' she said. 'Divorced?'

'Afraid not. She died a couple of years ago. So I'm widowered. Is that a verb? I should know that, shouldn't I?'

'I'm so sorry.'

He waved her apology away. 'You?'

'Divorced last year. Hence moving into a flat on my own at seventy-three.'

'Are you still working?'

'God, no. You know I had a vegetarian café around the back of Charing Cross Road?'

'Sheila used to love that place.'

She nodded. 'They knocked it down, to build Crossrail.'

'Bastards,' he said. Silence for a moment, apart from the kettle, which was roaring, shaking a little, too – probably time for a new one, he thought, as he poured boiling water into the pot. 'Sorry,' he said. 'I always forget how long tea takes to brew.'

'I'm not in a hurry. One of the perks of being retired. It's brilliant, you should try it. I've joined Extinction Rebellion.'

'Of course you have.' He sat down next to her.

'And now I've got my book club. You should come along.' She was sitting back in her chair, looking directly at him, which was disconcerting. 'Do you want to talk about it?'

'About what?'

She raised her eyebrows.

'You don't want to hear about my woes—'

'Try me.'

He straightened his back, formulating a lie. But Jessie's eyes were frank and wise and he decided to see what would happen if he told her the truth. So he told her, about the sperm donation, and the secret, and the DNA kit he had unwrapped on Christmas Day.

'Oh, Tom.' Jessie clearly pitied him. It was quite nice, actually, to be pitied, especially by someone with great tits. Every cloud, et cetera.

'Alison took it pretty well, considering. But Lena's on some great quest to find the sperm donor. She says she wants to know who she is. As if she isn't the same person she was in November, all of a sudden.'

Jessie sat up. 'You should help her!'

'What?'

'Find the donor! You could help her do it!'

'I'm not going to do that,' he said calmly, though he didn't feel calm.

'You should!'

'Absolutely not.'

'Why not?'

'Because I don't want her to find him.' How dare she? It was none of her business.

Jessie tapped her fingers on the table. 'You're jealous,' she said.

'Of course I'm jealous!'

'Why? What are you afraid of?'

'That she'll love him more than she loves me,' he said.

'You never struck me as the jealous type.'

'Well, monogamy is unnatural, isn't it? But one father is enough for anyone, surely.'

'I was very fond of my stepfather, as it happens,' said Jessie.

Tom grunted. His anger had dissipated. He felt weak without it. The tea was probably ready. He stood up and poured it, so he wouldn't have to look at her.

'Why do you think she'd like this stranger more than she likes you?' Jessie asked.

'He's never had to disappoint her, has he? He never embarrassed her by wearing a leather tie to parents' evening.' He handed Jessie a mug, then sat down again.

'He never actually had to be her father, you mean.' She sipped her tea.

He felt like he might cry. You're being self-indulgent, he told himself. Pull yourself together. 'It wouldn't be a fair fight,' he said.

'You're accepting defeat! Why are you accepting defeat? You've got the chance to reset your relationship with Lena from a place of honesty—'

He looked up at that, and laughed. 'Oh, I see! My kids finding out I'm not their biological dad is a *good* thing! Silly me—'

'It could be. Depends how you look at it.' She was studying him as though she liked his face, and he knew how rare it was, to find an interesting woman who wanted to look at him like that. He couldn't risk putting her off by being himself. So he said, 'I'll think about it.'

'Good!' she said.

He decided to change the subject. 'Are you in touch with anyone else from Haldane Road?'

'Just Jane and Norman. You remember the couple that ran the political theatre group? Norman owns a chain of estate agents now.'

They reminisced happily about their squatting days, and the various ways their old friends had sold out, until the teapot was empty. Jessie checked her watch. 'I've got to get back. The electrician's coming round in ten minutes. I think there's a family of mice nesting in the back of my oven.'

As he walked her to the front door, he asked, 'Could I tempt you to do this again one day?' He didn't want her to leave. He didn't want to be alone with his thoughts.

She smiled. 'You could.'

'Good. Great.' He put his hands on his hips, then crossed his arms.

'Why don't you come along to my book club? Thursday after next?'

'I thought it was women only.'

'Women *writers* only. Men are more than welcome to come to meetings.'

He felt deflated. He had pictured a proper date, pulling out a chair for her in a wine bar, sharing a charcuterie board, a kiss at the end of the night if things went well. Not hanging out in her living room with a load of old Germaine Greer types, moaning on about Jane Austen. 'What are you reading this month?'

'*Frankenstein*. We're going back over all the classics.'

He pulled a face.

'Not a fan?'

'I've never read it. I don't need to read it to know it's not for me.'

'You have to read *Frankenstein*. You're coming.'

He had missed women bossing him around. 'I'll think about it.'

'Don't think about it! I'm cooking. Bring your daughters!'

'Oh, god, no—'

'Why not? You want to bond with them, don't you?'

'I don't know about "bonding"—'

'Relationships get better the more you work on them,' she said. 'Trust me, take it from Ms Two Divorces over here.'

'Two?'

'This hasn't been my decade, let's put it that way.'

He opened the front door for her and she stepped on to the front path, saying, 'I'm making lasagne, for the book club meeting, by the way.'

'Well. Lena and Alison are partial to lasagne.'

'Well, then.' She smiled. 'That's settled.'

He broached the subject with the girls that Sunday, over dinner at a crowded, candlelit Italian restaurant in Queen's Park. 'I've been thinking,' he said, 'that we should spend more quality time together.'

Alison looked alarmed. 'Why?'

'So that Lena will love me again, and forget all about looking for the sperm donor' was the honest answer, but he didn't want Lena to throw a glass of wine in his face. He said, 'Because,' instead. Lena looked away, as though she knew what he was thinking. He soldiered on. 'Jessie's started a feminist book club. I thought that might be up your street.'

Lena started laughing.

'What?'

'Just the idea of you at a feminist book club—'

'I'm a feminist,' he said, and Alison started laughing, too, and for the second time in a week he felt as though he was seeing himself through a woman's eyes and finding himself lacking. 'I founded the Men Supporting Feminists Society at university,' he pointed out.

'Yes, you've mentioned that a couple of times over the years,' Lena said.

'Well.' He fiddled with his napkin, cheeks hot with humiliation. 'I thought it would be fun. And Jessie said she'd love to have you.'

'What's the book?' Alison asked. She had always been gentler than her sister.

'*Frankenstein*. By Mary Shelley.'

'We know who wrote *Frankenstein*, Dad,' Lena said.

'Ah,' he said, leaning forward, 'but did you know this? Mary Shelley's mother, Mary Wollstonecraft, developed a fever shortly after giving birth. And the doctors thought her breast milk was causing the fever, and they didn't want baby Mary to drink it. So guess what they did?'

'What?' Lena asked, putting the menu down.

He had her attention. 'They stuck a couple of puppies on Mary Wollstonecraft's nipples, to suck the milk out.'

'Did it work?'

'No. She died a few days later.'

Lena and Alison didn't seem to know what to say to that.

'So you'll come?' he said. 'To the book club?'

'As long as you don't tell everyone the puppy-nipple story,' Lena said.

'I won't.' He felt flushed with success, although perhaps it was the wine. Either way, he was on a roll. 'And I was thinking. Maybe we could all go on a family holiday this summer.'

133

Alison looked slightly desperate. 'As in – a long weekend? Or—'

'I was thinking a couple of weeks. The Algarve, maybe?'

'I always feel like families get on better when they don't have to share a bathroom,' Lena said.

'But there are lovely hotels out there, with en suites—'

'Me and Lena have already booked to go away, with Suria and Adam,' Alison said, apologetic, embarrassed on his behalf. 'And the villa only has two bedrooms – and I think it's non-refundable, isn't it, Lena?'

'Of course. Of course. Don't worry.' Tom nodded and smiled, trying not to look offended that his daughters preferred each other's company to his. That was the way it should be. 'Where to, this year?'

'Sicily,' Lena said. 'But maybe another time?'

'Yes, yes, maybe.' He snapped a breadstick in half. He should have quit while he was ahead.

'Maybe we could start with the book club,' Lena said. 'Build up to a holiday.'

'It was just a thought,' he said. And then he made his breadsticks into walrus tusks.

Still got it, he thought, making walrus noises as his daughters said, 'Dad, stop it—' (affectionately, they were rolling their eyes affectionately). But it was a bit embarrassing when the waiter turned up with their main courses. Tom opened his mouth and let the breadstick halves clatter soggily on to his side plate as the waiter presented him with a bowl of spaghetti alle vongole.

They ate in silence for a while after that, and his mind danced with memories of how proud they had been, once, to be his daughters, the way they had laughed at his jokes until they snorted orange juice, the way they had dragged him around their nursery by the hand, bragging 'This is our daddy. He's *ours*.' As though they were worried someone might take him away.

'So, Dad,' Alison said, eventually. 'Jessie, eh?'

Predicted relationship

Lena felt unsettled on the way home, a little guilty. Her father had always seemed so solid and permanent, an oak tree of a person, but he wasn't; he was weak, and old, and she had broken his heart the day she had told him he wasn't her father. She hadn't realized he could be hurt by words. He had always juggled with them, hidden behind them, but he had been hoist with his own petard (he'd taught her that phrase). Until Christmas, she had always craved his approval. She had tried (and failed) to get into drama school because he had said she was 'actually quite good' as Eliza Doolittle in the sixth form production of *Pygmalion*. At her university graduation, she had looked for him in the crowd as she walked up to collect her degree certificate, and tripped over her gown. And whenever she'd offered up one of her half-baked poems for his thoughts, he'd said, 'Not bad,' then corrected her scansion. But now she was the one with the power. He was afraid of her: she had seen it in his eyes, when she'd told him she was going to look for the donor, and again when he had suggested going on holiday and they had turned him down. She felt sorry for him, and angry with herself for feeling sorry for him, and angrier still with him for being weak enough to pity. But maybe being pitiable was a kind of power in itself, because she didn't want to go to the bloody book club, but she was going anyway, out of guilt.

She walked to Waterstones at lunchtime the next day and bought a copy of *Frankenstein*. She started reading it on the Tube home and laughed out loud when she read the epigraph on the title page, from *Paradise Lost*: *Did I request thee, Maker, from my clay / To mould me Man?* That morning, on the donor-conceived Facebook forum, someone had posted: *My parents just think I should be grateful to be alive, but I didn't ask to exist.*

She called Alison as she walked up Holloway Road. '*Frankenstein* is literally about donor conception.' She tucked the phone under her chin so she could find her keys.

'I don't think donor conception was a thing in – when was it written? The eighteenth century?'

'Nineteenth. But listen to this: it's about a scientist who creates this creature – basically his child – that should never have existed.'

'Yeah, I know the plot—'

'No, but listen! Frankenstein says about the monster, *I had selected his features as beautiful.* Doesn't that sound like someone choosing a donor from a catalogue?'

'I thought Frankenstein made the monster from dead bodies. Doesn't he dig up corpses from graveyards?'

'Yes—'

'And doesn't the monster go around murdering people?'

'Yes, but that's because his dad rejects him! Which is like

when sperm donors refuse to acknowledge their biological children!'

'Maybe don't bring up that particular theory in front of Dad?'

'I won't. I just – never mind.' She opened the front door and banged her way up to the flat. 'I want to be able to talk about this stuff with you.'

Silence.

'Are you still there?'

Alison sighed. 'Yes.'

Lena missed the days when she had always known what her sister was thinking. 'I'll see you at the book club thing, then.'

'Lena, wait—' Alison said, but Lena had already ended the call.

'It's been three months, Lena,' Adam said that night, as they lay side by side in bed, looking at their books instead of each other.

She put *Frankenstein* face down on the duvet. 'I know. I'm sorry. I feel too weird at the moment, still.'

'We don't have to have procreation sex,' he said. 'We could use a condom. Unless you've gone off me.'

'Of course I haven't!' Which was mostly true. She loved him still, as unequivocally as she loved her sister, Hampstead Heath, voting in general elections and salted butter on toast. She didn't want to have sex with buttered toast, though, that was the thing.

'Good. Because as far as I'm concerned, we've mated for life.'

'Like swans.'

'And grey wolves. And crows! And Laysan albatrosses.

They celebrate their anniversary every year by dancing together to solidify their bond.' He bobbed his head up and down.

'Are those your albatross moves?'

'Yep.'

'Not sure I find albatrosses very sexy.'

Adam looked deflated.

'Grey wolves, however—' She scratched his back. Sex was like exercise, wasn't it? The more you did it, the smugger you felt at parties.

She did feel better, once she'd got into it. They had the sort of sex they'd had when they first got together, biting each other and shouting 'Harder!' and more than one sexual position and hoping the downstairs neighbours could hear them, because they wanted other people to know they were good in bed.

'We won't have sex like that if we have children,' Lena said afterwards.

'We hardly ever have sex like that anyway,' Adam pointed out.

Afterwards, he fell asleep. Lena picked up her book and read until her eyes refused to stay open, and she dreamed that she was Frankenstein's monster, shouting at her father, *'You are my creator, but I am your master; obey!'*

Lena felt strange walking up Jessie's front path, as though she had got the wrong house. The tiles were just the same as her dad's, but they were cracked in different places. She rang the doorbell. She could hear voices downstairs – women, mostly, her father booming above them. She felt a nervous thrill, the sort she felt before a big client meeting. Her father answered the door. She was taken aback; things were clearly going well with Jessie. 'Come in!' he said expansively, ushering her to the warm, wood-panelled kitchen. He was in his element, she could tell: surrounded by women, talking about books. There were five of them (women, not books): Alison and Suria, sitting close together at the head of the table; Jessie, impressive in pink lipstick and harem pants, handing out bowls of lasagne; Asuka, Jessie's friend from a couple of streets away, who had made a lot of money from a vintage clothing app and seemed to have spent it all on bangles; and Roxanne, another friend of Jessie's, who didn't smile much but wore very colourful clothes, as if to make up for it. Jessie stood up when she saw Lena and hugged her hello. 'You look so much like Sheila!' Saying their mother's name seemed to summon her, and Lena felt like a traitor, telling this imposter how nice it was to meet her.

Alison pulled a chair out for Lena the way a stranger might. Lena felt shy as they smiled at each other. Things weren't quite back to normal.

Alison's copy of *Frankenstein* was suspiciously pristine. 'Have you read it?' Lena whispered, as Jessie said something about Mary Shelley being the first female science-fiction writer.

Alison shook her head. 'We watched the film last night, though.'

'Kenneth Branagh, with an oily chest,' Suria said, and pulled a face.

'I was just saying,' her father said, 'that *Frankenstein* is a funny choice for a feminist book club, in a way. Because it's narrated by men, and all the female characters are dead by the end.'

Lena flipped her phone to silent. She had one unread email, from Genealogy DNA.

Your DNA results are ready to view!

Lena put her phone back in her bag. She couldn't feel her fingertips.

'Isn't it a book about the dangers of men's ambitions?' Asuka was saying. Her jewellery rattled as she spoke.

'Yeah, exactly, which makes it feminist,' Roxanne said.

'I think it's a very female book, actually,' Jessie said. 'It's about birth – the monster is basically Victor Frankenstein's child, right? Mary Shelley wrote it while she was pregnant.'

Lena nodded, and she could feel Alison looking at her, warning her not to bring up the donor-conception theory, but she didn't trust herself to speak, anyway. She ate another forkful of lasagne instead.

Alison leaned forward. 'And there's that scene where Frankenstein and the monster wrestle in the vat of amniotic fluid—'

Jessie frowned. 'Is there?'

'I think that's just in the Kenneth Branagh film,' Roxanne said.

As Jessie cleared the lasagne plates away, Lena excused herself to go to the toilet. She locked the door. She took her phone out of her bag. She felt utterly sick.

Click here to view your DNA results.

There was a knock at the door.

'Someone in here!'

'Sorry!' It was Asuka.

'Don't worry!'

She looked at her ancestry report first. Ninety-three per cent European, mostly British and Irish. She was 2 per cent Native American, which was thrilling, and 18 per cent French, which explained why she liked eating brie straight from the packet.

141

View your DNA relatives.

She hesitated. She didn't want to find her biological father here, like this, sitting on a toilet, while her other father sat in the kitchen, debating nineteenth-century fiction. But she couldn't wait any longer, either.

She clicked.

She had 1,980 genetic relatives, living everywhere from Canada to Afghanistan. None of them was her biological father. She felt more relieved than disappointed – but only for a moment, because then she saw him, his initials shining up at her in a circle, like a No Entry sign.

D.G. 25% DNA shared. Predicted relationship: half-brother.

A shout from the kitchen. Her father. 'Lena? Do you want tiramisu? Shall we save you some?'

'Sorry! Coming!' She flushed the toilet.

'There you are!' her father said, smiling. Lena smiled back, like Judas. She took her seat, grinning away, hoping no one would notice her shaking hands if she kept them in her lap. There was a bowl of tiramisu on the table in front of her. She didn't trust herself to lift her spoon. She could see the tiramisu in supernatural detail, the individual grains of cocoa, the texture of the cream, too smooth where the knife had cut it.

'What I think's interesting,' Jessie was saying, 'is that Frankenstein never gives his monster a name. And Mary Shelley published the book anonymously. So maybe she identifies with the monster—'

'Oh, that's very good!' That was her father. She couldn't look at him. She couldn't look at Alison, either.

'And Mary Shelley *herself* wasn't given a name, was she?'

continued Jessie. 'Because her mother died so soon after she was born. So her name is stitched together from other people's names – Mary after her mother, Godwin after her father, and then Shelley, after her husband.'

'God, you're so clever,' Asuka said.

'Not really,' Jessie said. 'I got that from a *New Yorker* article.'

And everyone was laughing, and Jessie was pouring wine into Lena's glass. Lena didn't drink it. She didn't need to feel weirder than she already did.

'You OK, Lena?' Alison asked.

'I feel a bit sick actually, sorry. I think I'll just get some air—' She pointed to the garden.

'Sure, of course, go for it.' Jessie stood up to unlock the back door.

The moon was full over the rooftops. A plane hummed, somewhere in the sky above her. She checked her phone, to make sure she hadn't imagined her half-brother. She could see exactly which segments of DNA they shared. And his name: Daniel Gold. She had always wanted a brother. Like her, Daniel was 18 per cent French. He was 30 per cent Swedish, 14 per cent Danish, the rest British. She thought, I want to remember everything about this moment. She took in the temperature of the air on her skin, and the silver-white of the moon in the sky, and the way it reflected off the roof tiles.

'Lena.' Alison had followed her into the garden.

Lena jumped, caught in the act. She was grateful for the darkness. Her fingers fumbled as she pushed her phone into her pocket. 'Hey.'

'What's the matter?'

'Nothing.'

'You coming back in?'

'In a minute.'

Alison nodded and came to stand next to her. 'Reckon Dad's shagging Jessie?'

'Oh god.'

'He is, isn't he?'

'I don't think I want to know.' She laughed unconvincingly. She just wanted Alison to go inside and leave her alone. And maybe Alison could tell, because she stood there, hands on her hips, the shadows on her face intensified by the moonlight.

'What's going on?' she said. 'Tell me.'

A prickle of hope. Everything would be so much easier if she could talk about all this with Alison. 'This is something you've asked me not to tell you about,' she said. Change your mind, she tried to say, with her eyes.

But Alison drew back. 'I don't want to know anything about your DNA results. I don't want to know.'

'Which is why I'm not telling you.'

'Fine.'

'Fine.'

A beat.

'I really want to talk to you about it though—'

'Seriously, Lena, don't you dare—'

'But *why*?' It was breaking her heart already, having a secret that she couldn't share with Alison.

'I told you. I know who I am. I don't want to fuck myself up by seeing some weird man's face in mine whenever I look in the mirror. OK? And I don't want to hurt Dad's feelings—'

'But what about half-siblings?'

'I don't care if we've got half-siblings! They're just random people with, like, some of the same chromosomes as us!'

'Shh,' Lena said, looking back towards the house.

'Half-siblings are, like, basically just cousins we've never met. And we already have cousins, and we can't even be bothered to send them Christmas cards—'

'OK, OK.'

They looked at each other, distance stretching between them.

'I hate this, though,' Lena said.

Alison looked as sad as Lena felt. Almost as sad as James Van Der Beek in the Dawson crying GIF, which they had sent back and forth in happier times. Alison turned and walked back into the house. The garden door banged shut behind her.

Lena sat down on the steps that led down to Jessie's lawn. She took her phone out of her pocket again, and googled Daniel's name. There were thousands of results, dozens of LinkedIn and Facebook profiles, but as soon as she saw his face, she knew she'd found him. She was staring into her own eyes. He had dimples, like Alison. Daniel was an actor, a proper one with a blue tick and a Wikipedia page (a stub, but still). He'd had a small part in *Game of Thrones*. She'd actually seen him in a play at the Young Vic without realizing it. She scrolled through the Google Image results, photos of him with the Getty Images watermark, his arm around people she'd always wanted to meet: Maggie Smith, Mark Ruffalo, the bloke who plays the butler in *Downton Abbey*. He'd grown up in Westbourne Grove, according to IMDb – fucking Westbourne Grove! A thirty-minute bus ride from her parents' house! She wondered whether his parents had done the right thing and told him the truth. She wondered whether he would want to meet her. She was nervous about meeting him because he had 23.4k followers on Instagram.

The garden door opened again. Lena pushed herself to her feet and put her phone away. Roxanne lit a cigarette. 'I love a full moon,' she said. 'It makes me want to howl.'

They stood there in silence for a moment.

'I've just found a half-brother I didn't know about. On the internet.'

'Oh. Wow.' Roxanne carried on smoking.

'He was in *Game of Thrones*. As a wildling.'

Roxanne nodded.

'Don't say anything,' Lena said. 'To the others.'

Roxanne nodded again. She looked like she wanted to ask a question, but she stubbed out her cigarette instead. Lena was glad when she went back inside. She wanted to be alone in the moonlight, with her half-brother's Instagram account.

Adam was still out when Lena got home. She sat on the sofa with her laptop, opened her Genealogy DNA account and looked at the relatives she and Daniel had in common: distant cousins, mostly. She had no idea what to do next, no idea how to wrangle this sprawling list of faceless names into a family tree. According to Google, the police had used DNA matches to catch the Golden Gate Killer, but it had taken a team led by a genealogist months to do it. Her father would be able to help her, she was sure of it, but he was hardly likely to volunteer for the job. The roar of the traffic on Holloway Road seemed to be closing in on her and she was crawling with frustration and helplessness. She turned to the donor-conceived Facebook group for comfort. The names of the other frequent posters were familiar to her now. Brandon. Clover. Jake. She was always surprised by how human they looked, when they were made by science. But then she looked human, too, on the outside. She posted a message:

I've just got my Genealogy DNA results – I have one half-sibling match and a lot of third and fourth cousins. Just wondered if that's enough to figure out who my bio dad is?

She received a reply immediately, from a woman named Anne, who lived in Texas:

Hi Lena :) I'm a search angel (an amateur genealogist). I can help you find your bio dad (reuniting people with lost family members is kind of a hobby of mine).

Lena clicked on her profile. Anne's Facebook wall was filled with photographs of beaming people, their arms around each other, and posts thanking her for reuniting mothers with the children they had given up for adoption, sisters with long-lost brothers, fathers with adult children they had never met.

Yes please, Lena wrote. *That would be amazing, thank you. Just tell me what you need from me.*

Your turn

That night, Alison dreamed she was at her mother's funeral. The undertakers were lowering the coffin into the grave, and she turned to catch her sister's eye, only her sister wasn't there. She realized, with a jolt that woke her up, that Lena was the one in the coffin.

'Very Freudian,' Suria said, when she told her about it the next morning. 'Or is it Jungian?'

'It's unsubtle, is what it is. I'm a bit disappointed in my subconscious.' Alison was rifling through a pile of clean laundry for a shirt to wear to the fertility clinic.

'Lena's not dead, hen.'

'No, she just isn't speaking to me any more.'

'She is—'

'Yeah, but she's not telling me things. She used to tell me everything.' She found a shirt. She realized it was decorated with tasteful black-and-white illustrations of women's breasts. She chose a striped T-shirt instead.

Suria crawled across the bed towards her. 'Like – dirty stuff?'

'Like – apparently she and Adam talk in baby voices while they're having sex.'

'No!'

'Yep. Baby animal voices, mostly. Although, maybe they've stopped doing that. I wouldn't know.' Almost immediately, she felt the sting of guilt. She shouldn't have betrayed Lena's confidence. 'You have to pretend I never told you about the baby animal voices,' she said, pulling on the T-shirt.

'Easier said than done.' Suria was laughing, with the deep laugh she only used when something was really funny. It was worth the guilt, to hear that laugh again. Then Suria stopped laughing. 'Oh my god – what have you told Lena about us? You didn't tell her about the Elizabeth the First/ Francis Drake role play, did you?'

No one was laughing in the fertility clinic waiting room. There were two other couples, sitting as far away from each other as they could, leafing through interior-design magazines and drinking complimentary lattes. Alison preferred NHS hospitals. Sure, you might have to wait years for an appointment, but at least you know your taxes are going towards doctors' salaries and medical supplies instead of squeaky upholstery and a year's subscription to *World of Interiors*. Same-sex couples didn't qualify for IUI on the NHS, though.

'I feel like I've been called to see the headteacher for a bollocking,' Alison said, quietly, so the others wouldn't overhear.

Suria sipped her coffee. 'I feel like they're going to chuck us out for dragging down their results on the fertility-clinic league table.'

On the wall, above a vase of lilies, was a framed montage of baby photographs and thank-you cards. All the babies were white. Alison had pointed this out to Suria before their first appointment. 'Our baby can be the first, then,' Suria had said. She had been so certain the baby would exist.

The waiting-room door opened. Dr Pellici waved at them and smiled – a sympathetic smile, or maybe an apologetic one. Both undesirable types of smile, under the circumstances. 'Do you want to come through?'

As soon as they were all sitting down, Dr Pellici turned to Alison and said, 'I think it's your turn.' As if they were in the middle of a game of Monopoly. Alison's stomach dropped.

'Sorry?' Suria said.

'Well,' Dr Pellici said, 'Suria has tried three rounds of IUI, now. I say Alison tries a round of IUI next. Otherwise we have to move on to IVF, and that's very expensive and invasive.'

'As in – *I* would try and get pregnant?' Alison felt stupid and slow.

Dr Pellici smiled at Suria, as if they were sharing a joke. 'I mean – that's the general idea—'

'We're not doing that,' Suria said, and Alison was glad, because for a moment she had imagined being pregnant and she had jerked in her seat, as though her body was rebelling against the idea. She wanted to turn and run out of the clinic, the way she had run out of her Uncle Simon's wedding, aged seven, unable to bear people looking at her in a bridesmaid's dress. Her father had marched her back inside and she had cried all the way through the ceremony. Her mother had let her change into her favourite blue tracksuit for the reception. Being pregnant would be like being held prisoner in someone else's body, like being hijacked from the inside; she would turn into an archetype, a Mother-To-Be, and no one would be able to look past her swollen belly to see who she really was: Alison, an individual, a woman who wasn't altogether comfortable with being a woman. Maybe that made her a hypocrite, because she wanted to be a parent so badly. Not a mother, though. She had never aspired to be a mother.

'You're sure?' Dr Pellici said.

'Very sure,' Alison said.

The doctor folded her hands in her lap and turned back to Suria. 'OK, then! So! IVF!' She handed her a glossy brochure. 'I don't know how concerned you are about affordability. But have you considered egg sharing? You're under thirty-five, and you have decent hormone levels, so it's definitely an option.'

Alison was shaking her head, but no one seemed to notice. Suria was asking how egg sharing would work, and Dr Pellici was explaining that they'd harvest Suria's eggs and divide them between her and the person she was sharing them with, and Alison hated the way the doctor was shrugging, as though she was a car saleswoman, talking Suria into trading in a Renault Clio for a newer model.

'You'd be *donating* your eggs, Suria,' Alison said, quietly, because she didn't want to have an argument with her in front of Dr Pellici, but Suria ignored her. Alison tried again. 'They call it egg sharing, but really it's the same as donating them—'

'If you do egg sharing, you'll get a free round of IVF whereas if you don't, it could cost as much as £8,000, depending – it can add up,' Dr Pellici said, raising her eyebrows: good deal, limited time only. 'Plus you'd be helping another couple at the same time, so it's a real win-win.'

Alison couldn't believe what she was hearing. 'So you'd actually be *selling* your eggs.' She turned to the doctor, smiling, and said, 'Sorry – it's just— I thought it was illegal to pay donors for their eggs in this country.'

Dr Pellici was getting irritated. 'It's legal to compensate them for their time and expenses.'

Alison nodded, still smiling, though it felt like an effort. 'I thought the compensation was limited to £750, though—'

'There's a shortage of egg donors, so it makes sense to incentivize people,' Suria said, telling Alison to shut up with her eyes.

'Egg sharing isn't for everyone,' Dr Pellici said.

'I like the idea of doing something altruistic,' Suria said.

Alison didn't understand how the conversation had got so out of hand. 'Would you donate your eggs if you didn't need IVF? Would you?'

Suria breathed out, exasperated.

'Because if you wouldn't, it's not altruistic.'

Suria crossed her legs away from Alison and turned to Dr Pellici. 'Alison has just discovered she's donor conceived herself—'

'Suria!' How dare she bring that up? How dare she use it against her?

'What? It's not something to be ashamed about—'

'Why don't I let you talk about this between yourselves and come back to me?' said the doctor.

Alison waited outside the clinic while Suria put the £325 consultation fee on their credit card. She always felt under-dressed in this part of London – there were too many flagpoles and brass plaques, too many box hedges in the shape of pyramids. She had always been suspicious of topiary: it was the plant equivalent of a Hollywood bikini wax. A couple walked past her, down the clinic steps – a woman with an undercut, a man with a ginger moustache and impressive muscles. When the man turned and caught her eye, she realized she had admired those biceps before. Max worked at the eco-architecture firm that occupied most of the co-working space where she rented a desk. Being around the architects made her feel cool by association – they drank oat milk lattes and wore expensive jumpsuits; they designed buildings covered in plants, with beehives on the roofs. She pretended not to see Max, but he turned and waved.

'See you Monday!'

'Yes! See you!' she said, as Suria jogged down the steps, zipping up her puffer jacket.

'Who was that?' Suria asked, as they watched Max and his partner walk down Harley Street, hand in hand.

Alison was too angry with her to reply straight away.

The argument started on the Central Line, between Oxford Circus and Holborn. 'If we don't do egg sharing, how are we going to pay for IVF?' Suria asked, over the screeching of the train. 'Are you going to earn us the money, or what?'

A low blow. The *Inspirational Women* artwork was taking Alison longer than she had anticipated, and the publisher was always late paying her invoices.

'We would only have to donate once,' Suria said, her voice softer now. 'So it won't be a situation where our baby has hundreds of half-siblings.'

'Except the baby might have hundreds of half-siblings anyway, from the sperm donor—'

153

'Exactly,' Suria said, crossing her arms. 'So what's a few more? And I would be a good donor. Like, if the kid got in touch, I'd be happy to know them.'

The train pulled into Liverpool Street. They stopped arguing for a moment, drawing apart to allow the crowds to get off.

'Dr Pellici's right. *You* could try,' Suria said, quietly, as they came back together. 'We can afford another round of IUI.'

Alison bit the inside of her mouth. 'You know I can't do that. I'm not going to do that—'

'OK, so tell me, what other options do we have?'

Alison tried to turn away, but she was wedged between the door and Suria's rucksack.

'Aye,' Suria said. 'Exactly, hen.'

Alison silently hated the parents she passed on the way to work on Monday morning, hurrying their reluctant children through the streets of Hackney, anxious to be rid of them. She wasn't usually an envious person – she was always genuinely happy for her friends when they got promotions or pay rises, and she'd never needed more money than she earned, or a bigger house, or a Tesla (though, on reflection, it would be quite nice to have a Tesla). But every time she saw a parent with a child, her stomach twisted. She felt calmer once she was in the studio, surrounded by plywood furniture and succulents and architects' models, miniature buildings populated by tiny plastic figures living perfect lives. She sat at her computer, staring at the final spread of rough artwork for the *Inspirational Women* book: Zaha Hadid. She scrolled back through the InDesign document, looking at the fifty-two women she had drawn. There were a couple of queer women in there,

Josephine Baker and Virginia Woolf, both of them feminine and bisexual. Where was the representation for the boyish girls, the ones who hated wearing skirts and resented growing breasts, the ones who wore tuxedos to their school dances?

'Zaha Hadid!' Max was hovering behind her computer. 'My favourite architect. Queen of the curve.'

Alison twisted to look at him. Max dressed the way she would have dressed if she were a completely different person who didn't mind being stared at. Today, a floral shirt under a patchwork cardigan. 'Quite relieved you can tell who she's meant to be,' she said.

'She's very recognizable! But also – it says her name, at the top of the page.' He crouched by her desk, and lowered his voice. 'I wanted to clear the air. Bit awkward, running into each other at the clinic.'

'Oh. Yeah,' she said, as though she'd forgotten.

'It's shit, isn't it, fertility treatment.'

She nodded. Her eyes felt dangerously hot.

Max noticed. 'You need a hot chocolate.' He jogged to the coffee machine to make her one, while Alison wiped her eyes with the heel of her hand.

The hot chocolate was delicious, despite the oat milk. Max had sprinkled cinnamon and sugar on top. He sat on the empty desk next to Alison's, arms crossed, waiting for her to talk.

'I'd be able to handle the whole fertility thing fine, if I didn't think it was ruining my relationship,' she told him.

Max nodded. 'Me and Gemma slept in separate beds while we were trying for Seb. It took us two years to get pregnant with him.'

155

Funny, what people think you might find comforting.

'Are you doing IUI, then, or IVF?' Max asked, tucking his hands under his armpits.

'We're talking about starting IVF soon. I don't know, though.'

'We're on our second round. It's taken over my brain. I used to care about gardening and making jam—'

'I used to care who won *Strictly*.'

'Me too! And I used to get excited about golf.'

Which was surprising. He looked more like a skateboarder than a golfer.

'It's a great sport, when you know the rules,' he said.

'If you say so.'

'But now I spend all my time on fertility forums.'

'There are men on fertility forums?'

'About five of us.' He picked up a rough illustration from Alison's desk. 'Is this Beyoncé?'

'It is.'

'You've really captured her eyebrows.'

'Thank you.'

They lapsed into silence, then both rushed to fill it at once.

'You go,' Max said.

'I was just going to ask whether you and Gemma had thought about egg sharing. To get free IVF.'

Max shook his head. 'Gemma's thirty-seven, so. Too old.'

Alison flicked a pencil shaving from her jeans. 'We're going to a counselling session about it next week.'

'It's like a hurricane once you're in the system, isn't it? It's like you can't control it.'

'Exactly. And it's so expensive.'

He scratched his moustache. 'Fuck knows what we'd have done if Gemma's aunt hadn't lent us fifteen grand.'

'Wow.'

'I know. She bought shares in Apple in the Eighties.'

And then somehow it was the day of the implications counselling session, and Alison and Suria were walking hand in hand up the steps of the fertility clinic, and Alison's heart was speeding up, tick-tick-tick, as though she was approaching the top of a roller coaster, about to hurtle down.

'I should have worn brogues,' Suria said, as they walked across the marble entrance hall.

'Your brogues give you blisters.'

Suria looked down at her trainers, grubby against the marble.

'They're not going to turn your eggs down because you're wearing Converse,' Alison said, but Suria didn't look convinced.

The counsellor had grey hair and a deep vertical line between her eyebrows, probably from years of attempting to look sympathetic. She had a clipboard on her lap, and looked down at a form as she asked them questions.

'We're using a sperm donor,' Suria said smoothly when the counsellor asked why she wanted to donate her eggs. 'So becoming a donor myself feels like the right thing to do.'

Alison waited for the counsellor to ask how *she* felt about Suria becoming a donor, but the question never came.

The counsellor nodded and smiled and made a note on her form. 'And how do you think you'll feel if the woman you donate to gets pregnant and you don't?' She looked up at Suria.

'Disappointed,' Suria said, slowly, as though she was

thinking it through. 'But I know that's a risk, and I know the egg isn't my child.'

'Exactly,' the counsellor was saying, and Suria was smiling, because she'd got the answer right.

Alison could hear Lena's voice in her head, screaming that Suria would be the children's biological mother, that she would be passing on 50 per cent of her DNA, no matter whether she considered herself their mother or not. She made herself say, 'The children might think of you as their mother.'

'According to our research, that's very unlikely,' the counsellor said. 'But you do have to be prepared for the possibility that the donor children will get in touch with you when they're eighteen. And you should also ask yourself how you'll feel if you never hear from them.'

'That's totally their decision,' Suria said.

'You'd probably be quite upset, though,' Alison said.

'I wouldn't,' Suria said, her mouth a line. 'Because like I said, they wouldn't be my children.'

The counsellor nodded again. 'I suppose the way to think of it is, you're donating to help other parents. You're like a secret benefactor!'

Suria sat back against the sofa cushions, more relaxed now, because the counsellor's script was working the way it was supposed to. She was going to be a secret benefactor, jolly and red-cheeked, like a cheerful character from a Dickens novel. She wouldn't be a stranger's biological mother, even though that's what it would say on the DNA test, if the eggs she donated turned into children and those children signed up to Genealogy DNA. Amazing, Alison thought, the power words have, to transform what they describe.

'Well!' the counsellor said, when their fifty-five minutes were up. 'Have a good think about everything, OK, ladies? But it sounds like you're aware of all the issues already. It's the ones who don't have any doubts that I worry about. Because it shows they haven't thought it through, the way you have.' She patted Suria's arm as they left the room, as though she had done well.

'I'll do it on my own, if you don't want to go ahead,' Suria said that night, as they loaded the dishwasher.

Alison straightened up, a plate in her hand. 'As in – you'll break up with me?'

'I don't want to break up with you, hen. But I have to have a baby. I have to. So.'

Alison knew it wasn't an empty threat. If she didn't give in, Suria would pack up her Victorian nightie and her uncomfortable furniture and her collection of Buddhist self-help books and move into some other woman's house, or have children on her own. Suria would be fine on her own. But Alison – all her life, she'd been one half of a double act, the straight man (ironically), the rear legs of a pantomime horse (literally, in the sixth form pantomime. She had stood still while Lena – the front legs – had sung 'Horse With No Name' and performed a tap dance).

Suria put her arms around Alison's waist. 'What's the worst that can happen?'

'Lena will find out you've become a donor,' Alison said, quietly. 'And she'll never speak to me again.'

'Fuck Lena, if that's all it takes to ruin your relationship.' Suria kissed her, and Alison stopped thinking about her sister.

*

159

Three days later they were back at the fertility clinic, sitting in a consultant's office – a male consultant this time, with curly hair and a habit of tapping his biro on the desk when he spoke. He had signed Suria up as an egg donor with a sweep of his pen. Now he was helping them fill in the donor information forms. Alison felt as though she was watching the meeting in slow motion. It's not too late, she told herself. You could offer to carry the baby. But she thought about everything Suria had been through already, the catheters and the feet in stirrups and the latex gloves, and she remained frozen, silent.

'We recommend you write a letter for the recipient parents, just to give them some information about why you've chosen to become an egg donor.' He looked up. 'You know – *I want to give other people the gift of starting a family*—'

'No problem,' Suria said.

'But first, we have to get the basics out of the way.' He tapped his biro. 'What should I say your heritage is?'

'Half-Scottish, half-Malaysian.'

'And you're a social worker.'

'That's right.'

'And did you have to get an MA to qualify for that?'

'No, it's just – I did a second undergraduate degree.'

The doctor looked disappointed. Suria had panic in her eyes, as though she was taking an exam she hadn't revised for. 'Is that OK?'

'Of course it is,' Alison said.

The doctor was clearly surprised by the anger in her voice. Then, remembering that she was irrelevant, he turned back to Suria. 'How about hobbies?'

Suria looked at Alison. 'I haven't had a hobby since I was, like, twelve—'

'What were your hobbies when you were twelve?'

'I did ballet and tap—'

'Dance, great. And do you play an instrument?'

'No—'

'Yoga, sport, anything like that?'

'I do Park Run on a Saturday when Alison bribes me with coffee—'

'That's great, running, that's good.'

'And you like reading,' Alison pointed out.

'Brilliant!' the doctor said. 'Prospective parents love donors that read. Shall I say who your favourite author is?'

'I don't know – Marian Keyes?'

The doctor didn't write that down. 'OK, but for the form maybe we could put someone like – I don't know – just someone that doesn't write chick lit?'

'I felt like a product,' Suria said that night. They were sharing a bath.

Alison was at the tap end, as usual, leaning forward to avoid the drips from the shower head.

'Don't you dare say I *am* a product—'

'I didn't!'

'But you're thinking it.'

Alison reached for the soap. 'They've got to make you sound good, so people will buy your eggs. They're going to be charging, like, six grand for them.'

Suria closed her eyes and lathered her hair.

'I'm just saying.'

'But what's wrong with me the way I am?'

'Nothing,' Alison said. 'You're pure dead brilliant, by the way.'

'Your Glaswegian accent's atrocious, hen,' Suria said. She reached for the shower head.

'You don't have to go through with it,' Alison said, gently, allowing herself to hope. 'We can still pull out. It's not too late.'

Suria was rinsing her hair. She didn't say anything. She hadn't heard. Or maybe she didn't want to.

TELL THE TRUTH

Tom woke up early on Good Friday, though he didn't actually realize it was Good Friday until he turned on the radio. He turned it off again straight away: he couldn't deal with 'Lord of the Dance' on an empty stomach. He walked to the window. The flat next door was silent. He had picked up the phone several times, intending to ask Jessie out properly, but he couldn't get up the nerve. He wanted to be a better person by the next time he saw her. He had been reading *Mrs Dalloway* – the next book club pick – and he'd found himself enjoying it, though he didn't know what chapters had done to offend Virginia Woolf. He'd also been researching the climate crisis, seeing as Jessie was so worried about it. Now he was worried, too: the world seemed to be in a bad way, and it was so loud, once you started to listen, and everyone seemed to be angry, especially with people who looked like him. He still thought the Extinction Rebellion lot were naive – he knew from listening to climate scientists on Radio 4 that their demand for Britain to be carbon neutral by 2025 was unachievable, and he was very worried about their call for a People's Assembly – there was such a thing as too much democracy (had they learned nothing from the Brexit referendum?). But all the same, there was no doubt they were right in principle, and they were certainly getting attention and stirring things up, and once upon a time he'd enjoyed being someone who stirred things up. On the Ten O'Clock News, he'd seen an elderly man eating a sandwich on top of a DLR train, and he'd found himself moved to tears. He toasted a hot cross bun – what's the point of being a widower if you can't eat a hot cross bun for breakfast? As he buttered it, he made a mental note to tell Lena that hot cross buns were actually pagan, and represented the turning wheel of the year.

Three hours later, he was standing in the marble entrance hall of the Victoria and Albert Museum, waiting for his daughter. He looked up at the octopus-like glass sculpture suspended from the ceiling. The museum was full of mother–daughter pairs of various ages asking for directions to the Mary Quant exhibition. Sheila and Lena had gone to the fashion exhibitions together every year, then to the members' room for lunch. Sheila had always come home drunk on prosecco, no matter what time it was.

'Sorry I'm late.' Lena was pushing her way through the revolving doors. 'I shouldn't have got the bus. I forgot XR were occupying Oxford Circus.'

'Good for them, though, don't you think?' He held his arms out for a hug. They stood there for a long time, his head on her shoulder. If only she could absorb a bit of him, so he would be part of her. Eventually, she pulled away.

'I suppose we'd better go, before we miss our time slot,' he said. 'Through the gift shop.' He pointed the way.

'Last time we talked about Extinction Rebellion you said it was a load of old bollocks,' Lena said, as he showed his membership card to the gallery staff.

'Yes. But! Did you know that the extinction rate is around ten thousand times what it should be? And in 2030, if we don't do something soon, the climate will break down irreversibly, and it'll probably mean the end of civilization as we know it? That's not an exaggeration!'

'Adam told me that, yes.'

'All these bloody emergency Brexit summits and everyone's ignoring the climate emergency and just hoping it'll go away!'

'I think the North London Extinction Rebellion meetings are on a Wednesday, if you want to go along.'

'Yeah, yeah.'

They were in the exhibition now.

'Your mother would have loved this,' he said, as they admired a can-can line of disembodied legs in colourful tights. 'You remember the mustard tights she used to wear? She was always in miniskirts, when I met her.'

'She wore Mary Quant rouge,' Lena said. 'It came in a little compact, with a black daisy on the front.'

'How do you know that?'

'I found it, in her make-up case. I've still got it.'

'Well,' he said, gruff. 'Don't throw it away. It's a museum piece, clearly.'

They watched footage of a fashion show. Models had moved faster in the Sixties. Or had they? He couldn't remember. Maybe the footage had been sped up.

'Why didn't I know Mary Quant basically invented teenage fashion? And miniskirts?' Lena said.

'Probably because she's a woman, and women's achievements are always underrated,' he said, looking at her sideways.

'Very good, Dad.' She patted his arm as if he were a child.

Later, in the members' room, they ordered Niçoise salads and English sparkling wine, because there wasn't any prosecco on the menu.

'To Mum,' Lena said. They clinked glasses. He was just tucking his napkin into his collar when she said, 'I took the DNA test, by the way.'

'Did you!' A long sip of wine. 'Did you!'

'I found a half-brother.' She wasn't looking at him, which was lucky, because he could feel that his face was long with horror. She was fiddling with her phone, and then she held it out to him, and there, on the screen, was a photograph of a young man: tall, handsome, dark haired, smiling Lena's smile. The world seemed to shiver. The photograph was unnatural, uncanny, no good could come of it. He had to fight the urge to knock the phone out of her hand. He managed to smile and say, 'Well. That's fascinating. So interesting. Amazing.' But his voice wavered as he spoke, and Lena still wasn't looking at him. 'Have you been in touch with him, then?'

'No. I don't know what to say. And he last logged on to the DNA site two years ago, so, I don't know. He might not even know I exist.'

'Right.' He drank more wine.

'Apparently I'm eighteen per cent French.'

166

'Oh. Well. Much more exciting than being related to me. Boring and English, as far back as you can go.' He played with his fork, casual, and asked, 'Have you got any further with building your family tree, then? Are you any closer to finding this donor chap?'

'No.'

'Oh. Shame.' He tried to keep the relief out of his voice.

'But this genealogist from Texas has offered to help me.'

He put his fork down. Icy claws closed around his heart, his stomach, his throat. 'Texas?' he said, as though that was the part that bothered him. This was moving too fast.

She nodded. 'She's a retired police officer. She used to use DNA to solve cold murder cases for fun, but she said that was a bit depressing, so now she helps people find their relatives.'

'I don't think it's a good idea to give a stranger access to your genetic information, Lenny.'

'Why? I can't figure out how to build a family tree on my own—'

'I could help you.' He said it before he could stop himself.

'You don't have to do that—'

'I want to! I want to help!' No, you don't, his mind was screaming. What are you saying? But he couldn't think of another way to control the situation. If he helped her look for the sperm donor, then maybe he could get to him before she did. And then . . . what? Persuade this man to reject his daughter? Or be there when they met, like some sort of chaperone? No, that was too masochistic, even for a man who, in his heyday, had enjoyed a good spanking. He felt as though he was being wrenched in two, or like he

167

was imploding, he couldn't tell which, because if he helped her find her biological father, he might lose her, but if he didn't, he might lose her anyway. He heard himself saying, 'I don't want you to get your hopes up, though. The odds are we'll never find this bloke—'

'But— so— will you help me? Actually?' She was smiling at him the way she had the day he had come home from work early and presented her with a My Little Pony, much to Sheila's horror. 'You're spoiling her! I hope you got one for Alison, too?' (He hadn't. He'd got Alison an Action Man instead, because he knew his children, because they were *his* bloody children.) If he helped Lena, she would love him again. Properly, without reservations, the way she had back then, before she had known the truth. He felt himself nodding. He said, 'If you're sure this is what you want, of course I will.'

'Thank you,' she said, and she looked as though she might cry. 'Thank you.'

Lena had to dash off to meet some friend or other, but Tom wasn't ready to go home, to face the rest of the bank holiday weekend gaping before him, nothing to distract him from the promise he had just made other than an infuriating email Alison had forwarded, from Jim the stone mason: *Sorry it's taken me so long to send you the designs for your mum's headstone. I've been going through a break-up. Here's what I've got so far. I'd really appreciate it if you could pay me in full for the job now, because I'm having cashflow issues at the moment.* The cheeky bastard. He decided to visit the Extinction Rebellion camp to drown out the voice inside his head, the one screaming *WHAT HAVE YOU JUST*

DONE? Besides, it would give him something to say to Jessie, next time he saw her.

Oxford Circus was much more circus-like than usual, with flags and music and people on stilts, one man dressed as a magpie – *One for sorrow*, his sign read. Indeed, Tom thought. The protestors weren't as angry as he'd expected: they all seemed to be happy to be there, happy to be part of something. He envied them their optimism, their sense of purpose, their ability to wave tambourines unselfconsciously. They reminded him of himself as a young man (though he'd never waved a tambourine: the Rock against Racism crowd had been more into electric guitars and swearing). Grey-haired activists nodded to him in solidarity as he passed – he wasn't the oldest person there, not by a long stretch – and when he was offered a sticker he took one. He felt a pleasant sense of belonging. There were signs banning drugs and alcohol from the protest site, a craft area for children, an alarming number of yoga mats. And there, in the middle of it all, a salmon-pink boat emblazoned with the words *TELL THE TRUTH* in uncompromising sans-serif letters. Too late for that, he thought. Hindsight's a wonderful thing.

'No one's allowed past this point,' a policewoman with a Welsh accent said, as Tom edged closer to the boat.

Someone onboard was waving down at him, a blonde woman in a white T-shirt and dungarees. He waved back, then realized she was Emma Thompson. He'd have to text Lena – she loved a good celeb spot. 'Join us!' Emma Thompson shouted through a loudspeaker, and he was tempted, because he was lonely and he'd missed the camaraderie of being part of a cause. But then he was distracted by a surge of yells and cheers: police officers were carrying a white-haired man to a police van. 'We love you! We love you!' chanted the crowd, and Tom had the sudden urge to hurl himself at the line of police officers in the hope that he'd be arrested too.

#DanielGoldIsBae

It's funny, Lena thought, as she locked herself in a toilet cubicle during a work dinner and sobbed silently into a wad of toilet paper, how few people notice when you're unravelling. Her father hadn't noticed the way she'd panicked when he hugged her, that day at the V&A. Over his shoulder, she had seen the security guards watching them, probably wondering who they were to each other – father and daughter? Lovers? Because, biologically, he wasn't her father, and yet there she was, pressed up against a man almost forty years older than her, and she hadn't been able to breathe. When she'd pulled away, he'd said something about not missing their time slot and walked ahead of her into the gift shop. Lena had been amazed that she could move her legs and her arms, amazed that the screaming was only inside her head.

The screaming was loudest when she was with Alison, pretending to be excited that Suria was starting IVF treatment soon, or drinking smoothies after their kickboxing class, or arguing about the design of their mother's head-stone over pints in the pub after work.

'It's a bit tall and narrow, isn't it?' Lena said, one Friday night, as they looked at the sketch Jim had sent.

'I can't go back and ask Jim to change it. It's taken him literally four months to send me this. We just need to decide on the wording. Dad wants *Much-loved mother, wife and friend.*'

'But she had a whole career in biochemistry before she got married!'

'*Former biochemist, mother, wife and friend?*' Alison asked.

'Sounds shit,' Lena said, drinking her pint.

'It's a shame that gravestones never say what a person was actually like,' Alison said. '*Sheila Delancey. Very American, fond of cats, shit at washing up.*'

'*Lied to her children about their genetic identity for thirty-four years,*' Lena added.

'Don't be like that.' Alison pulled the headstone designs away from Lena, as though she'd forfeited her right to an opinion.

Why don't you care? Lena wanted to shout. Why does this whole thing bother me so much more than it bothers you? She had 2,027 new relatives on Genealogy DNA now (the numbers kept climbing) yet she'd never felt more alone. She couldn't tell her sister about Daniel – Alison had been very clear: she didn't want to know about their DNA results – but keeping his existence secret made her feel sordid, ashamed, and she hated that she would never be able to invite him to a party, or put a photo of him on her wall, or tell her children about their uncle in case one of them slipped up and said something. But she was getting ahead of herself. She didn't have children. And Daniel probably didn't even know he had a half-sister. She wondered whether he had received a perky email – *You have a new relative!* – or whether he had unsubscribed from notifications during the great GDPR purge of 2018. She checked his social media every morning before she got out of bed, looking into his eyes before Adam's were open, searching them for a secret sadness.

Did he know he was donor conceived?

After work each day, she snatched her phone from her desk with the urgency of an addict and checked Genealogy DNA over and over again as she walked down Old Broad Street, pulling her thumb down her phone screen to see if any more siblings had appeared the way she had once checked Deliveroo for new takeaway options. She spent most of her billable hours looking through her Instagram grid, trying to work out what Daniel would think of her if he found it. Her posts were mostly pictures of well-lit sandwiches and photos of her feet on beautiful tiles. She added a (flattering) selfie with her pro-bono team, to show she was a valuable member of society (plus quite photogenic, in the right lighting). Not that she wanted Daniel to fancy her, obviously. She just wanted to look like an appealing person to have as a sister.

'Just send Daniel a message,' Izzy said on the phone one night, as Peggy screamed in the background. 'Why shouldn't you be the one to get in touch first?' But she wasn't sure how to write to a half-sibling she'd never met. She had googled *Letter resigning from job* many times and she'd saved a template to her laptop, but there wasn't an accepted formula for writing to a long-lost relative who might not even consider themselves your relative. In the end, she sent him an email through Genealogy DNA one Monday night, eating a sandwich at her desk, when she should have been filling in her timesheet.

Hi Daniel, I thought I'd get in touch because it looks as though we're half-siblings. I hope this doesn't come as too much of a shock to you. I have to admit it was a huge shock when my dad told me I was donor conceived (on Christmas Day. He's never been great at presents). I'd love to hear from you, if you'd like to be in touch, but don't worry at all if not. A bit about me: I live in London. I have a twin sister, obviously from the same donor. I'm a lawyer, she wrote, and then deleted it, in case that put him off: people tended to glaze over when she told them what she did, at parties. She pressed send before she could change her mind.

'Has Daniel replied?' Izzy asked a few days later, as they drank coffees together in Pret a Manger.

Lena shook her head. 'Might have gone to his spam folder, though.'

'Have you had messages from other people?'

Lena nodded. 'Annoying fifth cousins from Hawaii who want to tell me all about our shared Irish ancestry. Do you want to see a photo of him?'

'Yeah!'

She scrolled to one of the pictures of Daniel she'd saved to her phone. 'Do you think we look the same?'

Izzy frowned. 'I mean—'

'It's the cheeks. And the eyes.'

Izzy wasn't convinced.

'There's a family resemblance.'

'If you say so.'

'I don't say so. There just is.'

Izzy nodded and offered Lena some of her almond croissant.

Lena was lonely, because no one seemed to understand why it was so important that she look like her brother, and her friends didn't even think he counted as her brother, because she'd never met him. Sometimes she thought she might have imagined the whole thing, or that Genealogy DNA had got it wrong, that the internet was gaslighting her. She felt lonely, because she knew she'd probably never meet her biological father, and even if she did, he wouldn't love her, because how could he love ten, twenty, thirty, fifty, ninety children at once? She felt lonely when her friends changed the subject when she tried to talk about being donor conceived, and lonelier still when they pointed out she wouldn't exist if her parents hadn't used a sperm donor, and asked whether she wished she'd never been born.

These days, Lena had heart palpitations when anyone mentioned DNA, and whenever she watched mothers pushing their children on the swings, or families screaming at each other in supermarkets, she wondered whether the parents were the biological parents and whether they'd told the children if they weren't. She checked Instagram one Tuesday morning as she left Liverpool Street Station and saw a message request: *Hello sister. How are you? Please reply to me.* Heart wild, she clicked on the profile: mostly women's arses or breasts. She probably wasn't this guy's sister. She deleted the request and reported the account and locked herself in the toilets as soon as she got to work, so she could fit a small panic attack in before her 9 a.m. one-to-one.

March turned to April, and Brexit didn't mean Brexit,

and Lena didn't find any exciting new relatives. Just a couple of fourth cousins on her mother's side who wanted to tell her all about their great-great-grandmother's emigration to New York, and a creepy Canadian named Jerry who thought, 'Hey! You're my sixth cousin!' was an excellent chat-up line. Her ethnicity shifted as GenealogyDNA.com updated her ancestry predictions. Eighteen per cent French one day. Twenty-three per cent Dutch the next. And just as she was getting used to being a quarter Dutch, googling flights to Amsterdam and wondering whether to buy a new bike, her Dutchness dropped to 2 per cent, and suddenly she was Basque, and Danish, and French again. Improbably, the one person who she could talk to about all of this was her father. Because he really was doing his best to figure out her family tree. She hadn't taken his offer of help seriously, but she'd given him the login details to her Genealogy DNA account anyway. And then he had started texting her daily progress reports. He was enjoying the intellectual challenge of working out who her paternal great-great-grandparents were. *Better than Sudoku*, he said it was. But she knew it must be painful for him; she knew he was only doing it to earn forgiveness. And she almost had forgiven him, because she could see how hard he was trying. Sometimes, she logged into her Genealogy DNA account and studied the family tree he was building for her, the branches sprawling outwards, weed-like, tying people together whether they liked it or not. *From the looks of it, the sperm donor is half-French*, he texted her. *Ignore the Dutch stuff. A lot of French surnames cropping up. More soon.* In the meantime, she stared at Daniel's face, making an imaginary e-fit of their biological father, mentally merging her features with his. Thick eyebrows. A big smile. Light green eyes. She found a photo of Daniel with his brother, Richard, at a premiere, both in jackets and open-necked shirts. Richard also had thick eyebrows and a big smile, but Lena couldn't get her brain to accept that he was probably her half-brother too. One unexpected half-sibling at a time seemed to be all she could handle. Either that, or she needed the internet to tell her they were related before it felt official, the way she hadn't truly felt secure as Adam's girlfriend until he'd updated his Facebook status to *In a relationship*.

One Wednesday morning, as she walked through the City with her coat slung over her arm for the first time that year, she realized Daniel would never reply to her message. He'd clearly taken the DNA test, looked at his results, and never logged into the website again. Her heart still raced every time she checked her emails, though, and the word *Daniel* jumped out at her in books and TV shows, bolder and louder than other names. Wikipedia said Daniel dated women. BuzzFeed told her he was single. She found his showreel one evening after work and stopped on a street corner to watch it. Daniel was a cop in *EastEnders*, a barrister with a drinking problem in *Silks*, a very moving Mercutio. Always a character. Never himself. She wished she'd never discovered he existed. She couldn't look away.

On a Thursday in the middle of April, Daniel posted a selfie outside the Barbican stage door. *So excited to share that I'll be playing Laertes in the RSC's production of Hamlet over the summer season!! #idieattheend #spoiler.* She watched him working out with a trainer on Instagram stories. She felt uncomfortable knowing what colour his chest hair was. You're not supposed to see your brother with his top off, are you, unless you're on a family holiday in the South of France, or something? She wasn't sure. She'd never had a brother before.

A couple of days later, just as she was wondering whether it was warm enough to eat her sandwich outside or whether she ought to stay at her desk so that James would think she was concentrating hard on disclosure for the Jerwood case, Abeo called. 'What did you say Daniel's surname was, again?'

'Gold.'

He laughed. 'It *is* him! Bella represents him!'

'Who?'

'Bella! My friend! At my agency! He's in *Hamlet* at the Barbican soon!'

'I know!'

'I can get comps, if you want to come with me?'

'Yes! Oh my god, amazing, thank you!'

In a week's time, she would see Daniel in person, onstage at the Barbican. And then she would stop following him on Instagram, and recommit to Adam, and spend time with people who actually knew and cared that she existed. That was the plan, anyway.

Lena and Abeo rarely did things together, just the two of them. Lena felt a little bit nervous as she arrived at the Barbican, and as she walked from the Tube station to the arts centre she tried to think of good topics of conversation. She was worried they'd resort to talking about how their jobs were going, or whether they had any holidays planned, which would mean acknowledging that they didn't really know each other any more.

Abeo was waiting for her outside, at a table by the fountains. His head was bent over his phone. He looked up when she approached. 'You look gorgeous!'

'Well. Thank you.' She had tried to dress like a person who goes to the theatre on a regular basis, in large earrings and an oversized shirt, but she had a feeling she looked like someone who sells necklaces on Etsy.

He offered her his arm. 'Shall we?'

'Oh god. OK.'

'You're just going to the theatre. Totally normal thing to do.' He pushed open the glass door.

The foyer was full of people clutching wine glasses, chatting and laughing. Abeo led Lena towards the stand selling programmes and ice cream. 'We can go backstage afterwards, if you like,' he said.

'No way.'

He bought a programme and handed it to Lena. 'It's a present,' he said, as she opened her wallet to look for cash.

'Thank you.'

He shrugged. 'I'm going to expense it.'

As they walked towards the stalls entrance, she opened the programme to the page with Daniel's headshot. The programme was glossy; his photo caught the light, so he disappeared for a moment, ghostly.

An elderly couple had to stand up to let them take their seats. 'I never sit in the stalls,' Lena said, as they edged past.

'I thought you'd want to get a proper look at him.'

The house lights dimmed. The murmuring of the audience intensified, then died away. Lena's heart sped up as two actors stepped on to the stage, then slowed down when she

179

realized neither of them was Daniel. Two more actors joined them, and the Ghost appeared, and she felt her mind wandering, the way it always did when she went to the theatre—

And then there he was. Lena sat up straighter. Abeo nudged her, but she ignored him, because her brother was beautiful, despite his ripped camouflage jacket and unflattering leather cycling shorts. She had stared at his face so long in two dimensions that three dimensions almost seemed too many. He crackled with charisma. She turned to her left, to see if the rest of the audience was as captivated by him as she was. Hard to tell.

'What do you think?' she asked Abeo during the interval, as they shuffled out of the auditorium.

'Not sure the post-apocalyptic thing really works.'

'No. I mean, what do you think of Daniel?'

'As what? An actor?'

'Just – in general.'

'I think he's extraordinary.'

'Extraordinary how?'

Abeo laughed. 'Surely the point is what *you* think of him?'

'I think he's amazing.'

Abeo put a hand to his forehead. 'Oh god.'

'What?' She felt like she'd been caught out, but she hadn't been caught out, because there's nothing wrong with admiring your half-brother's acting, is there?

'I suppose as long as you don't have kids together, there isn't really a problem.'

'I don't fancy him!'

'You one hundred per cent want to fuck him.'

They had reached the bar. Abeo ordered two gin and tonics.

'I do not want to fuck my brother—'

'This is *quite* a fun conversation to walk in on,' said a woman in a red wrap dress.

'Bella!' Abeo kissed the woman on the cheek. 'This is my very good friend, Lena. Bella Turner. Daniel Gold's agent.'

'Oh! Hi!'

Bella smiled briefly at Lena, then turned back to Abeo. 'Daniel and I are going for drinks later if you'd like to join us. With a couple of the producers.'

Abeo raised his eyebrows at Lena. Lena shook her head.

'Another time,' Abeo said. 'Tell Daniel he was wonderful, though.'

'Really wonderful,' Lena said, and Bella looked at her, slightly pitying, as if she were one of the teenagers who gathered at the stage door every night for his signature. Lena knew about the teenagers, because she'd set an alert for #DanielGoldisbae on Instagram.

'You're bright red,' Abeo said, as Bella walked away.

'Shut up.'

'Genetic sexual attraction is totally natural. No need to be ashamed—'

'OK, gross, that is *not* what's going on.'

Abeo didn't seem convinced.

Lena was one of the first on her feet for the standing ovation. Daniel bowed low, his hands sweeping the ground, as though he wanted to demonstrate how flexible his hamstrings were. This was the first time she'd seen him as himself, but of course he wasn't really himself, because he was still onstage. And anyway, Lena thought, as she clapped until her hands hurt, is anyone ever really themselves, except perhaps when they're asleep? Or a baby? Or dead? Still, she tried to pick up clues about his personality from the way he clasped the other actors' hands, the flourish with which he raised his head after each bow, the way he jogged to each corner of the stage. He looked into the audience, singling out certain people with a smile. There was a moment when she could have sworn that he was looking right at her, but the auditorium wasn't well lit, so she couldn't be sure. He reminded her of the drama students Abeo had hung out with at university, the ones who had spoken loudly as though what they had to say was important, the ones who had kissed each other on the cheek and slept with each other's boyfriends, their lives as dramatic as the parts they played. She wasn't sure she would actually like Daniel if she knew him, but she was drawn to him, biologically, hopelessly. Not in a sexy way – she knew Daniel was her brother, so there was no danger of that, whatever Abeo might say. Definitely not. But her chromosomes loved his chromosomes. They couldn't help it.

She couldn't sleep that night, so she watched Daniel's episode of *Game of Thrones* on her laptop, headphones on, so she wouldn't disturb Adam. The light from the screen woke him up, though.

'Pony! It's, like, two in the morning!' He leaned over to look at the laptop. 'Is that Daniel?'

She nodded. The wildlings were attacking Castle Black.

'You're turning into a bit of a stalker.' Adam lay down and closed his eyes.

'It's not stalking. It's research.'

'If you ever meet him, he'll be freaked out by how much you know about him.'

'He might be flattered. He's an actor, he wants people to know who he is.'

Adam rolled over. Onscreen, Daniel met a bloody death. Lena's phone buzzed with a new message. She half-expected it to be from Daniel, that she'd conjured a message from him by wanting one so badly, but it was her sister. *Suria's having her egg retrieval on Tuesday. Wish us luck. Xxx*

Lena spent ten minutes looking for an appropriate GIF before deciding it wasn't a GIF occasion. She replied with words, instead: *Good luck! Will be thinking of you!!! xxx* She wanted to be happy for them, but it was all so complicated. She watched the *Game of Thrones* episode again from the beginning to distract herself. Adam shifted in his sleep and she pressed pause on a close-up of her brother's face, his eyes fierce and green. She shut her laptop and closed her eyes, but Daniel was still burned into her retina, dancing, red, on the backs of her eyelids.

Calming breaths in the chilled goods aisle

Alison had been helping Suria inject herself every morning and evening for two weeks now, with drugs to suppress her natural menstrual cycle and hormones to stimulate her ovaries. They had cleared out a shelf in the kitchen to store the alcohol pads and syringes, and they kept the drugs in the fridge, between the mustard and an ancient jar of mango chutney. The sharps bin sat next to the fruit bowl, aggressively yellow, disrupting the calm of their kitchen. The first few mornings, Suria had rattled it like a maraca in time to whatever song was on Radio 2. The rattling had stopped when the hormones kicked in. On Thursday, Suria wept into her porridge to 'S Club Party'. 'I was young and beautiful when this song came out,' she said, as Alison patted her back and wondered what to say. 'I need these eggs out of me. I'm so fucking bloated. I can't do up my jeans.' There's no way I could do what she's doing, Alison reminded herself. She's sacrificing her mental and physical health so that we can have a baby. My wife is amazing, and I love her, and I can totally put up with her shouting at me for leaving my running shoes by the front door and storing balled-up tissues in my dressing-gown pocket and spilling tea on the stairs.

'How hard is it to actually clean the toilet every so often?' Suria had said that morning. 'What does it fucking take?' She lay on the sofa after that, holding a cushion to her face as though she hoped it would suffocate her. Alison sat down next to Suria and lifted the cushion. Suria was crying. 'Why am I like this?' Suria asked, as Alison stroked her hair. 'I'm horrible. I'm sorry. I don't want to be horrible.'

'I know.'

'All I can see at the moment is what's wrong with everything. The kitchen tap is leaking. And there's a red wine stain on the fainting couch.' She cried harder. 'I'm going mad.'

'You're not. It's the hormones.'

'But how will I know when it's not the hormones? How will I know when what I'm feeling is real?'

'I don't know. Shh. You just have to get through the egg retrieval and the embryo transfer and it'll be over.'

'If it works.'

'It will work.'

Suria looked up at Alison. 'It has to. I have to stop feeling like this.'

'Fucking cunts!' Alison opened her eyes and checked the time on her phone. One in the morning. Suria was standing by the bed, a syringe in her hand, sobbing. 'They've given me the wrong fucking needle! I can only do one of the trigger shot injections!'

Alison sat up. 'I thought the injection was – isn't the syringe preloaded?'

'Yes! And the first injection was fine, but the second one is different, and you have to attach a needle to it, and the one the nurse gave me doesn't fucking fit!'

Alison took the syringe from Suria's hand and tried to force the needle on to the end of it. No good. 'Fuck.'

'What are we going to do? If I don't do the trigger shot my eggs won't be ready to collect—'

'You've done half of it. So there'll be *some* eggs—'

'You don't know that!' Suria was hyperventilating, and Alison was panicking, too, because they had to give Suria the trigger shot. There must be somewhere they could get the right needle – even at one in the morning. Because everything Suria had been through couldn't be for nothing. Alison was pacing the room, staring down at the gaps between the floorboards, as though she might be able to conjure the correct needle from one of them, if she wanted one badly enough, if she thought magically enough.

Suria was calling someone now.

'The clinic's not going to pick up the phone at this time of night,' Alison told her.

'I'm calling Ed!' Suria said, but he didn't pick up either. She threw her phone on to the duvet, then buried her head in the pillow, sadness and anger spilling out of her into the goose down. 'Fuck!' she shouted, her voice muffled. 'Fuck, fuck fuck.' Alison stroked Suria's back and wished she was the sort of person who could shout into soft furnishings. But she wasn't, so she seethed silently instead, disappointment and anger burning away inside her, deadly as acid.

*

She was still vibrating with anger two days later as she sat in a curtained-off bay in the fertility clinic while Suria changed into a backless hospital gown and fantasized about the burgers (plural) she would order when the egg-collection procedure was over and she was allowed to eat again. Assuming there were any eggs mature enough to collect.

'I want the bacon cheeseburger with the pineapple relish, and you've got to order the blue cheese one so I can try that. And we'll need a wee McDonald's Quarter Pounder for the journey home.' She sat down on the hospital bed. 'And, like five portions of fries.'

'I can't believe no one's apologized about the needle mix-up yet,' Alison said.

'I know. But they're not going to, because that would be like them accepting responsibility.'

'They better give us some kind of compensation—'

'They won't. They're all cunts. Everyone's a cunt,' Suria said.

Which is when a cheerful-looking doctor whipped the curtain open. 'Sorry to hear that!' she said.

'Suria hasn't eaten in sixteen hours,' Alison explained.

'Let's get this over with then, shall we, and then you can have some lovely tea and biscuits. Have you signed the consent forms?'

Suria handed them over. 'Let's hope I'm not one of the ten in a million people that dies as a result of being sedated!'

'Oh no, you're not going to die.' The doctor paused. 'I mean, it's really unlikely—'

'I know,' Suria said, a little worried. 'I was joking.'

The doctor laughed unconvincingly. 'Most people actually love sedation. They say it's like the best nap they've ever had.' She looked down at her clipboard. 'I hear you had some trouble administering the trigger shot.'

'Only because the nurse gave me the wrong needle,' Suria said.

The doctor nodded. 'Well, we'll go ahead with the retrieval anyway, OK? Hopefully we'll still manage to get some eggs.' She checked the blood pressure monitor attached to Suria's arm. 'Your BP's slightly elevated.'

'Probably because she's stressed and upset,' Alison said. 'Because she couldn't do the trigger shot.'

'Alison. Leave it,' Suria said.

The doctor smiled at Suria. 'So the procedure only takes about twenty minutes—'

'Am I slurring?' Suria slurred afterwards, as Alison passed her a packet of Digestives.

'Only a little bit.'

Suria started to cry. 'Sorry.'

She cried even more when Emily, the embryologist, smiled her tight smile and handed her a print-out.

'We managed to get nine eggs,' Emily said.

'Is that a good number?' Alison asked.

'Yes—'

'But it looked as though there were going to be eleven, on the last scan,' Suria said. It took her a long time to say 'eleven'.

'Would we have got eleven if she'd managed to do the trigger shot?' Alison asked.

'More of the eggs might have been mature – but there's no way of knowing,' Emily said, head tilted. 'Still – five eggs for you!'

And four for the family Suria was sharing them with.

If they had retrieved fewer than eight, Suria and Alison would have kept them all. Alison felt that like a punch in the gut.

'That's amazing!' Suria slurred, but when she closed her eyes, her mouth turned down at the corners.

Suria woke up just after five the next day, too anxious to sleep, then took a Nytol and went back to bed. She wanted to be unconscious, she said, because if she was awake she would go mad staring at her phone, waiting for the fertility clinic to call to tell them how many of her eggs had become embryos. Suria's parents had come to London to look after her. They sat on the sofa all morning, watching television, while Suria slept and Alison made them tea and did the laundry. Alison welcomed the distraction, because she couldn't bear how powerless they were to affect the outcome. The embryologist told them she'd call between 8 a.m. and 10 a.m., but it was 12.15 p.m. now and still nothing. Alison felt sick with how badly she wanted the treatment to work. Maybe they would be parents soon. Maybe they would never be parents at all.

'Eh, Kirsty Wark is a looker, what do you think, Ali?' Ahmad said, nodding at the screen.

'She's not really my type,' Alison said, setting up the clothes horse.

'Enough of that, Ahmad.' Fiona batted his hand, then swivelled towards Alison and watched her hanging the laundry. 'Oh, you are good. See when I'm gone? Look after Suria for me, aye?'

'You're not going anywhere,' Alison told her.

Fiona laughed and settled back on the sofa. 'Aye, when I was your age, I thought I was gonnae live forever, and

189

all. I'd like to be cremated. Make sure you tell Suria.'

'Fiona,' Ahmad said. 'This is no the time or the place—'

'And I want an open coffin. Make sure I'm looking my best. McGoverns are the undertakers to go for. They tidy you up all nice.'

Ahmad shook his head at Alison, but Fiona hadn't finished.

'And I want a proper wake. Make sure there's enough steak pie for everyone.'

Ahmad switched channels, to *Songs of Praise*. 'Aled Jones! What does he want to be in a desert for?'

'That's the Holy Land, Ahmad,' Fiona said, holding her mug up to Alison. 'I don't suppose you'd be a darling and put the kettle on?'

They were running out of milk, which was a blessing, because it meant Alison could escape to Tesco and take deep, calming breaths in the chilled goods aisle. The leftover Easter eggs were half price. She considered buying one for Suria, but decided it wouldn't be very tactful to give her an edible fertility symbol. She was eyeing up the Lindt bunnies (a safer bet) when her phone rang.

'Four embryos,' Suria said, in a small voice.

'Oh my god, that's amazing! Four out of five!'

'But half of them will stop developing, which means we'll be left with two—'

'But it only takes one—'

'Don't say that. Everyone says that.'

'I'm coming home,' Alison said. She hung up the phone and jogged out of the store. She was escorted back in again by a security guard when the alarm sounded. She was still holding the chocolate bunny.

*

Just before Suria's parents left the following morning, Fiona presented them with a toy elephant, white and soft. 'For the wean,' she said, kissing Suria on the cheek. 'I didnae want to get anything pink or blue, you know, because we don't know what it'll be yet!'

The elephant sat, pathetic, on the sofa, mocking them, as the days passed and the embryos stopped dividing. By the fifth day, two blastocysts remained.

'Like cockroaches after the nuclear holocaust,' Alison said.

Suria was leaning against the dishwasher, her head in her hands.

'You'll get dehydrated if you cry every time we talk about fertility stuff. Do you want me to buy you some Lucozade Sport, to keep your salt and sugar levels up?'

'If you feel the need to make jokes, can you sign up for a stand-up comedy course or something, and leave me alone?' Suria said.

Alison shut the kitchen door as quietly as she could and went out into the garden. She sat on the bench. The neighbour's cat rubbed itself on her legs, as though it knew she needed the comfort. Her anxiety, always there in the background, was a constant companion now. Suria's sadness was soaking into her, too, and she felt saturated with it. She wasn't sure she could take much more. She ought to talk to someone about it all, but talking about her feelings to anyone other than Suria had always felt like doing a piss in the street – just about acceptable if you were drunk, or under the age of eight, but she was an adult, and she should be able to wait till she got home. When things got desperate, she usually turned to Lena. But she couldn't tell Lena about Suria being a donor, and

191

it was all Alison could think about, and Lena would guess. She'd hear the things Alison wasn't telling her in the silences in their conversation.

Instead, she threw herself into work. The roughs for the *Incredible Women* book had been signed off and she had started on the colour art, but the palette she'd chosen wasn't working. Everything looked too cold, too blue.

'Bad day?' Max asked one afternoon, at the coffee machine. He had caught her muttering at the milk frother.

'Shit day.' The tears were right there, behind her eyes, ready to fall. She concentrated on the bright green of Max's jacket, to distract herself. 'Nice colour, that—'

He touched her shoulder. She would have been able to hold it together, if he hadn't touched her shoulder.

'Sorry,' she said, angry with herself for leaking.

'Let's go to the pub,' he said.

She glanced at her watch. 'It's only four—'

'So? You're self-employed. And I'll just walk with authority, and everyone will think I'm going to a meeting.'

They walked with authority to London Fields, which was already crowded with groups of friends and couples, smiling at each other, optimistic the way people are when the sun shines unexpectedly. Alison waited, cross-legged on the grass, while Max bought beers from the pub. She felt calmer, less claustrophobic, now she was outside. She was just one of hundreds of people on the fields, walking their dogs and eating chips, shouting at their boyfriends, dodging cyclists, and her sadness seemed less important among the countless other private dramas taking place around her, inside these strangers' heads.

Max was carrying two pints in plastic glasses, walking

carefully. 'Cheers,' he said, as she took her beer from him. He settled on the ground opposite her, sipped his pint, and wiped the foam from his moustache. 'So,' he said. 'Tell me. How are you doing?'

'Oh, you know. On the brink of divorce.'

He nodded, like he wasn't surprised. 'Me and Gemma broke up for two weeks when we were trying for Seb.'

'OK, that makes me feel better,' Alison said, stretching her legs out in front of her. Then she realized how that sounded. 'Not that I'm glad you broke up, obviously—'

'No, obviously—'

'But at least it's not just us.'

'It's definitely not. It's amazing anyone makes it through IVF without getting divorced.'

His face was so kind, and he actually understood, so she said, 'Suria's driving me fucking crazy at the moment. Everything I do is wrong. I mean, it's not like I was willing to get pregnant, so I know I shouldn't complain—'

'Doesn't make it easier to deal with.'

And then the guilt kicked in. 'I know it's just the hormones, though. It's not her fault.'

Max nodded. 'The other day, Gemma started crying because I served her five bits of ravioli and I gave myself six, and she thought I'd done it on purpose, because I didn't love her.'

'Wow.'

'Yep.' Max leaned back on the grass. 'We've decided this is our last round of IVF. So if it doesn't work, Seb'll be an only child.'

'Sorry,' Alison said. 'I'm just wanging on about myself—'

'Don't be sorry. Seb's pretty cool.' He reached into his pocket for his phone. 'Want to see a photo of him?'

193

'Sure,' Alison said, because that was not the sort of question you could say no to.

He shuffled over to her and flicked through photographs of a little boy, smeared in tomato sauce, attempting to ride a tricycle, holding Gemma and Max's hands on a sunny day. Alison tried to make the right noises, though her heart was contracting with resentment, the way it always did when she looked at other people's children. Max paused on a picture of Seb beaming up at the camera in a *Love is Love* T-shirt. 'That was at trans pride, last year,' he said.

Alison took a while to get it. 'Oh!' she said eventually. 'Right!'

'I was trying to find a subtle way to come out to you.'

Alison tried to look cool with Max being trans, which should have been easy because she was cool with it, but she was embarrassed, too – embarrassed that she'd reacted with surprise, that she felt more comfortable being his friend now she knew he was queer. She wanted to ask him when he had known he was trans, because she had cried as a child when she'd realized she would never grow a penis, and she had been wearing boxers since the age of twelve. She still felt a little bit pleased when people called her 'Sir' instead of 'Madam', except when they were shouting at her to get out of the ladies' toilets. Sometimes she wondered whether, if she were ten years younger, her pronouns would be They/Them. But she wasn't ten years younger, and she didn't know how to have this conversation with him, so instead she said, 'I like your moustache.'

Max touched it. 'Thanks. I've always aspired to one.'

'It's a good one.'

'Not too Operation Yewtree?'

'No. Very hipster.'

He laughed at her, for saying hipster.

'It's weird now,' he said. 'When people look at me and Gemma in the street and think we're a cishet couple. It's good sometimes, though. You don't have to worry about being beaten up for holding hands when you're queuing for a kebab at two in the morning.'

'I got chased down the road by a kid on a mountain bike the other day,' Alison told him. 'He called me a "lezzie dyke".'

'The "lezzie" is a bit redundant.'

'Tautological, yeah.' They laughed, then sat in silence for a while, until Alison said, 'Can I ask you a question?'

'Go for it.'

She pulled up a handful of grass. 'Is Seb donor conceived?'

'Yep. Good old Danish sperm.'

'I'm donor conceived, too.' She looked up at him. 'I found out at Christmas.'

'No way!' Max said, delighted, apparently, that she wasn't related to her father. 'You're the first donor-conceived person I've met who isn't a toddler. How do you feel about it?'

'Mostly fine,' she said. But then she told him about Lena thinking donor conception was ethically wrong, and Suria becoming an egg donor, and how guilty she felt about all of it, and how angry she was with Lena for making her feel guilty.

'That's pretty homophobic of your sister,' Max said.

'Yeah. I know where she's coming from, though—'

'But things are so different than they were when you guys were born. Everyone tells their kids the truth.'

A prickle of anger. 'I'm not sure they do.'

195

'The clinics strongly advise you to.'

'My mum strongly advised me to get a pension when I went freelance, but I haven't got round to it. And even if you do tell the truth, it's not a guarantee your kids will be OK with being donor conceived.'

Max nodded, frowning. She could tell that he was wondering what Seb would think about his conception when he was old enough to understand. She felt bad for making him think about that, so she offered to buy another round.

A *chihuahua* named Janis Joplin

Tom had a purpose again, a routine: up at seven thirty, then an hour's research at his desk, trawling through historical marriage records. There was a sense of achievement in building his daughters' family tree, a dopamine hit whenever he added another name:

Aurelie Legard, 1880–1945
Bill Turner, 1882–1970

The task was abstract, intellectual, safe: the names on the tree all had death dates as well as birth dates. He tried not to think about the living man who might be out there, lying in wait, like a jellyfish lurking beneath the ocean's surface. He had pumped up the tyres on his old road bike – the doctor had told him to do more exercise – and he left for the library each morning at 8.30 a.m., wobbling along the Regent's Canal, tinkling his pathetic bell, dodging children on tricycles and tourists taking photographs of ducks. 'On your right!' he shouted to a jogger, on the last Thursday in April, but the jogger didn't hear him, and next thing he was lying on the ground, knees stinging. 'I'm fine! Absolutely fine!' he told the concerned women who helped him up – the humiliation – but the chain had come off his bike and he didn't want them to watch him struggle to fix it, or, worse, offer to help, so he lifted it up the steps and walked the rest of the way to the library, crying a little because of the shock.

At the issue desk, the Reader Services Assistants were debating which Pret sandwich was most delicious.

'Definitely the chicken and avocado,' Priya said.

'Veggie New Yorker, hands down,' Kwaku said, sipping his tea.

'I ordered the hot halloumi and falafel wrap the other day, and it burned my tongue, so not that one,' Brian said, eyes on his computer. 'Plus the bread was singed at the top.' He was wearing tartan shorts today. They were oddly flattering.

Most of the conversations on the issue desk revolved around food. On Friday, they had discussed the best cheap Chinese takeaway. The Wednesday before that, Aisha from Inter-Library Loans had wanted to know if it was possible to make vanilla essence without using alcohol.

'I prefer a soup to a sandwich,' Tom said, as he waited for his computer to boot up. 'Pret's Thai chicken soup is lovely with a baguette.' The others nodded, thoughtfully.

Priya leaned back in her chair to catch Tom's eye. 'You're on first lunch, aren't you? Me and Kwaku are going to one of those Indian buffets behind Euston if you want to come?'

He was flattered to be asked – fraternizing with the

supervisors wasn't really the done thing – but he had other plans. The Sussex Hospital Fertility Unit, where his daughters had been conceived, was now part of University College Hospital. And Elizabeth Sandringham, the doctor who had made him a father, was still the head of reproductive medicine. Amazing, how easy it was to find someone on the internet. 'I'd love to, another time,' he said.

Priya shrugged, as though it didn't matter to her either way.

'Don't go to the restaurant with the yellow door, is all I'll say,' Brian said. 'I found a cigarette butt in my korma once.'

At midday, Tom turned right on Gower Street and ambled towards University College Hospital, casual as anything. The building was clean and clinical-looking, white and pale green, as though it was on its way to a costume party dressed as a paediatric surgeon. He pushed through the revolving doors and approached the reception desk.

'Which way for the fertility clinic, please?' he asked.

'Women's health is on level four, outpatients,' said the receptionist.

'Lovely! Thank you!'

He had made it to the lifts. No one had stopped him yet.

The receptionist in Women's Health looked at him over her glasses, suspicious, as he approached. She probably didn't have to deal with 71-year-old men on a daily basis.

'I'm looking for Dr Sandringham,' he said. His palms were sweating slightly.

'Do you have an appointment?'

'No.'

She stared at him.

'At least – I *did* have an appointment,' he bumbled on, 'but that was thirty-five years ago—'

He had limited time, he realized, before she called security, or the psychiatry team, possibly—

'My daughters were conceived using donor sperm. In 1985. Dr Sandringham was our doctor. I was hoping to ask her a few questions about it—'

'We don't deal with that sort of thing here. And Dr Sandringham's very busy—'

He crossed his arms. 'I can wait.'

'There's no point waiting, Sir. She's not going to see you, unless you've got an appointment.'

His arms fell to his sides. He shouldn't have been surprised. He was used to women telling him, politely, to bugger off.

Just outside the Women's Health Centre was a glass-roofed atrium filled with bored-looking patients waiting on plastic benches. Tom sat down next to a young woman with a pierced septum. Dr Sandringham would have to leave the hospital eventually. He emailed Priya: *At the dentist. Appointment running over. Back ASAP.* He opened his copy of *Mrs Dalloway* and started to read, but the viewpoint kept slipping from one character's consciousness into another's and he lost his place every time the door to the Women's Health Centre opened.

It was ten past one, according to the clock above Tom's head, when Dr Sandringham entered the atrium. She was more stooped than she had been thirty-five years ago, and grey-haired now, but he'd have recognized her anywhere. It's hard to forget the face of a woman who once looked you in the eye and said, 'I'm afraid it's your sperm that are the problem, Mr Delancey. Or rather, your lack of them.'

His heart sped up as he pushed himself up off the bench and shuffled after her. 'Dr Sandringham!'

She stopped and turned, frowning, looking around for someone she knew.

'You probably don't remember me. You treated my wife, back in 1985.'

'OK—'

'I was hoping to have a quick chat with you, if I may—'

'I don't have time for a chat, I'm sorry.' She smiled an apology and lumbered off towards the exit.

Tom had to jog to keep up. 'It's just that my daughters were conceived with donor sperm. At Sussex Hospital. You treated my wife. They're twins – maybe you remember them—'

'Lots of women have twins after fertility treatment.'

'The thing is, one of my daughters is looking for the sperm donor. Who was used to conceive her. And I thought you might be able to help.'

They were at the top of a staircase. A man in blue scrubs edged past them into the atrium. Dr Sandringham looked tired. 'We didn't keep records of sperm donors in those days, I'm afraid.'

He felt pathetic, desperate, but he couldn't give up yet. 'I know that's the official position. But I thought you might remember—'

'I don't. I'm sorry. And I really have to go.'

'He would have been about my height, I suppose, and green eyed, because you matched by appearance, didn't you? Were they all medical students?'

'The only way for your daughter to find the sperm donor is to take a DNA test—'

'She's done that.'

'OK. Well.' She shook her head. 'That's her best bet. Sorry.'

He was a little disappointed. Part of him wanted to solve this puzzle, he realized; it was like an enormous, living cryptic crossword. Most of him was relieved, though. He felt almost faint with it. Or maybe he was just hungry – next time he accosted a medical professional, he'd eat a sandwich first.

Dr Sandringham was walking down the stairs, carefully, as though they couldn't be trusted. And as he watched her leave, Tom felt unexpectedly emotional, though perhaps he should have expected it, because he seemed to be emotional most of the time, these days. 'Dr Sandringham?' he called after her. She paused, hand still on the banister. 'I just wanted to say thank you. For helping me become a father. Having children was the making of me.' She smiled and nodded, and carried on down the stairs, as though people said that sort of thing to her every day.

As he turned his key that night, Jessie's front door opened. She was wearing a surprisingly short skirt for a woman her age. 'Thought that might be you,' she said, leaning on the railings. She held up a bottle of white wine. 'Opened this last night, and I'm not going to finish it on my own. Would you like to join me?'

They had finished the bottle and opened another, which went some way to explaining why Jessie was now telling Tom about her second divorce.

'It's the predictability of it all that bothers me. I wish he'd had a more original breakdown. Couldn't he have quit his job to become a water-skiing instructor, or something? Couldn't he have just started wearing leather trousers?'

Tom made a mental note to add his leather trousers to the Oxfam pile.

'If he had to have an affair, he could at least have gone for someone more interesting. Someone like – I don't know. Jane Fonda. Or Whoopi Goldberg!' Jessie picked up her glass. It was empty. Tom refilled it for her.

'It's probably hard to have an affair with a Hollywood legend when you're a transport administrator from Camden Town.' Tom noticed Jessie's red lipstick had left a mark on the rim of her glass. He felt the urge to run his thumb along it.

'But sleeping with a thirty-two-year-old—'

'At least she's not his secretary.'

'True. But she's younger than my daughters. And she has a chihuahua named Janis Joplin.'

'Weren't you a big Janis Joplin fan?'

'Yes! Still am! Salt in the bloody wound!' Jessie topped up Tom's glass. 'But you and Sheila had a good marriage, you say?'

He nodded.

'Nice to know they do exist.'

'Who knows what would have happened if she'd lived longer, though,' he said. 'She'd probably have left me.'

'Don't say that!'

'It's true. Not telling the girls about the donor thing was my idea, not hers. I can feel her judging me every time I visit her grave. Though maybe she's just pissed off it's taking so long to sort her headstone out.' He wished she hadn't

203

brought up Sheila. He could imagine his wife rolling her eyes: *Really, Tom? I know it's slim pickings, but Jessie? Doesn't she believe in aromatherapy?* Jessie glanced down at his knee. He realized he was jiggling it. Sheila had hated it when he jiggled his knee. He put a hand on it, to stop himself. 'Sorry. Wine always makes me feel sorry for myself.'

Jessie shifted closer. He was very grateful he'd drunk so much wine. No chance of a hard-on, even if he'd wanted one. 'And how are you feeling, about all of that?'

'Well.' He crossed his arms. 'I've started helping Lena look for the donor.'

'Oh! That's brilliant!'

'We'll see.'

'How far have you got with it all?'

'I think I'm closing in on one set of great-great-grandparents. They're French, I think. I'd show you, if I had my laptop with me—'

'Want to come upstairs and login on my computer?'

He laughed. 'Is that the twenty-first-century equivalent of "Let me show you my etchings"?'

Judging by the expression on her face, it wasn't.

Jessie's computer was squashed on to a dressing table in her bedroom, along with books, bottles of perfume, hairbrushes and boxes of paracetamol. Tom had to force himself to concentrate on the screen – her double bed was just behind them, the duvet rumpled and inviting.

'This is what I have so far,' he said, clicking through the branches on the family tree. 'Not sure how much further I can get without another lead.' He was stuck on a woman, Cécile Legard, who disappeared after the 1912 census and never seemed to have died.

Jessie reached around him to take the mouse. Promising – he'd used that move once, to teach Sheila to use a pool cue. That night, she'd given him a blowjob.

He could feel Jessie's breath on his cheek as she clicked on a marriage record. 'There you go.' Cécile Legard had married not once, but twice, it turned out. She had become somebody else, and died as Cécile Marion, and she was Alison and Lena's great-great-grandmother. Jessie looked at him.

'You made that look easy,' he said.

'It was easy.'

He shifted in the chair. 'Maybe subconsciously I didn't want to get any further—'

'Subconsciously. Sure.'

Tom leaned forward. Now that they had identified Cécile Marion, they had unlocked a new branch of the girls' family tree. Name after name stretched out on the screen in front of him.

'Don't you think this would make a good book?' Jessie asked.

'What would?'

'You, searching for the sperm donor. It could be a sort of whodunnit, but true—'

'I'm not a memoirist. I write fiction. Anyway, the girls would kill me.'

'Oh, yeah. I suppose they might.'

He hoped she wouldn't notice the heat rising up his neck, because the truth was he would write about anything and anyone if it would get him a glass of prosecco in a publisher's office.

Jessie yawned, stretching her arms above her head.

'Better let you get to bed,' he said, hoping she'd object.

'Yes,' she said. 'Got to be up early tomorrow, for a mammogram.'

He wasn't quite sure what to say to that.

'So,' she said, as she walked him to the door. 'I'll see you at book club, if not before.'

'Indeed you will!' Ask her out, he told himself. What's the worst that can happen? If she says no, you'll have a few awkward encounters when you're emptying the recycling. But she wouldn't say no, if the wine and the length of her skirt were anything to go by, though naturally you weren't supposed to assume women were dressing for your benefit—

'Unless you'd like to do something before then? Just the two of us?' she asked.

'Yes,' he said. 'Yes, I would.'

She nodded, and they were too close together, standing there on her doorstep, so he stepped on to the path. 'I could come and meet you one lunchtime, near UCL,' she said. 'There's a café in the back of Planet Organic. I've been meaning to go there, anyway, to buy their hummus. It's the best. Really garlicky.'

Perhaps Jessie wasn't suggesting a date after all – the garlic comment wasn't promising. Nor was the location. Eating lunch at Planet Organic involved sitting at a communal table at the back of the supermarket, eating textureless vegan food out of a biodegradable box.

'I was hoping we could go to a restaurant,' he said. 'Somewhere with proper cutlery.'

She laughed. 'All right then. If you insist.'

He thought about the way she'd smiled as she'd said that, as he shut his front door. It made it easier to bear the echo of his footsteps as he walked upstairs, the chill of the sheets as he got into bed, and the realization that came as he closed his eyes, jolting them open again, that his research was working, that he might actually find his daughters' other father.

A bit of a mindfuck

'I miss you,' Adam said to Lena, one Sunday morning in early May. They were sitting at the kitchen table, eating breakfast. Adam had bought the paper, because he had always wanted to be the sort of man who read the paper on a Sunday morning, though he only ever looked at the news and culture sections and discarded the rest on the kitchen floor, along with the leaflets advertising Stannah stairlifts and organic vegetable boxes.

Ella Fitzgerald was playing on the radio and sunlight was dancing benignly on the kitchen table, and Lena had been feeling more content than she had in weeks. But now Adam was picking a fight. She didn't want to fight, so she pretended she hadn't heard. She carried on flicking through the *New Review* – she wanted to see if the television critic had anything to say about Daniel's latest part, as a corrupt cop on *Line of Duty*. The episode got a rave write-up. Daniel's name wasn't mentioned.

'Hey.' Adam pulled down the top of the *New Review* so she had to look at him.

'What?'

'I said, I miss you.'

'You can't miss me, Donkey,' she replied, as calmly as she could. 'I'm right here.'

'You know what I mean.'

She dropped the paper to her lap. 'You mean I'm not paying you enough attention.'

'Don't say it like that.' Adam's voice was sulky.

'Like what?'

'Like I'm needy. I'd just like to have sex once in a while, maybe have a conversation with you that isn't about your half-brother.'

That hit a nerve. 'Yeah, well, you're always out playing the fiddle with a load of Jeremy Corbyn lookalikes.'

He held his arms out for a hug. His anger never lasted more than a few minutes. 'Come here,' he said, in his baby animal voice; he only ever deployed that as a last resort. So she sat on his lap and seethed silently as he stroked her back.

'We were supposed to be having kids this year,' he said, into her shoulder.

'I told you. I don't want to pass on my genes until I know whose genes they are.'

'But what if you never find out?'

She didn't know what to say to that, so she kissed his cheek instead.

'You should just tell me if you've gone off me. I can go and find someone who appreciates me.'

'A sexy birdwatcher,' she said.

'Exactly. A really attractive birdwatcher who loves Lithuanian folk music and is really worried about Arctic sea ice decline.'

She kissed him again. Properly this time. 'I haven't gone off you. I love you, silly.' And she did love him. It was just that she had always been drawn to people who were hard to get: the Romantics lecturer who'd written *Quite good* in response to her final-year coursework; the kickboxing instructor who remembered Alison's name but always called her 'Laura'; the half-brother she'd never met.

'It's transference,' Ed told her later that week, as she sat next to Abeo on their sofa, drinking wine, scratching Oscar's head. 'You don't know who your sperm-donor dad is, so you're fixating on Daniel instead.'

Lena liked that idea. Transference was normal, and she didn't feel normal at all. She felt perverted. She never pictured Daniel with his clothes off, or anything like that – that would have been wrong. Disgusting and incestuous and wrong. But still, she thought about him too often. She dreamed about him. She imagined him thanking her in a BAFTA acceptance speech. He took up too much space in her mind. She wished she could evict him.

'It'll go away once you meet him,' Ed said.

Abeo touched her arm. 'Come to our summer party next Friday. Daniel will probably be there.'

'Whose summer party?'

'Milton Rye's.'

'Oh. Right. I thought you two were having a summer party you hadn't invited me to.'

'You can be my plus one instead of Ed,' Abeo said, holding out a bone to Oscar.

Ed laughed. 'Charming.'

Lena shook her head. 'I can't talk to Daniel and not tell him who I am.'

'You don't have to talk to him if you don't want to.'

'But what if we end up reaching for the same canapé?'

'Not sure your genetic history will come up during small talk about vol-au-vents.'

The party was held in the bar of the Ivy, which was very exciting: it was the sort of place national treasures took their mothers for dinner. Lena's name was on the list. Her name hadn't been on a list for a good ten years. She felt young and alive as she walked (slowly, impeded by high heels) upstairs to the bar. Abeo was waiting for her just inside, in a floral shirt and bow tie.

'Is he definitely here?'

'He RSVPd yes.'

There were waiters standing around with trays of red wine and white wine, smiling at each other when they thought the guests weren't looking, pretending not to be impressed by the famous faces. Milton Rye represented everyone, it seemed. YouTubers-turned-cookery presenters. A Scottish Shakespearean actor who had won an Olivier for his Lear and was now playing a mafia boss in an Emmy-award-winning thriller. Several comedians who had written children's books were laughing together in a corner, probably about how much money they had made over Christmas. But Lena was looking over their shoulders.

Abeo offered her a glass of red wine.

'I don't think I should.'

'Really?' he said, unconvinced. 'You're going to do this sober?'

'I'm trying to make healthy choices.'

He laughed. 'Nothing about coming here tonight is healthy.'

He had a point. She took the wine. It was thick and delicious and it dulled the thudding of her heart.

And that's when she saw him, queuing at the bar, laughing with a woman who'd played a Gryffindor in the Harry Potter films, head tilted back, wanting people to notice him (there was no other explanation for his paisley trousers). Looking at him was like looking into a distorted fairground mirror. His hair was straighter than hers, and darker. He was wearing brass-framed glasses. He was taller than she'd thought he would be, probably six foot two, and he had to bend down to hear what the barman was saying over the buzz of the crowd. He thanked the barman for his martini and walked across the room, eyes on his drink. He was walking in her direction.

She couldn't help it. She smiled at him. 'Hello,' he said, wedging himself into their conversation, as though she and Abeo had been waiting for him. This was what it was like to be famous, Lena realized. It gave you the confidence to talk to people you'd never met before, assuming they'd be delighted to meet you.

Lena had fallen in love three times. Four if you included James Rochester, her hard-to-impress Romantics lecturer, which she definitely did, because she still thought about him when she masturbated. Her first love was Solomon, the bassoonist in her school orchestra, who had touched her breasts on Hampstead Heath while their friends smoked weed and pretended not to watch. He'd dumped her three weeks later because she wasn't ready to have sex, and she still had to change the station whenever she heard a bassoon-heavy concerto on Radio 3. Then there was Owen Jenkins, her first university boyfriend (gorgeous eyes, wrote long poems about geographical features, not very good at sex). And then Adam. That love had crept up on her gradually, so that she'd hardly noticed it until it was a fact, something she took for granted but would be lost without, like her kidneys, or her ability to make people laugh. Seeing Daniel felt like falling in love at first sight. But it wasn't. Her attraction to him wasn't sexual – she was drawn to him because he was part of her and she was part of him. She felt like she'd known him all her life. She should have known him all her life. Maybe this is how people feel about newborn babies, she thought: overwhelmed with joy, but also anxiety and pain, because every love story has to end sooner or later. Now that she'd found him, she could lose him.

Daniel sipped his martini. 'You work at Milton Rye, right?' he said to Abeo.

'Yeah, I'm an agent. Abeo Manso. And this is my friend, Lena Delancey.'

Daniel moved his martini into his left hand so he could shake hands with Abeo. Then he reached his hand out to Lena. She half-expected to get an electric shock when their palms touched. 'I saw you in *Hamlet* at the Barbican. You were brilliant.'

He smiled, flicking his eyes down to the floor, then up again. 'Thanks. Don't think I was fantastic in that part. But thanks.'

'You were! You were wonderful!'

He looked up at her. 'Are you an actor?'

He said actor, not actress. A good sign. 'I wish. I'm a lawyer, boringly.'

'Not boring.'

'But I write sometimes, too.'

She could see Abeo sniggering into his wine, because she had hardly written anything other than witness statements and letters to clients and the odd terrible poem. She did have lots of ideas for novels, though – really literary ones. She was going to write dialogue without speech marks, so everyone would know how literary they were.

Daniel nodded. 'I'm a playwright as well as an actor.'

Lena already knew that, because she'd read an interview with him in the *Stage* that morning. 'What are your plays about?'

'I'm writing my first at the moment. It's about a boy from West London who hates that he's a privileged straight white man, because that means he's everything that's wrong with the world.'

'Must have been a stretch.'

'Touché.'

Lena had never met anyone who said 'touché' in real life. But then Daniel had just spent two months speaking iambic pentameter. Allowances had to be made.

'It is a pretty personal piece,' he said. 'But authenticity's what it's all about.'

'And making your own work gives you much more control than sitting around, waiting for the right part to come along,' Lena said, because she'd heard Abeo say that to his clients.

'Exactly.' Daniel held her gaze. He was wearing some kind of expensively androgynous fragrance but underneath she could smell his sweat, and something else, something chemical.

'I'm just going to—' Abeo pointed at the bar.

And then they were alone.

'Let's sit down,' Daniel said, and he walked towards a couple of armchairs beneath a stained-glass window, certain that she'd follow.

'You don't have to hang out with me,' Lena said, sitting down. 'I'm sure there are loads of other people who want to talk to you.'

'But I want to talk to *you*,' he said, like it was his decision alone. He was slightly camp, the way he moved his hands when he spoke, the way he tilted his head. He put his martini down and crossed his legs. 'Tell me about yourself.'

'Not much to tell,' Lena said.

'What kind of lawyer are you?'

'A litigator. Honestly, it's so boring—'

'And where did you grow up?'

'London.'

'Me too!'

'And— OK, here's something interesting about me.' This was her chance. 'At Christmas, I found out I'm not related to my dad.' She watched his face for a reaction.

'Oh my god.'

'I know.'

'How did you find out?'

She told him.

'Fuck. And you had no idea? You didn't feel different from your family growing up, or anything like that?'

'No idea at all.'

He had no idea either. That was obvious. She'd watched enough of his work to know he wasn't that good an actor.

He took a sip of his drink. 'I took a DNA test a few years ago but it just told me I was half-Greek, which I

215

knew already, and that I have the muscle composition of an elite athlete.'

'It told me I'm more Neanderthal than most people.'

'Neanderthals were actually more intelligent than homo sapiens.'

'I know!'

They had the same laugh.

Lena forced herself to say, 'You didn't get any messages from random relatives?'

'One from a third cousin in Greece. Maybe more, I don't know, I haven't checked the website for years.'

And she was about to say something – but he said, 'Must be a bit of a mindfuck, finding out you're not related to your dad.'

'Massive mindfuck.'

'What do you know about your biological father?'

'Nothing.'

He leaned forward, so that the stained-glass window cast a pattern on his face. Green, red, yellow. 'If he's anything like you, he must be pretty cool.'

'I'm not cool—'

'I think you are.'

Oh god. 'Thank you.'

Daniel frowned. 'Have I met you before?'

'No.'

'That wasn't a chat-up line.'

'I didn't think it was.'

That was her cue. She missed it.

'This is going to sound weird, but I feel like I've known you for ages.'

'I know what you mean—'

But she couldn't tell him here like this, at a party, in

front of an ex-*Blue Peter* presenter and half the cast of *Coronation Street*.

'I swear I'm sober. Sort of.' He drained his martini.

'I'm not.' She reached for her wine glass. Someone had topped it up without her noticing. 'So,' she said, 'which part of London are you from?' As if she didn't already know.

And they were off, heads close together, comparing notes on their childhoods, discussing the TV shows they'd watched when they were young, telling each other about their siblings, delighting in each other for hours, or was it minutes? She had no idea, because time had dissolved and all that mattered was this moment with him. They had so much in common. Their love of London. Their ambivalence about having kids. Twenty-five per cent of their DNA.

'We should hang out some time,' he said at last.

'I'd love that.' She'd noticed him noticing her wedding ring. So it wasn't like she was leading him on.

'Give me your number.'

She typed it into his phone.

He was smiling. 'You have beautiful eyes.'

'Thanks.' And then, because of the wine: 'So do you.' And she really was about to say something – about to explain, to point out that they had the *same* eyes, actually – when his agent walked over to them, shimmering in a green-black sequinned dress like a glamorous fly. 'Hello,' she said, recognizing Lena.

'Hello.'

'Abeo's friend.'

'That's right.'

'Sorry to interrupt.' She turned to Daniel. 'The Bright Eyes producers are here. Can I borrow you?'

'Sure.' Daniel stood up. 'Sorry about this.'

'It's fine!'

'I'll text you,' Daniel said. He leaned in and kissed her on the cheek, and she realized his scent reminded her of the aftershave her dad used to wear in the days when he'd kissed her goodnight and she'd begged him to read her just one more page of *Alice in Wonderland* because he did the voices so well, especially the White Rabbit.

On the Tube home, she thought a lot about glass houses and stones and pots calling kettles black. She could understand, now, why her father hadn't got around to telling her they weren't related. Not telling people crucial information is horribly easy, it turns out. Or telling them is impossibly difficult. She sent her dad a drunken text as she stumbled out of the station at Holloway Road. *Just to say, very grateful to you for helping me with my search xxxxx* And then she stepped out in front of a motorcyclist, who pulled over at the side of the road to shout at her.

That night, as she lay in bed, the world lurching from the wine, her phone lit up with a message from Daniel.

Let me buy you a drink next weekend. I think you're magical.

Fuck, she thought. But she replied, *OK.* She would explain everything when she saw him again. Everything would be easier when it was just the two of them.

Last hoorah

'I tell you, I've got a feeling it's going to work,' Suria said. The afternoon sun was beating down and the heat was reflecting off the pavements as she and Alison approached the fertility clinic, clutching takeaway iced coffees. They associated the clinic's hot drinks machine with sympathetic smiles and doctors offering them boxes of tissues. They were doing things differently this time.

'Hello, Ms Syed! Ms Delancey!'

'Quite impressive that the receptionist knows our names,' Alison said, as she sat down in the waiting room and tried to find a magazine she hadn't read yet.

'Depressing, you mean,' Suria said. 'This place is our equivalent of the *Cheers* bar. What does that say about our lives?' She curled up on the shiny leather chair. 'It's going to work, though. So we'll never have to come back here again.'

'Exactly,' Alison said, leafing through a copy of *What Car*. Her palms were slippery on the pages.

Aoife, the nurse, smiled at them from the doorway. 'We're ready for you!'

*

They watched the ultrasound screen as the consultant injected a potential baby into Suria's uterus. Suria was digging her nails into Alison's palm. Alison didn't want to blink, in case she missed it. But the image was shifting and grainy and black and white and there was a white dot at the end of the syringe – was that it?

'That bright flash, that was the embryo,' the consultant said.

Alison's heart hurt with how tiny it was. Too little to carry the weight of all this hope and expectation.

Suria was still staring at the screen, frowning.

'You didn't see it, did you?' Alison asked.

Suria shook her head.

'I didn't, either,' Alison lied.

Suria turned to the consultant, eyes wide. 'Is it definitely in there?'

'Yep. Definitely there.' The doctor pointed at the grainy image. 'Right there.'

Suria nodded, scanning the screen. She still couldn't see it, Alison could tell. She started to cry.

'You don't need to be able to see it for the transfer to work,' Aoife said. She rubbed Suria's arm. 'Remember to think positive, yeah? It's much harder to get pregnant when you're stressed.'

'Think positive. What does she think I'm doing?' Suria muttered. They had stopped off at the Conran Shop on the way home to look at pasta bowls they couldn't afford. Luckily, the Conran Shop is one of the most calming shops in London: smooth jazz, low lighting, plenty of sofas, and bed sheets in soothing shades of blue. There were two other couples in the kitchenware department, turning wine glasses

upside down to check the prices. Alison watched them, as Suria checked the price of a turquoise vase. A man and a woman in their twenties were holding hands, laughing at each other's jokes, agreeing about cereal bowls – probably moving in together for the first time, Alison thought. The couple in the bathroom section, two men, looked more established. They were comparing bins, and everyone knows you don't jointly purchase a bin until at least three years in. 'Does Aoife think I'm stressed on purpose?' Suria said. 'Does it not occur to her that those fucking injections have a negative impact on my mood?'

'She was just trying to help,' Alison said, in her most soothing voice. 'Optimistic people have higher success rates.'

'Or maybe optimistic folk keep trying to conceive after everyone else has given up.'

They moved through to the furniture department and sat side by side on a large wooden-framed bed.

'Whatever happens,' Alison said, 'in two weeks, we'll buy this bed to celebrate you, and how amazing you've been through all this.'

'You're kidding on.'

'I'm serious. We're in our mid-thirties now. We deserve a king-size bed.' She felt expansive and generous, saying that. Though she'd need to use the money in their joint account.

Suria kissed her shoulder. 'I haven't been amazing.'

'You have. There's no way I could have done it.'

'Well. Thank you.' Suria bounced a little on the bed. 'See if it works? Maybe we could get the pink linen bedsheets, too.'

'Maybe we could. If they're on sale by then. And some tea towels and a carrot peeler—'

'We're not made of money, hen,' Suria said. 'A carrot peeler's the sort of thing you should get at Robert Dyas.'

This is the most middle-aged conversation we've ever had, Alison thought happily. She had always fancied being middle-aged. When she had realized she was gay she'd worried she'd always be an outsider, but look at her now, having a boring conversation with her wife about kitchen utensils, trying for a baby, like most other thirtysomethings in London. She loved it when she felt just like everyone else.

Suria nudged her and pointed.

'Is that—?' Alison asked.

Suria hushed her and nodded. Benedict Cumberbatch was in the kitchen department, examining a serving dish in the shape of a cabbage. Alison texted Lena, as Suria took a surreptitious photograph with her phone.

OMG Lena replied. *What does his hair look like? Is it long and curly? I love it when his hair is long and curly.* And then, as an afterthought, *And how was the embryo transfer???*

OK, I think, Alison wrote.

Fingers crossed!!!!!! Lena typed back. She wasn't used to being insincere. She hadn't learned that exclamation marks were a giveaway.

'Bet Cumberbatch has lovely kitchen utensils,' Alison said, as she put her phone away.

Three days after the transfer, Alison was woken up early by Suria, who was doing something annoying with her elbows.

'I feel pregnant,' she said. She was running her hands over her stomach and her breasts, tenderly, as though they belonged to someone else.

'How do you know?' Alison asked. 'You've never been pregnant before.'

'My boobs are sore. And my belly's big.'

Alison put her hand on Suria's belly. It did feel bigger than usual. It was also more bruised than usual, though. She was still injecting herself with progesterone every morning. Don't get your hopes up, Alison told herself, because anxiety was already stirring in her stomach.

'Don't press,' Suria said, sitting up. 'I need a wee.'

'OK. Let's see if you still feel pregnant after you've been to the toilet.'

Suria looked disappointed when she came back to bed. 'I think I pissed the baby out.'

'Not sure that's how it works.' The anxiety subsided.

Suria rolled on to her side to look at Alison. 'I've started to have cravings.'

'You haven't. It's way too early.'

'OK, then,' Suria said, shifting on to her elbow, 'why do I want to eat steak and chips for breakfast?'

'Because Phil was making that on *Masterchef* last night.'

'No, he wasn't.'

'He was. You'd fallen asleep by that point. It must have crept into your subconscious.' Suria lay down again, forehead creased. She was finding the waiting unbearable, Alison knew. 'I can go to Tesco and get a steak if you actually want one.'

Suria shook her head.

'Shall I make you porridge instead?'

'Yes, please.' Suria rolled on to her back again and pressed the heels of her palms to her eyes. 'What are we going to *do* with ourselves for two weeks?'

'Yoga and meditation and positive thinking,' Alison said. Suria threw a pillow at her.

*

Luckily, Suria had to work twelve-hour days over the next couple of weeks, preparing for a child-protection inquiry, though, as Suria pointed out, it wasn't lucky for the children involved. Alison stayed late at the studio most nights, colouring Coco Chanel's pearls, her heart pounding. She had to hurry up and finish the artwork so she could move on to the next project, a non-fiction book about rocks and minerals – in nine months' time, she might be a parent, and it would be up to her to provide for her family. Or perhaps she'd never be a parent. And then – what? Would she and Suria carry on as they had before? She didn't see how they could. They had made space in their relationship for a baby, and without one it would be empty, a failure, like a badly reviewed restaurant.

'The two-week wait is the worst,' Max said, as they ate lunch together on London Fields, waving away the barbecue smoke floating towards them across the grass. 'Apart from finding out the transfer has failed.'

'I don't know,' Alison said. 'I've never been good with uncertainty.'

'It's like Schrödinger's cat, isn't it? The baby exists and doesn't exist at the same time until you know one way or the other.' Max and Gemma had started their final round of IVF – a new egg collection cycle, days of waiting to see how many turned into embryos, more implantations, more money.

'Suria says she doesn't want to go through it again if this embryo doesn't stick.' Alison offered Max a crisp.

He took one. 'Fair enough,' he said, crunching it. 'She doing quite a lot of shouting?'

Alison nodded. 'And crying. I wish I could offer to have

a go if it doesn't work, but the idea of getting pregnant makes me want to boak.'

Max looked blank.

'That's Scottish for vomit.' She looked down at her phone. Lena had texted her. *Went to a party with Abeo last night. Celebrity spots galore. Ps want to go out tomorrow? To the Royal Vauxhall Tavern? With Ed and Abeo? Adam's coming too. Xxx*

'We should go,' Suria said, when Alison got home. She was sitting at the kitchen table, eating a piece of toast, replying to work emails on her laptop. 'If we have a baby it'll be twenty years till we can go out partying till three in the morning.'

Alison pulled out a chair and sat down. If she had her way, she would never stay out till three in the morning again. She was happiest on the sofa of an evening, a bowl of leftovers on her knee, one arm around her wife, watching moodily lit detectives investigating high-concept murders. God it would be great, to have a baby as an excuse not to go out. 'I'm up for it, as long as we can get the last Tube home,' she said.

'Alison!' Suria said, through a mouthful of toast. 'This is our last chance to be young!'

'We're not young,' Alison pointed out. 'We say things like "go out partying".'

Because they weren't young, they got to the Royal Vauxhall Tavern as soon as it opened. The disco ball scattered light around the room, from the stage, where a drag queen was adjusting a microphone, to the dance floor, an empty circle enclosed by glossy red pillars. 'Who wants a drink?' Alison asked the others, and then remembered she hadn't been paid for three months, because she was a freelancer, and people didn't seem to feel the need to pay freelancers – or indeed reply to their emails asking why they hadn't been paid. The round was cheaper than she'd feared it would be, though, because Suria and Lena both ordered Diet Cokes.

'Do you have something to tell us?' Suria asked Lena, when she heard her drinks order.

'No. Just overdid it a few nights ago—'

'But you and Adam are trying for kids, aye?'

Alison glanced across at Adam, who was leaning against a pillar, smiling, desperate, as a man in a leather waistcoat shouted into his ear.

'We've decided to wait, actually.'

Suria looked disappointed. 'I was hoping we'd be on maternity leave together. I was thinking we could get a joint membership to the Tate and hang out in the members' room while everyone else is at work, and compare notes on the state of our vaginas.'

'Lena can hang out with you in the Tate members' room without a baby,' Alison pointed out, handing them each a Diet Coke.

'It was the vagina-comparing bit I was really looking forward to, to be honest,' Suria said.

They stood in the middle of the empty dance floor, swaying to Lady Gaga, arms crossed against the cold. Clubs were only sweaty when they were filled with people, Alison realized. Around ten, other people drifted in: a group of grey-haired queers, a young lesbian couple holding hands, five gay men, all wearing glasses. Ed and Abeo turned up, drunk, at ten thirty – 'Sorry. The dog sitter was late' – and by eleven, the dance floor was rammed, everyone jumping up and down, arms around each other.

'If we don't have kids, we could do this every weekend!' Suria shouted.

'You don't want to do this every weekend.' Alison couldn't stop thinking about Max. Max and Seb. She wanted to know what that kind of love was like.

'I do! I do!'

'You'll be knackered in the morning.'

'I won't!' Suria put her arm around Lena. 'See queer folk?' she yelled into her ear. 'We get to choose our family, and you're my family.'

'You're my family too!' Lena said.

Abeo leaned across to Alison. 'I haven't given them any MDMA, I swear.'

'And even if me and Alison never have weans, it'll be OK, because we already have a family.' Suria was always extra Scottish after 11 p.m.

'OK, Suria,' Alison said, tugging her arm, because Lena wasn't smiling any more.

Suria was still shouting into Lena's ear. 'I know you don't think using a sperm donor is a good idea. But love makes a family, is all I'm saying.' Suria took Lena's hand between both of hers. 'And the donor won't love the baby, and the baby won't love the donor, because they won't know each other—'

'Come on, let's go,' Alison said, pulling Suria away.

'What've I said?'

'Nothing.' But Lena had turned away. She was looking at her phone, Alison realized. And Alison didn't mean to look, but she couldn't help seeing the message: *When can I see you? I'm taking you to Soho House. xxx*

227

'Who's that?' Alison asked her.

'No one.'

'No, seriously, who? Are you—' She looked around for Adam, but he was sitting in a booth at the edge of the club, having an intense-looking conversation with Ed. 'Are you shagging someone else?'

'No!' Lena said, exactly the way she would have done if she had been shagging someone else.

'I wouldn't judge you—'

Lena laughed.

'OK, I'd judge you a bit—'

'I'm really not,' Lena said. 'Unless you count having the occasional wank with my electric toothbrush.'

'Lena, gross, seriously – you'll never get the brush properly clean—'

'You take the brush head off first! Obviously!'

'But the pointy metal bit could do you some serious damage—'

'You don't use it on the inside—'

Suria draped an arm around Alison's shoulder. 'Who's Lena shagging?'

Lena sipped her drink. 'Jamie Dornan.'

Suria frowned. 'What – from *Fifty Shades of Grey*?'

'Yep. It's just casual, obviously, because he's in LA all the time—'

Suria looked at Lena. 'Is this like when you said you were going to be a judge on *The Apprentice*?'

'No. I am genuinely shagging Jamie Dornan. Don't tell anyone. The *Daily Mail* will have a field day if they find out.' She glanced across at Adam, who was showing Ed something on his phone.

'You're lying.'

'Of course I'm bloody lying!'

'Fuck!' Suria said.

'I'm honestly not having an affair. If I was, I would tell you.'

'She would,' Alison said, though she wasn't sure any more. But it was natural that they were growing apart like this. Once they had children, they would be incapable of discussing anything other than mastitis and childcare arrangements and the cost of three-bedroom houses in East Sussex. They were branches on a family tree, moving away from each other. 'I'm just going to sit down,' Alison shouted to Suria over the music.

She joined Adam and Ed in their booth at the edge of the room. They looked up, awkward, when she sat down.

'I was just saying to Adam,' Ed said. 'I still feel shit about not giving you and Suria my sperm—'

'It's fine!' Alison waved her arm, and was glad the room was dark, that they wouldn't see her blush, because why did people think it was appropriate to have this sort of conversation in public?

'It was just a bit complicated—'

'I know. I get it.'

Ed had pulled his sleeves over his hands. 'Maybe we could talk about it again, though, if Suria's embryo transfer doesn't work—'

'Ed, no,' Alison said. 'Honestly, it's fine. Let's just forget about it.'

Ed nodded. There was a strained silence.

'I might get going,' Adam said. 'I'm leading Assembly in the morning.' He stood up.

Lena and Suria were arm-wrestling, now, as a crowd gathered around them, whooping and cheering. Lena pushed Suria's arm down, her face tight, shaking with the effort.

'I'll make sure Lena gets home OK,' Alison said.

Adam pulled on his jacket. 'I mean – she can clearly look after herself.'

Alison woke up the next day, heart pounding, mouth dry. She decided to work from home instead of going into the studio, but she was too distracted by her emails to get much done. She had been copied into an exchange between her father and Jim:

Hi Jim,

Tom here (Alison's dad). It's been four months now since we commissioned you to make my late wife's headstone. I was hoping to have it installed by her birthday (June). What are the chances? What's the hold-up? Can you send us pics of your progress?

Looking forward to hearing from you soon!

Best

Tom

Dear Tom,

I'm very sorry. My own granny died in March and so I had to take a break from working on the head-stone. Then I moved studios, from Surrey to Devon, and the headstone hasn't arrived at my new studio yet. June might be ambitious, to be honest.

Yours

Jim

She was writing a passive-aggressive reply to Jim when Suria texted her.

Want to go to Marylebone after work?

You better not have taken a pregnancy test, Alison replied. *Wheesht and meet me in the Conran Shop.*

She knew for sure as soon as she saw Suria sitting on the bed.

'You were supposed to wait!' Alison sat down next to her. 'You should have waited for me!'

'I know! But I was going nuts!' Suria showed her the pregnancy test. There was a cross, but it was very faint.

'We should do another one to make sure,' Alison said, but her heart was already dancing.

'The packet says it doesn't matter how faint the line is.' Suria was shining with happiness. 'I can't believe it worked! Must be because I've been so relaxed and good-tempered.'

Alison couldn't make herself feel it was true. Suddenly, having children seemed like the sort of thing other people did, like winning the lottery and voluntarily going to an Angus Steak House.

'Aren't you happy?'

'Of course!' She hugged Suria and pulled her down to the king-size bed and they lay there, staring up at the ceiling, eyes narrowed against the halogen lights.

'This time next year, we'll be parents,' Suria said. 'Aren't you glad we went out last night? That was probably our last hoorah.'

'Fuck.' Alison was dangerously happy.

'I feel like jumping on a sofa.'

'Don't. Only dickheads jump on sofas.'

'Arseholes,' Suria reminded her. 'Gender-neutral insults only.' She bounced on the mattress. 'You haven't changed your mind?'

'About—'

'About the bed.'

'No. We're going to need all the help sleeping we can get.'

Suria stopped bouncing. 'We'll like the baby, won't we?'

'Hope so,' Alison said.

'I'm terrified.'

'Me too.'

'But I'm the one that's got to keep the wean alive, and push it out.'

And I'm the one who's not going to be related to it, Alison wanted to say, but she didn't, because it was a bit late to worry about that. She worried anyway, though. She worried that the hormones wouldn't kick in because she wasn't the one giving birth, that she'd look at the baby and the baby would be a stranger and she'd realize she'd made a horrible mistake. She worried that she'd been so caught up with the expensive waiting rooms and copies of *Elle Decoration*, the drugs and the tests, that she hadn't really thought about what it would be like when the baby actually arrived and looked at her with someone else's face. She wished they hadn't had to outsource the sperm. She didn't believe in outsourcing. She wouldn't even let Suria hire a cleaner.

Suria pushed herself off the bed and consulted the price tag. 'You do know this is two grand, just for the mattress?'

'What?'

'But you said we could get it! Too late to back out now!'

An endangered species

Tom wished he had ironed his shirt. He had never really seen the point of ironing, but that afternoon, as he looked in the mirror that stretched the length of the restaurant, comparing himself to the pristine waiters and the starched businessmen in the booth by the door, he felt like a piece of paper, one that had been scrunched and thrown in a bin, then unfolded and smoothed out. His heart felt like that, too; just a few months ago he had felt a failure of a father – a failure in general, really, with no one to love him and no career to speak of – and now he was drinking whiskey sours with an attractive environmental activist (his favourite kind of environmental activist). His lack of an impressive career mattered less now that Jessie was next to him, pulling the cherry from the cocktail stick with her teeth.

'I haven't had bourbon before 5 p.m. in about twenty years,' she was saying.

'Don't tell Lena I'm drinking spirits,' Tom said. 'She's obsessed with me eating healthily. She came over a couple of weeks ago and threw my chorizo in the bin.'

'Because she loves you.'

'Or maybe she just doesn't fancy any more death admin. Did I tell you about the nightmare we're having with Sheila's gravestone? Apparently the stonemason's too upset to finish it, because he had to put his pit bull down. Last time, his excuse was that his granny had died, and before that he was too heartbroken to use a chisel because his girlfriend had dumped him—'

Sheila took a long sip of her drink. 'This is a cheery conversation.'

'Sorry. My small talk is a bit on the rusty side.'

She smiled. She had lipstick on her teeth. A small, re-assuring flaw. 'You don't need to make small talk, Tom. We've known each other for years. Just be yourself.'

He nodded and sat back in his chair, arms limp. He wasn't sure how to be himself. He wasn't entirely sure who that was. He picked up the menu – when in doubt, reach for a prop – and considered the starters. Gazpacho soup with raw bream, or crispy chicken skin with an egg cooked at 62 degrees Celsius. 'They don't seem to be very into heating up the food, do they?'

Jessie laughed.

'You're wondering why I've dragged you all the way to South Kensington for a lukewarm meal,' he said. 'But there's method in my madness.'

She leaned forward. 'Is there, now?'

'This is just the first half of the date.'

He felt pretty good about himself, suave and seductive, sexy even. Until his phone rang, and Alison told him he was going to be a grandfather.

*

'Where are you taking me, then?' Jessie asked, as they walked up Cromwell Road.

'Here.' He stopped outside the Natural History Museum. Extinction Rebellion protestors milled about on the steps, eating sandwiches and giving out leaflets. 'They're holding a mass die-in, under the blue whale skeleton. Thought it might be up your street.'

'Well!' Jessie said. 'You have surprised me, Tom Delancey.'

Tom offered her his arm. 'Shall we?'

He felt older and stiffer and slower than he had that morning as they walked into the glorious gothic hall and stared up at the bones of the whale, soaring above them, bleached and beached.

'An endangered species, just like me,' Tom said, pointing up at it.

'Oh, come off it,' Jessie said, hitting his arm.

'A bloody grandfather! I'm not old enough to be a grand-father!'

'Last time I saw you, you were moaning about your daughters leaving it so late to have children—'

'Yes, in theory. Everyone wants grandchildren in theory. But in practice, it's quite – confronting.'

The protestors crowded together beneath the whale. A man in yellow rang a bell. Everyone lay down at once. Jessie and Tom were a little slower than the others.

'I'm not sure I'll be able to get up again,' Tom whispered.

'Shh,' she said. 'We're dead.'

He closed his eyes and rested his head on his forearm. He could smell Jessie's perfume. He could hear her breathing. 'Never thought I'd get to lie next to you on a first date.'

'Shh.'

'You know they've named the whale Hope?' he whispered.

'I know. Stop trying to impress me.'

'I'm not.'

'Oh.' She nudged him. 'Shame.'

The protest lasted half an hour. Afterwards, they went to the café for a slice of lemon drizzle cake – the desserts at the restaurant had been foam and dry ice, mostly.

'That's the most relaxing protest I've ever been on,' he said, pouring Jessie a cup of Earl Grey.

'I love a good die-in,' she said. 'I've told you about that lovely one I went to outside the Treasury a couple of years ago, about traffic pollution and cyclist deaths?'

'You haven't.'

'Well. It was less relaxing. Everyone was shouting and ringing their bicycle bells.'

So many causes. He was getting too old for this nonsense (a *grandfather*). She was exhausting. Exhausting yet magnificent.

'What?' she said, because he was smiling at her.

'Nothing. I was just thinking that you're magnificent.'

She laughed. 'All right, then,' she said.

'All right then what?'

'All right then, I'll come back to yours.' She could obviously see the panic in his eyes, because she said, 'Unless you don't want me to—'

'No, no! I do! I'm just – not very good at cooking.'

'I don't need dinner. I'm stuffed.'

'Well. I'm going to need to eat at some point.'

'We could get takeaway pizzas?'

'We could,' he said slowly. He could install her in the living room with a glass of wine while he sorted out the house. There was a fortnight's worth of Y-fronts scattered across the bedroom floor, and he couldn't remember the last time he'd cleaned the toilet.

The living room made much more sense with another person in it. They ate their pizzas on separate sofas, plates and wine glasses on the coffee table, listening to Joni Mitchell (Jessie's suggestion. She'd dug through Sheila's old LPs while he stuffed his dirty underwear into the chest of drawers). The silence was companionable at first, but by the time the pizzas were finished and the wine glasses were empty, Tom realized he couldn't think of anything to say that wasn't innuendo or a pun. Perhaps Jessie felt the same, because she smiled at him, opened her mouth, shut it again, and said, 'I was just going to ask how your sperm donor research is going. Unless you don't want to talk about it.'

He didn't, really. Being reminded that he had defective sperm didn't do wonders for the old libido. He cleared his throat. 'I've hit a wall, I think,' he said. 'But I did find out that one of the girls' ancestors was a British painter of some renown. Not a very good one, though. A lot of dreary-looking fields and bowls of fruit, by the looks of it. But one of his paintings is in the National Gallery.'

'There are a lot of very brown paintings in the National Gallery,' Jessie said.

'I know! Endless horses and bales of hay! Anyway. That's probably where Alison gets it from. I always thought she was artistic because I dragged her around the Tate a lot when she was a toddler.'

Jessie pushed herself up from her sofa and moved across to sit next to him. He realized he was jiggling his leg. He wasn't really sure what the rules were, but she had invited herself to his house and now she was sitting provocatively close to him. Except she wasn't being provocative, obviously, he needed to stop thinking like that—

'Are you going to kiss me, or what?' she said.

Which cleared that up.

A little later, he pulled off her skirt, there on the sofa. She was wearing lacy underpants. Nice ones, like she'd expected this to happen.

'This isn't pity sex, is it?'

She laughed. Which wasn't, he realized later, a denial.

He turned the overhead light off before he took off his own clothes. No one had seen him naked since Sheila.

'What are you doing?'

'I'm about to become a grandfather. Everything about me is droopy.'

'Shut up and get over here,' Jessie said.

He pulled off his T-shirt and resisted the urge to cross his arms. She pushed him on to the sofa and climbed on top of him. She undid her bra.

He looked at her breasts and he could think of so many similes to describe them, so many metaphors, but luckily, before he could say them out loud, she kissed him. And then she unzipped his trousers. 'Not everything is droopy,' she said.

Later still, he read James Joyce out loud to her in an Irish accent, until she asked him to stop.

'You can be my muse!' he said, the next morning, as he lay in bed, watching her get dressed.

'You can fuck off.'

She zipped up her skirt slowly, like she wanted him to unzip it again. Except she didn't, because she batted him away when he tried.

'You already inspire me, whether you like it or not.' He sipped his coffee. 'You've inspired me to read more women writers.'

'Oh yeah? Like who?'

'Well – just Mary Shelley and Virginia Woolf so far. But that's given me a taste for it! I thought I might try a bit of Sylvia Plath, maybe one of the Brontës—'

'Woah,' she said, opening her make-up bag. 'Steady on.'

'And I've started writing a short story, like you said. About – you know.'

'You looking for the sperm donor.'

'Exactly.'

She twisted to look at him. 'Can I read it?'

'God, no.'

'Why not?'

'It's just a first draft. It's shit. And far too personal.'

'The best books are personal, I've always thought.' She bent towards the mirror, to apply her lipstick. He had literary thoughts about her buttocks.

She kissed him on the doorstep, and her lipstick left a mark.

He went upstairs to his office after she left and re-read the first draft of his short story. He'd used the word 'sanguine' more than anyone should ever use the word 'sanguine', but still. Nice, clean prose. He sat down at his laptop and carried on writing, about what it meant to be a father, how it had changed him, given him something to live for, something real to do. The seal was broken and more words were coming, about how vital he'd felt for those twenty years the girls had been at home and how faded and used up he felt now, like they had juiced him, taken the best of him, leaving him a husk on the side of the kitchen counter, suitable only for composting or boiling down into soup. How grateful he was, to have lived long enough to become a husk. How meeting someone new had rehydrated him. (Had this metaphor run its course? That was a question for the second draft). He was so excited he didn't even notice he had switched to writing in the first person – he hated the first person – until he was a thousand words deep, and when he read it back he found he actually liked the personality it gave to the prose. For the first time in a long time his writing felt alive, and he felt alive, and he sat back and checked the word count and he felt dazed, as though he'd become someone else for a moment. He didn't want to carry on, in case he jinxed it, so he opened Lena's Genealogy DNA account. Someone had sent her a message. A man named Jonathan Green.

Hello! Genealogy DNA says we're second cousins! Do you know how we might be related? I've given you access to my tree in case you want to look at it.

Tom clicked on Jonathan's tree, and there they were, the names of his daughters' relatives, Greens and Marions and Reids and Butlers, hundreds of them, and some of them were still alive, men who were the right age to have donated sperm in the Eighties – and before he could stop himself, he was searching medical school graduation records for doctors named Green or Marion or Reid or Turner, and then it happened very quickly, and Nick Turner's name was right there, he'd graduated in 1988, and he was a cardiologist living in Cambridge, and he had light-green eyes, and it was him, it had to be him, and Tom Delancey slapped his laptop shut, because he was starting to hyperventilate. He felt the way he had the one time he'd tried jogging on a treadmill, like his feet were being pulled out from under him, like he was about to fall and break his nose.

Bloomsday

Alison told Lena that Suria was pregnant one sweaty Sunday in June as they sunbathed on the hot concrete at London Fields Lido, slightly self-conscious in their swimming costumes. They'd swum twenty lengths in the slow lane, their heads above the water, making inane small talk about the boring-sounding book Alison was illustrating – she was drawing pictures of stones, apparently – and the hours target Lena was expected to hit before getting a bonus. She wasn't going to make it this year. She couldn't bring herself to stay at work past 8 p.m.; she had lost the ability to concentrate. It was too quiet in her office, and her thoughts were too loud. But she didn't tell Alison that, and Alison didn't tell Lena that she was going to become an aunt until their costumes were almost dry, and their hour-long slot at the lido was almost up.

'I'm so happy for you!' Lena said, thinking: I feel like I barely know you any more.

'You don't have to say that.' Alison hugged her knees.

'No! I am! I am! I am, honestly!' She leaned over to hug Alison. Their skin, tacky with sweat, stuck together as they pulled apart. 'These are happy tears!'

Lena went home and replied to a donor-conceived Reddit thread called *AIBU? My queer friends are pregnant, and I'm happy for them, but when they say things like, 'this baby won't have a father' I find it really triggering.*

'Suria's pregnant,' she told Adam that evening, when he came back from a folk session at a pub in Lewisham. She was standing at the hob, making dhal, even though it was thirty degrees outside. She needed comfort food.

'Oh!' Adam said, taking off his bike helmet. He was struggling to settle on an appropriate facial expression, she could tell. 'IVF?'

She nodded, and scraped the lentils from the bottom of the pan.

He sat down at the table. 'I don't actually know what IVF is.'

'They took her eggs out and fertilized them, and waited for them to turn into embryos, and now they've put one of the embryos back inside her.'

'We could try IVF too,' Adam said. 'Then you wouldn't have to have sex with me at all.'

She turned to look at him. 'I didn't say I don't want to have sex with you—'

He laughed, looking at his knees.

'Let's have sex tonight,' she said.

'Maybe I don't want to have sex with *you*,' he said, standing up and heading to the shower.

*

But he did, when it came down to it.

'Maybe we should schedule sex in,' he said afterwards, as they lay in bed. 'Every Saturday and Monday?'

'Sure,' she said, but she wasn't really listening, because Daniel had texted her again. She glanced at Adam. 'Daniel wants to meet up with me on Sunday. At his private members' club.'

Adam pulled a face.

'I know.'

'You have to tell him it's not a date.'

'Of course it's not a date.'

'He clearly thinks it's a date.'

'It doesn't matter if he thinks it's a date. He's my brother.'

'Yeah, well, make sure you tell him that,' Adam said, pulling her closer. 'And tell him about me too, and how virile and good in bed I am.'

'Obviously.' She leaned across and kissed him. She definitely would.

Lena met Daniel outside his club as the sun turned Soho Square pale pink. He was wearing shorts, which was reassuring. People didn't usually wear shorts on dates, did they?

The receptionist recognized Daniel and waved them through to the bar, which was filled with curved sofas and squashy armchairs, as though it had been designed by someone with a phobia of corners. Lena had assumed the place would be full of cigar-smoking Old Etonians, the sort that have secret children scattered all over London, like business cards. But there were women in this club, too, and men with exciting facial hair.

'It's kind of a media hangout,' Daniel said, as he pulled out a chair for her. She tried to sit down the way a features journalist would. He went to buy her a drink. Shorts aside, it was beginning to feel uncomfortably date-like.

'Just so you know,' she said, as he came back with two martinis, 'I'm married.'

Daniel sat down, slowly. 'Well, yeah. You're wearing a wedding ring.'

'I wasn't sure. If you thought this was a friends thing, or a more-than-friends thing. So I just wanted to tell you. To be clear.'

'Happily married?'

'Yes.'

'I guess it's a friends thing, then.'

'Yes.'

And that's when she was going to tell him the other thing, except he said, 'That's not what I was hoping for, though. To be clear.'

And obviously it was wrong. Obviously, completely, totally, legally, morally, biologically wrong. But GOD it felt good, the way he looked at her, like he wanted to look at all of her, like he wanted her. How wonderful to be wanted. Adam wanted her too, of course, on Saturdays and Mondays, but most of the time he wanted her to make him toast or sign a petition about the destruction of skylark ground-nesting sites.

Daniel was wanted by half the people in the club, it seemed. Most of them knew his name.

A waiter touched his shoulder as he passed and said, 'All right, mate?'

A young woman with Sixties eyelashes ambushed him on the way to the toilet and kissed him on the cheek.

A stand-up comedian with a Netflix special came over to say he'd missed seeing him around.

'I know, man. Work's been wild, recently.'

Then Daniel and Lena were alone at last.

'It's Bloomsday today,' she said, to fill the silence.

'What?'

'Bloomsday. Sixteenth of June. It's from *Ulysses*.'

He nodded.

'By James Joyce.'

'What do you do on Bloomsday?'

She tried to remember. She couldn't. 'Pretend to be Irish?'

'Or maybe read one of James Joyce's books.'

'Or maybe that.'

They sipped their drinks.

'It's also the date Sylvia Plath and Ted Hughes got married.'

Daniel laughed. 'That ended well.'

'And it's the date Mary Shelley came up with the idea for *Frankenstein*.'

He had nearly finished his drink. He turned around and caught the barman's eye.

'Sorry,' she said, 'I'm like my dad. Telling you things you don't want to know.'

'No! Go ahead! I'm interested!'

'OK. I just want to tell you one more thing—'

'Tell me loads more things!'

'It's a bit gross.'

'I love gross.'

'OK. So. Mary Shelley's mother, Mary Wollstonecraft, died eleven days after she gave birth, of some kind of fever – and they thought the milk in her breasts was causing the fever, so to try and cure her, the doctor brought puppies to her house, to suck the fever out of her breasts.'

A beat.

'I told you it was gross.'

'Poor puppies.'

'Poor Mary Wollstonecraft, I was thinking.'

He laughed.

'But the infection actually came from the doctor's fingers, when he reached inside her to remove the afterbirth. So.'

'You're a woman—' Daniel began, as the barman put another martini down in front of him.

'I am.'

'Tell me. Why the fuck do women have kids? Why would you do that to yourself?'

'I actually don't know.' As she said it out loud, she felt lighter, and everything felt simpler, and all at once her mind was swept clean of the questions that had been clattering around in there since she'd turned thirty – when's the right time, and what if I leave it too late, and how the fuck are you supposed to be a City lawyer and a mother at the same time, and what if I hate the baby, and what if the baby hates me, and what if becoming a mother ruins my life? She could opt out of all of it.

She needed to talk to Adam.

He raised his glass to her. 'Happy Bloomsday.'

'And happy *Frankenstein* day.'

'And happy doomed poetic lovers' day.'

She took a swig of her martini and revelled in the sting of it. She was going to stay out late and get drunk and no one could tell her not to, because she wasn't responsible for anyone else, and she never would be.

'And from now on the sixteenth of June will be remembered as the day the great actor and playwright Daniel Gold first went for a drink with the world-renowned lawyer, Lena—'

'Delancey.'

'Delancey, great name.' He smiled at her over his martini. 'How do you know so much about Bloomsday, anyway?'

'It's my mum's birthday.'

'You didn't want to hang out with her tonight?'

'She died two years ago,' she said, looking at her hands. 'Feels like a really long time ago, actually. It was quick, she didn't suffer.' She always said that, to make people feel better. Bit of a conversation killer, a dead mother.

'I'm so sorry,' Daniel said, like he actually meant it. And then a man shuffled up to ask him for a selfie, and told him he was great in *Killing Eve*. When he left, Daniel leaned across and said, 'I wasn't in *Killing Eve*. But it's too embarrassing to say that after you've posed for a picture, know what I mean?'

She did know.

They spilled out into Soho and marched down Greek Street, arm in arm, singing at the tops of their voices like 21-year-olds. Lena smiled at the people they passed, who turned to look at them, and wondered if they were staring because they were being outrageous, or because they recognized Daniel, or both. Her phone rang a couple of times. Alison, probably. They always spoke on their mum's birthday. But she didn't want to think about death today, because she was alive, and giddy, and *free*, and she was never going to be a mother, so she would always be free, and nothing else mattered but walking through Soho, tipsy and happy, with her secret brother.

'You know the mnemonic for how to remember the order of the streets in Soho?' she asked him.

'No.'

'Going For Dinner With Billie Piper. Greek, Frith, Dean, Wardour, Berwick, Poland.'

'I've actually been for dinner with Billie Piper. On Wardour Street.'

'No!'

'Yeah. She's a friend of a friend. Total babe. She ate a lot of chips.'

'Fuck! I want your life!'

'It gets quite lonely sometimes.' He glanced at her, half smiling.

Outside Balans, a man with greasy hair touched Daniel's arm. 'Sorry to interrupt. Just to say. Loved you in *Game of Thrones.*'

'Thanks! Such a small part. But.'

'You nailed it.'

'Do you think so?'

'Yeah!'

Daniel smiled, impish, humble. 'I really appreciate that.'

'Can I get a selfie?'

'Course!'

Lena stood there while the two men posed for the camera, proud to know Daniel, feeling famous by association.

Daniel linked arms with her again and they ran up Charing Cross Road and paused outside a second-hand bookshop. A man was wheeling the discounted books inside. Daniel said, 'Are you still open? We need a copy of *Ulysses.*'

'If you're quick.'

'*Ulysses* is very long,' Lena told him, as they walked into the shop. 'And famously hard to read.'

'I want to be the kind of person that reads *Ulysses,* though.'

'Me too.'

249

She found an old Vintage Classics edition of *Mrs Dalloway* while Daniel browsed the shelves for *Ulysses*. She turned it over to read the back cover copy. *The events in Virginia Woolf's fourth novel occupy a single June day in Central London.* 'This takes place over one day in June, too!' she said, holding it up to show Daniel.

He wasn't listening. He was flipping through a pristine, unread, copy of *Ulysses*. 'You know what? You're right. I can't be fucked with this.' He put it down and picked up *Portrait of the Artist as a Young Man*.

'My dad read me that when I was little, as a bedtime story,' she told him.

He studied the cover: James Joyce in black and white, legs apart, staring down the camera. 'Quite fit,' he said, turning the book so she could admire him too.

'Definitely.' She looked at him, her opinion of him shifting and deepening as she took this in. 'Are you bi?'

'I don't like labels.' Daniel fanned the book, stopping on a page with more white space than the others. 'A poem!' he said, and started to read: '*Are you not weary of ardent ways, / Lure of the fallen seraphim? / Tell no more of enchanted days.*' He looked up. 'I'm not weary of ardent ways.' He looked back down. 'But I'm starting to think you might be a fallen seraphim.'

'Stop it,' Lena said, moving away without consciously deciding to, the way you drop a pan before it scalds you.

'Stop what?' He was still smiling. How amazing, to be able to flirt with someone that shamelessly, to be that comfortable in your own skin.

'You *know* what.' Lena's skin was prickling – Run, her body was saying. But instead, she took the book from him and read the villanelle, to change the subject. 'I thought that was the most beautiful poem in the world, the first time I read it.' It was more pretentious than she remembered.

He took the book to the till.

'You're buying it?'

He nodded. He held out his hand for the copy of *Mrs Dalloway*. 'And I'm getting you that one, too.'

'You don't have to—'

'But I want to. That way you'll think of me as you read it. And I'll think of you when I read this.'

'Well, OK. Thank you.' She walked out into the street, away from the heat and the intensity of him.

'Come on, one more drink,' he said, when she told him she ought to go home. They were passing a club on Berwick Street, and someone recognized him and came out to say hi. His life was so glamorous, and she felt intoxicated by it, and her body was beating with adrenaline, and she felt reckless, the way she always did on her mother's birthday. So when the doorman waved them inside, she let Daniel lead her into the darkness.

'London's like a village when you're famous, isn't it? Everyone knows you,' Lena said, as they pushed their way to the bar, where flutes of cava were lined up, sparkling, like an alcoholic chorus line. 'And everything's free,' she observed, as he handed her a glass.

'I'm not that famous,' he said, but he smiled, like it was just a matter of time.

'What was he like?' Adam asked, as she put her rucksack down on the kitchen floor. He was frowning at his laptop, drinking coffee.

'Fun,' she said. 'Maybe a bit of a twat.'

Adam shut his computer. 'How did he react?'

Lena sat down. 'React to—'

'When you told him. That he's your brother.'

She took a sip of his coffee and wondered what to say. Adam's hands were in his hair. 'Lena!'

'I didn't know how to tell him!' She stood up and started opening and shutting cupboards, looking for food.

'Did he think you were on a date?'

'No! He knows about you!' She was staring into the fridge, eyes narrowed against the light, wondering what to eat.

'I don't want you seeing him again, unless you tell him you're his sister. It's too weird.'

She turned to face him, one hand still on the fridge door. 'You do not get to tell me who I can and can't see!' She said it with a ferocity that alarmed them both.

'You're wasted,' he said, eventually.

'So?' There was a bowl covered in cling film on the first shelf of the fridge. She picked it up. Chickpea curry. He had saved her dinner. A hit of guilt.

'Don't try and make out like I'm a male chauvinist, when you've been out drinking with a bloke who probably thinks he's in with a chance—'

'I know. I know.' She sat down with the cold curry, hating herself. 'Thanks,' she said, holding up the bowl. 'Sorry I'm home so late.'

He nodded. 'It's a shitty day for you.'

She started to cry. 'She would have been sixty-eight.'

He put an arm around her and kissed the top of her head. She loved Adam. She would stay away from her half-brother. She had no idea what she was doing. She would stop doing it, whatever it was.

But that night, she dreamed about Daniel. They were at a house party together. He was wearing a denim jacket. His hair looked awful; he was wearing so much gel in it that it was sticking out from his head, spiky, and when she looked more closely, she realized each spike was actually a tiny knife. He had his arm around her all night, and they went into the kitchen together and made drinks, and there was an understanding that they couldn't have sex, but that they wanted to. And then the birdsong of her alarm woke her, and the feeling of the dream was still in her body, and she reached for Adam, who was lying next to her, eye mask on, and she straddled him.

'What are you doing?' he asked, pushing up the mask so he could see her.

'What do you think?' She pulled the mask back over his eyes.

She moved against him till he was hard, then pushed herself down on to him, and she closed her eyes and fucked him, and she didn't have to pretend to be anyone else for once because she was so turned on, and for once she came before he did, which made him come, inside her. As she lay down next to him, he laughed and ran a hand over his face. 'That was amazing.'

And she felt dirty, and guilty, and overwhelmed.

And that's when she realized they hadn't used a condom.

Eyes like ceviche

Lena often found it hard to get around to things. She wrote letters, intending to buy stamps for them, and found the envelopes months later, crumpled at the bottom of her rucksack. She'd never had a flu jab. Amazon had once sent her a lawn mower instead of a ceramic mixing bowl (26 inches), and she'd tried to call their helpline to figure out how to return it, but after forty-five minutes on hold, she had given up. The lawn mower had sat, dusty and silent, in the corner of the spare room for a year, like a sulky guest, until Alison asked if she could have it. And that Monday morning in June, as she walked down the hill towards the Tube, she fully intended to go to Boots in Moorgate before work, but she walked to the office on autopilot. She worked through lunch, and her head was so full of thoughts about Daniel that everything else was squeezed out, including her password for Lexis®Library. She spent an hour on the phone to IT, trying to reset it. And it was only that night at ten thirty when she finally got home from work and Adam asked, 'How was your day?' that she realized it hadn't been great, but that it had started well, and that Adam's sperm were probably still swimming up inside her, determined and exhausted, the way she felt at the end of a 5k run.

Lena Delancey said she would buy the morning-after pill herself, Lena thought, as she walked into Boots the next morning: she had started reading *Mrs Dalloway* on the Tube. She had never bought the morning-after pill before. She hadn't realized it involved a mandatory consultation.

'I'm sorry,' said the pharmacist, tucking her hair behind her ears. 'It's the law—'

'I don't have time,' Lena said. 'I have a meeting in fifteen minutes—'

'I promise it won't take long.'

The consultation room was more of a cupboard than a room, really: just enough space for a computer and two chairs. No window. Bright overhead lighting. Perfect for an interrogation.

'So,' said the pharmacist, looking down, awkward. 'Do you actually know how human reproduction works? And why it's important to use contraception if you don't want to get pregnant?'

Lena laughed. 'I am literally thirty-four years old.'

'I'm sorry. I have to ask. Is there a reason you're not on the pill?'

'The pill makes me insane.'

'There are various different kinds—'

'I don't see why I should have to ingest loads of hormones when my husband doesn't have to.'

'Right. OK. So what kind of contraception do you use?'

'We use condoms.'

The pharmacist nodded.

'Apart from on Monday morning.'

The pharmacist nodded again. Lena had a feeling she was picturing her having sex. 'Bit silly.'

'Sorry?' Lena was sure she must have misheard.

'I just said – it was a bit silly. Not to use a condom. If you don't want a baby.'

Lena arrived at work fifteen minutes late, £30 poorer, and twice as humiliated as she should have been.

'Nice of you to join us,' James said, as she tried to slip unnoticed into the meeting room.

Afterwards, back in her office, she stared at the pill for a good ten minutes before she could bring herself to take it. She washed it down with a glass of water, then opened her emails and tried to concentrate, ignoring the low thrum of shame. At lunchtime she checked Instagram to see where Daniel was and what he was doing. Seeing his face made her pulse race, and she felt sick with herself, sicker the more she stared at him, because he was her fucking *brother*. Not that she was attracted to him – she really wasn't attracted to him at all, honestly.

But now that Daniel was in her life, she understood why people felt moved to write rhyming couplets. She wanted to write great poetry about him, poetry that would be studied by students in hundreds of years, as academics debated the identity of her 'forbidden fruit'. Unfortunately, as her poems contained phrases like 'forbidden fruit', she knew they weren't likely to stand the test of time. But she wrote them anyway, because she couldn't tell anyone what she was thinking, and what she was thinking at any given moment was DANIELDANIELDANIELDANIEL, which made it hard to concentrate during client meetings, and when she was having sex.

'Your sex drive's gone up,' Adam said one Sunday as they lay in bed, drinking a post-coital cup of tea.

'You're a very sexy man,' she said.

He smiled, surprised. 'Thank you.'

'You're welcome.'

'You're very sexy too.'

'Thanks.'

'We're having a sexual renaissance, aren't we?' he said. 'Do you think maybe it's time we tried—?'

'What?'

'You know.'

'If you're too embarrassed to say it, how are we supposed to do it?'

'Anal,' he whispered.

She laughed so hard she spat PG Tips on the pillow.

'I'll take that as a no.'

'No!' she said. 'Not a no!'

She wrote a Haiku about that conversation:

He wants anal sex
I want to silence my thoughts
So we've bought some lube.

She tried out sestinas and sonnets, typing them into one long Word document on the Piccadilly Line, about how uncomfortable Daniel made her and how impossible it felt to stay away from him. She didn't have words for the way he made her heart race, the sense of danger she felt when she was near him. Because he's my brother and he doesn't know, she reminded herself, and he thinks we're going to get together, and it's all completely fucking wrong. But she kept writing, kept trying to capture the curl of his lips when she made him smile, the exact colour of his eyes: *like oxidized copper*, she wrote, in one particularly poor villanelle, but that made them sound cold and old and cloudy. How to describe how naked and raw they were, when she looked into them? *Eyes like ceviche*, she typed, as the Tube pulled into Holborn. The man in the blue suit next to her stifled a laugh, and she realized he was reading over her shoulder. She stuck to prose after that.

She wrote, just to get the secrets out of her. She couldn't tell Alison that Daniel existed, because Alison didn't want to know anything about their DNA results. She couldn't tell Daniel that she was his sister because she had left it too late – he had basically told her he fancied her. And she couldn't tell Alison how she really felt about Suria being pregnant – that she was jealous, because Alison would love the baby more than she loved Lena – and she couldn't tell Alison she felt sorry for the baby, because they would be brought up without their biological relatives. She wrote about that on the train home one night, a stream of consciousness, full of guilt and capital letters.

The text messages were the hardest things to write. Daniel's were flirtatious, insistent, direct.

When can I take you out again?

What you doing right now? I can send a cab to get you.

I've got an invite to the Summer Exhibition private view. Wanna come?

Her replies were short, casual, no kisses at the end. She just needed to hold out for a few weeks longer and the crush would fade, not that it was really a crush at all. It was just transference. Totally natural and normal and nothing to be ashamed of. She distracted herself with work and drinks with friends and buying jumpsuits from ASOS, even though she didn't have anywhere special to wear them, because Suria was pregnant and knackered, and Alison felt she ought to stay home and keep her company, and Lena was working past 9 p.m. most nights now anyway, and Adam was so exhausted in the run-up to the end of term that he was usually asleep on the sofa by the time she came home, a bowl of half-eaten stir fry balanced on his chest. One night, when she was feeling particularly weak, Daniel texted again. *Please come to the Summer Exhibition with me tonight. Desperate to see you.* And he made her feel young and reckless and beautiful, so she replied, *OK*.

He was standing outside the Royal Academy of Arts, one leg crossed over the other, in ripped jeans and a bright-pink blazer. He dressed more like Jackie Collins than any man she'd met before. Compared to him, she felt dowdy and conservative – she had come straight from work, and she was wearing her most boring navy-blue suit – but when he looked up and smiled at her, his face matched hers, their smiles too wide to be platonic. She ran across Piccadilly to meet him, narrowly avoiding a honking taxi and a swearing cyclist. He caught her in a hug. 'This is going to sound nuts,' he said, 'but I've missed you.'

She laughed instead of replying. He held out his elbow – not his hand, thank god, because she'd probably have taken it – and they linked arms.

The champagne was free. So was the food: cheese boards and grapes, crisps and crusty bread. She was pleased to see that even at private views, people crowded around the buffet tables. 'Got to soak up the champagne,' she said to Daniel, who had taken two flutes from the bar and was drinking them both himself.

The art was packed tight on the walls, oil paintings of landscapes next to photographs of naked women fellating cucumbers. 'The pieces hung at eye level are the ones the gallery thinks are the best,' Daniel told her. But Lena's favourite pieces were the paintings of pigeons hung near the cornicing, as though they were trying to fly away.

Daniel followed her gaze. 'Now those I like. I've always had an affinity for pigeons.'

'Because you're a Londoner?'

'No. Because I'll eat anything, and I've been known to shit in the street after a particularly wild night.' He checked the price in the catalogue. 'Only £450. We could get one each.'

She laughed, then realized he wasn't joking.

'Not sure Adam would be pleased with me if I bought a picture of a pigeon for literally the same price as a return flight to New York.'

'I thought he didn't believe in air travel.'

'That's true, actually—'

He stepped a little closer. 'I'll buy it for you.'

She moved back, repelled by him, attracted to him. 'You're drunk.'

'I'm serious!'

'That is very kind of you. But I can live without the pigeon.'

He shrugged and strolled to the opposite wall of the gallery, hands in his pockets. Two women in their twenties recognized him but pretended not to, and Lena wanted to be next to him again, for other people to notice that she was with him. He paused in front of a border-patrol office that jutted out of the gallery wall, as though it had been picked up and dropped there. 'That's a Banksy,' he said, consulting the catalogue.

'Is it for sale?' she asked, sauntering over.

'If you've got a spare half a million.'

'Not sure it would fit in my flat, on reflection.'

And then, from behind her, a familiar voice: 'Thinking of buying something?'

'Hey, Karla!' Lena could tell her cheeks were red, and thinking about how red they were was making them redder—

'All right, mate? Good to see you!' Karla slapped Lena on the back. 'If I'd known you were coming this arvo we could have got the Tube together!' She held her hand out to Daniel. 'Are you Lena's brother?'

'No!' Lena said, before he could answer.

'Daniel,' he said, shaking Karla's hand, smiling.

'Nice to meet you,' Karla said, looking him right in the eye. How could she do that? How could she stand the intensity of his gaze? 'I'm a friend of Lena's from work. You're an actor, right?'

'Yeah,' Daniel said, shrugging.

'Yeah. I thought I recognized you.' She was looking at Lena, eyebrows raised. 'See you in the office. Send my love to Adam.' Karla slapped her on the back again and walked up to the Banksy, so close that one of the gallery staff asked her to take a step back.

Lena tried to draw Daniel's attention to a painting above the door, of a man with the head of a blackbird, but Daniel put a hand on her forearm. 'Why did she think I was your brother?'

'Because you're not Adam.'

That seemed to please him. He linked his little finger through hers. Her body lit up. A waiter approached with a champagne bottle, and she let go. Her finger felt cold where it had touched his.

'I've got some coke, if you want some,' he said, when the waiter had left.

She shook her head. 'I'm working tomorrow—'

'Come back to mine.'

She turned to make sure Karla wasn't watching. 'I can't. I told you, I'm working—'

'Why aren't you single?'

Her heart was hammering. 'You have to stop this—'

'Seriously, why?' He looked hurt, confused.

She knew she had to tell him, but she couldn't do it here, in front of all these people, within earshot of Karla, who would get the wrong idea and announce to the office that she was cheating on Adam. So she said, 'I don't want to be single.'

He pouted. 'I don't like Adam.' The danger had passed.

'You would, if you met him. Everyone likes him.'

'When can I meet him?'

'Soon.'

His eyes were still on hers. She stared at a portrait of a family – mum, dad, two children – until he looked away.

Adam was lying in bed when she got home, watching a documentary about the Dalai Lama on his laptop. She kissed his cheek.

He pulled away. 'You taste like a pub carpet.'

'Sorry. Free bar.' She sat down on the bed next to him.

He shifted to face her. 'How did Daniel take it?'

She hesitated.

'You did tell him, this time?'

She shook her head.

'What the fuck? Why not?'

'Don't be angry—'

'Lena! Jesus Christ! This is not OK!'

'I know. I know. But I've left it so late now—'

'So what, you're just going to keep hanging out with him? Until he makes a move?'

'No, of course I'm not!'

'But that's what's going to happen!' He was sitting up now. 'It's like you want that to happen!'

'Of course I don't! He's my brother—'

'Yeah, but he doesn't know that!'

'What are you actually accusing me of?'

'I'm not accusing you of anything. I'm just saying— He's going to be so humiliated when he finds out. He's going to be furious with you. You're not being fair—'

'I know. I know. I'll arrange to see him again and I'll tell him. I promise.' She reached out to touch his leg. He didn't move away.

'You promised last time.'

'I know. I'm a terrible person.'

'You're not. But just – try to be better.'

She lay back on the bed and let the world and the guilt and the adrenaline spin around her.

Tissues

The first few weeks of Suria's pregnancy reminded Alison of the beginning of their relationship, when the world had seemed electric, when every text message had been like a little present and they had stared into each other's eyes walking down Hackney Road, oblivious to the traffic and the noise and occasional shouts of 'Dykes!' Except back then they'd had sex in the shower, in art gallery toilets, once even behind the trolleys in a supermarket car park, until they had both ended up with urinary tract infections. Now, they didn't have sex at all: Suria was worried about poking out the baby. Ed, at Alison's request, had called Suria up to reassure her that it wasn't possible to 'poke out a baby', and that the baby wasn't a baby yet, anyway – just a collection of cells – but Suria didn't want to take any chances. No hot baths, no alcohol, strictly no orgasms. Still, she was happier and more affectionate than Alison had seen her since those early days, when they had been so in love that nothing had existed outside the present tense. Now, though, they were thinking about the future, googling baby yoga classes and car-seat reviews, having good-humoured arguments about the Ofsted ratings of local schools.

'The only "Good" secondary is a boys' school, and it's a science academy, so we'll have to move if we have a girl, or a boy who wants to go into the arts,' Suria said one morning over pancakes.

'The arts might not exist by the time he's eleven, the way the government cuts are going,' Alison pointed out, sipping her coffee. But Suria was already on Rightmove, looking up house prices in Margate.

Alison was happy, too, so happy that she'd have skipped down Mare Street to the studio every morning if she had been a skipping sort of person. She wasn't, so she skipped internally instead, and put her arm protectively around Suria's waist whenever they were out together, and winked knowingly at babies, until Suria pointed out that was quite a creepy thing to do. She saw babies everywhere: in buggies on the street, in the park, eating bananas messily, screaming from nearby flats. She saw parents, too, and looked closely at them to check whether they were younger or older than her. She was so happy and so grateful that Suria was pregnant, but sometimes she felt too young to be a parent, and sometimes she felt too old: she couldn't exist on three hours' sleep the way she had in her twenties, when a quick shower after a night at Dalston Superstore had been enough to sort her out before work. She started to notice non-parents everywhere, too, eating tapas on Broadway Market, riding their bikes on the Heath, playing tennis on Highbury Fields, and though she was so happy, and so grateful, when she thought about the life she was about to lose, her throat closed up. She had never actually played tennis on Highbury

Fields, true, but she liked the idea of being able to, if she ever got the urge.

They told their friends and family the good news, even though it was early days, because they would need their support if things didn't work out. Besides, Suria said, people should talk about pregnancy more, talk about miscarriage more, talk about everything more. But talking had its downsides. Once the news was out, it seemed to transform Suria from an individual to an archetype, her body into public property. Colleagues touched her belly before she could stop them, and the sales assistant in the maternity-wear shop called her 'Mum', and everyone, whether or not they had ever been pregnant, wanted to give her advice. 'Sleep when the baby sleeps!' everyone said. 'Sleep as much as you can now, because you won't sleep once the baby comes!' When she ordered a coffee one afternoon, after lunch with Ed and Abeo, Ed turned to the waiter and said, 'She'll have a decaf.' And then, later in the same conversation: 'If I were you, I'd have a C-section. Much less risky for the baby.' As though she was just a vessel now, a piece of meat, rather than one of his oldest friends.

'Why didn't you tell him to fuck off?' Alison asked Suria, in bed that night.

'Why didn't *you*?' Suria rolled on to her side.

'I didn't want to be all macho. You can stand up for yourself—'

'Oh, aye, is that right,' Suria said, pulling the duvet up to cover her shoulders.

The questions were even worse than the advice and the unsolicited touching. From Alison's point of view, at least.

'Who'll be the mammy?' Suria's father asked, over FaceTime.

'Well, I'm carrying the baby—' Suria said.

'Aye. So Alison's the daddy.'

Alison wasn't sure what to say.

'There'll no be a daddy,' Suria said, squeezing Alison's hand, out of shot. 'We're using a sperm donor.'

He frowned. 'A wean should have a daddy.'

'That's homophobic,' Alison said, too quietly for him to hear.

And, when Alison went to her publisher's office for a meeting about the *Incredible Women* book, Jeanette, the art director, asked 'Can I ask where you got the sperm from? Did you go through the whole fertility clinic rigmarole? Or was it a DIY job?'

Alison opened her mouth, then closed it again, too stunned to know what to say.

'Jeanette!' said Emma, the senior editor. The three of them were sitting around a table in Jeanette's office, looking at printouts of the artwork, eating Jaffa Cakes and drinking tea. Emma looked as appalled as Alison felt.

Jeanette glanced up at Emma. 'What?'

'You can't ask people that sort of thing!' Emma turned to Alison, as though asking for back-up.

Alison laughed uncomfortably and fiddled with the printouts.

'Alison doesn't mind!' Jeanette said. 'Do you?'

Alison hated conflict of all kinds, particularly conflict with people who had the power to stop commissioning her artwork. But she was going to be a parent soon: she had to get better at boundaries. So she said, 'I guess it is quite a personal question.'

Jeanette pulled a tissue from her cardigan sleeve and polished her glasses with it. 'Well. I'm sorry if you're upset.'

She took the printouts from Alison and turned to the spread featuring Coco Chanel. 'Now, I know this is annoyingly late in the day, but the Americans have asked us to cut Coco Chanel from the book. Apparently she was a Nazi collaborator! Oops! So we're going to swap her with Aretha Franklin.'

Alison wanted to cry. She had spent half a day colouring Chanel's jacket, and about three hours getting the texture of her hair just right. 'No problem, that's fine!' she said. 'Can I have another week to do the artwork, though?'

'Afraid there isn't any room in the schedule if we want it out for Christmas,' Jeanette said, pushing her glasses on to her nose. 'Cutting it fine as it is.'

Emma pushed the Jaffa Cakes towards Alison. She should have known the Jaffa Cakes were a bad sign. There wasn't enough money in children's publishing for unnecessary premium biscuits.

As the weeks passed, the novelty of the pregnancy wore off, and soon Suria was too sick to get out of bed in the morning without eating Jacob's Cream Crackers first. 'My brain isn't working,' she said one night, dropping on to the sofa as soon as she got home from work. 'And my boobs are so massive that I keep whacking them off walls. And the whole of London stinks of petrol. Can you help me take my shoes off?'

Alison took deep breaths to calm herself, because Suria's bad mood was contagious, and knelt down at Suria's feet.

'And FYI, there are so many pregnancy symptoms folk don't talk about. Like – I've started dribbling all the time, and I hate all human beings. And sometimes I wake up at night and it feels like someone's stabbing me in the vagina. Like, pure shoving a knife right up inside me.' Suria covered her eyes with her hand. 'I hate it, hen.'

'I know,' Alison said, in her most soothing voice.

'But I'm supposed to be happy. And what if I have a miscarriage?'

'Don't think about that,' Alison said.

'Don't tell me what I can and can't think about.' Suria walked out of the room.

Alison closed her eyes and told herself that anxiety was like bad weather, and that it would pass, and that it would all be worth it when the baby arrived – everyone said there was no joy like it, so she was hanging on to that – and then she went upstairs to sweep the cracker crumbs from the mattress.

'How have you been feeling?' Aoife asked, rolling a condom on to the ultrasound wand. They were back at the clinic for their eight-week scan. If all was well, they would graduate to the NHS.

'We've both been pretty anxious,' Alison said.

Aoife laughed. 'I was talking to Suria.' Alison stood there in silence, pulsing with embarrassment, as Aoife asked Suria, 'Do you still feel sick?'

'I feel like shit.'

'Grand. That's what I like to hear! The sickness is a good sign!'

The grainy image on the screen shifted and bloomed.

'That's the head,' Aoife said, pointing to a lump like the head of a shrimp. 'And there's the heartbeat.'

The foetus pulsed in black and white, and Alison's embarrassment was washed away by relief, and her heart beat harder, reminding her what it felt like to be alive. Suria took her hand and held it hard, and started to cry.

'Oh, love.' Aoife passed her a box of tissues.

'Sorry,' Suria said, taking one and covering her eyes. 'I'm just so relieved. I'm so relieved. My stupid body works.'

They strolled through Regent's Park to celebrate, where the roses were blooming, an unnecessary number of them, like bouquets thrown onstage after an encore, and children were running back and forth along the paths, collecting pebbles, holding them close to their faces, then putting them in their pockets, guarding them like secrets, and an elderly woman, bent-backed, walked slowly, arm in arm with a younger woman – her daughter? Her carer? – and Alison felt connected to all of them, and she wanted to expand and take in all of it, this moment, this happiness, this feeling of being in love with her life and her wife and the new life growing inside her wife, and then she realized she was thinking in rhyme and she really ought to get a grip. Early days, she told herself. But Suria was infected with joy, too, and as they headed back towards the Tube she said, 'Shall we buy just one thing for the baby?'

'We shouldn't,' Alison said.

'But it might make it feel more real.'

'But it's tempting fate.'

'But we don't believe in fate,' Suria said. 'Please?'

So they walked along Marylebone High Street to a French baby-wear shop and spent half an hour muttering under their breath about the cost of the newborn cardigans.

'The clothes on the rack by the door are all in the sale,' the shop assistant said, eventually.

They bought a tiny yellow raincoat at 60 per cent off.

It was still more expensive than most of the clothes in Alison's wardrobe.

'It'll fit the baby for approximately four weeks,' Alison pointed out, as they queued at the till.

'Aye,' Suria said, taking out her credit card. 'But we'll keep it forever.'

They were at Jessie's house when it happened, discussing whether or not the book club ought to be discussing *Mrs Dalloway* at all. The pasta plates had been cleared, and Tom was drunk, or perhaps he was just irritated, because Roxanne was leaning across the table towards him, saying, 'But everyone knows she was a racist!', her bangles clattering as she spoke. 'And an antisemite—'

'But her husband was Jewish!' Tom said, his knee bouncing up and down.

'Doesn't mean she wasn't antisemitic, darling,' Jessie said, putting a hand on his leg. Alison caught Lena's eye and they were both overcome with laughter, snorting and pinching their noses to hold it in, and then Alison noticed Suria was staring at her, because how could she be laughing during this conversation? Alison looked away from Lena, digging her nails into her palm to control herself.

'Listen to what Virginia Woolf wrote in her diary,' Roxanne said, brandishing her phone like a weapon.

'I don't think we need to hear what she wrote,' Suria said.

'And god forbid we ever write anything unpalatable in our diaries,' Tom said. 'God forbid we ever have an impure thought!'

'Dad, stop it, you sound like Nigel Farage,' Lena said.

271

'Why don't we go back to the book club questions,' Asuka said, holding up a printout from the internet. 'We could talk about the motif of flowers in the novel? Or the theme of uncertainty? Or death?' She looked up, blinking. 'Wasn't it horrible, when Septimus threw himself out of the window and impaled himself on the railings?'

Which was a bit of a spoiler: Alison was only halfway through the book.

'Just going to the toilet,' Suria said, pushing her chair back, as the others discussed the meaning of the red-and-white roses that Mr Dalloway brings home for his wife.

The conversation had moved on to whether or not Virginia Woolf approved of the British Empire by the time Suria sent the text.

Am in the bathroom. Please come. I think I'm having a miscarriage.

The world around Alison expanded, then contracted. She felt very calm and very steady as she stood and walked to the bathroom, as behind her, the book club meeting continued, her father's voice booming above the others, Jessie's laugh low and rich, Asuka, nervous and high-pitched, and Lena asking, 'Where's Suria?' as Alison knocked on the bathroom door. Suria let her in, and it was horrible, horrible. Alison would never forget it: the shock on Suria's face, her trousers around her ankles; the sheen on her cheeks from the tears; the white of the toilet paper she was holding, the redness of the blood.

'Fuck,' Alison said. 'Fuck. OK. I'll call the midwife—'

'I'm sorry.' Suria covered her face. 'I'm sorry, baby.'

And Alison wasn't sure which of them she was talking to. She wasn't sure how many of them there were, in that room, in their family, any more. She knelt in front of Suria and took the toilet paper from her hand. 'Some people bleed when they're pregnant, don't they?'

'Not like this—'

A knock at the door. 'Are you guys OK?' Lena.

'Not really,' Alison said. 'Do you think anyone's sober enough to drive us to A&E?'

Her father drove them to the hospital. He smelled like a brewery, but he drove very slowly, his eyes unnaturally wide, as though that would make up for it. 'I'll wait outside,' he said, as Alison slammed the car door shut. She waved at him as if she was nipping into the petrol station to buy a bag of Starburst and a lottery ticket.

Alison kept her eyes fixed to the ultrasound screen as Suria pulled the paper sheet over her lap. Her shoulders were up around her ears with the effort of wanting everything to be OK.

'We're going to do an internal scan,' the sonographer said, 'because it's still very early.'

Suria flinched as the sonographer pushed the wand inside her.

'It feels like I'm rummaging around for something in my bag, doesn't it? Sorry, I know it's not very nice.' The silence grew, though it wasn't silent in Alison's head – thoughts rushing, blood rushing, worst-case scenarios tumbling over each other, competing for her attention like buskers – and surely the sonographer should have said something by now?

More rummaging.

'What it is, I'm struggling to find the heartbeat just at the minute.'

Suria's head fell back against the pillow. Her eyes were

closed. 'No,' she said. 'My baby.' She put her hand on her belly, and Alison thought her heart would break.

'I'm so sorry,' the sonographer said.

Alison nodded. She couldn't speak. Her mind felt clean and empty.

A nurse led them into a windowless room. There were four plastic chairs and a box of tissues on a table. 'This is the fifth miscarriage I've seen this week. Sorry, I don't know if that's a helpful thing to say or not, but like – you're not alone.' She passed Suria a box of Kleenex, and handed Alison leaflets about baby loss and support groups, one after another, as though pieces of paper could make up for what they had lost.

She left the room and Suria bent double, clutching herself. 'I can't bear it,' she said, again and again. But Alison had to bear it. She had to get them home somehow, to make the dinner, to get out of bed in the morning and make Suria a coffee, even though she couldn't imagine wanting to get out of bed ever again.

They stopped at Sainsbury's on the way home and bought five packets of maxi pads. The cashier nodded, knowingly. 'Got to love that heavy flow.'

'Actually, I'm having a miscarriage,' Suria told her.

'Oh my god. I'm so sorry.' The cashier stared down at the till. 'That'll be £10.69.'

Suria cried all night and all through the morning and fell asleep in front of the television just after eleven. Alison pulled a blanket over her. The toy elephant Suria's parents had bought sat on the mantelpiece, mocking them. Alison picked it up and closed the living-room door softly. As though Suria were a sleeping baby, she thought, and she had to sit down in the hallway, because her legs had given way, because it was so horrible, so unnatural, even though it happened all the time. She hoped the baby hadn't felt any pain. She took the tiny yellow raincoat out of the wardrobe in the spare room and folded it into one of the storage boxes under the bed, along with the elephant.

She needed air after that, so she walked out into the garden. The sky was defiantly blue, the sun unforgivingly bright. She heard children kicking a ball back and forth in a neighbour's garden and wondered whether she would ever have a child to kick a ball back and forth with. She didn't need to worry any more, about whether the baby would look like her or love her. She didn't need to worry about losing her old life, about losing sleep or dealing with a teenager or not being able to play tennis in Highbury Fields. What a selfish, shallow fool she had been. How naive, without realizing it.

Suria spent a week lying on the sofa, wearing big T-shirts and sanitary pads, watching Nineties sitcoms. Alison cooked, and filled hot water bottles, moving slowly, heavy with grief. She felt utterly useless. Lena came round on Saturday morning, with bagels, on her way to the office – she had a trial coming up and was working all hours, which was probably why she hardly ever answered the phone any more.

'I'm sorry,' Lena said as she hugged them hello, the way people do at funerals. 'I'm so sorry.'

'Thanks,' Suria said, nodding.

'Maybe Sicily will help take your mind off it,' Lena said.

'I don't think anything's going to "take our mind off it",' Suria said, her voice cold.

'No, of course it won't.' Lena cringed and hid her face in her hands. 'God. Sorry. I'm such an idiot.'

Alison put a hand on her sister's shoulder, because she knew what it was like, not knowing what to say.

Ed and Abeo turned up after Lena left, with dahlias and a large box of expensive chocolates. They always spent money when things were terrible.

'I feel like I let the baby down,' Suria said. Alison picked a white feather from a hole in the sofa.

'You didn't,' Ed said. 'I don't know if this is going to be a helpful thing to hear, but from a medical point of view, it was just a bunch of cells that didn't divide properly. That's what happened. It's not your fault.'

'It was going to be a baby,' Alison said, furious suddenly.

She could see Abeo scowling at Ed, warning him not to say anything else, not to make things worse. 'Sorry,' Ed said.

'It's fine,' Alison said, but she couldn't stand it any more. She couldn't handle another minute of her friends telling her in soft, strange voices how sorry they were for her loss instead of screaming in pain and outrage, because surely there should be at least a little screaming, when something as awful as this happens to someone you love? She walked into the hall and stood there, hands on hips, concentrating on breathing, when Suria ran past her into the bathroom, slamming the door shut behind her.

Alison tried the door, but it was locked. 'Suria?'

'It's in my pants,' Suria said.

'As in—'

'There's a miscarriage. In my underpants.'

Alison leaned against the door, eyes closed. 'What does it look like?'

'Like a— like a miscarriage. Like guts. Like my uterus has fallen out of me. But it's done, it's gone, it's out.'

Ed was there, taking charge, knocking on the bathroom door. 'Suria? It might be good to take it to the hospital for genetic tests—'

'Yes, I know, we're going to do that,' Suria said, snappishly.

Abeo was hovering in the corridor, arms and legs crossed. 'Shall I— get some Tupperware?'

'Yes,' Ed said, taking charge. 'And some freezy packs.'

'We don't have freezy packs,' Alison said.

'We have a wine cooler,' Suria called through the door.

'Perfect,' Ed said.

'Not perfect,' Suria said. 'Horrible.' And she started to cry.

Self-flagellating bollocks

'I feel responsible,' Jessie said, when Tom dropped his keys on her kitchen table, later that night. 'I know that's ridiculous, but Suria had a miscarriage in my house—'

'*In the middle of my party, here's death,*' Tom said, twisting the cap from a bottle of wine.

Jessie looked appalled. 'Please tell me you didn't quote Virginia Woolf at Suria and Alison—'

'I managed to restrain myself.' He looked into his wine glass as the blush seeped up his neck into his cheeks. Why did he resort to other people's words during moments of emotional intensity? He was a vulture – his whole life had been one long act of appropriation. He would never have got his job at the library if Sheila hadn't known the head of HR. He had inherited the house on Dyne Road. He had raised someone else's children. And now, one of his daughters was experiencing a crisis, and it had been an effort not to recite Modernist prose at her. At the hospital, he had resorted to his own words and realized he didn't have any. 'I don't know what to say,' he'd said,

278

and 'I'm sorry.' Words which did, at least, have the virtue of being true.

All week long, another phrase from *Mrs Dalloway* had been rattling around his skull: *The world has raised its whip: where will it descend?* He hadn't told Lena he had found her biological father, yet. The whip was still hovering up there somewhere, and he knew he wouldn't be able to stop it falling; all he wanted was to delay the moment, to extend the silence between the ticks of the clock, so that he'd be braced for the sting of the impact.

'We'll send them flowers,' Jessie said.

'What?'

'Flowers. To Suria and Alison—'

'Of course. Yes. Yes. Good idea.'

'I'll do it, if you give me their address.'

'Thank you. That would be lovely.'

'Or chocolates, if you think they'd prefer them?'

'Sorry?'

Jessie put her wine glass down on the table. 'Tom.'

He looked up at her. 'Sorry. I'm just distracted.' He told her, about being a vulture.

'Nonsense,' she said. 'That's self-flagellating bollocks. You haven't done anything wrong. Apart from making everything about you, when your daughters both need you to step up and be a father—'

'I've done plenty of things wrong—'

'Fine, you've done lots of things wrong. For a start, you haven't offered to make me a coffee yet this evening.'

'Sorry.'

'And you're going to let me buy the flowers for Alison and Suria, when really that's your job, Tom—'

'But you offered! You just offered to do it!'

'And you should have turned me down!'

So many rules! How was he supposed to understand the rules? He felt like Alice, playing croquet in Wonderland, and then he realized he was identifying with a literary character by a problematic author again. He gave up and closed his eyes. 'I think I've found the sperm donor,' he told her.

Jessie reached for his hand. 'Oh, Tom—'

'I haven't told Lena yet.'

'She'll be very grateful.'

'Yes, well. Let's hope so. Let's hope she still wants to be my daughter, after she's met him.'

'She might not want to meet him.'

He laughed, once. It came out like a bark.

'I told you, my mother was adopted,' Jessie said. Her voice was gentler, now.

'You didn't tell me.'

'Well, she was. She met her birth mother once, in a pub in Land's End. I think it was quite an uncomfortable experience for her. My grandparents were wonderful, and she wouldn't have had it any other way. Your daughters love you.'

'Yes, well.'

'They do.'

'We don't go in for saying that sort of thing out loud in our family.'

'You poor things.'

He poured himself another glass of wine. 'I think they're pleased about us, by the way.'

'There's an "us"?'

'Oh god. I've put my foot in it again.'

'No, you haven't! I just wasn't sure what our status was.'

He glanced at her sideways. 'What would you like it to be?'

'Well. Would you like to be exclusive?'

He started laughing, which turned into coughing. Jessie passed him a glass of water. 'Sorry. It's just – the idea that more than one woman would want to have sex with me, at this stage in my life—'

'I didn't want to presume.'

'Just the idea is exhausting.'

Jessie looked pleased. 'I'll tell my daughters, then. That we're seeing each other. I'm sure they'd love to meet you.'

He couldn't believe his luck, that a woman like Jessie, so beautiful, stately looking, principled, would want to be connected with him – was prepared to tell her family about him.

'What's wrong?'

'Nothing! Everything's right! Just – a bit of an emotional night.' He cleared his throat. 'Tell me what they say.'

'They'll be thrilled for me.' She kissed his nose. 'Would you like a celebratory blowjob?'

'Let me have a shower first.'

'Very considerate of you.'

On Sunday, Jessie invited Tom to Sunday lunch with her daughters. Tom lied and said he was meeting Lena and Alison. He didn't feel solid enough, yet, to meet Jessie's family. Besides, he had a phone call to make. He had put it off for long enough, and he could feel the whip descending, making his heart stutter and stop and start again, like a car engine, badly in need of a service. He waited until he had eaten lunch: everything felt more achievable after a decent lunch. But Lena didn't answer, and the distant ringing of her phone made him feel as though a bell was tolling for him, and he hung up; he couldn't trust his voice not to wobble. He texted her instead, and sent her the YouTube video he'd found of Nick Turner talking about NHS waiting times for heart surgery and tried to make it casual. *Hey Lena. Here's suspect number 1. Not 100% sure, but this could be your biological father. Give me a bell if you want a chat. Love, Dad xxx.* His heart swelled and stung as he pressed send and he remembered Lena's last day at primary school, how he'd helped her pick out an outfit – a pink-and-white striped T-shirt and black leggings – and the smell of the hall during her final assembly, baked beans and warm plastic, and the song the children had sung, 'One more step around the world I go,' and the way Lena had rolled her eyes when she had seen him crying.

Suspect number one

Lena's phone was on silent; she was walking past the pagoda in Kew Gardens with Daniel. She had taken him there because she was going to tell him the truth, today, and she had to make sure he didn't say anything romantic before she got the nerve up. Kew Gardens was the most platonic place she could think of: it's hard to feel sexy in a greenhouse. Unfortunately, Daniel wasn't interested in the greenhouses. He kept taking her by the hand, leading her deeper into the gardens, far away from the safety of the roses and the orangery and the gift shop with its chaste floral tea towels.

'Where are we going?' Lena asked, as she followed him down an avenue of holly trees, away from the Sunday-morning crowds.

'You'll see.' His hair shone red in the sunlight, like hers did. Because he was her brother, which she was going to tell him, just as soon as they were somewhere private. 'Does Adam know you're here?'

'Yes.' She pulled a leaf from a holly tree, pricking her finger.

'With me?'

'Yes, with you.' She sucked the blood from her fingertip.

The blood made her think of Alison and Suria and the miscarriage. She felt a sting of guilt, because she ought to be focusing on her sister rather than hanging out with Daniel, but she had to tell Daniel the truth, she just had to – and what could she really do for Alison and Suria, anyway? Make them cups of tea and send them flowers that would wither, reminding them? Pretend there wasn't a part of her that was secretly relieved?

They turned a corner. A thatched, red-brick house stood in a clearing.

'Queen Charlotte's Cottage,' Daniel said, opening his arms wide, as though he owned it. 'Smaller than I remembered it. I used to play here all the time when I was little.' He led her inside. Her eyes took a while to adjust to the darkness.

'I still can't believe you grew up in London too, and we never met.'

'Plenty of people grow up in London and never meet.' He climbed the stairs, two at a time. He was too tall for the house. He bent to walk through a doorway.

'Yes,' she said, and she would have added a 'but', but now they were in a dining room of some kind, with spindly wooden chairs set around a table.

A guide was standing with her back against the wall, in an eighteenth-century dress and Nike trainers. 'Just let me know if you have any questions!'

Lena moved to the window. She looked across the grass to the river and wished she was out there, on the distant riverbank. Daniel's arm was hot against hers. He nudged her with his hip. 'I've got a historical fact for you. Guess who died today, in 1817?'

'Queen Charlotte.'

The guide stepped forward. 'No! But very close! She died in 1818!'

'A writer,' Daniel said, to Lena.

'William Blake.'

'Nope.'

'Austen!' said the guide.

Daniel looked at her. 'How did you know that?'

'I'm doing a PhD in English literature at Queen Mary's.'

'Oh. Cool.'

The guide smiled up at him. 'I loved you in *Line of Duty*, by the way.'

'Thank you,' Daniel said. He turned to Lena. 'Shall we – let's get some fresh air.'

They stepped out into the sunlit clearing. Daniel reached into his back pocket, checked his phone. He stopped still beneath an oak tree. 'Fuck.'

'What?'

'I was up for a film. Didn't get it.' He shielded his eyes and typed a reply to the email, leaving her standing, stupid, on the grass, and Lena registered that this was something she didn't like about him: his self-absorption, his lack of concern for other people's time. She would tell him the truth, right now, she'd rip off the plaster. She said, 'Daniel?'

'Hang on a minute.' He was still tapping at his phone. Lena checked hers, to pass the time. And that's when she saw the text from her father. *Suspect number one.*

'Oh my god.' She clicked on the YouTube video, but the doctor's face was fuzzy with bad reception. 'Oh my god.' She waved her phone around.

'What?'

'I don't have 4G. Fuck!'

'What is it?'

'My biological father. Maybe.' She wanted to be alone. She ran across the clearing, to a patch of long grass.

Daniel followed her. 'How do you know?'

She waved a hand to silence him. The video was loading. Dr Turner's eyes were light green – or were they blue? – and he raised his eyebrows whenever he made a point. He was saying something about heart surgery, but she wasn't paying attention to his words. She was paying attention to how he said them, to the way his mouth moved.

'He doesn't look that much like you.' She hadn't noticed Daniel coming up behind her.

She held her phone to her chest, terrified he'd recognize himself.

'What?'

'It's just – private.'

He shrugged. 'I've seen it now.'

She looked back at the video. 'His mouth's like mine.'

'And his eyes are the same colour.' He placed a hand on the small of her back. 'But not as beautiful.'

'Oh god.' She closed her eyes. She sat down on the grass. 'This is such a fucking mess.'

She didn't tell him.

She stayed on the train until Camden Road, hating herself all the way. She needed Adam. Folk music needed Adam too, and he was playing at a session at Cecil Sharp House. She could hear the scraping of fiddles and the warbling of elderly voices as she walked down Regent's Park Road. She bought a cup of tea from the café and pushed open the door. The room was crowded and sweaty, and the seats were all taken, so she stood at the back. A grey-haired woman was singing 'All Around My Hat'. The singer had a cold and kept hitting her chest to try and clear the phlegm. The crowd stamped their feet in time to the music and the whole room shook.

The song ended. Adam looked up and saw Lena, and waved, delighted. 'I'm up next!' he called. He put his fiddle on his chair and jogged to the stage. 'This is an old song from Lincolnshire, about Jesus's childhood.' He smiled at Lena, proud she was there to hear him. The song was strange and haunting, all the more so because of the way he sang it. He sang about Jesus, who was a poor maid's son, and the way the rich boys in the neighbourhood wouldn't let him play with them, so he drowned them. Adam looked out at the audience as he sang. He looked over at Lena. He was singing right at her, right into her, and she felt sick with self-hatred.

'We're going to play another tune, now, from America,' a ukulele player said, as the applause died down. 'Join in if you know the words.'

'Pony! I can't believe you came!' Adam said, as they walked out into the late-Sunday sunshine.

'You were brilliant! Why didn't you tell me you were so good?'

'I wouldn't need to if you came to more of my gigs.'

'I will,' she said, and took his hand.

He turned to face her, swinging her arm. 'How was Kew Gardens? What did Daniel say when you told him?'

'He was weirdly OK about it.' She looked at her shoes, so that he wouldn't see the lie in her face. And then, to change the subject, she handed him her phone. 'I need you to watch this.'

287

'Wait. Tell me more about Daniel.'

'After you've watched the video.'

He frowned at the screen. 'Why am I watching a video about heart surgery?'

'The doctor might be my biological father.'

He looked up at her. 'Fuck.'

'Exactly.'

A Morris dancer waved at Adam, the bells on his ankles jangling as he walked through the garden. Adam was still squinting at her phone screen. 'I can't see a family resemblance.'

'But he's in his fifties. Maybe I'll look like that when I'm in my fifties.'

'You're going to look lovely when you're in your fifties,' he said, and she hugged him, and hated herself.

'Did you show Daniel this?'

She shook her head. She felt like she was falling. If she didn't actually speak, she wouldn't technically be lying.

'Did he already know he was donor conceived?'

'Yes.' So far, she had tried to stay close to the truth, or only tell lies of omission. But now—

'OK, so he didn't freak out completely, then?'

'I mean, obviously he thinks I'm a dickhead for hanging out with him and not telling him I'm his sister.' She was freestyling, flailing, out of control.

Adam pulled her down to a bench. 'How are you feeling?'

'Shit. Guilty.' Which was true, at least.

'So you're going to stay away from each other for a while?'

'Yeah.'

'Probably for the best.' He hugged her. 'Can't have been easy. I think you're very brave.'

'I'm not.'

'You are.' He kissed her head. 'Told you he fancied you. He probably needs at least six months' worth of therapy before he sees you again.'

She was a different person than she had been that morning. The daughter of a cardiologist, probably. And a liar. She marvelled at how easy it was, just to make things up. She felt the way she had, aged sixteen, when she realized that if she made herself sick after eating a KitKat, it was as though she hadn't eaten it at all.

That night, once Adam was asleep, she stared at her face in the bathroom mirror until it was a series of shapes, until she didn't recognize herself any more. She held up the screenshot on her phone, comparing her mouth to the doctor's, trying to mimic the shapes his mouth made when he spoke. They both had defined cupid's bows. Then again, there were probably a limited number of possible mouth shapes, like lottery-number combinations. If she could just be certain he was her biological father, she'd know who she was, and she would be a better person, a more honest one. She googled his name and found a video of him encouraging medical students to specialize in cardiology. She willed him to smile – she was sure she'd know him if he smiled – but it's hard to look cheerful when discussing heart attacks. She read his CV. He had studied medicine in London and now lived in Cambridge. Izzy probably passed him in the street all the time. He enjoyed playing badminton. Maybe he'd teach her about shuttlecocks one day, if he ever agreed to meet her. She wouldn't blame him if he didn't. He seemed like a nice person to have as a father: intelligent, selfless, successful. She was starting to feel attached to him.

She dreamed of a father who was Tom and Dr Turner and Daniel and Adam all at once. They were walking together through a garden when he cried, 'Lenny!' and split into four different people, and she wasn't sure which one to look at, and then she realized she was naked and she woke up, choking, it felt like, and Adam rolled over, unaware. The sun was rising over the rooftops. Just after 6 a.m. She texted Tom.

Are you awake?

He called ten minutes later, as she was making a cup of tea. 'Good morning, daughter of mine. How are you feeling?'

'Not great.'

'No. No, of course.'

'Do you think I should email the doctor, then?'

'I don't see why not.'

'What if he tells me to fuck off?'

'Then you'll know that he's a tosspot, and you can move on.'

Dread rose through her, like damp.

'I can help you write the letter if you want,' he said.

'It's fine, don't worry. I can do it myself.'

'I know you can. Of course. Just, if you want someone to read it over. I'll keep my phone on, at work.'

She sat at the kitchen table, writing and rewriting the email, as cars roared past and Adam's alarm bleated, muffled, from the bedroom. He shuffled to the kitchen and made breakfast as she spellchecked the letter. She cried when he kissed the top of her head, and he thought she was crying about the doctor, which was only partly true. She held his leg the way she'd held her father's when he dropped her off at nursery and she didn't want him to go. Adam offered to read her letter, to make sure it didn't sound as though she was after Dr Turner's money, or his kidneys.

'It's perfect,' he said, spooning honey into his porridge. 'He'd be lucky to have you as a daughter.'

She cried again when he said that.

He left for work at eight, and Lena emailed the letter to Tom.

He called her when he'd read it. 'Very good.'

'You think?'

'I do think.'

She felt the dopamine hit of his approval. 'You don't think it'll freak him out?'

'You've been very measured. He'll probably be shocked, but it's not as though you're asking to move into his spare bedroom.'

'No. You're right.'

'Really, all you want is to know your medical history. He can't say no to that, surely.'

Had she told her father that all she wanted from this man was information about his blood type, his cholesterol levels, his parents' causes of death? 'I don't know if that is all I want,' she said to him now.

She could hear him breathing on the end of the line.

'I'm late for work. I'm going to send the email.'

'Hang on, Lenny—'

'I've just sent it.'

More breathing. 'Well then. The die is cast.'

She wore her most cheerful yellow trousers to work, and her biggest earrings, and she smiled and waved at the paralegals as she walked, jauntily, to her office. Another kind of lying. James knocked on her door just after ten and

291

sat on the edge of her desk, swinging his legs, as though he belonged there. 'Listen – I have to leave early today. Business development meeting in the West End.'

'OK.' They both knew that business development meetings involved taking university friends to Michelin-starred restaurants and charging them to the expense account.

'I haven't had a chance to write up the witness statement for the Jerwood case. Would you be a star and do that for me? End of the day will be fine.'

'Sure,' said Lena. You couldn't say no to a partner.

For eight long hours she worked on the witness statement, ignoring her writhing insides, the dread that made it hard to lift her feet. At lunch she ate a sandwich at her desk, refreshing her email every two minutes, but Dr Turner didn't reply. Daniel texted, though, asking if she wanted to go for Korean food one night. She texted back, *Why not?* She felt self-destructive, wild. She wouldn't tell Adam, she decided. She'd already lied to him about Daniel. Might as well tell a few more lies, to make the first one worthwhile.

She woke at six again the next morning and checked her email in bed. Among the ads for summer sales and property alerts from estate agents was a reply from Dr Turner. *Not me, I'm afraid. Never been a sperm donor. Sorry I can't be more help.*

She read the email again, then a third time. She deleted it. 'It's not him,' she said, out loud. She felt winded. Empty.

'I'm asleep,' Adam murmured.

'Dr Turner's not my biological father.'

Adam opened his eyes. 'Oh.' He touched her back in the place Daniel had, two days before. 'I'm sorry.'

She nodded. Relief. Then grief. She lay back on the bed. She turned towards the window. She couldn't see the sky, just the ghost of her own reflection.

'He might be lying,' Adam pointed out.

'He might be.'

'Be stupid to deny it, though, when it's probably just a matter of time before enough people take DNA tests to prove it is him.'

Lena nodded. But people did stupid things all the time. And it was easy, not to think about the consequences.

'He didn't have your smile.' Adam used the past tense, as though Dr Turner was dead. Which he was, in a way.

Lena picked up her phone again and texted Tom. *He says it's not him.*

Fuck. I'm sorry, Lenny.

It's not your fault.

Disappointment settled, like snow, or ash. But that was better than the slow creep of foreboding, better than uncertainty. She deleted the screenshots of the doctor's face, the way you try to erase someone who's broken your heart, as though that can take away the fact you'd ever cared.

Tom sat up in bed, staring at his phone. 'I got it wrong.'

Jessie flung an arm over her face. 'What time is it?'

'I got it wrong,' he said again. 'About the sperm donor. Lena just emailed an eminent cardiologist and accused him of being her biological father. Imagine getting that email on a Monday morning.' He lay back and stared at the ceiling. 'I shouldn't have told her till I was absolutely sure.'

She sat up. 'You were trying to do a good thing.'

He pressed his palms into his eyes. 'She used to think I could do no wrong.'

'And then she grew up.' Jessie began to play with his chest hair. Almost entirely silver now. He was amazed anyone could stand touching it.

Il Padrino

It was a summer of extremes, of rage and complacency, of Leavers and Remainers marching through the streets, of 38-degree weather, of having a father for twenty-four hours, then losing him. Lena had received another email from Genealogy DNA – thirty-eight new relatives had joined the database – but she couldn't face contacting any of them, not just yet. She needed a break from reality, a break from the unknown, too, and so on a sweltering July evening, Lena met Daniel for Korean food in Waterloo. He ordered two kinds of glass noodles, bibimbap, kimchi pancakes and seafood stew, so they could try everything, and when Adam called to check in, she told him she was with Izzy. Which meant she had to ask Izzy to cover for her. She met her in a Pound Shop during her lunchbreak the next day: Izzy needed to buy pass-the-parcel presents for Peggy's birthday party.

'You're having an emotional affair with your own brother,' Izzy said, as they browsed the craft aisle.

'I'm not. Don't say that. I don't find him attractive.' Lena picked up a packet of fuzzy pipe cleaners. Life had been so simple, the last time she had held a fuzzy pipe cleaner. She wished she was eight years old again.

'But – doesn't he think you're dating?' Izzy asked, as Joe pawed at her breast.

'No! I've told him about Adam.'

'But you're lying to Adam about meeting up with him.'

Lena put the pipe cleaners down. 'I know. I'm a terrible person.'

'You're not. You're just *behaving* like a terrible person.' She shifted Joe on to her hip.

'That's the last time.' Lena nodded, making the decision. 'I'm going to ignore his messages from now on.' She held up a packet of felt-tip pens. 'What about these, for the middle of the parcel?'

'The other parents would go nuts if I gave the kids felt-tip pens. They'd draw all over the walls.'

'I didn't think of that. This is why I can never have kids. I'd be such a shit mother.'

Joe was crying now. Izzy began to wrestle him back into his buggy. 'Have you told Adam? About never wanting kids?'

Lena shook her head. Adam kept talking about moving house when they had a baby and the low-emissions holidays they could go on when they had a baby, and she had never felt less maternal, and Joe screaming and squirming as she helped Izzy strap him into the pushchair wasn't helping, and fixating on literally the one person she wasn't allowed to fall for was the opposite of settling down and having children with her husband, and so she let herself fall.

*

She silenced her brain with sex.

'What's got into you?' Adam asked, when she came on to him for the third night in a row.

'Shh. Just fuck me.'

'With a condom?'

She opened the bedside drawer and held one out to him.

'You'd tell me, wouldn't you, if you knew for sure that you didn't want kids?' he asked, afterwards.

She nodded, slowly. She wasn't being fair to him. She'd tell him today, she'd do it right now—

But Adam was already saying, 'You said – before Christmas, you said you wanted them—'

'I know, I'm sorry, but that was before I realized my children would be one quarter a stranger.'

'That doesn't matter!'

'It does to me—'

'I want to be a dad, Lena!' Adam said, standing up, hands in his hair. 'I've always been upfront about that!'

'And I always said I wasn't sure!' She felt claustrophobic, but she made herself take his hand. 'If I could get pregnant right now, would you be happy to have a baby in nine months?'

'Yes.'

'Honestly?'

'Yes!'

'Would you take paternity leave?'

'Of course.'

'As in – not just two weeks.'

'I'd add my annual leave on to it. So that would be a whole month—'

'But what about shared parental leave? Would you take six months? Share it fifty-fifty?'

He sat on the edge of the bed. 'I'd have to look into it. It's not easy for a teacher just to bugger off for half the school year—'

She dropped his hand. 'Right. OK. Well. When you've done that, we can have this conversation again.'

'But none of this mattered to you before! We were trying!'

'I have the right to change my mind about something with life-altering consequences, Adam—'

'So you *have* decided.' His eyes were ugly with anger. 'You have.'

His fury felt like the beginning of a farewell, and she didn't want it to be, she realized, now that she was faced with it. She reached for him, like a commuter fighting to hold the train doors open. His arms hung at his sides as she hugged him. And then he turned to look out of the window, as though at other possibilities.

She forced herself to say, 'Would you leave me? If I said I definitely didn't want children?'

He cleared his throat. The way her father did, when faced with a difficult question. There was something Freudian in that, but she decided not to think about it. 'I don't know,' he said. 'Maybe. Probably.'

'OK. We should both think about it, then.'

'We should.'

'OK.'

He crossed his arms.

'I love you,' she said.

He left the room without saying it back.

*

Adam went away for a two-week folk workshop at the beginning of August, so Lena was free to hang out with Daniel. They got drunk together, mostly. When she was drunk she didn't miss Adam and she didn't feel guilty or anxious, though she did afterwards as she sweated through the night, her body burning, cramps in her stomach and lower down, too, waking up with the sort of constant nausea she hadn't felt since she'd discovered her mum's supply of pre-mixed gin and tonics, aged twelve. One afternoon, Daniel asked her to go shopping with him: he had a credit card and a fondness for Selfridges' gender-neutral department. 'If I go on a red carpet wearing one of these,' he said, holding up an oversized hoodie that cost £800, 'I know no one else will be wearing the same thing.' For good reason, she thought, but she didn't say that out loud. Because she'd noticed that Daniel didn't like people to contradict him. He had flecks of darkness. He wouldn't have glittered the way he did without them.

Fleck one: he was rude to shop assistants and waiters and taxi drivers when he didn't get his way.

Fleck two: he loved being recognized, but he was dismissive of the people who approached him, as though he respected them less for caring who he was.

Fleck three: his fondness for drugs. Lena hadn't taken drugs since Ed and Abeo's New Year's Eve party in 2017: after two lines of coke, she'd spent the evening claiming that her job was 'actually quite important' until Abeo's friend Muriel told her she was 'actually a tosser'. She'd resolved to avoid drugs (and Muriel) after that. But Daniel didn't think a night out was complete without a line or a bump or a pill. She took ketamine with him in a pub toilet, and had to feel her way along the walls to make it back to the table. She checked the mirror when she got home. White powder crusted around her nostril. Bruises on her arms and legs she didn't remember getting. She resolved to be stronger after that.

But she had flecks of darkness, too. The grief she didn't feel any more, most of the time, until something caught her out of nowhere. The fact that she was his sister and she hadn't told him. The lies she was telling, great teetering towers of them. But she and Daniel had settled into friendship – it had been weeks since he'd last stared meaningfully into her eyes or joked about paying for her divorce lawyer – and telling the truth didn't feel quite so urgent. So she let herself accept his invitation to the last night of the *Hamlet* run, and the party afterwards, and she didn't stop herself buying a leather skirt for the occasion. She didn't need to lie about where she was going, because Adam was two hundred miles away, sharing a bunkbed with a viola player from Totnes.

The party was a mistake. The other actors asked too many questions about how she and Daniel knew each other, and Daniel slipped to the toilets every hour with the actor playing Polonius, and emerged sniffing and rubbing his nose. His agent, Bella, trapped Lena against the wall for a good half an hour, raving about how gorgeous Abeo was and how many of his clients wanted to shag him, and then Daniel came up behind her and put his arms around her waist and asked Bella if he could steal her, and she could feel the room turning to watch them, and it felt like infidelity.

'My parents are here,' Daniel said, as they leaned against the bar, watching Ophelia make out with Claudius.

'Fuck.' Lena looked around the room. 'Where?'

He nodded to a booth at the edge of the bar, where a smart, grey-haired couple were sitting, straight-backed and awkward, not speaking to each other. Daniel's mother had very solid-looking hair and immaculate make-up. Daniel's father was red-faced and white-haired, with expensive-looking teeth.

'Want to meet them?'

'Absolutely not.'

'Why not?'

'Because I don't like meeting my friends' parents when I'm drunk.'

He sighed, frustrated, and put his hands on her hips. 'When are you going to stop pretending there's nothing happening between us?'

Her stomach dropped. She was so fucking stupid. She pushed his hands away. 'I don't want to talk about this.'

'Too bad.'

Bella was looking at them. There was a change in the air. Quiet, at their end of the bar.

'Bella's listening—'

'So?'

Lena had to get away from him. She pushed her way through the crowds to the exit, but Daniel caught her hand before she got there, pulling her back into the room. 'Out here,' she said, leading him through the double doors into the foyer, to privacy. She dropped his hand. 'You've got to stop it, Daniel—'

'You wouldn't keep hanging out with me if you didn't feel what I feel.' He took a step towards her. 'It's driving me mad, not fucking you.'

And there was no going back, now that he'd said it,

and no going forwards, either. His words were like a pin, fixing them in time and space, trapped and doomed as butterflies.

She looked at the ground, heart racing. 'I'm not interested. I've told you, I'm married. I just want to be friends.'

His hands were on her shoulders and she looked up, right into his eyes, and she couldn't look away as he said, 'I'm not interested in being your friend.'

'Listen, it's never going to happen. Ever. There are, like – a thousand reasons it's never going to happen—'

'Give me one.'

And she stared at him.

And the words wouldn't form in her mouth, because she knew how much damage they would do – she couldn't tell him, she would never be able to tell him—

And then the director swung through the double doors, saying, 'Dan! We've been looking for you everywhere!', and pulled him back into the bar, into a loud, theatrical conversation.

Lena left without saying goodbye. On the Tube home, she deleted Daniel's number. If she couldn't tell him, she could never see him again. He was bad for her. Her heart felt black and damaged, like a lung in an anti-smoking campaign. She wrote a short story in the Notes app called 'French Exit'.

She'd write every morning in Sicily, she decided. She'd write and she'd sit in old stone churches and ask for forgiveness and she'd come back cleansed, and she'd go back to being the person she had been before she realized she didn't know who she was.

*

A week later, as the plane to Sicily was taxiing down the runway, she took out her phone to turn it off and saw a message from an unknown number.

I'm sorry, Seraphim. I miss you.

Objectively the most revolting nickname of all time. If she hadn't been related to Daniel, she'd have thought he was awful. If she hadn't been related to Daniel, she wouldn't have felt this pull towards him.

Adam was reading the safety card. Alison and Suria were consulting the inflight menu. The cabin crew were pointing out the exits. She messaged Daniel back – she wasn't being fair, cutting him out of her life with no explanation. *I'm sorry too. I really didn't mean to lead you on. I think it would be easier for both of us if we didn't see each other any more.*

Grey dots. He was replying.

Adam slid the safety card back into the seat pocket. 'We're about to take off.'

'I know.'

The cabin lights dimmed. The light from her phone seemed brighter than ever.

'Who are you texting?'

'Izzy.'

Dots, still.

'If we crash it'll be your fault.'

'That's a myth.'

They were taxiing down the runway. Daniel still hadn't replied.

'Put it away.'

'I just want to see what she says!'

'About what?'

Her phone buzzed.

303

If that's what you want. But I would like to try and be your friend, if you're up for it. I really am sorry.

'Excuse me?' A female flight attendant, scarf tied at a jaunty angle, was leaning over the seat. 'You can't use your phone during take-off?'

'Told you,' Adam said, turning towards the window.

'Just turning it off.' Lena put her phone in her bag and took out a novel. She stared at it, unseeing. She was alive with relief, drunk with it. Daniel was sorry. The danger had passed. She turned to Adam. 'Shall we do a digital detox this week?'

He smiled at her, surprised. 'Yes! Good idea!'

She kissed his cheek. No more lying. The plane took off with a roar, like a distant crowd, cheering for her.

The holiday villa was browner than it had looked in the photographs, with wood-panelled walls and dark furniture, nothing in the cupboards but a bottle of vegetable oil, a pair of binoculars and a two-thousand-piece jigsaw of *The Last Supper*. Still, it had a pool, and the sea stretched calm and still beyond black-sand beaches and cactus-covered cliff faces. The villa was part of a hotel complex perched at the end of a twisting road that ran up through Savoca, a beautiful village famous for being the location for a shooting in *The Godfather*. Tourists posed outside the church where Michael Corleone got married, and queued up to buy *Il Padrino* T-shirts in the village shop, which also sold cigarettes and lemon granita. *The Godfather* theme tune wobbled through the hot, still air from cafés and bars and buskers' violins, ominous.

The minor key felt appropriate; Suria and Alison had barely smiled since they'd arrived. After dinner on the first night, Suria went straight to bed and Adam set off up the hill with the binoculars in pursuit of a Eurasian scops owl. Alison and Lena sat outside by the floodlit pool, drinking red wine and eating cannoli – a stomach-curdling combination. Alison was monosyllabic, and Lena was talking too much to fill the gaps in the conversation. She had known what to say when Alison had cried over disappointing exam results, girlfriends who turned out to be straight, their mother's death, the ending of *Beaches*, but now Alison was experiencing a kind of grief Lena had never experienced, and she felt useless in the face of it.

'Is Suria OK?' Lena asked, after a particularly agonizing pause in the conversation. 'I mean – I know she's not OK, obviously—'

Alison shook her head. 'We had our second embryo transfer last week. We found out this morning that it didn't work.'

'Oh god. Alison, I'm so sorry.'

Alison drank her wine and stared into the pool.

The silence was roaring now. 'Are you going to try again?'

'We don't have any embryos left. So we'd have to start from square one, with more injections and another egg collection. And it's thousands of pounds.'

Lena couldn't bear it, the silence and the awkwardness, dangerous as taut elastic. She said, 'I wish you'd told me you were having another transfer.'

'It's fine, Lena. I'm not sure you're the right person to support me with fertility stuff.'

Lena nodded. 'Am I—' she started. Then she shook her head.

Alison looked up from her glass. 'What?'

'Am I still in the centre of your onion?'

Alison laughed, a sad sort of laugh. 'Course you are.'

Lena leaned over to give her sister a hug. Alison patted her back, like a dad greeting another dad at an under-eights football match.

They spent the next day by the pool. Suria slept on a sun lounger, a copy of *Girl, Woman, Other* face down on her thighs. Lena lay in the shade of an olive tree as Alison ploughed through the water in her old black Speedo.

'You're going to burn,' Lena called.

'I'm wearing factor fifty.' Alison carried on swimming.

Adam leaned over from the sun lounger next to Lena's, proudly showing her a blurry video on his phone. 'You can't really see the owl, but do you hear that? That's its call!'

Lena thought about how many times the four of them had played out this scene over the years, lying by pools in Italy and France, Croatia and Spain, eating crisps and swimming and reading and talking. Their reading material had become slightly more sophisticated over the years – fewer Jilly Cooper novels, more books in translation – and they started drinking at lunchtime now, rather than straight after breakfast. But this might be the very last time. Suria and Alison weren't the sort to give up on things. They would probably have children eventually.

But maybe she and Adam would have children, too – maybe she was wrong to rule that out completely. She hadn't checked her phone in three days, and Daniel was fading into the background. She felt calmer than she had in months. She read three chapters of a novel in one sitting, without losing concentration. Now that her heart wasn't beating out of her chest, there was more room inside her for Adam, for his kindness and silliness and gentleness, and the idea of starting a family with him felt sane and comforting. An ordinary sort of adventure.

'I like you in Sicily,' he said, as they lay on the beach that afternoon.

'I like you in Sicily, too.'

He put his hand on her thigh, and it felt electric.

She kissed him in the water, long, slow kisses. Then they floated on their backs near the shore, little fingers linked, staring up at the uncomplicated blue of the sky, until a sunburned man swam past them shouting 'Jellyfish!' They splashed on to the shore, kicking up black sand, laughing the way you do when you've had a narrow escape.

The sunburned man stood on the sand, chest heaving, examining the welts on his legs from the jellyfish tentacles.

'Do you think I should offer to piss on him?' Adam asked, quite seriously.

Lena felt a rush of love, the sort you get when you've come close to losing someone. She kissed him and said, 'I don't deserve a husband as lovely as you.'

Adam laughed. 'You're lovely too.'

'I'm not, but thank you.'

'You are.' He put his arms around her waist. 'I've been doing some thinking, actually. About how lovely you are.'

'The best kind of thinking.'

'And I've been thinking that it's OK if you don't want to have children.'

'Adam—'

'It is, it's fine.' He looked shy and a little sad.

'You don't have to say that,' she said, but still, it was a relief to hear it.

'No, I know. I know I don't. But the children don't exist and you do, and I really, really love you, and I'd be an idiot to give that up. Wouldn't I?'

His hair and skin were golden in the late-afternoon sunlight, and Lena had never met anyone with a better heart, anyone more beautiful. She hugged him, her face on his chest, breathing in the salty, familiar scent of him. He smelled like home.

Maybe it was the sea air, but Lena was so exhausted by the time they got back to the villa, she went straight to bed. She slept by the pool the next day, too, while the others played card games and drank negronis. Suria seemed to be coming back to life, though she was spikier and meaner than usual, grumbling about the beach towels being damp and Alison leaving dirty underwear on the floor of their room.

'Sorry I've been such a miserable cunt all week,' Suria said that night. They had walked, single file, down the cobbled hillside to a bar in the centre of the village, and now they were sitting outside, drinking wine and watching tourists posing in the doorway, pretending to be Al Pacino and Robert De Niro, their fingers cocked like guns.

'You haven't been miserable!' Adam said.

'I have. It's fine, I can take it.' She poured herself more wine. 'It's just – we've just had some shitty news.'

Lena nodded. 'Alison said.'

Suria turned to Alison, surprised. 'Did she?'

'I told her about the second embryo transfer not working,' Alison said.

'Oh. Aye. Right.' Suria sat back in her chair. 'But anyway. Fuck it.' She drained her glass. 'Everything happens for a reason. What's for ye'll no go by ye. As my mother would say.'

'Enough wine, now,' Alison said, moving the bottle away from her.

It was Suria's idea to go skinny dipping on the last night of the holiday. They streaked from the villa to the edge of the pool, arms crossed over their chests, and hurled themselves into the water, pretending not to look at each other's bodies. They each took a corner of the pool. They looked like different people in the moonlight. Adam and Alison were splashing each other. Suria was swigging from a bottle of Campari.

'We wouldnae be able to do this, if we had babies!' Suria shouted. She put the Campari down on the edge of the pool and did a handstand in the water.

Lena flipped and floated on her back. No stars tonight. The pressure in the air felt like a threat. A waiter at the bar had said something about a storm. Suria was swimming over to her, saying something. She lifted her head out of the water. 'Sorry?'

'I was just saying,' Suria said, slurry, 'that your tits look fucking great.'

Lena laughed and looked at Alison, who said, 'Suria! Gross!'

'What?' Suria said. 'They do! Look at the size of them!'

Lena looked down at her breasts. 'Premenstrual,' she said. Which is when she realized she couldn't remember the last time she'd had her period. Her bras had become tighter over the past couple of weeks. She'd assumed that was because she kept forgetting to put her underwear in the delicates wash. She pushed herself out of the water. She walked back to the villa. She couldn't feel her feet. She picked her phone up from the chest of drawers and opened her period-tracking app. Almost a week late. She googled *morning after pill effectiveness*. Eighty-five per cent effective, if taken twenty-four to forty-eight hours after sex. Only 85 fucking per cent.

The pharmacy in the village was open till eight. She could still make it if she hurried. She pulled on a dress and walked as quietly as she could past the pool—

'Lena?' It was Alison. She was out of the water, back in her shorts and T-shirt.

'Just going for a wander.'

Adam swam to the side of the pool. 'You shouldn't go on your own in the dark!'

'I'm fine. I just feel sick, I need some air—'

'I'll come with you,' Alison said.

'OK, what's the hurry?' Alison asked, as Lena marched up the stone steps, up through the village towards the church tower. Bats ruffled across the fat moon, then disappeared into the darkness.

'I want to go to the pharmacy before it shuts. I've run out of painkillers—'

'I've got paracetamol.'

'I need ibuprofen.'

'I've got that too.'

Rain had started to fall.

'Lena. Let's go back—'

'You go back.'

'What's going on?'

'It doesn't matter. Seriously, leave me, I'm fine, I just fancy the walk—'

'In this?' Alison pointed to the sky: the rain was falling properly now. They had reached the church. Alison stepped into the shelter of the doorway. 'Let's wait here till the rain stops.'

Lena kept walking. 'I'll pick you up on the way back.' She had less than five minutes to get to the pharmacy. She wasn't going to make it—

'Lena!' Alison was jogging after her up the hill.

Lena didn't want to tell her, not until she was sure, but if Alison was going to follow her to the pharmacy—

'Seriously, what's going on?'

Lena turned to face her sister, her vision blurred by the rain. 'I need to buy a pregnancy test. OK? I think I might be pregnant.'

Biblical

Suria drank too much on the last night of the holiday, and Alison couldn't blame her. They should never have come, so soon after the embryo transfer. They should have thought about how it would feel to sit around, grieving, in a Sicilian villa while Lena and Adam splashed about in the pool, pretending to be bottlenose dolphins. Alison was humiliated, now, thinking back to how hopeful they'd been as they left the clinic, like they hadn't learned anything. 'Fingers crossed!' Dr Pellici had said, which Alison had found irritating – there shouldn't be any room for superstition in science, especially when science cost as much as this did – but Suria had given in to the superstition too, to the pregnancy vitamins and acupuncture, the meditation sessions and special diets, and Alison had caught herself praying to a god she didn't believe in that this time it would work, that they would be enough for each other if it didn't.

Suria had cried when she had taken the test, but Alison found herself wanting to punch a wall. She managed to restrain herself by remembering how pathetic people looked on television when they punched walls. Instead, she had gone swimming in the black Speedo she had been wearing since university, which was fine for Leyton Leisure Centre but almost see-through with age, she could see now, in the unforgiving Sicilian sunlight. She cried at night though, as the moon sliced through the curtain. Suria slept – the doctor had given her sleeping pills after her miscarriage – but Alison lay awake until dawn, pretending she couldn't hear Lena and Adam having sex.

The next morning, before they drew the curtains, Suria called the clinic to let them know the pregnancy test had been negative – and she asked whether her egg donation had resulted in a pregnancy. The answer was clear, from the way Suria's knees crumpled. 'Amazing! That's amazing! No, no, I'm fine, that's brilliant, wonderful news, aye.' She hung up, eyes closed, mouth open, her face a silent scream.

'We knew it was a possibility,' Suria said, as the tears rolled steadily down her cheeks. 'We knew it was a possibility.'

Alison paced the gloomy bedroom, because standing still felt unbearable; if she kept moving, perhaps she could dodge the reality of it, stop the truth catching up with her.

'We have done a good thing,' Suria said, arms wrapped tight around her chest, as though she was holding herself together. 'We have helped another family become a family.'

It's not my child, Alison reminded herself. It's not Suria's child, either. But she knew that she would look at every pregnant woman she passed in the street, wondering, and in nine months' time she would stare into every bassinet, looking for Suria's eyes, and then at every toddler, every teenager, every twenty-something.

Now, the holiday was nearly over. Just one more night of pretending to smile in photographs. At lunchtime on the final day, Alison received an email from Jim about her mother's headstone that, in ordinary circumstances, would have left her white-fisted with fury, but she couldn't bring herself to care. She went for a long, exhausting walk in the hammering heat down the twisting roads to the beach and back again, and the Campari went to her head quicker than usual when she got back, which is how she ended up naked in the pool. The four of them were passing a bottle of Campari back and forth, when Lena climbed out of the water. She disappeared into the villa and emerged a few minutes later, an unfamiliar wide-eyed look on her face.

'Just going for a wander,' she said.

The pharmacy was shut by the time they reached it. 'Fuck!' Lena said, shaking the door, her face sickly in the light from the green cross above the storefront. She sank down to the step. Alison sat next to her. They tucked their feet under the porch, to keep them dry: rain was streaming past them down the hillside. 'I can't believe this. I took a morning after pill. Sorry, you don't want to hear this.'

I believe in a woman's right to choose, Alison told herself, and she did, of course she did, but she couldn't stop herself saying, 'Don't do this, Lena.'

Lena looked at her. 'You're not seriously about to say what I think you're about to say?'

'Is it Adam's?'

'Of course it is! Who do you think I am?'

'Then—' Alison stopped herself.

'Don't tell me to keep it,' Lena said, and Alison recognized the look of panic in her eyes, because she felt it too, whenever Suria suggested she try to get pregnant.

'Just – wait. You're getting ahead of yourself. First things first. Take a test.' If Lena was pregnant it would be like a slap in the face, the awful irony of it, the utter unfairness. But life is unfair, isn't it? That's what their mother had always said. And then she had proved it by dying for no reason before they could say goodbye.

Lena was crying. The rain was falling harder, too, slapping the steps. 'I thought you'd understand!'

'I do. It's just – you're thirty-four—'

'So? It's my fucking body, Alison!'

'I know it is. I know.' Alison pressed her hands against her eyes. 'It's just – it's not that easy to get pregnant—'

'But I don't want to be pregnant!'

'Are you sure, though? Are you sure you're sure? Because it's happened naturally now, and if you change your mind, there's no guarantee – fuck, Lena, you have no idea what Suria has been through—'

'I *do* know!'

'No! You don't! You don't have a fucking clue! Do you know how much IVF costs? It costs eight grand a go! Do you think we've got eight grand?' Lena was staring at her. She should stop talking, but she didn't want to stop talking now that she had started, and the rain was falling too fast, streaming past them down the hillside. There would be a flood.

'How did you pay for it?' Lena asked.

And Alison didn't know how to tell her – she should have kept her stupid mouth shut.

315

'How did you pay for it?' Lena asked again. 'Suria didn't do egg sharing, did she?'

'We had no other option!'

'Oh my god. Oh my god—' Lena started to walk away, but as soon as she stepped outside the shelter of the pharmacy she was soaked through.

Alison followed Lena into the rain, which was wetter than any rain she'd felt before, her hair heavy, sticking to her cheeks. 'We were desperate—'

'I can't believe you didn't tell me.'

'It's not about you, Lena!' Alison was furious now, and vicious with it. 'Not everything is about you! I knew you'd react like this—'

'No, you're right, it's not about me, it's about your future children, having loads of half-siblings out there—'

'We're not going to have any children!' The rain on her cheeks felt like tears, clogging up her eyelashes, and she could hardly see her sister, and it felt biblical. 'If we want to do another round of IVF we have to donate more eggs unless we pay for it, and we don't have the money—'

'I can lend you the money! I could have lent you the fucking money! If you'd just asked me—'

'You have eight grand lying around?'

'I have savings!'

Alison couldn't hear that. She couldn't let that be true. 'How could I ask you for money? I know how you feel about us using a sperm donor—'

'Oh, no, yeah, you're totally right, I'd much rather that Suria became an egg donor, too, that makes total sense.' Lena walked down the hill, but she slipped on the wet cobblestones and stood up again, sodden. She returned to

316

the pharmacy steps and sat there, staring out at the rain, as though she couldn't believe it, as though she couldn't believe any of it.

Am I in the wrong? Alison wondered. Maybe. Fuck, it was all so chaotic, life, wasn't it? When your sister was pregnant and she didn't want to be, and your wife's baby was growing in a stranger's womb, and your friend could give birth even though he was a man, and you, a woman, didn't feel female enough to be pregnant. 'Suria will be a brilliant donor, Lena,' she said, unsure of herself, unsure of everything. 'She'll be there, if the kid ever wants to meet her—'

Lena was shaking her head, her eyes closed. Alison sat down next to her, and her sister shifted away.

'Please don't be like this. Have you got any idea how shit we already feel?'

'Let's just – not talk to each other right now.' Lena turned to face the pharmacy door, like a child who thinks that if they can't see you, then you no longer exist.

And Alison was raging with her sister's self-righteousness, her lack of empathy, but she couldn't go away, because the water was a river now, and Adam and Suria were too drunk to pick them up. She called a taxi.

The minutes stretched and contracted, the way time does when everything is awful. Sometime later, headlights swept around the curve in the road. The taxi slowed down. Alison stepped into the roar of the rain, slamming the taxi door behind her.

Lena climbed into the front seat. She didn't turn around. Alison focused on the squeak, squeak of the windscreen wipers, and she thought about the way Lena had said she would always be in the centre of her onion. She started to cry, but they weren't real tears. That's just what happens with onions.

Pyrrhic victory

Back in London, Tom was having a wonderful August, which made a change: he had never really enjoyed the summer before. He had always preferred the autumn, the shorter days, when the leaves had fallen and the woollen coats had returned, when the cloudy skies excused his melancholy. What were you supposed to wear in thirty-degree heat, once you were over the age of fifty? Not shorts, not unless you wanted people to think you were a Scout leader or a professional geologist. Not linen (too easily creased) or straw hats (the preserve of professional cricket commentators) or baseball caps (ruined by Jimmy Savile). He had never got the hang of picnics; they were for young people who hadn't yet developed sciatica. The youthful bodies sprawled all over Primrose Hill, flaunting picnic hampers and bottles of cava, friends and flat stomachs, reminded Tom that he wasn't young any more. And even as a young man, he hadn't known that many people – there were picnics involving frisbee and bunting, with fifty, sixty guests. Where did they meet each other, these twenty-something frisbee players? At some sort of frisbee convention?

This summer was different, though. This summer he had company as he walked up Primrose Hill, panting and cursing it for being so steep, and sure, his hip wouldn't allow him to sit on the grass, but Jessie had invested in two collapsible picnic chairs, and they sat in them on Sunday evenings on the quiet side of the hill, drinking more expensive wine than the young people could afford, then going back to his for sex, or to watch something French on Netflix. He was taking August off from his genealogy research. The case of mistaken identity had knocked his confidence – and anyway, the winter was a much more appropriate season for moping around the house while his daughter and her fit, attractive biological father drank mulled wine on an ice rink, or whatever it was long-lost relatives did when they met for the first time. For four glorious weeks, while the library was quiet and the sky was clean and blue (the clouds must have buggered off to the French Riviera, along with everyone else with an up-to-date passport), he spent every day with Jessie, thinking of nothing but whether he was boring her yet and what colour bra she was wearing under her silk shirt and what Sheila would think about them being together and when it would end, because everything came to an end, eventually. Except he wasn't thinking about that because he was taking the summer off from worrying.

Now that they were officially a couple, Tom and Jessie bought cheap seats to the opera, and read the papers together over breakfast on a Saturday, and made plans for two weeks ahead, certain they'd still want to spend time with each other. She even invited him to Devon, to spend the weekend at her youngest daughter's house. He bought pyjamas especially for the occasion – he had slept naked since the Eighties – and he felt a little awkward shaking Amelia's hand on the doorstep, as though she was the parent and Jessie was the child and Amelia might, at any moment, ask him about his intentions. They went hiking up steep hills, Tom panting and trailing after the others, pretending to stop and identify butterflies when it all got too much, while Jessie and Amelia waited for him, hands on hips. They swam in the sea, too, or rather Jessie and Amelia swam while Tom thrashed about and tried to remember how to tread water. He and Jessie had silent sex on the Saturday night, and as Tom was hugging Amelia goodbye and telling her what a lovely time he'd had, she told him she was 'chuffed' to have met him, an old-fashioned word that made him think of small birds and wheat and steam engines. He felt a stab of pointless regret that Jessie had had children with another man, even though he and Sheila had been very happy, even though Lena and Alison were the best things to ever happen to him. And then he remembered that, even if he'd had kids with Jessie, he wouldn't have been related to them.

Strange and new, this jealousy: he had never been jealous of Sheila, even though, before they'd met, she'd slept with at least half the Revolutionary Communist Tendency. Maybe it was because so much of his life was in the past, but he felt retrospectively jealous of every man Jessie had ever been with, particularly Ray, Amelia's father, who had been keen on doctors and nurses role-play, and Lewis, her second husband, who had been into tantric sex. 'It was a pain in the arse, quite honestly,' she told him, one night in

321

bed. 'So boring. It went on for hours – endless stroking and heavy breathing. Once, I asked him to hurry up and come so I could put on a load of laundry, which didn't go down well.'

'I can imagine.'

'I think he started seeing the 32-year-old quite soon after that.'

He wanted to hear about her past – he wanted to know everything about her – but the problem was, there was a lot of it, years and years of happiness he'd had nothing to do with, shelves full of photo albums showing her aged 5 and 9 and 16 and 20, a teddy bear under her arm, waving from the top of a sand dune, clutching a mortar board, gut-twistingly beautiful. '*You contract my heart by looking out of date*,' he told her, as she showed him her wedding photographs, one evening in early September. 'Philip Larkin.' She rolled her eyes and called him a pretentious old bastard, and then she reached for his hand and told him she loved him anyway.

The leaves were curling on the trees now. In the library, freshers staggered to the issue desk with piles of books they would never read, and Brian was wearing three-piece suits again. Lena and Alison were back from Sicily, and he had received a notification from Genealogy DNA – Lena had a new first-cousin match – but he couldn't bring himself to look at it. Maybe Lena felt the same, because she didn't answer the phone when he called to discuss it. Alison came for tea one afternoon, though, with a lump of rock from Mount Etna, and news.

'Mum's headstone's finished.'

He laughed. 'Well, I'll be buggered.'

'But.'

'Of course there's a but.'

'Jim took so long to make it that the cemetery has changed the rules on headstone dimensions in the meantime. And it's too tall. So we can't have it installed, unless we basically chop it in half, in which case the date'll be cut off the bottom—'

'This is ridiculous.' He put his head in his hands. That bloody man.

'So basically we own a very expensive lump of sandstone with Mum's name on it.' Alison sipped her water. 'We could put it at the bottom of the garden, or something. Stick a hose behind it, turn it into a water feature.'

Breathe, Tom told himself. His neck muscles were stiffening, he was so furious, and he couldn't afford a massage, not when he'd wasted thousands of pounds on a pointless bit of rock. 'That bastard needs to give us our money back—'

'I'm pretty sure he's already spent the money—'

'We can't just let him get away with it – fucking bastard!'

'Calm down, Dad—'

'I am calm!' But his hand shook as he picked up his water glass. 'What's Lena saying about all this? We should get her to write to him and threaten to sue. She could use her firm's letterhead—'

'I haven't told her yet.' Alison was fiddling with her placemat. 'We had a bit of a falling out in Sicily.'

'Oh dear,' he said. 'When you say a bit of a falling out—'

'A massive falling out.'

'Right. Do I want to know what it was about?'

'No.'

'I won't take sides,' he said, but she shook her head. Then she looked at her watch and started muttering about

323

how long it would take to get back to Leytonstone. He had pushed her too far.

'Well,' he said, as she stood up. 'Thanks for coming to visit your old dad. And thanks for this.' He held up the lump of volcanic rock. 'It'll make a lovely paperweight.'

'I wanted to bring you back some Sicilian wine,' Alison said, as she put on her jacket. 'But Lena wouldn't let me.'

'I'll call the cemetery,' he said. 'I'll cry down the phone at them, do my grieving widower bit, persuade them to make an exception for us.'

'Pretty sure everyone with a non-regulation gravestone is grieving someone,' Alison pointed out.

He called Lena again on Monday afternoon. She answered this time, at least, but she said, 'I'm actually in Boots, Dad, and my reception's shit. Can I call you later?'

The house was too quiet, after she hung up the phone. He did a couple of cryptic crossword clues, and left an angry voicemail for the Kensal Green Cemetery board and an even angrier one for Jim, the hopeless stonemason. He turned on the radio after that, but Boris Johnson's voice did dreadful things to his blood pressure, so he turned it off again. Rain was falling, and his melancholy had returned along with the autumn weather, and he wanted to wallow in it, to pick an emotional scab. Upstairs in his office, he opened his laptop and logged into Lena's Genealogy DNA account. And there she was, his daughter's first cousin, a woman helpfully named Calypso Jennings – there couldn't be too many of those knocking about on social media. He clicked on her family tree, but it was private. Her Facebook was private too. She did have a Twitter account, but she used it exclusively to complain to supermarkets about dodgy vegetables in her click and collect orders. He dialled Jessie's number as he scrolled back through Calypso's Twitter feed.

'Hello, darling,' Jessie said. Her voice was echoey. He heard a splash. 'I'm just this minute getting in the bath—'

'I've found Lena's first cousin. On Genealogy DNA.'

More splashing. 'The bath can wait. I'll be round in five minutes.'

After that, everything happened too quickly, before he could really understand it was happening, the way it had that day when Sheila had started shivering uncontrollably and told him she felt like she was going to die. Jessie sat at his desk chair, eyes inches from the screen – 'You ought to get your prescription checked,' he told her, but she hushed him and said, 'I've narrowed it down. The sperm donor must be one of these two blokes here. They must be this Calypso character's uncles.' And before he could stop her, she was googling their names, and one of them was a property developer named Hugo Martin and the other, Dexter Campbell, seemed to run some sort of jam-making business, and neither of them was a doctor, neither of them had ever been to medical school, so the hospital must have lied to him—

'Tom? Are you OK?'

'I'm fine.' But he was struggling to regulate his breathing.

'Shall we leave it for today?' Jessie was frowning, concerned.

'I can't just leave it.' She offered him the desk chair. He sat down and clicked on Dexter Campbell's website.

'I hope it's him, don't you?' Jessie said, peering over his shoulder. 'You can't be a total bastard if you make jam for a living, can you?'

'I wouldn't be so sure,' Tom said. 'There's a fair bit of child labour involved in the chocolate business, isn't there?'

He opened a new tab and searched for the property developer's website. There was a YouTube clip of him talking about his commitment to social housing. There was something familiar about the way his nose moved up and down, very slightly, as he spoke.

'Click on *Contact*,' Jessie said. 'We can message him and ask if he ever donated sperm—'

'No. Absolutely not. Look what happened last time we did that.'

'What do you want to do, then? Are you going to call Lena?'

'She's busy.'

'You could leave her a message—'

'No. I want to tell her in person.'

'You're procrastinating—'

He crossed his arms. 'I'm not.'

'You can't stop her finding him—'

'I'm not trying to!' he said, more snappishly than he'd intended. 'I just want to – I just want to be sure. When I tell her. Which one he is.'

Jessie was squinting at the computer screen again. 'Well, according to the Campbell Jams website, Dexter has been living in Devon since 1976. Whereas Hugo Martin has been living in London since the Sixties. And we think whoever it was donated sperm around 1986, don't we? So unless Dexter had a penchant for taking four-hour journeys to London twice a week to masturbate into a specimen cup, I'd say Hugo's our man.' She beamed at him. 'You've found him. You *did* it, Tom!'

'I did it.' He resolved to look up 'pyrrhic victory' in his

etymological dictionary. His eyes were hot, and he was wearing too many clothes all of a sudden, and his heart was jumping arrhythmically, the way it did whenever he was forced to dance at weddings.

Fuck fuck fuck fuck fuck

Lena waited until Monday to buy the pregnancy test: she didn't want to do it when Adam was around. She went to Boots during her lunch break, casually sauntering down the aisle the way she used to peruse the condom display as a teenager. She felt as though she was playing at being another person as she put two tests in her basket, along with some shower gel (Mint Source), deodorant (Sure: Cotton Fresh) and a packet of gum (Extra, spearmint) to dilute the gravity of the purchase.

The cashier barely looked up as he scanned the items. He was a teenager still, with spots and a downy moustache. 'You need a bag?'

'Yeah, actually, I do. Sorry. Thanks.'

He did glance at her, when he came to the pregnancy tests. Probably trying to work out whether she wanted to be pregnant or not.

And that's when she noticed James, the bloody senior partner, in the pain relief aisle, deciding between Nurofen and own-brand ibuprofen. He'd been out for drinks with

328

clients the night before. She turned away before he could see her.

The cashier was staring at the code on the back of the pregnancy test, frowning. 'Sarah?' he called to a woman with a grey ponytail who was kneeling in the Revlon aisle, restocking the eyeliners. 'Can you have a look and check the SKU code for these?' He waved the pregnancy tests in the air.

'The Clearblue ones?' shouted Sarah, heaving herself to her feet.

'Yeah. There's a two-for-one offer, but it's not coming up.'

James glanced over to the cash register. Lena turned away.

'I always have that problem with the pregnancy tests!' yelled Sarah. 'One minute, I'll have a look at what's going on.' She walked over to the till, slowly, left hand on her lower back.

'I'll just leave it,' Lena said.

James approached the till, carrying Nurofen, a Coke and a packet of ready salted. 'Hello.' He looked down at his phone. She couldn't be sure whether he'd seen or not.

'This'll just take a minute,' Sarah said, entering a code.

'It's fine, really, I'm in a rush—'

'There.' Sarah smiled up at Lena, victorious. 'That'll be £27.89.'

'Do you have a Boots card?' asked the boy with the moustache.

'No,' Lena said. She couldn't look at James.

'You honestly save loads of money if you have one,' Sarah told her. 'I'll give you a leaflet.'

'I've got a call in five minutes.'

'The Boots points do actually add up very quickly,' said the boy.

'Fine. The leaflet would be great, thanks.'

Sarah smiled and handed her one. 'Good luck!'

Lena stuffed the leaflet and her shopping into the bag, then finally tapped her card on the reader.

James raised an eyebrow at her as she backed out of the shop saying, 'Thanks! Bye! Bye! Thank you!'

She locked herself in a toilet cubicle. She could hear Angela and Karla chatting by the sinks.

'You going Carnival this year?'

'Nah, I can't be doing with crowds, mate.'

She pissed on the stick. On her hands, too. Then she waited, ignoring the voices outside the cubicle, the impatient rattling at the handle.

'Is someone in that one? The door's been locked for ages.'

Two minutes later, two blue lines later, she was on her knees, heart hammering, head on the cool of the toilet lid, trying not to vomit.

Someone knocked on the door. 'Are you OK?' It was Karla.

'I think I've got food poisoning,' Lena said. The excuse she had always used aged 24, when she called in sick with a hangover. Only this time she didn't need to fake the shaking in her voice. 'Can you tell James I'm going to have to leave early?'

'Yeah, course.'

She rang Izzy as she ran down the escalator. No answer. She ought to call Adam, obviously, but she knew he'd be happy, and she couldn't deal with his happiness. Not when she knew, as certainly as she knew she was a woman, a daughter, a friend, that she wasn't supposed to be a mother. She knew it the way you know you've picked the wrong lottery numbers as soon as the draw has been announced.

She stood on the corner of Old Broad Street, in the shadow of a fire escape, and googled the number for Marie Stopes. A woman with a kind voice answered the phone. She must have had this conversation thousands of times, must have practised sounding sympathetic, soothing, non-judgemental when a voice high and wobbly with panic says, 'I'd like to talk to someone about having an abortion.' The woman asked a few questions and invited Lena in for an appointment in a week's time. Lena entered the date in her calendar and then scrolled to Adam's number, but she couldn't tell him over the phone. She was just about to ring Abeo when her phone started vibrating. She had deleted his number, but she knew it was him. Fuck, she thought as she wondered whether to pick up. Fuck fuck fuck fuck fuck fuck fuck fuck fuck.

'Finally,' said Daniel.

Daniel had free tickets to *Fleabag* in the West End that night. Lena agreed to go with him because she had to do something, to see someone, to distract herself, to make her forget about the cells dividing inside her, blossoming like mould. And so it was that she found herself sitting in Wyndham's Theatre, row D, seat 24, waiting for the play to begin. Her elbow was touching Daniel's. The atmosphere was electric. The audience members were practically hovering above their seats, primed for a standing ovation, but the play began with a jolt and a flash and Phoebe Waller-Bridge was already talking, fast, and the audience fell back into their seats, delighted. Lena watched the audience as Fleabag killed the guinea pig. They were horrified by her, but they loved her anyway. Which gave her hope.

'I thought it was better on television.' Daniel said, as they filed out of the theatre.

'It definitely loses a bit of power if you know the twist.'

She noticed people noticing Daniel, nudging their friends, as they sauntered down Charing Cross Road. His hands were in his pockets. He was floodlit by the West End lights. 'Let's get some food,' he said.

'OK,' she said.

He held her hand. Which was fine, she told herself, because friends – and brothers and sisters – hold hands all the time.

Daniel was very discerning when it came to restaurants. He wanted tacos, proper ones, but all the places he wanted to go – the loud restaurants with short menus – were full, with obnoxious queues stretching down the street.

'There's an amazing Mexican place in Borough Market.'

'That's miles away.'

'We can hire bikes. Come on.'

Lena wasn't a great cyclist – she tended not to look behind her when pulling out into traffic, and taxi drivers swore at her as she wobbled to a stop at traffic lights – but fuck, it was exhilarating, speeding along Victoria Embankment, lights from the National Theatre and the OXO Tower reflected in the river, and across Blackfriars Bridge, flinching as vans shrieked past. She was unsteady with adrenaline by the time they reached the market.

'A margarita will sort you out,' Daniel said, noticing the way her knee shook as she stepped off the bike.

*

332

Her body didn't want the margarita but she made her body drink it anyway, because it was still her body even though there was something else living inside it, and she was in charge. They ordered and sat at the metal table, knees almost touching, staring into each other's eyes.

'I find Phoebe Waller-Bridge so inspiring,' Daniel was saying, eating corn chips. 'She just fucking wrote a play and put it on. And now look! She came from absolutely nowhere—'

'From a middle-class family, and RADA—'

'Yeah, well. So did I. And I'm just sitting here, with you. Which I want to be, by the way. Nowhere I'd rather be.'

He reached out and ran his fingers lightly over her forearm, so that the hairs stood on end.

'Daniel,' she said, pulling her arm away. 'You said you were fine being my friend.'

'Yeah, I know. I know. Sorry.'

The tacos arrived, saving them from another argument. Between bites of pork pibil, Daniel told her about the play he was trying to write, and how fucking hard it is to write plays. She passed him a napkin because juice from his taco was spilling down his chin. She told him she'd started writing poetry and short stories but didn't think she'd be giving up the day job any time soon. He asked if he could read her writing, and she said, 'Absolutely not. Under no circumstances.' The lights were bright in the restaurant, and the acoustics were bad, and they were shouting at each other over their food.

'Let's get out of here,' he said, once they'd paid. 'Let's go for a drink.'

'I should go home—'

'No, please. We haven't seen each other for weeks.'

She let him take her arm and walk her into the deserted market. The empty stalls crouched, silent. She imagined them watching, judging her, an inanimate Greek chorus.

'There's a pub just around this corner,' Daniel said, pointing to a side street. 'Or.' He paused in front of a green doorway. 'This is my flat.'

'Just friends,' Lena said.

'Just friends, yeah.'

She looked up at the dark windows. 'Who lives in Borough Market? Literally just you and Bridget Jones.'

He nodded. 'My dad bought it for me when I left drama school.'

'Lucky bastard.'

'You haven't met my dad.'

Nor have you, she thought, as he unlocked the front door.

His flat wasn't as flashy as she had expected it to be. Just one room, mostly taken up with a bed, a kitchen on one side, a bathroom behind a door on another. The sink was piled with plates.

They sat on the bed. They drank Rioja.

Blood was beating in her ears. Tell him, tell him, tell him. She decided to start with the easier confession. She looked down at the duvet. 'I'm pregnant,' she said.

'No.' He said it quietly. He shifted away from her, slightly disgusted, or maybe she was just disgusted with herself, projecting that on to him. He looked at the wine glass in her hand. Another reason she could never have a baby: people judging what she put into her body, as though it wasn't her body any more.

'I'm going to have an abortion.' She took another sip of wine.

'Fuck.'

'I know.'

A beat.

'What does Adam think?'

'Adam doesn't know. You're the first person I've told.'

'How do you feel about it?'

She shrugged. 'Shit. Awful.'

'I'll go with you, if you want me to.'

'Thank you. I'll be OK.'

His gaze was too intense. She kept her eyes on her knees.

'Are you going to break up with Adam?'

She shook her head. She didn't want to think about Adam. 'I think he'll break up with me, when I tell him.'

He breathed out. He had been waiting for this. He turned towards her—

'Stop it—'

'I can't. I don't want to.'

And then kissed her. Of course he fucking did. What had she expected? An ambulance was driving past, the flashing light brilliant against the white walls, its siren warning her to pull away. But she couldn't seem to move fast enough. Or maybe she didn't want to – because she had imagined this moment, and hated herself for imagining it, and now it was happening, and she leaned away, but he thought she was lying back on to the bed, and he climbed on top of her, still kissing her, even though she was pushing him away – not quite forcefully enough – and she could feel him hard against her, and his hand was up her shirt, and she looked up at him, into his eyes, which were her eyes, and the awfulness of what was happening crashed into her and she shouted, 'NO!' She was disgusting, unnatural, a monster. Her *brother*. He would never forgive her. She would never forgive herself. The kiss had broken the spell, the way kisses do. She could see him clearly now. The acne on his cheek. The glassiness of his eyes. He wasn't beautiful to her any more. It was the strangest feeling – like flicking a switch and realizing the sinister figure in the corner is actually an overcoat, hanging harmless on a hook.

She found the strength to push him off her. 'Fuck's sake! I said no!' She sat up.

He groaned in frustration. 'Why not?'

'Daniel! No means no!'

His head was in his hands. 'Shit. Sorry. I know. Fuck!' He stood up. He kicked the wall. 'You're killing me.'

'You're being really Hashtag-Me-Too about this, Daniel—'

'But you want me! I know you do—'

'No, I don't! I told you! I *told* you—' But she stopped, because she hadn't, not really. She needed to leave.

He was in the kitchen, opening and closing drawers and cupboards. 'I need some fucking drugs.'

She felt around for her phone. She couldn't find it. Fuck. It was on the bed somewhere—

'Poppers.'

She was face down on the bed, reaching down past the mattress, feeling on the floor for her phone.

She felt him sit down next to her, heard him sniff from the bottle. 'Have some.'

'No thanks.' No phone. Just dirty socks and what felt like crisp packets.

'Come on.' He grabbed her shoulder and pushed her on to her back.

And before she could sit up he was moving the bottle towards her nose

And she flailed her hand to stop him and knocked the cap from the bottle

And the liquid spilled into her mouth and it was freezing, burning

And she didn't mean to swallow but it was a reflex

And he held up the bottle and it was empty

And she said, 'Fuck'

And thought, So this is how I die

And the world went black. And then flashed back into place. And then everything was black again. As though the world had eyes and it was blinking

And she ran to the toilet, tripping over the detritus of his life

And she shoved her fingers as far down her throat as she could manage, and she was sick.

The world stopped flashing.

Her head started pounding.

She stumbled back to his bed.

'I'm so sorry,' he said, trying to put his arm around her. 'I'm so, so sorry.'

'It's fine.' She leaned away, desperate not to touch him, and put her elbow on something hard, under the pillow. Her phone. Thank god.

'Stay the night,' he said.

'We can't do this.' She tried to stand up. She was still unsteady on her feet.

'We haven't done anything.'

'You know what I mean.' More ambulances outside, but

the sirens were inside her head too. Rushing to the scene of the accident, too late.

He leaned in and kissed her again—

'Get off me! Fucking hell!' She managed to stand up, this time. She picked up the bottle of Rioja and swigged from it, an attempt at absolution. 'I'm going to walk home. To get the alcohol out of my system.'

He pushed himself off the bed. 'I'm not letting you do that. It's too dangerous.'

'You don't get to "let" me do anything. You're not in charge of me.'

He moved to block the door and took both her hands in his so she had no choice but to look into his eyes. He said, 'I'm in love with you.' She jerked away from him, repulsed, at last, the way she should have been all along. She had to get out of there.

'You're not. You just think you are.' She tried to edge around him, but he followed her.

'I know there are probably annoying things about you—'

'Thanks.'

'There are annoying things about everyone! But I don't care.'

'You do not want to be with me.'

'That is literally all I want.'

'It's never going to happen.'

'Why not, though?'

'I don't need to give you a reason!'

'Tell me. Lena. Please.' His voice cracked.

She closed her eyes. She couldn't say it. She'd never be able to say it. She lifted his arm, and he didn't try to stop her. 'Check your Genealogy DNA account, Daniel,' she said, as she opened the door.

'What?'

'Just – login. Check it.'

She slammed the door as she left. She walked unsteadily to Borough High Street, ignoring the drunk men catcalling younger women (not her, not any more). She hated him. She hated herself. She didn't walk home – too drunk, too horrified to navigate. She sat on a night bus, her mind blank, her heart loud in her ears. She missed her stop.

She was back home, unlocking the front door, when the phone rang.

She could hear him breathing on the line, before he spoke. 'You're my fucking sister?'

The truth had caught up with her and it took her breath away, though she had been standing in its path, waiting for it to hit her, deadly as a train. She shut the front door behind her. She slid down to the floor and leaned against the door, the doormat prickling her thighs.

'How is that even possible? You're my *sister*? And you didn't tell me?'

'Half-sister.'

'Oh, fine, OK, that's cool then – what the *fuck*?'

'I was going to tell you. I sent you a message on Genealogy DNA—'

Thumps on the other end of the line. He was kicking a wall, or throwing things against it, his voice high and harsh. 'You're a fucking stalker! You're a – you fucking *psychopath*!'

'I'm not!' But maybe she was. Maybe that was fair. She made herself hear what he was saying, made herself feel it, because she deserved it, because she hated herself more than he possibly could.

'Who are you? Who even *are* you?'

She didn't have an answer to that. She hugged her knees.

'Who does that? Who comes on to their own fucking brother—' The smash of glass.

'I didn't come on to you! You came on to *me*!' A floorboard creaked, somewhere above her. She had to keep her voice down. People were asleep. Adam was asleep—

'You wanted me to! You're disgusting! I can't even—'

'I'm sorry. I'm so sorry—' Her voice didn't sound like hers.

'Stay away from me! Stay out of my life! Just fucking – just fucking disappear!'

He hung up. The hallway was tangerine in the sodium light. She couldn't bear the silence. She couldn't believe the stairs didn't give way beneath her, after what she had done.

The flat smelled of Adam. She was ready to tell him everything, to get it all over with in one terrible night, to get what she deserved. But she couldn't bring herself to wake him up. She sat down at the kitchen table. She felt as if she might float away, or dissolve. But she went on existing, having a bath, getting into bed as quietly as she could, falling asleep, dreaming about Daniel, waking up, sweating, from a nightmare into a nightmare.

'Lena?'

She opened her eyes. Adam. Lovely, familiar Adam, who wasn't biologically related to her in any way, who had never poured poppers down her throat.

'You're back!'

'Sorry. I didn't mean to wake you—'

'What time did you get home? It's nearly four.'

She began to cry.

'Hey.' He frowned and touched her cheek.

She shook her head and rolled over.

'What's wrong, Pony?'

'I'm pregnant.'

She turned to look at him. He was smiling, but then he stopped, because she wasn't. 'This is a good thing, Lena. I know we said we weren't going to do it. But it's actually a good thing.'

She shook her head again.

She watched his face change. Disbelief, anger, fear, confusion, disgust. 'Lena—'

'I can't do it.' She said it like it was a question, even though it wasn't. She needed him, now. She needed him to hold her and kiss her hair and tell her everything was going to be OK, the way he always did.

But he said, 'You have to do it.'

'No. I don't.'

'No, of course you don't – that's not what I meant—' He sat on the edge of the bed. 'We're married.' His voice was softer. 'We can do this, Pony.'

'I can't. I can't. I'm so sorry.'

He raised his arms and lowered them again, looking around as though appealing for help.

'I'm so, so sorry.'

'Please don't do this. Please don't do this to our baby—'

'It's not a baby yet, Adam, don't say that, don't make this harder than it already is—'

She could see him wrestling with himself, trying to

341

work out what to say, how to say it, how to change her mind.

She reached for his hand. She was desperate for him to absolve her. 'Please, Adam. I just can't be a mother.'

'You can!'

'I can't. I don't— I'd be no good. I'm no good—'

'Is it mine?' He said it quickly, like he didn't like the taste of the words in his mouth.

'Of course it's yours!'

'I'm not an idiot, Lena—'

'I'm not cheating on you, Adam! I love you!'

'Then why?' His eyes were wet. 'Don't do this, Lena. It's one thing, not trying for a baby, but getting *rid* of one—'

'It's my fucking body, Adam!'

'It's my fucking baby!'

'It's not a baby!'

'You're drunk, aren't you?' He was disgusted with her.

'I've had a drink—'

'What's going on?'

'Nothing.' She couldn't meet his eyes.

'You're being weird. Did something happen tonight?'

'What do you mean?'

'This has got something to do with him.'

'With who?'

His mouth twisted as he laughed.

'It has nothing to do with Daniel—'

'But you were with him tonight. Weren't you?'

She didn't move. She didn't want her body to betray her any more than it had already.

'Fucking hell. Did something happen?'

'What are you saying?' But her voice was too loud, and she had never been a good liar—

'Oh god!' His hands were in his hair. 'Something *did* happen!' He stood up. He opened the wardrobe.

'What are you doing?'

'You're the best person I've ever met,' he said, and she realized he was crying. 'The very best. The most fun. The funniest. But I can't do this any more.'

'Don't say that.' She grabbed his arm and rested her head against it, desperate to feel the warmth of him, desperate to stop him saying what he was about to say. She was broken, and awful, and the only good thing inside her was her love for him.

He snatched his arm away. 'Your own brother, Lena—'

'I'm never going to see him again. He knows now—'

'You said you'd already told him!' The hurt in his eyes. She had done this to him.

'I know I did—'

He turned back to the wardrobe and started throwing clothes, apparently at random, on to the bed.

Her heart was wild. 'I'm sorry—'

'You didn't tell him you were related to him till you'd *kissed* him—'

'He kissed *me*!'

'Why did he kiss you, Lena? Hey? Have you asked yourself that question? Have you considered, for a single moment, that you might be in some way responsible for the fucking mess of a situation you've got yourself in?'

'Donkey, please, don't be mean!' She said it in her baby animal voice. She thought he might soften.

'Of course you don't want kids. You're never going to grow up.' He was ramming the suitcase full of T-shirts, odd socks, a pair of goggles. He had never been good at packing.

343

'Those are my pants—' she said. And then she realized all the clothes were hers.

'You're the one with family in London,' Adam said.

She felt like he'd skinned her alive, but she deserved it. She deserved it. She wrestled the suitcase from him. She opened the chest of drawers violently, bras and socks spilling on to the floor.

'You're the one making this decision, Lena, not me, you're the one who doesn't want to be a family, so don't you dare make me out to be the bad guy. You're the one having an affair with your own fucking *brother*.' He was standing at the side of the bed, face red, as though he couldn't believe the words that had just come out of his mouth. 'I can't—' he was shaking his head. 'This is like something out of *EastEnders*.'

She wanted to apologize and take it all back and tell him they could have the baby after all, so that he would hug her again and be the gentle man he had always been. She had always been irritated by how gentle he was. What a fucking idiot. 'Donkey—' she said, but he was already slamming out of the room.

She zipped up her suitcase, which took a while, because her hands were shaking so badly. He stayed in the kitchen as she made her wobbly way out of the flat.

The Overground was shut: it was 5:01 a.m. She sat on the pavement, watching the sun stain the sky, until a tired-looking TFL employee unlocked the station.

On the way to her father's house, she stopped on a side street to cry into a hedge.

*

Her mother had always been the one to answer the front door. Lena felt her absence as she waited for her father to let her in. Her face crumpled when she saw him.

'Oh dear,' he said. He held the door open, and she was home.

A couple of hypocrites

On the other side of London, Alison was sitting on the fainting couch, listening for Suria's key in the lock. She was trying to be positive, for Suria. She was devastated, but she knew her grief was nothing compared to Suria's, so she kept quiet about it and tried to smile. She was learning to anticipate her wife's mood by the way she closed the door when she came in from work. If Suria slammed it and went straight to the bedroom, Alison took her a cup of tea, then went for a run to calm down, and spent the evening watching *EastEnders* on her own. If Suria closed the door quietly, that probably meant she'd spend the evening lying on the sofa, weeping while watching the news, which Alison had to admit was fair enough, because the world was falling apart, just like they were.

'The climate crisis!' Suria wailed, waving an arm in the direction of the television. 'Boris Johnson! No-deal Brexit! Kashmir!'

'There's nothing you can do about any of that.' The sun

was out, but the curtains were drawn. Alison pulled them open.

'Don't!' Suria shielded her eyes. 'Now there's a glare on the TV.'

Alison shut the curtains again.

'Maybe it's a good thing,' Suria said, 'that we can't bring a wean into this world.'

'Don't say that—'

'I can't do it again. No way am I putting my body through all that again. Even if we could get the money for the treatment. I'm done.'

Alison felt something heavy drop down inside her. They couldn't stop trying. They couldn't just – not be parents. 'You might feel differently in November,' she said. 'It'll be cold then. I can't even imagine feeling cold at the moment, can you?'

Suria shrugged, miserable.

Alison sat on the arm of the sofa. 'What's for ye'll no go by ye,' she said. She tried to keep the desperation out of her voice.

But Suria wouldn't look at her. 'I was sure this was for me. I was sure of it.'

'I'm still sure of it,' Alison said, but Suria was shaking her head. 'Hey.' Alison knelt in front of her wife, a supplicant. 'Don't give up.'

But Suria closed her eyes.

Suria spent the next two days in bed. Alison brought her breakfast on a tray, fixed the leaking kitchen tap and did three loads of laundry – she even hung it out to dry, rather than leaving it mouldering in the washing machine – but Suria was trapped inside the blackness of the loss and hardly

347

seemed to notice. On the third day, Alison stayed home from the studio and took Suria to see the GP. They sat in the waiting room between an elderly man with gauze over one eye and a woman with twin boys in a double buggy and two older girls, who were squabbling over a plastic walrus.

'Careful with that,' the woman said to the girls, rubbing her face over and over again, as though she was trying to feel it. 'You could take your sister's eye out with those tusks.'

Alison nudged Suria and said, 'Shall we ask if we can have one of her kids? Maybe one of the twins. They seem nice and placid.'

Suria looked at her, disgusted.

Alison composed a text. *Help. Am turning into Dad. I just made a joke about stealing someone else's children and now Suria hates me.* But she and Lena weren't speaking, so she deleted the words one by one until just *Help* was left on the screen, the cursor flashing. She wondered whether Lena would respond if she pressed send.

Suria emerged from her appointment with a prescription for fluoxetine and a handwritten list of books to borrow from the library.

'As if *The Power of Now* is going to do me any fucking good,' Suria said, as they walked up High Road Leytonstone towards the pharmacy. 'You know how I feel in this present moment? Like I want to throw myself under that bus—'

'Don't say that.' The dreadful, dropping feeling was back.

'I do, though. I do.'

Alison took her arm and held it tight. 'You don't have clinical depression, though?'

348

Suria laughed. 'They don't just give Prozac out to folk who are having a bit of a shit Wednesday.'

Alison didn't know why she was surprised. Suria's sadness had coated everything since the miscarriage, like the grease you can never get off the cooker hood.

At the pharmacy, Suria asked for a glass of water, so she could take her first pill straight away.

After one week on fluoxetine, Suria started showering again, voluntarily. Alison heard the running water and Suria humming 'Lady in Red' – her karaoke song of choice – and it felt like the first day of spring. When Suria went back to work, Alison started cycling to the studio again, to work on the colour art for the book about rocks and minerals. *Hope you can find a way to make it look dynamic and colourful!* the art director had written, in the illustration brief about metamorphic rocks. Life was almost back to the way it had been, before they had started trying, except that there was a gap where a child should have been. She felt the baby's absence like a physical presence, following her around, ghostly. She avoided the park on weekends, because whenever she saw a child tottering towards its mother, unstable on chubby legs, she had to hide behind a tree and take deep breaths. She tried to persuade herself she would be fine if she never became a parent. She and Suria would be free to lead selfish lives, to move to Paris and become the sort of elegant older lesbians that have enough disposable income to shop at Agnès B. Alison would have the brain space to write picture books as well as illustrating them, and Suria would train to be a cheese-monger, and they would read the papers over coffee every morning, and own some sort of spaniel—

'I love rocks and minerals.' Max was hovering behind her desk, holding a mug of coffee. He was wearing mustard dungarees.

'You wouldn't if you had to draw them.'

Max leaned over her desk and picked up a sketch of a lump of granite. 'Nice,' he said. 'Igneous rocks are my favourite.'

'I'm more of a sedimentary woman, myself.'

He smiled, and put his mug on her desk. He crouched down, his voice low. 'Listen. I've got some news: Gemma's pregnant.'

'That's wonderful!'

'I hope it's OK that I told you—'

'Of course it's OK! It's brilliant news! Amazing!'

'Anything might happen, still,' Max said. 'But she's four months now, so. Fingers crossed.'

'Fingers crossed!' She felt as though she'd had the guts scooped out of her, leaving her clean and ready to eat, like a melon.

That night, she found Suria in the kitchen, making Empire biscuits from scratch, whistling to herself. She seemed so much stronger now that she was on the drugs. Alison had a vision of a little girl next to her in a Mickey Mouse apron, sticking her finger in the icing.

'Can we have a chat?' Suria said.

Alison crossed her arms. 'OK, that sounds ominous.'

'No, it's not. It's not.' Suria sat down at the kitchen table, brushing icing sugar from her jeans, waiting. 'I've been thinking.'

'OK.'

'About the baby thing.'

Alison nodded.

'I've been thinking—'

'Yeah, you said that bit—'

'That we can't just give up on it, after everything we've been through.'

Alison laughed with relief. 'Oh my god, I'm so glad you feel like that.'

'Because I need to be a mother.'

'Exactly! And I need to be a parent—'

'But I can't get pregnant again, hen.'

Alison nodded again, slowly. She could sense, now, where this conversation was going.

'So I was thinking,' Suria said, 'that we should have another conversation about *you* starting treatment.'

But Alison could barely stand a hairdresser touching her head – she wouldn't be able to bear the injections and the midwives forcing their fingers inside her, never mind moving through the world as a pregnant woman, with breasts and a bump, the most womanly kind of woman – she wouldn't be able to stand it.

'Say something,' Suria said.

'I wish I could do it,' she said, at last, and she felt as though her heart might break.

Suria nodded. 'Then we can't have weans,' she said. She sounded so calm about it.

'Maybe we should think about adoption again—'

'No. It's too complicated.'

'But you only see the worst side of it. Most adoptions don't fail—'

'I don't want to adopt. OK?'

Alison dropped her head to her chest. Quietly, before she could stop herself, she said, 'You're *sure* you don't want to do another round?' A mistake, she knew, before she'd finished speaking. She braced for the impact.

'I can't believe you – you expect Lena to keep her baby, but you're not prepared to get pregnant yourself. You expect me to go through all the IVF shit again just so you can have a wean—'

'So we can both have one!'

'This isn't *The Handmaid's Tale*! If you want a baby, you can have treatment yourself—'

'You know I can't do that—'

'You could if you wanted to. We're in a two-womb relationship.'

'I'm not doing it. I'm sorry.'

'Well then!' Suria's shout echoed against the kitchen walls.

Alison covered her face with her hands.

Suria moved behind her and kissed the top of her head. 'We've rubbed along OK all these years just the two of us, haven't we? Hey?'

'Yeah, of course,' Alison said. But the future stretched out before her, terrifying, empty as a blank page, except the opposite of that, because a blank page suggested possibility. Empty as a vacuum, then. Empty as a grave.

Alison poured herself a glass of wine and carried it out into the garden. She sat on the bench, sipping it, and felt steadier. The neighbour's cat ran across the wall at the back of the garden, its bell tinkling. The tinkling made Alison think of Christmas and how shit it had been last year. This year they still wouldn't have a baby, and Tom was the only member of her family she was speaking to, and now that he was with Jessie, he would probably be spending Christmas Day in Trafalgar Square, shouting, 'There's no planet B!' at carol singers. Alison needed her sister.

She sent Lena a GIF: a cat with revoltingly large eyes, hugging the words *I miss you.*

Lena wrote back immediately: *I miss you too. I'm sorry for being such a dick.*

No, I'm sorry. Alison replied. Suria was right, of course she was. What had she been thinking, trying to talk Lena out of ending her pregnancy, when she couldn't face carrying a baby herself?

She was desperately sad. Desperate to be a parent. Desperate enough to force herself to consider, for a moment, what it might be like to go to clinic and go through the tests, and move through the world as a pregnant person. Why couldn't she bring herself to do it? She wouldn't be the first butch woman to have a baby. Her body would change, yes, but it wasn't as though she loved her body the way it was. She would hate being pregnant, almost certainly, but plenty of women hated being pregnant, and they went through it anyway. What made her so special?

The cat tinkled back across the wall, eyes flashing. The sun had set without Alison noticing and the trees were skeletal against the sky. Her phone buzzed, but it wasn't Lena – it was an email from her father.

Alison. Wankers at the cemetery have agreed – after much shouting and screaming and pleading (me) and grovelling and begging (also me) to let us install your mother's headstone. But apparently Jim doesn't have the qualification he needs to do the installation.

ABSOLUTE WASTE OF CUNTING SPACE. *Thinking of doing the qualification myself. Will look into it and keep you informed.*

Dad.

PS – Give your sister a call. All sorts going on but not my place to fill you in.

'Alison?' Lena's voice was higher than usual when she picked up.

'Lena? What is it?'

'Adam broke up with me.'

'Oh. Jesus.' The news was a jolt, a sort of bereavement. Adam had been irritatingly polite, hopelessly scared of their father, and unfailingly kind to Alison for nearly fifteen years. He was part of the family. 'What happened?'

'He didn't want me to get an abortion. Not just that. But it was my fault. I'm awful.' Lena was crying.

Alison's eyes filled with tears in response. All she wanted was to see her sister again. 'You're not. Don't say that.'

'Sorry,' Lena was saying. 'I haven't stopped crying, in, like, three days—'

'No, *I'm* sorry—'

'Let's not do this.'

'OK. OK.'

Silence, for a moment.

'Are you at home?'

'I'm staying with Dad.'

'Have you had your— Have you had the procedure yet?'

'It's on Tuesday.'

'Is anyone going with you?'

'Dad said he'd drive me—'

'Send me the address, OK? And the time. I'll meet you

there.' She was so glad there was something practical she could do. 'Only if you want me to, obviously—'

She could hear the smile in Lena's voice when she said, 'Of course I want you to.'

The clinic was in a run-down Georgian house, with red geraniums in the window boxes. The magazines in the waiting room were several years out of date. There was no expensive coffee machine.

'Are you sure you're OK, being here with me?' Lena asked.

Alison nodded. And she was. She was just sad. She felt heavy and slow with it, like she was wading through water.

'I know you think I'm making a mistake—'

'I don't. I was being a hypocrite.'

'And a bad feminist.'

'I'm really sorry.'

Lena took her hand. 'I'm sorry I was such a dick about Suria being an egg donor. I had zero right to judge you. I'm a terrible person.'

'Shut up, no you're not—'

'No, I am. I really am. You have no idea.'

They sat in silence for a moment.

And then Lena turned to face her. 'I wish I could tell you—'

'Is this about – is this stuff I've asked you not to talk about?'

'Sort of—'

'Then don't. You promised.'

Lena looked as young, as heartbroken, as the day they had both left for university. Back then, they'd never spent more than a few nights apart. And now they were almost strangers.

I could just let her tell me, Alison thought. Maybe I could fix this, if I let her tell me.

But then a doctor came out of a consulting room and smiled at Lena. 'Do you want to follow me?'

A slap in the chromosomes

Lena woke up at dawn and watched the light creep around the curtains and slide across the floor. *Unresting death, a whole day nearer now*, she thought. A line from a poem about ageing that her father was fond of reciting at birthday parties. Except death was already happening inside her, and she was still living. Rain was falling. She was pleased about that. She opened the window and lay back down on the pillow and let it spit on her, because she deserved it.

On the second night she had a shower, then brushed her teeth before changing her sanitary pad and putting her pyjamas back on. She didn't notice the bloody trail she'd left from the shower to the sink until the morning: scarlet circles, satisfying as gunshot wounds.

On the third morning, on the way to the kitchen for a glass of water, she heard raised voices.

'If you don't tell her, I will.'

'But she's vulnerable, Jessie—'

Lena pushed open the door. Jessie was sitting at the table,

eating porridge in a patterned kimono. Tom seemed very busy with the coffee machine.

Jessie patted a chair. 'Would you like some porridge?'

'Oh, no thanks, not very hungry.' She filled her glass at the kitchen tap. Her father turned away, clattering mugs.

'I've got some codeine, if you need any,' Jessie said. 'Codeine's the thing for the womb. I've had two abortions myself, so I know what I'm talking about.'

Tom looked at her.

'I told you about that.'

'You didn't.'

'Well. There you go. One when I was sixteen, one after I'd already had two kids and couldn't face another. Never regretted it.'

Back in her room, Lena wondered what Tom and Jessie had been arguing about. Then she decided to stop thinking about it, because her brain was already too full, and she didn't want it to overflow and ruin everything, like an oil spill.

Lena bled for a week. Then it was over. Almost as if it had never happened. Except that Adam hadn't called. On the Sunday, she walked to the corner shop with Jessie, to buy milk.

'You really never felt guilty?' Lena asked.

'I did. I still do.' Jessie stopped at the corner of Dyne Road, bending to smell a stubborn October rose. '*Abortions will not let you forget. / You remember the children you got that you did not get.* That's by Gwendolyn Brooks. Do you know her? Brilliant American poet. The first black person to win a Pulitzer.'

'I can see why you and my dad get on so well.'

'Except that he's barely read a single female poet.'

'True.'

Jessie offered Lena her arm. 'Just remember, my dear: guilt isn't the same as regret.'

That night, after her father tucked her in, and stroked her hair, and read to her from *The Wasteland*, the way he had when she was seven, she picked up her laptop and deleted her profile from Genealogy DNA. Then she removed her DNA from the other websites where it had been sitting for months in a great genetic ocean, a whistle and a light for attracting attention. She felt lighter, knowing her chromosomes were no longer out there for everyone to see, but she couldn't get rid of the shame. She slept solidly and when she woke up, she couldn't remember her dreams, and she was glad. Sometimes it was nice, not knowing things.

The shame propelled her to work and kept her at her desk from 9 a.m. till 9 p.m., only leaving for a lonely lunchtime sandwich. There was plenty to do, because a court date was looming, and James was pleased with her for once, smiling as he passed her office on the way home each day around seven. She was more grateful than ever for her predictable, stable career which paid a decent salary and provided her with free bottled water and mini-yoghurts and an air-conditioned room of her own that she never had to leave if she didn't want to. She was grateful for her family, too, just the three of them, a nice, manageable number of people to buy Christmas presents for. She ordered sushi for dinner every night because Adam hated sushi, and she ate at her desk, jumping whenever her phone rang. But her phone didn't ring, except when Ed and Abeo called to apologize for adding Adam to their Halloween party WhatsApp group. He didn't stay in it for long. *Adam left*, the notification said, pithy but accurate. It hurt, seeing it written down. He emailed two days later, asking if she'd like to buy him out of the flat.

'You sure you don't mind if I stay here a bit longer? Till Adam finds a new place?' she asked her father one Saturday morning, as he put on a load of laundry and complained about his back.

'Stay as long as you like! This is your home!' He breathed out heavily as he sat down. 'Anyway, I'd been hoping for a spinster daughter to turn up and be my amanuensis.'

She laughed, which seemed to please him.

'Are you out tonight?' he asked. 'I bought lamb chops at the farmers' market at the weekend. Thought I might char them into oblivion, serve them with an undressed salad.'

'Your signature dish.'

'Indeed.'

'Sounds lovely,' she said, and he nodded, like he was making a decision.

She went kickboxing with Alison as usual. She jabbed the punchbag and pretended she was punching herself. Izzy and Abeo had called several times in the weeks since everything had happened, asking if she wanted a drink, and why she wasn't returning their calls, and whether she was still alive, but Lena couldn't face seeing them or telling them about the disastrous night with Daniel. She didn't need to tell Alison – though she longed to – because as far as Alison was concerned, Daniel didn't exist.

'Suria sends her love, by the way,' Alison said after the class, as they queued up to order smoothies.

'She doesn't hate me?'

'Of course she doesn't hate you. She hates me a bit at the moment, though.'

Lena's smoothie was ready. She took a sip, wishing it were a milkshake.

'I did a bad thing,' Alison continued.

'I'm sure you didn't.'

'I did. She said if I want a baby, I'll have to carry it myself—'

'Fair enough—'

'And I sort of tried to persuade her to do another round of IVF, even though she doesn't want to.'

'OK, that is a bit bad.'

A woman walked past the window, chatting away to a baby in a sling. What did that feel like, that love? Lena didn't want to lose her sister to the other side of that divide. 'Don't have a baby,' she said. 'We could grow old and weird together. Like Big Edie and Little Edie. Or Muriel Spark and that woman she lived in Tuscany with—'

'Yeah, really appealing. A childless, sexless future.'

But Lena couldn't think of anything better than living with her sister for the rest of her life, going on driving holidays to Europe, staying in hotel rooms with twin beds and dying in adjoining rooms in an upmarket care home. 'It's an option,' she said. 'If you and Suria break up, you can move in with me—'

'We're not going to break up.'

'Then Suria's welcome to join us. We could start a commune, adopt a few chickens. Much lower maintenance than children.'

'Until they get murdered by foxes,' Alison said, paying for her smoothie and stepping into the street.

Lena knew something was up as soon as she walked into the kitchen. Her father looked uncharacteristically tidy. He was wearing a linen jacket she hadn't seen before. He appeared to have washed his shirt.

'That's nice,' she said, nodding to the jacket.

He pulled the jacket open, so she could admire the yellow lining. 'Bit snazzy, innit. I bought it from a shop on Lambs Conduit Street.'

'What brought that on?'

'Jessie told me I looked good in it.'

He had laid the table with the good china. Lena looked around, confused. 'Is – is Jessie joining us, then?'

'No, no!' He pulled out a chair for her to sit down. 'Can't I make a fuss of my eldest daughter every now and then?' His smile didn't reach his eyes.

Her skin prickled. 'Dad?' she said. 'What's going on?'

The conversation lasted less than a minute, but at the end of it she was a different person, with a new surname. A surname that would have been hers, if things had been different. But she would never have existed if things had been different.

Her father slid a piece of paper across the table, with her biological father's name, phone number and email address on it. Hugo Martin. She felt as though she had known his name all her life. 'He's a property developer,' her father said.

'Not a doctor?'

'Not a doctor. Sorry about that.'

362

Lena nodded, and felt her identity shift, adjust, deflate. 'Are you sure it's him this time?'

'Ninety-nine per cent sure.'

Tom stood up, to baste the lamb chops. 'I have a request to make of you,' he said to her, his back turned. 'I've done what you asked me to do. You know who he is now, so you can ask him about your medical history and all that bollocks.'

'Knowing my medical history isn't really bollocks, Dad—'

'I know. I know.' He turned to her, a spatula in his hand. 'I just – please don't go and meet him. Please? You don't need to meet him.'

She felt as though a hand was closing around her throat. 'You can't ask me not to.'

'But *I'm* your dad, Lena.' The lamb was spitting in the pan behind him. 'Doesn't that count for anything?'

'Don't guilt-trip me—'

'I'm not! I'm not!'

'You are!'

'I just don't think – you don't need him in your life. Do you? You don't need more than one grumpy old bastard commenting on your haircut—'

'That's for me to decide—'

'He's probably twenty years younger than me. He might be good at tennis.'

'So? You know I hate sport—'

'I don't want you to get hurt, Lena!' He flicked the spatula as he spoke. Grease spattered on to the floor. 'I've looked this guy up. You won't like what he stands for! You won't be able to un-meet him—'

'Stop it.' She pressed her hands to her face. 'You're just worried about getting hurt yourself.'

He turned away and leaned on the kitchen surface, and said, 'Touché,' and the last person she'd heard say that out loud was Daniel, and the smoke and the heat from the lamb and the intensity of the conversation were all too much, and she picked up the piece of paper and opened the kitchen door.

She sat on her bed and opened her laptop. She Googled *Hugo Martin* and waited for her future to change forever, for her past to change forever, too.

On the donor-conceived forums, people talked about feeling peace when they saw their biological father's face for the first time. They said they felt happier with their features, more comfortable in their own skin. Lena didn't feel any of that. Just a vague unease, and a huge sense of anti-climax. Of course it's you, she thought, when she saw him. But how eerie, to recognize a stranger, to see her features in a white-haired man's ruddy face: her cheekbones. Her teeth. Her sister's eyes. She sat back in her chair. Her face was reflected in her computer screen. She liked it a little bit less than she had that morning.

She called Izzy as she scrolled down the donor's LinkedIn page. 'His company built the flats in Nine Elms with the flammable cladding.'

'Sounds like he's loaded, at least,' Izzy said.

'That's not really the point—'

'Could be worse, is all I'm saying. He could be in prison. He could be a men's rights activist.'

Lena found Hugo Martin's Facebook page, which was private: but she could see his profile picture, and he'd decorated it with a Leave EU rosette.

'He's a Brexiteer!'

'Lots of people are Brexiteers,' Izzy said. 'What's his name again?'

Lena told her, and a moment later, Izzy said, 'Oh.'

'What?'

'Doesn't matter.'

'Tell me!'

'Well. There's an article about him in the *Guardian*. He's being sued for failing to build the contractually agreed number of affordable housing units in his developments.'

'Oh god.' Lena looked down at her body and she hated it; she was tainted.

'You don't inherit political opinions,' Izzy pointed out. 'You don't inherit dodgy business decisions.'

But it wasn't just that. She'd felt special, before, when she'd been Tom's daughter, the daughter of a writer, even if he wasn't a successful one. And although she had been devastated to discover she was donor conceived, there was something special about that, too, because it meant she was a designer baby in a way, a product of the very finest sperm, from a medical student – a 'man of science', the fertility doctor had told her parents. When her biological father had been a mystery, he could have been anyone. But he was an average-looking man, potentially a criminal, with problematic politics and bad taste in cufflinks. Which meant that she was average, too.

Tom knocked on her door half an hour later. 'You're disappointed,' he said.

'I thought he'd have green eyes,' she said, and she began to cry.

He bent down to hug her. 'I told you. Your granny had the most beautiful green eyes when she was younger, everyone said.'

But her granny had died when Lena was a baby, and her eyes had been so watery by then that you couldn't see the colour, and all of the photographs of her as a young woman were in black and white, and Lena had never really talked to her mother about her grandmother, because she'd been so convinced she took after Tom's family, and now it was too late. It had always been too late.

Tom let her go and straightened up. He stood in the doorway, hands on hips. 'Are you going to email him, then?'

She nodded.

'What are you going to say?'

She shrugged.

'I'm sorry,' he said. 'I'm sorry about all of this. I'm sorry about my stupid useless bloody sperm—'

His voice was wavering.

'Don't say that, Dad—'

'But I'm not sorry we used a donor, even if he is a total bastard. I'm not sorry you exist.'

She lay awake that night, questioning everything she had ever thought about herself. Until this dreadful year, she had believed she was a good person, but recent events had proved she wasn't. No wonder she was selfish, when her biological father was an unscrupulous property developer who, according to an online petition he'd signed, believed in privatising the NHS. She emailed him anyway, though, short and to the point. *I'm not looking for a father figure*, she wrote. *But I'd really appreciate knowing my medical history. And I would love to meet you and ask you a few questions, if that's something you'd be open to.*

*

Hugo's reply came two days later, as cold and official as an email from opposing counsel.

Dear Lena (if I may),

I always wondered if this day would come. Let me give you some information: when I was a young man, I had a friend from medical school, who told me about the sperm donation programme at the hospital where he worked. They advertised it as a way to 'make ends meet', and I was assured that I would always remain absolutely anonymous. I realize that things are very different now. I understand your curiosity in your biological origins. Let me assure you that there are no major medical issues in our family and I myself am in rude health. My father died at the respectable age of 89. My mother is still with us.

Since I became aware of your existence, I have thought long and hard about the situation and I have taken the views of my family, particularly my wife, into account. This email will be the first and last communication between us. I hope you can respect my privacy.

With best wishes for a long and happy life,
Hugo Martin

A slap in the chromosomes. She wished she could cut him out of her, but he was everywhere, in every cell of her body, and she wanted to float away.

In a way, the news affected her less than she'd thought it would. That first week, she barely thought about Hugo.

She barely looked in the mirror, either, because she didn't want to see him looking back at her. Jessie asked how she was feeling. Lena told her she didn't want to talk about it, and caught her exchanging looks with Tom over the apple crumble. She told Ed and Abeo about Hugo in a loud bar in Brixton, but she told it like a funny story, and they laughed, and she was annoyed with them for not taking it more seriously.

'Everyone's got a dodgy racist uncle,' Ed said.

'But he's not my uncle. He is my actual father.'

'My actual father believes that all homosexuals are going to hell,' Abeo pointed out.

The second week, she felt nothing at all – until Thursday, when she was preparing the trial bundle for the Jerwood Case, and it crashed over her without warning. She stood with her back to the door so no one would see her through the windows and felt tears rise from the well of disappointment that had sprung up where the mystery had been. Once they came, they didn't stop. She locked herself in the bathroom, her sense of self leaking out of her, salty.

She was back at her desk by the time her phone rang. Louder than it usually did. Vibrating more violently in her hand. A number she had deleted but couldn't forget: Daniel's.

She locked her office door. Her heart was beating in her ears. She answered the phone. This was his news, too, after all.

He didn't speak for a few moments. Then he said, 'Listen. I need to talk to you.'

'I need to talk to you, too.'

'I've found out who the sperm donor is.'

'So have I. Hugo Martin.'

'Yep. He's my dad.'

Lena didn't understand, at first. 'As in—'

'As in my actual dad, yeah, the one who brought me up.'

Her heart was beating in her mouth. She had been in the same room as her biological father, that night at the *Hamlet* cast party. She had looked right at him, and she had felt nothing.

She walked to the window. 'Your surname's Gold.'

'I changed it when I started acting. There was already someone called Daniel Martin with an Equity card. Listen, I asked my parents what the fuck was going on and why I have a half-sister I didn't know about. And Dad told me he used to be a sperm donor.'

She didn't know what to say.

'I just wanted to tell you.'

'Thank you—'

'Yeah. Well.'

'He doesn't want to meet me, though. He already told me.'

'I know. I told him to stop being a cunt. He's going to get in touch.'

A beat.

'Daniel,' she said, because she might never get the chance again. 'I'm sorry—'

The phone beeped twice, and he was gone.

London was still the same, gleaming in the sun.

Her desk was still there, still sticky with salad dressing.

And James still let himself into her office to say, 'Hey, Lena, I need to catch up with you before you go about the

369

Jerwood case. I'll be out of my meeting at about six thirty so don't shoot straight off.'

And she sounded the same when she said, 'Sure! No problem!' But when Alison called, she didn't pick up.

Masc as fuck

Alison imagined Lena sitting in her office, deciding not to answer her phone. Something was going on with her sister, she knew, and their father was in on it. Alison had dropped round unexpectedly for breakfast that Sunday and caught them arguing. They had put on a show of unity as she sat down at the kitchen table, Lena turning away to dry her eyes with the back of her sleeve, Tom talking too loudly about the undertakers who had agreed to install their mother's gravestone, but not until December, because they had to take care of their own clients first.

'We'll be able to visit your mum on Christmas Day! She'll love that!'

'I mean – she won't really, will she, Dad. Because she's dead.' Lena cracked an egg into a bowl, not looking up.

Tom had picked up the cafetière and waved it desperately. 'Coffee, Alison? Fresh beans! Just ground them!'

Alison left Lena a voicemail. 'It's me. I just wondered if you're around for a drink after work? Or a walk? Would

371

love a drink or a walk, if you're free. Or both! OK, I'll go away now. Bye. Bye.' She put her phone on her desk and tried to concentrate on a full-bleed illustration of the Grand Canyon. She added a tiny figure, arms raised, at the bottom of the valley, for scale: herself, in the future, alone. And then she sat back and thought, Oh god, my self-pity is seeping into my artwork. The art director probably wouldn't notice, though: it's hard to make rocks look sorry for themselves.

Max put a hand on her shoulder. 'Hey, mate. Fancy cheap noodles for lunch?'

'I'm always up for cheap noodles, yeah.'

Alison told Max about her argument with Suria as they edged their way past office workers and women with yoga mats queuing for toasted sandwiches and protein boxes. 'Literally no part of me wants to be pregnant. But I'm starting to think, fuck it, maybe I should do it anyway.'

They were passing a bookshop. Max stopped outside the window. 'Is that one of yours?' He was pointing at a fairy-tale search-and-find book she had illustrated.

'It is.'

'Seb's getting that for his birthday,' Max said, pushing the door open.

'He probably won't like it—' she said, but Max was already in the children's section, a copy of the book in his hand.

'Will you sign it?'

'You should probably pay for it, before I write in it.'

'They won't mind. You should tell them you did the pictures! They'll want you to sign all the copies.' He pulled a biro out of his rucksack and handed it to her. 'Sorry. You

372

were saying, maybe you should try getting pregnant, even though you don't want to.'

'It just feels wrong to me. It would be like expecting a man to carry a baby.' Alison opened the book and scribbled her signature on the title page.

'Men can carry babies,' Max said.

Alison looked at him for a moment. Then realization burst in her brain like a firework. Which is when a book-seller jogged up to her, alarmed. 'Sorry – are you writing in that book?'

'She's the illustrator,' Max said. 'She's signing copies.'

'Just one copy. He's going to buy it—'

'But she can sign the others too, if you like—'

The bookseller pulled a face. 'Let me go and check with the manager.'

They were alone again.

'So – did you—' She couldn't say it, just in case she'd got it wrong. She didn't want to offend him.

'Did I carry Seb?'

'Sorry—'

'Why are you sorry? Gemma didn't want to take time off work, and I was well up for getting pregnant. I reckon most people thought I'd just let myself go and had a massive beer belly.'

She didn't know what to say. 'Before you—?'

'After I transitioned. I stopped taking T. It messed with my head, not going to lie. The gender dysphoria was real. And obviously the language around it all is really gendered – the midwife at my antenatal class kept calling pregnant people "ladies". But it was worth it.'

Alison stared at him, then realized she was staring.

'What?'

'Nothing! That's amazing!' Her thoughts were racing and she crossed her arms over her chest as though she wanted to protect it from what he was telling her.

'If you want to do it, you shouldn't be put off by what other people think.'

'It's not what other people think,' she said. 'It's what I think of myself.'

He was watching her, frowning. 'Having a baby doesn't make you femme.'

'I know that.' Her voice was defensive.

'The way I see it, giving birth is masc as fuck – blood and guts and endurance. And let me tell you, anyone who can push another human being out of their body – or have a baby cut out of them, or whatever – is fucking powerful.'

But she wasn't as brave as him – was she? Would she be able to get over the horror of it, of something growing inside her for almost a year, of not being in control of her body, of risking death at the end of it all? Maybe. Because the look on his face, when he talked about Sebastian—

The bookseller was back. 'The manager says he'd rather you didn't sign the books if that's OK? Just because we can't return them to our wholesaler if they don't sell, if you've signed them—'

'That's fine! Of course! No problem!'

'Sorry about that—'

'Don't worry!' Alison's cheeks were hot with all kinds of shame. She pointed to the door. 'Max, I'll wait outside while you pay.'

The cheap noodle place was empty, apart from a group of teenagers making a TikTok video in a neighbouring booth.

While they waited for their pho, Max pulled a book out of a paper bag and slid it across the table. A graphic novel. The illustration on the front showed a short-haired woman in a checked shirt and baggy jeans: a masculine woman with a pregnant belly.

'*Pregnant Butch*,' she read. She felt less alone, just looking at it.

Max pointed to the subtitle: *Nine Long Months Spent in Drag*. 'That's basically how I felt.'

The waiter arrived with their soup.

'I can tell you which clinic I went to, if you're interested,' Max said, as Alison twisted noodles on to her chopsticks.

She nodded. She had put too much chilli in her pho. She reached for her water.

'Honestly, it's an exciting time to be alive. We're redefining what it means to be a family.'

Alison tried to feel excited. She felt terrified instead. But they were two sides of the same coin, weren't they, fuelled by adrenaline—

'Anything you want to ask, any time.'

'I do have a question, actually.'

'Go for it.'

'Where did you buy your maternity clothes?'

Max threw back his head and laughed. 'First of all we say pregnancy clothes, not maternity clothes, because I'm not a mother—'

'God.' Alison hid her face in her hands. 'I'm such an idiot. I'm so sorry—'

'It's fine.'

'It's not. I'm sorry.'

'Honestly, mate. You didn't mean it. I went heavy on the

tracksuit trousers. Also, workmen's clothes come in big sizes. Just FYI.'

Alison nodded, her cheeks still burning. 'I really am sorry—'

'Alison. Drop it.' He nudged her hand with his. 'We're all on a journey, aren't we?'

Alison's brain was buzzing as she walked down Mare Street into the grey October afternoon. She usually plugged into podcasts on the way home, but she didn't today. She listened to it all, the traffic, the shouts of teenagers, the sirens, and she kept going as she passed Bethnal Green station, because she wasn't ready to stop walking. Her body was pulsing with possibility. She felt as though she was expanding, but nobody was looking at her, not even when she laughed out loud at nothing. Nobody gave a shit. On a bush outside a house, spiderwebs were beaded with water droplets, like temporary pearls. Just nine months. She could do it, maybe, just for nine months.

'Does Suria know you're thinking about it?' Abeo asked, the following weekend, as they walked Oscar up Parliament Hill.

'Not yet. I want to be sure, before I say anything to her.'

'I think it'd be good for you, my love. People touching you all the time, not being able to stop your tits getting big. It would be like exposure therapy.'

'I'd hate to be pregnant,' Ed said, bending down to take Oscar off his lead.

'I wouldn't,' Abeo said. 'Sometimes I wish I had a womb.'

'You wouldn't be able to hack childbirth, babe,' Ed said, as Oscar bounded off through the long grass.

'Excuse me?' Abeo said.

'Have you ever been on a labour ward? I have. Shit and blood everywhere—'

Abeo pulled a face.

'Screaming and forceps and women being rushed to theatre for emergency abdominal births—'

'OK, enough, Ed,' Abeo said.

'No, no,' Alison said. 'It's good to be prepared.' They were at the top of the hill, now, London spread out before them like it was theirs for the taking, and Alison thought of all the people out there in the city giving birth at this very moment – hundreds of them, maybe thousands – and imagined what it would be like if she could hear them all, screaming and crying out and laughing with pain and delight.

That Sunday, Alison went to visit her mother's grave. As she walked from the Tube to Kensal Green, the sky darkened and rain started to fall. She bought two African violets, in pots, from the flower stall outside the cemetery gates.

'You've picked a right old day for it!' the flower seller said, counting out her change, a newspaper held over his head. 'Tell you what, though, the rain hasn't kept anyone away. It's like Piccadilly Circus in there!'

Alison picked her way across the grass to the quiet corner of the cemetery where her mother was buried. The wooden cross was leaning drunkenly to one side, the way her mother had at New Year parties. Alison put one of the violets on her mother's grave, and the other in the empty vase at the foot of Barry and Nigel's. Alison had googled them; she had found an article about their experimental theatre company and a photograph of them with their arms around each other. She liked to think of her mother and Barry and Nigel hanging out together in the afterlife.

'Not long now, Mum, till we get your actual headstone installed.' She felt silly, speaking out loud, but no one was listening. The rain stopped, and Alison had to remind herself it was unlikely that one dead person controlled the weather for the whole of London when all over the city, people were having conversations with friends and family who could no longer answer back.

She walked back through the cemetery, past families sitting on memorial benches in their Sunday best, or sweeping dry leaves from headstones. She read the words on the graves, blurred by age and acid rain, but still bearing testament:

Beloved mother
Much-loved sister
Brother
Husband
Father
Daughter
Son

She wondered what would be written on her grave, who she would be in relation to others when her time came, and she thought about the baby who never was, and the baby that could exist in the future, and she stood, silent, and sobbed.

She stopped at the flower stall again on the way out and bought the most expensive bunch of flowers they sold: red and white roses. She ran home from Leytonstone High

Road Overground to get rid of the adrenaline and put the flowers in a vase on the kitchen table.

Suria was home from work already, singing in the shower: 'Total Eclipse of the Heart'.

A wall of steam hit Alison as she opened the bathroom door.

'You're home!' Suria said, washing under her armpits.

Alison pulled back the shower screen and kissed Suria's cheek, and the water soaked her hair and her cheeks and her jacket, and she hated getting wet, usually, but she could deal with it.

'What's going on?' Suria asked.

'I've just been thinking.'

Suria turned off the shower. 'Thinking what?'

'Thinking, fuck it.'

Suria stood in the shower, dripping, hands on her hips. 'As in—'

'As in fuck it. I'll give it a go. I'll try and have a baby.'

'Fuck off.' Suria looked almost scared.

'I'm serious.'

'You're kidding on. You said—'

'I don't *want* to do it. But I *can* do it—'

'Are you sure? Are you *sure* sure?'

Alison nodded, even though she wasn't, because it wasn't the sort of thing you can really be sure about, is it? Suria screamed, then laughed, and stepped onto the bathmat, and hugged Alison chaotically, pulling her down to the floor. 'Thank you,' she said, and they were both crying, now, and Alison felt the future open up in front of them again, beautiful but terrifying, too, the way beautiful things often are.

The potato masher of fate

September had been like one long Sunday afternoon, sunshine and golden leaves and drinking tea with his daughter, but now it was October, and Lena had moved back to her flat. The house felt cold without her there, and the sky was overcast most days. Tom's mind felt cloudy, too, as he sat behind the issue desk, putting the finishing touches to the short story he was writing about being a father, the one he was writing in the first person. The words weren't flowing the way they had in the summer, though he had more time to write now; the freshers had realized they would never get around to finishing all the books on their reading lists, and the Extinction Rebellion protestors had been moved on from the quad. The library was peaceful, but Tom wasn't. He was furious – Hugo Martin, the bastard sperm donor, had emailed Lena, refusing to meet her. Tom had never been angrier, not when he had been made redundant from *Literary Review*, not when a UCL English student sold her first novel for six figures, not even when the doctors told him there was nothing they could do for Sheila. Nobody

380

had been to blame for that, no matter how much he wanted them to be. So many people were to blame for this. Hugo the bastard, of course, but also Dr Sandringham, and whoever had written the laws around donor conception, and himself, himself most of all.

He was doing his best to comfort Lena, but inviting her over for roast dinners and calling Hugo Martin a fucking scumbag didn't seem to be working. So he turned to Proust. '*We are healed of a suffering only by experiencing it to the full*,' he told her, one afternoon, passing her the horseradish sauce.

'Please don't be literary at me,' she said.

'Give me Hugo's email address. I'm going to write to him.' He was going to tell this bastard how lucky he was that wonderful, clever, fiery Lena wanted to meet him. He wanted to let him know just how much he was missing out on.

'Please don't,' she said. 'Just leave it. It'll make it worse.'

The phone rang. He answered. 'Alison! Hello, love! Oh yes, all fine here. Fine, fine, fine.'

He had just got home from buying croissants at the corner shop that Sunday when the doorbell rang. Lena was standing on the doorstep. 'He's changed his mind,' she said.

'Who?' he asked, though he could tell from her anxious smile.

'Hugo the scumbag.'

The bag of croissants hung limp in his hand.

Lena took them from him – 'You're not eating these, Dad, sorry' – and handed him her phone, so he could read the email for himself. *I am prepared to meet you, once, to give you some closure and to answer any questions you might have. I am often away on business, but if you are free on Friday 11 October, I will be in Gail's Bakery on Portobello Road at 5pm. My son Richard will be there, too.*

'Well!' he said, handing the phone back to her. 'He sounds like a right arsehole. Are you going to meet him?'

She nodded.

'I suppose you'll have some answers, at least.'

'Exactly. And – can I come round for dinner afterwards?'

'You don't have to do that—'

'I want to.'

'Well. That would be very nice.'

He rattled the radiator and whistled as he walked to the kitchen, so she'd know he was absolutely fine with the whole thing, not threatened in the slightest.

'Hey,' Jessie said that night, as he stared at the ceiling, his breathing shallow, imagining Lena meeting Hugo the scumbag, imagining the bastard hugging his daughter, imagining them clutching each other, weeping, the way fathers and daughters did on that *Long Lost Family* programme he watched when no one was around to judge him. Jessie touched his hand. 'She's just going to meet him once, for a coffee.'

'He *says* he just wants to meet her once. But he'll want to be in her life, when he realizes how brilliant she is—'

'You're getting yourself into a state.'

'I'm not!' He sat up and tried to breathe.

'What are you going to do while she's having coffee with him? To distract yourself?'

'I don't know. Drink myself into oblivion?'

'You could come to Trafalgar Square with me. There are going to be lots of writers reading their work at the Extinction Rebellion camp. Ali Smith's going to be there, and Simon Schama—'

'Bloody Simon Schama.'

'What's wrong with him?'

'He just gets on my tits.' He cleared his throat. 'It does sound interesting. I'll think about it.'

He felt out of breath that Friday morning just swivelling to the edge of the bed, sliding his feet into his slippers. He wondered how Lena was feeling, whether her heart was racing too, or whether he had just overdone it on the whisky the night before.

In the library, the Reader Services Assistants were discussing whether it was possible to make a pumpkin spice latte taste anything other than revolting.

'If you order a flat white and ask for just one pump of syrup, it doesn't taste that bad,' Priya said.

'But not as nice as an ordinary flat white,' Kwaku said.

Tom left work at 5 p.m., and as he walked down Gower Street he wondered whether she had met him yet, whether they had shaken hands, whether he had turned up to meet her at all. He carried his phone in his hand as he walked to the bus stop, sound on, in case she needed him.

He put his phone away when he reached Trafalgar Square. You never could tell how safe your belongings were, with activists. He met Jessie outside Waterstones and they crossed the street to the Extinction Rebellion camp, which was a thousand kinds of loud. He counted them down as he followed Jessie through the chaos of tents and police officers and bongo drums to the base of Nelson's Column, where the Writers Rebel event was taking place. Anything to distract him from his thoughts. Fifty drummers drumming. Twenty loudspeakers blaring. Thirteen singers singing: 'There's only one planet Earth.' Two police sirens wailing. One helicopter juddering overhead. The crowd was shifting and changing as people joined and others left. Everything was in motion, trees swaying, flags and banners fluttering (like his stomach), people dancing and twirling hula-hoops, one man canoeing in the fountain. Except the police, who stood as still as Nelson, outnumbered, disapproving, and the protestors chained to plywood plinths, as peaceful as the stone lions.

At the Writers Rebel tent, the crowd sat like well-behaved primary school children as A. L. Kennedy conducted them in a furious chant: 'Tell me lies about climate change.' Jessie huddled closer and raised her umbrella, because it was raining. The sky would have been dark, if it hadn't been for light pollution.

The readings paused as a protestor appeared at the side of the stage and said, 'We need some arrestables. Who's up for it?'

The cross-legged people looked shifty. A woman in an anorak whispered to her friend, 'I'd do it if I didn't have kids.'

'Anyone?'

'What are they asking for?' Tom asked Jessie.

'They need people who are willing to be arrested. Tempted?'

'Got to get home and put the sausages on for Lena, but maybe next time.' He checked his watch. Almost six thirty. 'I should probably get going now, actually.'

Jessie nodded and picked up her rucksack.

'You stay here!' he told her.

'You sure?'

'Yes. You have fun, listening to Simon bloody Schama. Give me a ring when you're back.'

He waved as he backed away towards a group of protestors, dressed all in red, performing a silent masque at the centre of the square.

He was on the Tube at Charing Cross by the time he realized something was wrong. He was dizzy, exhausted, his chest was tight. He wasn't sure he'd have the strength to get off at Kilburn Park. He'd have to find the strength though, because he had a whole meal to cook before Lena turned up. He put an arm out to steady himself as he left the station. His phone started to ring.

'Lena!'

'Dad!'

'Are we still on for dinner?'

'Of course! How was he? What's he like?'

'Bit of a twat. I'll tell you more when I get there.'

Tom smiled, which turned out to be a bad idea. The pain was spreading to his jaw. 'Jesus,' he said, before he could stop himself.

'What?'

'Nothing. I've just pulled a muscle or something.'

'Where?'

'My neck. I don't know why it hurts so much.' He rubbed his neck and the pain released him, as though he'd loosened a noose.

'Dad.'

'I'm fine.' His neck twanged again. 'Fuck. Jesus. This is agony—'

'You sure you're OK?'

'I'm fine. I need to stop going to climate change protests, I'm too old—'

A pause. 'We can cancel if you like—'

'No, no. Bring a bottle, if you want wine.'

'OK. See you in, like, half an hour.'

'Before you go – can you remember which recipe your mum used to use, for mash? Was it Delia?'

'You don't need a recipe for mash, Dad.'

'I'm sure there was one. Delia, or Nigella, or one of them.'

'Just google it,' she said. 'Mash it for longer than you want to. And don't put too much butter in it.'

The mash was the final straw. He stood over the pan, pushing down on the King Edwards, swearing under his breath, and the pain came back again, as though he was the one being crushed, by the great potato masher of fate. He stopped and leaned against the kitchen counter, and the pain in his chest eased again, and it finally occurred to him that he might be having a heart attack. But he didn't have time for a heart attack, not when his daughter was due any minute, and he still hadn't put the sausages in the oven. He pricked their skins and slid them on to a baking tray, and he knew he'd regret not lining it with foil first, but he really didn't have the energy, not when opening the oven had caused him to break out in a sweat.

He needed a sit-down, so he dragged himself to the living room. The sofa was further away than it had been the day before. He just needed to relax, take his mind off things. He opened *The Times* and started the cryptic crossword. He was pondering five down (*Forgiveness for a second-rate answer (10)*) when the pain came back, coursing down his arm. He was an idiot. He was definitely having a heart attack. And now it was too late. It was too late, because he no longer had control over his body, and he tried to stand up and walk to the phone, but his legs weren't his legs any more and the carpet came up and smacked him in the face, and his back arched, and his hands were curling into fists against his will, and this was it, it was all ending with a whimper.

His life didn't flash before his eyes. Instead, his spiteful subconscious served him visions of what he could have done with his time on Earth, if he'd just made more of an effort. There he was, playing Woodstock '79, women screaming and weeping and calling his name. There he was at the launch of the novel he'd never got around to writing. He saw himself in a gown, at his MA graduation, giving a speech at his twenty-fifth wedding anniversary party. He'd always refused to celebrate wedding anniversaries; being married was embarrassingly conventional. 'Marriage is a wonderful institution. But who wants to live in an institution?' he'd always said, when friends announced their engagements. All his best lines had been somebody else's first. No one but his daughters and Jessie and a couple of colleagues from the library would even remember him. His daughters would be furious, because he never had written that bloody will, and they wouldn't even be orphans, because Hugo was waiting in the wings. The only slight consolation was that Lena was coming for dinner, so at least he wouldn't lie there until the police broke the door down because the smell had got too much for the neighbours.

As his eyes started to close, he saw faces: his daughters first, Lena, with her intense green eyes, and Alison, wiry and dark-haired like he had been, before the colour had drained out of him along with his youth, then Sheila, then Jessie, and he wasn't going to get to say goodbye to any of them, because he was dying right here, right now, on the living-room carpet, which could do with a Hoover, he realized, now that he was writhing on it. The last thing he remembered was the bell that started to ring somewhere in the distance, over and over again. It's tolling for me, he thought, and then, in a final flash of consciousness he realized it was the alarm on his phone, telling him to turn the sausages. They're going to burn, he thought. My daughter will be hungry. And then he stopped thinking altogether.

Staying alive

Most people don't have to worry about their appearance, when they meet their biological father for the first time. They go for the natural look, smeared in blood and bodily fluids. Lena wanted to look intelligent and respectable, beautiful and approachable. Neutral, above all. She dressed in jeans and a white T-shirt. A blank slate. She didn't want to say anything or be anything that might push him further away.

She watched YouTube videos of people meeting their long-lost parents to work out how to behave. She found footage of a 32-year-old woman running up to her father, hugging him, both of them sobbing, while their partners stood around, awkward, filming the encounter on their iPhones. But the 32-year-old woman wasn't donor conceived. It wasn't socially acceptable to care that much, if you were donor conceived. The meetings between donors and their offspring were much more casual. Older men and younger women meeting at airports, shaking hands, making small talk about their journeys. A teenager sitting

389

between her mother and her biological father for the first time, saying, 'This is blowing my mind. This is blowing my mind,' over and over again. Groups of three, ten, forty-three, fifty-six half-siblings meeting up, comparing the size of their hands, laughing at how similarly they laughed. She found herself down a sperm-donation YouTube rabbit hole. She watched an American sperm donor saying, 'There are thirty-five kids so far. I hope that'll be it. It's just not possible to care about that many people. I donated about four hundred times, though, so I guess there might be more of them out there—' and a British man on the *Victoria Derbyshire* show, talking about how he donated sperm at motorway service stations. 'I do my business in a toilet stall, I pass it straight to her, and she goes into the Ladies and squirts it up there. I reckon I've got about eight hundred kids at this point. I'm hoping to break the world record and hit a thousand in a couple of months. Buying sperm is expensive, and I give it away free. I'm just helping people out.'

Abeo called as she was putting on her make-up, to ask how she was feeling. 'I could come with you,' he said. 'In case he turns out to be a murderer.'

But Lena didn't want a witness. She already felt exposed. 'Thank you, though.' She had too much blusher on. She wiped it off with a tissue.

She turned down Portobello Road and dodged the crowds of tourists admiring second-hand teapots and brass door-knobs. She was stopped by a woman wanting to find the blue door from *Notting Hill*, and a man with two children looking for Gruber's Antiques from *Paddington*. She did her best to help them with directions, and said, 'Have a lovely day!' They didn't know that for her it was a red-letter day. She felt sick as she approached the café, so sick she thought she might actually vomit from nerves, which she had thought only happened in films and novels, but here she was, clutching her stomach, and she resolved to give writers the benefit of the doubt more often. What would Hugo and Richard think of her? And what had Daniel told them? Not the whole story, presumably, or they wouldn't have agreed to meet . . .

Gail's was fairly empty but she could see two men at the back, heads close together, talking.

The door tinkled as it opened.

The men at the back table looked up.

'Hello,' she said.

The three of them stood there, at the back of the coffee shop, staring at each other. Lena could sense the baristas behind the espresso machine, drying coffee cups, watching them, wondering.

'You have the same eyes as Daniel,' Richard said, smiling Lena's smile back at her.

Hugo made a sort of harrumphing noise, as though he wanted to disagree but couldn't. He was even more red-faced than he had been at the *Hamlet* cast party. She could tell he couldn't bring himself to look her in the eye.

She had assumed she would feel a connection as soon as she met them, because of Daniel. Thank god she didn't. This time, there was just an overwhelming feeling of strangeness.

'Hi.' Hugo held out his hand and shook hers, and then – as though he couldn't help himself – he went in for a hug. The hug felt better than the handshake because she didn't have to look at his face.

Lena pulled out a chair and sat down, folding her hands on the table the way she did in meetings when she wanted to look more confident than she felt.

'This is so weird,' Richard said, in Daniel's voice.

Lena laughed, pleased someone had said it out loud. 'So weird.' She turned to Hugo. 'Thank you for meeting me.'

'Sorry about that first email,' Hugo said. He adjusted his shirt sleeves. 'I was just—' he shrugged.

They stared at each other for a moment. 'Shall I get us all a coffee?' Lena asked. She wanted to do something ordinary.

'I'll get them,' Hugo said, standing up. He was wearing an expensive watch.

'Thanks, Dad,' Richard said. 'Could I have a flat white?'

'Me too, please,' Lena said, and Richard smiled at her, as though they had something in common already. 'My DNA test said I was genetically predisposed to drink more caffeine than most people,' she told him.

Things were easier, now it was just Lena and Richard. He was Daniel diluted. Shorter hair. Duller clothes. Paler eyes. A kinder smile.

'We have the same sticky-out tooth,' he pointed out.

'Has Daniel said anything about me?' she asked.

He frowned. 'He just said you'd met. Why?'

'Nothing. No reason.' She laughed, she was so relieved.

And her new brother laughed, too, as though he got the joke.

Hugo was back. He put the coffees on the table. 'So,' he said. 'Where do we start?'

They started at the beginning. Hugo had told her the story already, about needing money and the friend who went to medical school and the promises the doctors had made him, but he told her again – and this time he was appealing to her, asking her to understand. She told him the story of how she'd discovered she was donor conceived, how she'd found Daniel through Genealogy DNA. She skipped the next bit. 'And then my dad helped me, with research.'

'Your other dad,' Richard said. 'So weird!'

Hugo coughed, frowning, then turned to Lena and asked, 'So, what is it you do?'

'I'm a solicitor.'

Hugo nodded when she said that, as though he was proud of her, as though he'd had anything to do with it. She understood why Daniel didn't like him. She didn't like him either, objectively, but an electric current was running through her, because this was happening, this was him, the man who had given her 50 per cent of her DNA. Hugo took out his phone and flicked through family photographs. His grandparents, at home in the South of France, fuzzy, black and white. His parents on a farm in Surrey. She had his mother's cheeks. 'I know they're not very interesting,' he said. But they were interesting. No photographs had ever been more interesting. She was feeling things, but she wasn't sure what. Her brain had never felt so small, so inadequate.

She showed Hugo and Richard photos of her family, too. Her father at home, waiting for someone to cook him dinner. Her mother, before she got ill, at the Notting Hill Carnival, dancing the samba. Photos of her fifth birthday party, blowing out candles with Alison. She felt guilty for showing them pictures of her sister, because Alison wanted to pretend they didn't exist.

Richard took the phone from her to look more closely

at a photo of Alison at a gallery opening. He shook his head. 'So I've got two sisters. Wow.'

Hugo shifted, uncomfortable with the intimacy of the word. 'Alison does something arty, does she?'

'Yes, she's an illustrator,' Lena told him, but she was smiling at Richard. Her heart let him in; he'd opened it when he called her his sister.

Clouds were gathering, but the unusual family at the back of the coffee shop didn't notice. Two of the baristas left and the third locked the front door and closed the cash register. When they didn't take the hint, the barista asked them to leave.

'I've got to get back, anyway,' Hugo said, smiling at Lena sadly – or maybe she was imagining that. He stood up, his arms slightly out from his body, as though he wanted to hug her again. She opened her arms and he patted her on the back.

'I'm glad we did this,' he said.

She looked at him, and told herself to remember what it was like to look at him, because this might be the last time. She wanted to ask if it definitely was the last time, but she didn't want to hear the answer. He hugged his son, too, and left, and Lena wanted to laugh as she watched him leave, because it was so strange, so strange and so terrible.

'Are you in a hurry?' Richard asked, once his (her, their) father had left. 'I told Daniel I'd meet him for a pint.'

'I can't,' she said, too quickly, shame rushing to her cheeks. 'Sorry, I'd love to, I've just – I've got to be some-where.' She waved her phone, vaguely, then checked her messages. Texts from Izzy, Abeo, Ed and Karla, checking in. And one from her dad. *What's he like? What time will you get here? I'm making sausages.*

'Another time,' Richard said, smiling at his knees, a little bashful. She felt like she'd known him for years. She wished and wished she had.

Lena felt lightheaded as she walked down Portobello Road, but other than that, her body didn't seem to recognize what had just happened. She called her father, because she knew he'd be anxious, but she was too jittery to really take in what he was saying to her – something about his neck – and she checked Citymapper even though she already knew the way to the Tube. As she jogged down the steps she wondered how many of the other commuters had experienced life-changing events that day, deaths or births or engagements or redundancies, and she felt connected to all of them, and perhaps she was, because she probably had other half-siblings out there, and she missed them, though she'd never met them.

Her father took even longer than usual to answer the door, so Lena called his landline. She could hear it ringing, muffled, from various rooms in the house, and another noise – a smoke alarm, maybe? – bleating and insistent. Something was wrong. She bent down and shouted through the letterbox. 'Dad?'

No answer.

She knocked on the living-room window. Through the grimy glass, she could see something on the floor behind the coffee table, out of place. A shoe.

Panicking, she felt her pockets, but she had left her key behind when she had moved out – but then she realized

Jessie would have one, and she was running up number 12's front path, and ringing the bell, but there was no answer—

She dialled Jessie's number. 'Are you home? Dad's not answering the door, and the smoke alarm's going. I'm a bit worried—'

'Oh, fuck. No, I'm just on my way – but try number 16 in the meantime—'

Gladstone Vernon – Mr Vernon – opened the door to number 16, slowly, in a caramel-coloured cardigan and brown flares. The little hair he had left was turning white.

'You'll have to come in and have a look,' he said, when she asked him for a key. He shuffled slowly down the stairs ahead of her, painfully slow. It took everything not to push him out of the way. 'How you been keeping?' he asked, as he reached the landing. 'You still working, lawyering and whatnot?'

The air in the house was sweet and thick. A clock ticked on the kitchen wall, too fast.

He nodded to the drawers next to the sink. 'The keys are all in there. Do you want a biscuit while you're here?'

'No, but thanks,' she said, as she opened the drawer. There were hundreds of keys, keys on loops of ribbons, keys to padlocks and safes and long-rusted Volvos—

'I've got custard creams,' Mr Vernon said, flicking on the kettle.

'I don't really have time for a biscuit – Dad's not answering the door, and I think something might have happened to him, so—' Yale keys and Chubb keys and tin openers and flyers for Chinese takeaways—

Mr Vernon made an understanding noise. 'Oh dear. That happened with me mum. No answer on the phone for a couple of days. The neighbour found her on the bathroom floor. Blue, she was. But I'm sure your dad'll be OK. I've got bourbons, if you prefer those?'

'Really, I'm fine—' a key ring made from shells, *A present from Cyprus*—

'Or— what are them biscuits called, the chewy ones? With the currants? It'll come to me.'

The kettle was rumbling.

And then, thank god, three keys on her mother's old work lanyard. 'Got them. Thank you so much—'

'You know the ones. They come in a big sheet, and you pull them apart—'

'Garibaldis,' Lena said, as she ran up the stairs. 'Thank you! Sorry! Bye!'

The front hall of her father's house smelled of charred pork. The smoke alarm was screaming. Radio 4 was burbling up the stairs – 'Welcome to *Any Questions*, which comes to you this week from Christchurch College, Oxford' – and, in the living room, a newspaper was open on the sofa. There was a cup of tea on the coffee table, half-full. Half-empty, actually, considering the circumstances.

He was spreadeagled on the carpet.

'Dad!'

Nothing.

She couldn't touch him, because her mother had felt like an empty glove, so shockingly cold that Lena had jerked her hand away as though she'd been burned. She put her hand on the doorframe to steady herself, because without her father in the world any more, she felt she might dissolve. He had taught her to read and let her stay up and watch late-night sitcoms when her mother was out, and if she fell asleep on the sofa he would stroke her hair and carry her back to bed. 'Don't go,' she'd say, and he would sing, 'Stay' by Frankie Valli & the Four Seasons and kiss her on the forehead.

There was a voice behind her in the hall. 'Jesus, where's that smoke coming from?' Jessie. 'Tom? Tom?' She edged past Lena into the room. 'Can you hear me?' She knelt down beside him. 'He's moving—'

Lena heard herself saying, 'Oh god,' again and again.

Jessie looked up at her. 'Lena, go and see what's burning. Go on.'

Lena followed the smoke to the kitchen, glad there was a real adult in charge. She turned off the oven. The sausages were black on one side, pale on the other. She threw them in the bin.

She ran back upstairs to the living room. Jessie was on the phone now, still crouched at Tom's side. 'Yes, hello, yes, we need an ambulance. I think my partner is having a heart attack.' She nodded, then held the phone away from her face and said, 'We're meant to do CPR.'

Lena tried to remember what she'd learned at the three-day first-aid course she'd attended in 2015. 'I can only remember how to do it on babies,' she said. 'Fuck. Why can I only remember how to do it on babies?' She googled *how to do CPR*, but her phone autocompleted the sentence to *how to do CPR on a dog*. 'For fuck's sake,' she said, and threw her phone on the sofa. The buttons on her father's shirt were too fiddly, or maybe it was her hands that were too unsteady, so she tore the shirt, and his chest hair was white, which shouldn't have been a surprise, but it hadn't been, the last time she'd seen it, on a camping holiday to Germany in 1992.

Jessie was still on the phone. 'He says place your palm

on the breastbone and put your other hand on top and press down with your body weight, 120 times a minute. To the rhythm of "Stayin' Alive".'

Lena remembered doing this on the dummy in the meeting room, only the dummy had been smooth and soft and cold and it had never kissed her knee when she'd grazed it, or carried her to school on its shoulders. 'What about the kiss of life? Do I have to do the kiss of life?'

'He says no,' Jessie said. 'The ambulance is on the way, they're coming.' She hung up. She looked completely lost. 'Do you want me to sing the song? To help you keep time?'

Lena shook her head. 'Dad hates the Bee Gees.'

Lena did CPR as vigorously as she could, but it was exhausting. She couldn't help slowing down, so Jessie took over, and Lena stood up, catching her breath, looking down on them – her father, unconscious; Jessie, pressing down on his chest, muttering the song lyrics – two lovers, locked in a kind of disco pietà. She couldn't stay in the room. She walked out into the hall and tripped on the Turkish rug, on the rip she'd made as a child, playing tag with her sister. She had to make sure Alison got there in time, but Alison wasn't answering the phone.

'That fucking alarm,' Jessie called from the living room. 'Turn it off, Lena, would you?'

Lena fetched a broom from the kitchen and prodded the smoke alarm into submission. Then she stood there in hallway, listening to the thrum of the boiler and the babble of the radio and the barking of a dog in a neighbouring garden and the awful, rhythmic wheezing and crunching coming from the living room, until the doorbell rang.

The paramedics tramped past her into the living room, and she could hear them discussing whether to work on him there, or whether to transfer him to hospital. They decided to stay.

'Wait, is that because you think he's dying? Or because he's going to be OK?'

They didn't say. Lena watched them work, vaguely aware of Jessie's hand on her shoulder as they injected something into her father's arm and attached the stickers of the defibrillator to his chest, calmly, matter-of-factly, like it was something that happened every day. Which, of course, it was. You don't understand, she wanted to say, he's different, he's not an old man, he isn't ready to die. He wears Doc Martens and leather trousers and earrings, and at university he founded a society called Men Supporting Feminists, and he met my mum at a squat party in the Eighties. He fancies Judi Dench, and he's had several short stories published in literary journals, and he works in a library, and he sometimes gets in trouble for whistling too loudly at the issue desk. I've already lost my mum, she wanted to say. I spent today with a stranger instead of him, and I didn't get the chance to tell him that he's my real dad, that he always will be. You have to save him, please, you have to save my daddy—

'Tom?'

Her father groaned and tried to take off his oxygen mask. Lena's heart sped up, now that she knew his was beating.

'It's all right, Tom,' one of the paramedics said, moving his hand away from the mask. 'Leave that there for now, OK? You're at home, you've had a heart attack, we're taking you to the hospital.'

Lena was surprised how light he seemed, as they lifted him on to a stretcher.

'Your daughter's here,' they told him as they wheeled

400

him out, and he touched her hand, and he was shaking, but then the paramedics manoeuvred him into the hallway, knocking the stretcher's wheels on the skirting board, and he was out of reach.

She and Jessie followed them out into the street. Mr Vernon was watching through his curtains as they loaded Tom into the ambulance.

'We're taking him to the Royal Free, so you can follow us there.'

The paramedics slammed the ambulance door, which made Lena realize the front door to the house was still open. She went to shut it. Then she tried Alison's number again. No answer.

'I can't get hold of my sister,' she said to Jessie.

Jessie said, 'Come here,' and hugged her, and that's when she started to cry.

Basically Jesus

Alison didn't pick up because she was gripping the edges of a hospital bed, trying not to scream out loud as the nurse pumped dye through her fallopian tubes to check they were working properly. She felt like someone was stabbing the very essence of her, and she couldn't stop herself saying, 'Oh my god. Oh my god,' over and over again, as the nurse smiled at her, apologetic, and Suria stroked her hand.

'I know,' said the nurse. 'It feels like a bad period. You're doing very well.'

But Alison had never experienced a period, or anything else, as painful as this – she could barely see or think and she couldn't take it any more— 'Could you stop? Please?'

'Done,' the nurse said. 'Your fallopian tubes are working perfectly, so that's good news, isn't it? Just lie there for now. You'll probably feel dizzy for a while.'

Alison opened her eyes, her body still shaking with the shock of the pain. But it was over. She could do this.

They were at an NHS hospital this time, though they

402

were paying for the treatment themselves. Alison felt more comfortable now that they waited in rooms with faded carpets and municipal plastic chairs, the only reading material a sticky copy of *The Watchtower*. She still felt a little unsteady on her feet as she and Suria made their way out of the hospital into the street. She checked her phone as they walked towards Upper Holloway Overground. Eleven missed calls from Lena, and two from Jessie.

She stood outside Sainsbury's to call Lena back and waved to Suria to stop walking. The line was bad. 'Lena? Sorry, can you say that again?' A red Mini Cooper pulled up as Lena told her the news – she particularly remembered that it was a red Mini Cooper, because it was such a cheerful car, and what Lena was saying was so terrible. She could only make out the words, 'Dad' and 'hospital' and 'heart attack', but they were enough.

Outside the Royal Free, patients in gowns and slippers smoked cigarettes, leaning on their drip stands. Alison half expected to see their father among them. 'Why did they have to take him to the Royal Free?' she said, as they walked through the doors.

'See just because it's the same hospital?' Suria said, holding her hand. 'Doesn't mean the same thing will happen.'

They sanitized their hands and walked towards the lifts, past the café where she had sat with her father and sister after her mother's death, three of them at a table for four, drinking cappuccinos. She remembered the way her dad had stared into his coffee, muttering, 'I don't know what I'm going to do without her. I don't know what I'm going to do.'

'Can I help you?' A nurse wearing a lot of eyeliner approached them as they walked on to the cardiac ward.

'Yeah, I'm looking for my dad, Tom Delancey,' she said, and the tears were right there, and she couldn't speak any more.

Suria took charge. 'They're opening his artery, he had a heart attack—'

'Right, of course. They're operating on him now, so if you'd just like to take a seat—' The nurse showed them to a windowless corridor, lined with moulded plastic chairs.

Lena and Jessie were already there. Jessie stood as Alison approached, and hugged her – a warm, woolly, perfumed hug. 'I'm so sorry.'

'Nothing's happened yet,' Lena said, her voice sharp.

'I'll go and get you guys some food,' Suria said.

'I'll come with you,' said Jessie.

Alison and Lena sat side by side in silence. A couple of seats away, two women about their age were eating samosas, paper napkins spread on their laps. Sisters too, perhaps. Or wives, maybe. Across from them, an old man sat dozing, his chin jerking up from his chest every now and then. Everyone seemed determined to avoid eye contact. Just like in the fertility clinic waiting room, where couples sat in corners, whispering about IVF cycles as though they were at a pub quiz and didn't want anyone to overhear their answers.

'Hello.' A doctor with a ponytail was smiling down at them, sympathetically. She was wearing pearlescent clogs, which looked a lot more cheerful than she did. 'I'm Doctor Barker. Are you Tom's family?'

Lena stood up. 'What is it? Is he OK?'

The doctor beckoned them further down the corridor, away from the anxious eyes of the other waiting relatives. 'Can I just check what you know already?'

'He had a heart attack,' Alison said. 'They were going to operate—'

'Is he dead?' Lena asked, voice unsteady.

'Your father had what we call an acute myocardial infarction, which is a heart attack, exactly. The cardiac team here operated to insert a balloon into the blocked artery, but the heart muscle was already very damaged, and he had another heart attack while they were operating—'

Lena was covering her mouth with her hand and shaking her head, like people do on daytime television. React, Alison told herself. Stop thinking about daytime television when you know what the doctor is going to tell you—

'I'm so sorry.' Dr Barker looked down at her ridiculous clogs, and Lena cried out, and Alison felt like she was falling— 'I'm afraid Mr Smith died today.'

Alison looked up. 'Mr Smith?'

A beat.

'You're Mr Smith's daughters,' the doctor said. 'You're—'

But the nurse they'd met earlier was running towards them, shaking her head, pointing to the two women still waiting on the moulded plastic chairs, paper napkins on their laps.

'Oh, no,' Dr Barker said. 'No, no.' Her hands were in fists.

'He's not dead?' Alison asked. 'Tom Delancey?' Best to be clear about these things.

'He's not dead,' Dr Barker said.

405

'Fucking hell—'

'I'm so sorry. I'm so, so sorry – it's been crazy in here tonight, and there were two Toms with two daughters admitted at the same time. I can't apologize enough.'

She offered them a leaflet about how to complain, but Alison didn't like living in the past, and she just wanted to see her infuriating, non-dead dad, and the nurse was leading them back to the land of the living, and there he was, looking smaller and paler than usual, sitting up in bed, saying, 'That wasn't nice.'

They tried to hug him, but he batted them away, like wasps from a sandwich. 'All right, all right,' he said. 'Save it for when I've actually popped my clogs.'

The nurse asked Alison and Lena to leave after half an hour. Suria met them on Pond Street, with cardboard bowls of ramen steaming in a paper bag.

'Where's Jessie?' Lena asked.

'She's gone to your dad's house, to get him some clothes and that.'

They sat on a low brick wall and started to eat. 'Jesus,' Suria said, when they told her what had happened.

'He basically is Jesus. This is basically Easter Day,' Alison said.

Lena twisted noodles on to her chopsticks. 'The look on the nurse's face when she realized. She was so horrified Dad wasn't dead.'

They laughed so hard that Lena spilled soup on her legs. Alison helped her mop it up. The paper napkin made her think of the other family, the two women with their samosas, the pity on their faces, before the blow landed on them.

Lena must have been thinking the same thing, because she said, 'Poor other Tom.'

They sat in respectful silence until a car honked them. Lena raised a middle finger to the driver.

'Where were you earlier, anyway?' Lena asked, after a while. Alison told her.

'That's wonderful news!' Lena said, hugging them both. 'I can't wait to be an aunty!' She seemed genuinely pleased for them, this time. Though maybe she'd just got better at lying. She opened her mouth, as though she wanted to say something else, then stopped herself.

'What?' Suria said.

'I was just thinking – it must be quite hard for you. Alison having treatment.'

Suria shrugged, then nodded. Her face crumpled.

Lena passed her the last of the paper napkins. 'Sorry, god—'

'No, you're fine. It's just – the baby won't look like me.'

'We're using the hospital's sperm bank,' Alison explained.

'That's great! That's brilliant!'

'But guess how many donors they have. Total.'

'How many?'

'Seven.'

'No!'

'And all of them are white, except for two.'

'And none of them is half-Malaysian, clearly,' Suria said, fiddling with her chopsticks.

'We've found a guy who's half-British, quarter-Indian and quarter-Chinese, though,' Alison said. They were 60 per cent comfy with their choice.

'Honestly, it won't matter that you're not related,' Lena

said, as Suria blew her nose. 'I promise. You're going to love the baby and the baby is going to love you.'

'Yeah?' Suria looked up at Lena, as though she had the power to make it so.

'Definitely,' Lena said. 'Apart from when the baby turns fourteen and wants to get a septum piercing.'

A *twenty-first-century*
Ebeneezer Scrooge

Tom woke up after his operation, blinking in the strip lighting, and realized he wasn't dead; heaven probably wouldn't involve lying half-naked in a hospital bed, a cardboard bedpan within arm's reach. He cried when he realized he was alive, partly with relief, partly with guilt. Why had he been granted extra time by the great referee in the sky when Sheila hadn't? He wasn't a man who spent much time thinking about heaven and hell or god or indeed referees, but there's nothing like a heart attack for changing your stance on the afterlife. He felt like a twenty-first-century Ebeneezer Scrooge, determined to seize his second chance and give himself a happy ending. Happyish, anyway; he wouldn't be able to avoid the inevitable coffin, the ceremony at Kensal Green, the dry sandwiches at the pub afterwards, but perhaps he could put them off for a while. Now, life was shiny and precious again, like new skin under a blister. And his daughters were with him, and Lena was in floods, and she wouldn't have been if she didn't love him, and wasn't he lucky to have them both, though he did wish they'd stop fussing over him as though they were auditioning for yet another adaptation of *Little Women*. Even the doctors were at it, talking about him over his head like he wasn't there, speaking too loudly when they addressed him, as though the heart attack had damaged his hearing. 'You gave us quite a fright there, Tom!' 'No driving for you, for a few weeks, OK? And no sex.'

'Jessie won't be happy,' he said.

'God, Dad,' Alison said, and covered her eyes with her hand.

An old man, a couple of beds down, died that night. The staff just pulled the curtain around his bed and waited for the funeral home to collect him. Tom heard the whole thing, because he couldn't sleep: the man in the bed next to him had such severe dementia that he shouted, 'Is it Shabbat? Is it Shabbat?' every few minutes, even though his family had stuck a notice to his bed tray: *YOU ARE IN HOSPITAL. YOU HAD A HEART ATTACK. IT IS NOT SHABBAT. RACHEL AND DAVID ARE COMING TO VISIT YOU IN THE MORNING.* He was relieved when he was discharged the next day.

Jessie arrived in the morning, to help him get dressed – honestly, the indignity of the whole thing. 'Nothing I haven't seen before, Tom,' she said, patting his arse as she helped him pull his trousers up. His daughters turned up after lunch, too. Apparently he needed three people to help him get home.

'Which of you is going to stay with him, for the first couple of nights?' the doctor asked.

'I am,' Lena said. Tom thought his heart might explode

again. It was dangerous, loving people, when you had high blood pressure.

'I'll do it, love,' Jessie said, touching Lena's hand. 'I'm there most nights anyway.'

'No, it's fine, he's my dad.' They were fighting over him! He forced himself to frown, to hide his delight.

'Go on, let me help,' Jessie said. 'You have enough going on.'

'Fine. Thank you,' Lena said stiffly.

'I don't need anyone to look after me,' he said.

'All right. You can cook all your own meals, and call the ambulance yourself if you have another heart attack,' Jessie said.

He didn't argue, after that.

Alison carried his bag to the taxi, and he held tight to Lena's arm. Everything looked piercingly beautiful to him now – the concrete car park, the trunks of the trees shining in the winter sunshine, the few wrinkled leaves that still clung to the branches, the way he was clinging to life. 'It's funny,' he said, 'knowing you wouldn't be alive if it wasn't for medical intervention.' Jessie touched his arm. It was tender where the cannula had entered it.

The house felt like a crime scene. There were muddy foot-prints on the carpet where the paramedics had worked.

'Still smells of sausages,' Lena said, as she picked up a cushion from the floor and placed it back on the sofa.

'Not sure I'll ever eat a sausage again,' he said. Alison helped him lower himself into the armchair, the one Sheila had liked to sit in.

'Might be time to try the Linda McCartney ones,' Lena said.

411

'Bugger off.'

'You're going to have to walk up and down stairs after lunch,' Jessie said.

'Oh, come on, all of you. Give it a rest.'

'You are,' Lena said. 'You're going to get better. Dad?' She was holding his gaze. 'You have to.'

He looked up at the three of them, at Alison, picking up the dirty cup from the coffee table, and Jessie, lining up his drugs on the mantelpiece, and Lena, who was arranging a blanket over his legs as though he was a bloody invalid. He had never told Sheila how much he had appreciated her. He cleared his throat. He was going to say it.

He couldn't.

'Tom?' Jessie put a hand on his arm.

'I'm fine. Sorry I'm such a grumpy old bastard.'

'You're not,' Alison said.

'I am.'

'OK, you are,' Jessie said. 'But we love you anyway.'

Why was it so easy for her to put it into words? Say it back, he told himself, but Jessie had turned away, and the moment had passed – except it hadn't, because his heart was still beating. He could say it now, he could just open his mouth and say it— 'I love you.'

They all looked at him.

'All of you. I love you. Very much.'

Alison frowned. 'They did say a heart attack can lead to a change in personality—'

'I'm serious! I do!'

'Well. That's very nice, Tom,' Jessie said, patting his hand.

'Yes,' Alison said, though she couldn't look at him. She had inherited something from him, after all. 'We're very glad you decided to stick around.'

But Lena bent down to kiss him on the forehead. She said, 'I love you, Daddy.' He hadn't heard those words in a good three decades. He wasn't sure he had ever been happier.

Bugger off

They visited the cemetery on Christmas Day, after the pudding but before the presents. Jessie decided to stay behind – 'Thought I might make some mulled wine,' she said, which was tactful, though she was wearing an old apron of Sheila's as she said it. Lena felt a little swoop of grief and anger, but told herself not to be a hypocrite. She had received a Christmas card the day before, a glittery one with a snowman on it:

Love from Richard, Daniel and Hugo.

Richard had written all of the names, trying to vary the handwriting so it looked as though it was signed by different people. But Lena was an old hand at that trick. Adam had never been one for signing birthday cards. She didn't have to worry about that any more, though.

She had met up with him a couple of weeks before, for an awkward walk around Highbury Fields. He was taller than she remembered. He smelled different.

'I've started using one of those shampoo bars,' he said, when she told him. 'No plastic packaging.'

He had always been too good for her. She could hardly bear it, how kind he was.

'I'm glad your dad's on the mend,' he said, gruffly, staring into his takeaway cappuccino.

'Thank you. He'll miss you at Christmas. No one else will put up with him quoting medieval poetry at the dinner table.'

He laughed. She risked reaching for his hand. He put it in his pocket.

'I'm so sorry, Adam—'

He nodded. 'You were going through a tricky time.'

'That's no excuse.'

'And we'd been growing apart, anyway. So it's not your fault—'

'That's not true—'

They moved away from each other to let a woman with a buggy walk between them.

'OK, it was mostly your fault,' he said, once they were side by side again.

'No, I mean— I still think we might be able to fix it.'

His breath made a cloud in the December air.

'We could go to couples' counselling?'

He shook his head. 'I've actually met someone—'

'Oh! Brilliant! Great!'

'It's very new. But she plays the cello, so that's nice—'

'That's wonderful!'

'And she wants children.' The winter sun picked his profile out in gold. God, she had missed his warm, familiar, handsome face. She had stopped noticing what he looked like, when they were together.

She was crying, now. The flat wasn't a home without him in it. There were three wine glasses in the kitchen cupboard instead of six. Three dinner plates, three cereal bowls, three knives, three forks. She even missed his music stand, which had cluttered up the living room, and the sound of Eastern European fiddle tunes at 8 a.m. on a Sunday morning, and being embarrassed when he called her 'Pony' in Tesco. There were too many spare hangers in the wardrobe. She missed not having enough room to hang up her clothes. She hadn't realized how much she had loved the ordinariness of marriage – taking it in turns to make dinner and reminding each other to buy light bulbs and the comfort of being loved by someone and never having to doubt it. But she didn't miss the claustrophobia she'd felt every time she thought about becoming a mother. 'I'm sorry,' she said. 'I was such an idiot.'

He didn't say anything.

'I love you.'

He put an arm around her. 'I love you, too,' he said. 'Best person I've ever met.'

'But you still want a divorce.'

''Fraid so.'

She let out a desperate, involuntary cry. She tried to turn it into a laugh.

He said, 'Come on, now. Come on.'

She nodded. She heard herself say, 'Unreasonable behaviour?'

'No rush. If we wait for two years, no one has to take the blame.' He squeezed her arm, then let her go.

The headstone *was* quite tall, Lena realized, now it was in situ. Barry and Nigel's grave looked squat by comparison. She pulled the ivy from their column, by way of apology.

'Very smart,' Tom said, gruffly. 'Plenty of room for my name underneath.'

'Don't say that,' Lena said.

'Mum would have liked it,' Alison said.

'It's lovely,' Lena agreed. She had brought her mother a mince pie. She laid it in front of the headstone.

'That'll encourage rats,' Tom said, but he left it on the ground. 'Reminds me of when you used to leave snacks out for Father Christmas. You were always so excited when they were gone in the morning.'

They were silent for a moment, as they stood back to admire the lettering.

Sheila Delancey
1952–2017
Biochemist
Beloved mother, wife and friend

'This puts me in mind of one of my favourite Philip Larkin poems,' Tom said, crossing his arms.

'Here we go,' Alison said.

'It's a poem about a fourteenth-century tomb that shows a husband and wife holding hands. And the last line is, *What will survive of us is love.*'

'Getting a bit sentimental in your old age, aren't you, Dad?' Lena said.

'Oh, bugger off,' Tom said.

'Jim didn't do a bad job in the end, did he?' said Alison, bending down to clear the rotten leaves from the grave.

Lena looked at her. 'I mean—'

'He's asked me for a testimonial for his website.'

Tom laughed. 'Tell him to get fucked.'

*

Alison was still the youngest member of the Delancey family, so she was in charge of handing out the presents. With any luck, though, she wouldn't be the youngest for long: twenty-four hours earlier, she had been lying on a hospital bed, feet in stirrups, as the embryologist had injected a stranger's sperm into her uterus. 'Little pinch!'

'A man's sperm inside me,' Alison had said, as she and Suria walked home from the clinic, down the hill, past last-minute Christmas shoppers and buskers dressed in cheap Santa costumes. 'First time for everything.'

And as she said that, a man hurried past her up the hill, late for his appointment at the Women's Health Centre. Alison glanced at him, and wondered. Don't be stupid, she thought – but she was right to wonder. His name was Jamie. He had been a blood donor and a platelet donor, and now he was a sperm donor. He was 24 years old, gay, happily single. He didn't want kids of his own, but he wanted to help other people conceive: he'd watched his sister go through fertility treatment and he knew how awful it was, and how easy it would be for him to help. He said hello to the receptionist and walked to the waiting room, where he leafed through the copy of *The Watchtower* until the embryologist said, 'Jamie? Do you want to go straight through?' Meanwhile, five streets away, Natalie, a single mother by choice, was breastfeeding the babies she had always wanted, the twins she would never have been able to have without him. And in Hastings, Bilal and his wife Angela were arguing about whether to tell their newborn baby he was donor conceived, and how to do it, and when. Jamie, the baby's biological father, snapped the cap on to his donation, and zipped up his trousers. And in the kitchen of a terraced house in Brixton, Nur, eight months pregnant

418

with her first child, bounced on a birthing ball as her husband packed her hospital bag. She had been devastated when the doctors told her she wouldn't be able to conceive without using donor eggs. Until she'd found the ideal donor – a social worker, half-Scottish and half-Malaysian, who loved running and ballet and George Eliot novels, who wanted to help other people have a family because she was using donor sperm to conceive a child with her wife.

But Alison didn't know any of that. She passed Lena a present.

'*Inspirational Women*. Illustrated by Alison Delancey. Just what I've always wanted!' Lena kissed Alison on the cheek and flicked through the book. 'Beyoncé! Looks just like her. Hillary Clinton, nice. Malala, obviously.'

'It's very impressive,' Tom said, leafing through the book, which had come together nicely, Alison thought, though she couldn't bear to look at the pages too closely in case she spotted a mistake. 'I just have one problem with it.'

'I'm not sure Ali's interested in your notes, darling,' Jessie said, opening a present from Lena. 'A checked scarf! Lovely!'

Tom ignored her and smiled at his daughters. 'You two ought to be in it. You're the most inspirational women I know.'

'Oh god.' Alison couldn't get used to her father's post-heart-attack sentimentality. That morning, she had found him on the sofa, eating a mini-panettone and weeping at the Heathrow arrivals scene from *Love, Actually*.

'Boak,' said Suria, as Alison handed her another parcel.

'Ignore them, Dad,' Lena said, patting her father's hand. She wondered how many families were sitting around Christmas trees unwrapping DNA test kits this year. She wondered how many new members would request to join the donor-conceived Facebook group in the morning. *Hi everyone, I've just found out I'm not related to my father.* She sipped her champagne and decided to write a poem about it, after she had watched *It's a Wonderful Life*. The *Call the Midwife* special had just started and the Christmas-tree lights were reflected in Jessie's glasses, and everyone was pretending that last Christmas had never happened. Suria ripped the paper from a present. 'A tartan scarf! Thank you!'

'Thought I'd get everyone something nice and inoffensive this year,' Lena said.

'But this is Campbell tartan,' Suria said, 'And my mum's a MacDonald, so I cannae let her see this—'

But Lena wasn't listening. On the TV, a lighthouse keeper was radioing to the coastguard for help because his wife was in labour, and the actor had eyes the colour of oxidized copper, and when he frowned he looked like Alison—

'Who's that bloke?' Alison said, nodding at the screen. 'What have I seen him in?'

'Whoever he is, his Scottish accent's worse than yours,' Suria said.

'*Game of Thrones*,' Lena said.

'Maybe that's it.'

'But he's been in loads of stuff—'

Alison was opening her present. 'A tartan scarf. What a surprise!'

'You're welcome!' Lena said, trying to resign herself to the doubleness of her life, the ripping reality of not being able to share all of it with her sister.

Except Alison wasn't her only sister any more. That morning, she had reactivated her Genealogy DNA account and found a message in the inbox from a woman named

Nicola, who shared 26 per cent of her DNA. *Hi Lena, Happy Christmas. You're coming up as a close family match. Do you have any idea how we're related?* Lena had locked herself in the bathroom and googled her new sister's name. Nicola had green eyes, like hers, and a degree in journalism from City University. From what Lena could tell from Instagram, she lived in Nottingham and had two children, and she had no idea she was donor conceived. Lena had written to her straight away: *Hi Nicola, it looks as though we're half-siblings. I was conceived using donor sperm. I know this might be a massive shock.* The story was beginning all over again a few miles away in a different family that was also the same family, whether they liked it or not.

Tom stood up and turned off the television. Daniel flickered and disappeared. 'Right, you horrible lot,' he said. 'Who's up for a game of literary charades?'

Acknowledgements

Thank you to my mum and dad, who always told me the truth. Their names are Liz Davies and John Collier, and they are excellent parents and people in general – I appreciate them even more now that I'm a parent myself. When I showed my dad the dedication to this novel, he said 'I'm very honoured to have been the one to fuck you up.'

Thank you to my wonderful editor, Suzie Dooré, and everyone else at The Borough Press and HarperCollins, especially Jabin Ali, Sarah Foster, Maud Davies, Sian Richefond, Sophie Waeland, Harriet Williams, and Alice Gomer.

Thank you to my brilliant (and extremely patient) agent Judith Murray, Kate Rizzo, and everyone else at Greene & Heaton. Thanks also to Emily Hickman, Seàn Butler and everyone else at The Agency.

Huge thanks as always to Sarah Courtauld and Zanna Davidson, who are my family as well as my friends and colleagues (literally in Sarah's case, according to 23 and Me). They are always the first people to read my writing, and I would be lost without them.

Thank you so much to the people who read early drafts of this book and gave me notes (or just encouraged me to keep going): Victoria Fitzpatrick, Erica Gillingham, Hanna Johnson, Alexia Korberg, Owen Nicholls, Matthew Oldham and Nick Sharp. Thanks also to Ian Campbell-Fitzpatrick and Kimmy Rajasagaran for your medical expertise, and thank you to Caroline Campbell for the immortal sentence about sausage rolls and funerals.

Thank you to the Hawthornden Fellowship: the most inspiring month away from all distractions. Thank you to the directors, to Hamish, Ruth, Mary and Debbie, and to the writers I met there: Penelope Pelizzon, Marin Sardy, Penny Shutt, Royston Tester and Diana Wagman. My conversations with all of you made this a much better novel.

Thank you to the British Library, the London Library, Forest Gate Works and the Arvon retreats at Totleigh Barton and the Clockhouse.

Thank you Lynton Pepper, for letting me write in your wonderful studio and for letting Alison rent a desk there in the novel.

Thank you Maria Peters for the brilliant An Artist's Adventure course. Thank you Sylvia Bishop and Writers with Faces for keeping me company during lockdown.

Thank you to Team Ivandoe – Christian Bøving-Anderson, Eva Lee Wallberg, Daniel Lennard, and everyone else at Sun Creature/ Hanna Barbara Studios Europe/ Cartoon Network – working with you while I was writing this novel was SUCH a joy.

Thanks to Paul Burston and the Polari Prize for your incredible support and encouragement. Thank you to Erica, Jim, Uli and everyone else at Gay's the Word.

Thank you to the friends I haven't mentioned already, particularly Naomi Baars, Laura Barnicoat, Annabel Bligh, Florence Bullough, Megan Cullis, Zoë Ellings, Michelle Erodotou, Harriet Evans, Ellie Farrell, Fenke Foss, Alex Gillingham, Ahmed Ghazal, Joanna Glen, Steffi Hunt, Cath Hunter, Rachel Jones, Rachel Korberg, Ilana Gordon, Nell Guy, Amanda Harrington, Ray Lee, Luke Leighfield, Hannah

Lewis, Laura Macdougall, Aurelie Marion, Marina McIntyre, Karen McLeod, Luke Massey, Sinead MacCann, Alice Morrissey, Anna Nagy, Elise Neve, Albi Owen, Amy Perkins, Alice Sanders, Debbie So, Matilda Tristram, Leyla Turkoglu, Jo Wickham and Marcia Williams.

Thanks to Jack Davies, Tanya Freeman, Charlie Freeman, the Collier family and the wonderful Campbell and Fitzpatrick families.

Thank you, as always, to Will Tosh and Piers Torday for being our family as well as helping us become a family. Thank you also to Norma Clarke, Barbara Taylor, Jane Torday and John Tosh.

Thank you to Louise McGloughlin, who I met as I was starting to write this novel. Her perspective and experience made me look at donor conception in a new light. I recommend Louise's podcast, *You Look Like Me*, to anyone interested in hearing more about donor conception from a donor-conceived person's point of view. Thank you to the donor-conceived community on Facebook, particularly We Are Donor Conceived.

Thank you to the man who donated sperm anonymously so I could exist, and a general sort of 'hello' to my half-siblings, most of whom I'll probably never meet.

The biggest thank you to my amazing wife Victoria, the very best person to share life with. And thank you to Felix, our son, who is joy and sunshine. I can't believe how wonderful you are.

Finally, thank you so much to the readers, booksellers and writers who supported *In at the Deep End,* and all the people who read the novel and got in touch to tell me they liked it. Your messages really kept me going while I was writing *Nuclear Family* – sorry it took me so long.